Dedicated to Erin and Candy, whose

support made this book possible

PART ONE

"Salt and Smoke"

"In salt and smoke, the Prophetess's path was begun
Beside warm waters, soon stained red,
Returning home at the setting sun,
Woe, for blood and tears, both shed.

Reiki, the revered, the holy, Terra's vengeance,
Was born anew in a baptism of sorrow,
Her harpoon, her bow, her persistence,
Readied, she set sail toward the morrow."

-The Tale of Reiki-
Priam the Skald

Chapter I

"Serenity Village"

"When you tell the tale of a savior, a prophetess, a hero, it is tempting to embellish. They have a miraculous birth, or they slew a fantastic beast all on their own at the age of three. They ran four thousand kilometers to fetch water for a dying woman who blessed them with immortality.

What rubbish! I have heard skalds and chroniclers from the city of Sychak, all the way to the southern bay of Chekhov, east to Sakawat, and beyond the oceans to the far flung corners of our world. They will all claim Reiki the Prophetess, the Savior, Favored of Terra, was born to a virgin and harpooned a great turquoise dragon when she was but five years old. Nonsense.

She was born and raised in a typical village in the Islands. She was a gifted navigator and a prodigious fisherwoman, but she was not so different from any other young Islander. She was not touched by the divine but was rather a normal young woman who was touched by tragedy. What she did after was entirely a product of her most astonishing assets: she was exceedingly clever and, perhaps more importantly, she refused to accept defeat."

-On Reiki: A Factual Telling-
Horace the High Chronicler of the Kingdom of Hastra

The skalds of Sychak would later tell increasingly ludicrous tales of the birth of Reiki, the Islander woman who is now known by such an abundance of names and titles as to require almost a book of its own to list and explain them. Some claim she washed upon the shore on a raft of tree bark pulled by a giant eel in the year 2286 under the light of a burning comet. Some claim she was found at the rim of a volcano, the fire mountains so common in the islands where she was born, a seashell in her hand and a silver spear by her side.

The truth is less exciting and fanciful, perhaps, but more encouraging for mere mortals. She was born uneventfully, the first child of a fisherman and a rice farmer in the village of Serenity on the fourth day of the sixth month, called June, of the year 2286, by the reckoning of the Sychak standard calendar. Her father, Harald, was a doting man who instantly fell in love with his daughter. Her mother, Lia, was a strong and dedicated woman who taught Reiki the importance of community, providing for one's neighbors, but also self-reliance. Together, they lived in a six-room hut made from the wood from the island's forests, tree fronds, and woven sea grasses. Harald fished the seas, Lia worked the fields, and together they helped care for Harald's aging mother, as was the custom.

The Islands, though referred to as a nation throughout known history, are a strip of thousands of islands stretching roughly north to south over an expanse of ocean nearly five thousand kilometers long and about a hundred kilometers wide with no ties to each other beyond those of a shared culture and geography. There are hundreds of little villages on hundreds of little islands all throughout the vast archipelago, and it is unknown how many villages or people, for that matter, there are in the islands. Each village is essentially a self-contained society that will readily assist outsiders in need, especially other villages, and gladly trade, but seldom goes out of its way to involve itself in the private business of others. They are a friendly but insular people with no currency and no government beyond a loose affiliation of village councils of elders that met on the rarest of occasions for matters that concerned the Islands as a whole. Of war, they know little, though each village keeps a handful of trained warriors to defend them against the predations of brigands, pirates, and the rare band of raiders from the far eastern nation of Sakawat.

Reiki was raised like any child in the Islands. Young children are tended to by the grandmothers of the village, a dozen or so elderly women who no longer could work the fields, work the nets, or work any of the other jobs that needed doing in the village, but they still had the ability to chase after a rambunctious toddler or two. Reiki was a curious but well-behaved child who would explore Serenity if she was left unattended. She was ever drawn to the lagoon where the fishermen worked on their trimarans and their nets or else cleaned and prepared their daily catch. Once she was able to listen and comprehend and communicate with adults, Harald took her under his wing and began the most joyous period of both their lives—he taught her to sail, to fish, to work harpoon and bow and net. He showed her how to build a trimaran and to fashion new sails. She learned to navigate by sun and stars, by maps and compass, and even by the flight of birds or paths of fish. Reiki took to the sea eagerly, her eyes wide with delight, and as he poured out his knowledge, she drank it up greedily.

There's no question Reiki was a gifted mariner, but where Reiki differed most from her peers was her insistence on studying the skills and trades of as many people as would teach her. At the age of seven, she appeared before the home of the village's chief priest, Ichiro, her eyes wide with excitement, and exclaimed, "I am going to learn about the gods now! You're going to teach me. My mom and dad said I should ask, but then you could say no. So, I'm telling you instead." She grinned a shameless toothy grin and before the priest could reply she spun on her heels and ran off, shouting, "Okay, thank you! We can start tomorrow!"

The priest might have said no if he weren't too busy laughing at the time. He assumed she wasn't serious, or, like so many children, she would simply find something else more amusing or interesting and forget. Yet, he awoke the next morning to find Reiki banging on the door of his hut, insisting that her lessons start right away. The first lesson he taught her was that he did not arise until after the sun did, and so she should let him sleep until at least after breakfast. Many other lessons followed. He started with the tale of the dawn of their world, a planet they called Matria. He told the story from memory and with great solemnity, though she later discovered a roll of parchment in his hut where the tale was written and illustrated with beautiful black ink drawings that Reiki found entrancing. She memorized it and later recited it back to Ichiro, mimicking his own solemn demeanor as she did:

"Long ago, Matria was born from the cosmos. It sprang from the void lush with life: plants, the bounty of the sea, great diggers beneath the earth, the wandering herds of great scaled beasts, and furred monstrosities of tooth and claw in the far east. Finally, after many an age, the gods descended from the heavens in fire and ice and emerged from the sacred cryopod gardens. Only holy mother Terra remained above, guiding the lesser gods, her children, on Matria below. The gods gave birth to mankind in their respective domains and mankind multiplied. Then, after a time, a great fiery star fell from the sky and holy mother Terra fell silent, never to be heard from again. The gods themselves left their mortal vessels on pyres, and their souls were carried back to the stars from whence they came as ash and smoke. Mankind was left to live and toil on Matria while the gods watch from above."

Ichiro smiled at her recitation and sent her on her way so he could take a nap. Reiki thought the story had a beautiful symmetry to it even then, though she spent many nights wondering over what became of Terra, mother to all. When she asked Ichiro later, she was surprised to learn that he did not know.

"Perhaps she was the fiery falling star and she fell to Matria at last, though none have ever found her. Or maybe she faded away alone in the sky. Who can know the ways of the gods? Why did they surrender their mortal vessels and return to the sky in ash? There are always more questions, Reiki, though there are not always answers. Do not trouble yourself too much. Curiosity is a good thing but not at the expense of happiness. Live. Love. Do good. Have a family. Strengthen the village through your works and your voice. These are the ways to a good life." Ichiro's advice usually came back to those key points, regardless of where the discussion began. Well, that and his beloved Toki, a potent spirit fermented from rice and the succulent fruit found in the forests on Serenity. He never let her try any, no matter how often she pestered him. Ichiro was a quirky old drunk, but she loved him, even though his answers often left her with even more questions.

She learned the rites and responsibilities owed to the gods of the cryopod garden and holy mother Terra. She learned some astronomy. She learned a little about herbology and healing. She pestered the small number of warriors in Serenity until they begrudgingly taught her to fight with a harpoon, a knife, and a bow. She followed around several of the older men as they went foraging in the trees and bushes and the three hills of her island. She was an avid learner and by fifteen she was known by all in the village as one who could be relied on to help with whatever task they required and to do it well.

Still, for Reiki, the greatest moments of her childhood were going out to sea with Harald, the first time she went out alone on her trimaran (a rite of passage for fishermen in Serenity), and, most of all, the birth of her little brother, Tova, when she was ten years old. Lia had spent the whole night in labor, hours and hours. Reiki thought her mother was dying and had rushed into the hut before being rushed out by the midwives. Her father had sat beside her on a log next to their fire and explained to her what was happening. Reiki was calmed somewhat, but her mother's cries continued for what seemed to Reiki to be countless hours. Then, the next morning, her father brought her into the hut to see her mother and little Tova. Reiki had never felt about anyone or anything what she felt for that tiny little boy with his mop of black hair slick to his head, his tiny bulbous nose, and toes, and his high-pitched cry. As she stared down at him, resting in his woven crib, he opened his eyes, stopped crying, and, for a moment, he smiled a gaping toothless smile. She was immediately and irretrievably smitten with him.

When he was old enough to learn to fish, she went with her father to teach him, and she comforted him when he wept in terror at the sight of his first garatha eel, even though it was a small one, five meters long and without its adult teeth yet. She bandaged his scrapes and tended to him when he was ill, which was often. Tova was a small and sickly child, but Reiki only loved him more for it. As far as Reiki could see, he was also loving, slow to anger, and kind to everyone. As much as Reiki loved Tova, Tova loved Reiki as much, if not more so. It was a common sight to see them walking together hand in hand, sixteen and six years old, along the beach at night. Reiki delighted in pointing out the different constellations she knew and telling the stories of each. Tova would smile and look up at her, his eyes full of adoration and wonder.

"That's the Eel, Tova. See how it snakes its way across the sky? The garatha eel is a great terror, it's true, but also a great boon to our people. Its hide makes the best clothing and sails. Its teeth can be used as spear points or knives. Its flesh can feed the whole village if you find a big one. They are dangerous, though."

Tova squeezed her hand tightly. "They scare me, Ray-Key. Tell me about a nice one!"

Reiki smiled and squeezed his little hand gently. "Okay. See that one there?" She pointed to a cluster of stars, five forming a cross and a curve of six stars below them. "That's the great boat! Do you see how it looks like a small boat with a mast and spar? That's the boat of the great hero Matsui, one of the gods of the cryopod garden. He had it burned with him when he left this world and returned to the sky. You can see him there, just to the right of it."

Tova nodded. "That's better, Ray-Key. Mat-soo-ee is way better than eels."

Reiki laughed. "Alright, Tova. I won't try to convince you that eels are good. We'll stick to the other constellations instead."

The other children would sometimes bully Tova. At first, Tova responded with tears. He was a sensitive child, and the other children could be so cruel. Reiki defended Tova when she could, but this seemed to only increase the bullying. As Tova grew, the bullying grew with him until, at the age of nine, he decided it was time to stop relying on Reiki to protect him. He decided to focus on training with the harpoon and began to spend hours practicing every day when he was not busy helping Lia or Harald around the hut. Reiki understood the impulse and even recognized the wisdom of it, but she missed the sweetness of his tiny little hand in hers, the way he would fall asleep on her chest, and the way he would smile when she told a story. Now, he was growing, and she knew those days were gone.

She also knew that it was time for her to decide her future in the village. The Islanders attained adulthood when they turned nineteen years old. Now, it was October, and she had passed that milestone four months ago. Islander women were expected to choose a profession and a mate, both within a year of becoming an adult unless there were extenuating circumstances. To Reiki's knowledge, "I don't want to" was not considered to be an extenuating circumstance.

Reiki was happy to contribute to the success of the village, but Serenity had enough fishermen as it was. What Serenity needed was a new high priest and a new trading chief to make voyages to other villages and even some foreign lands to trade excess goods for things the Islanders could not make for themselves, such as steel tools. Reiki was torn between her sense of duty, which would have her adopt the robe and headband of the high priest and spend all her days in service to the gods of the cryopod garden, for she was one of only a handful of Serenity's citizens who had trained under Ichiro. Yet, her heart belonged to the sea. She had journeyed with her father as part of a trading expedition on several occasions as a child and her young mind had relished every moment. The current trading master was now in his sixty-third year and had crippling arthritis. His son, Malek, was eager to fill the role, and he was not an incapable sailor or trader. However, it was generally agreed that Reiki was in another class altogether where mastery of the sea was concerned.

Reiki felt fairly certain she knew what she would ultimately decide, but choosing a mate was a greater challenge. Reiki had no interest in any of the young men of

Serenity, nor the women, for that matter. She remembered the first time she kissed a boy. His name was Alexei and he had long flowing black hair that felt warm and smooth in her hands. She remembered the kiss had felt awkward to her, a wet and meaningless act that she had only done because the other girls on the island had made fun of her because she had never done so. Then she remembered the first time she kissed a girl. That she had done because she had been curious if the problem with that first kiss was that it was with a boy. Her name was Kelli, and she had smelled and tasted like the whistle fruit[1] she had been snacking on that morning. Reiki liked the sweet taste of the whistle fruit, but she found the kiss as empty of feeling as the one with Alexei. After that, she had never felt the desire to try again and had since come to the conclusion that her life was fine without the addition of romance. She worried, not without reason, that her decision to forgo choosing a mate could jeopardize her place in the village and potentially lead to being shunned by her people.

These concerns plagued her each night when she finally laid down on her cot to try to sleep, the snores of her father and the soft breaths of little Tova drifting through the walls. She would lay awake as her mind raced, and she agonized over her future. Every day brought her closer to having to make a decision, until she could no longer keep putting it off without the risk of being shunned or banished from her village; Serenity was a tight knit island that could

---

[1] Whistle fruit is a yellow and green oblong fruit with a natural slit in its stem that makes a whistling noise as the wind passes through it. It is quite sweet and has soft mushy flesh.

not suffer an excess of individualism. She had pushed her luck for as long as she could.

So it was that she fell asleep one cool night in autumn, the seventh day of the eight month, called October, of the year 2305, fretting over the distance in her relationship with her brother and the uncertainty of her place in Serenity and dreading the decision she knew she must make. When she finally fell into a deep sleep, she did not suspect that by nightfall the following day her entire life, her world, everything she had known, would be irrevocably changed; all would be burned and washed away in a torrent of fire and blood.

Chapter II

"A Day Like Any Other"

"I wonder what we might do differently, how sweetly we might speak to those we love, were we to know what horrors the day might bring and what lasting yawning chasm of silence might be forced upon us by our inscrutable fate."
Celia, High Priestess of Emerald Village

The worst day of Reiki's life began like most days in Serenity. As Reiki left her hut, she was greeted by the sound of her brother's practice harpoon striking a wooden post. Tova was nearly ten years old now and practiced every morning as soon as there was light enough to see. Reiki smiled at her mother who was tending to the breakfast, eggs, seared Seajack[2] and a few of the delicious purple tubers that grew on the hillside above her village. She waved to her mother and saw it returned, with a smile.

"Good morning, Reiki!"

"Good morning, Mom. That smells delicious."

Her father was sitting on a thick log just outside the ring of stones and still smoldering coals of their fire pit. He was weaving a net from hair shorn from their flock of

---

[2] The Seajack is a delicious saltwater fish of about one meter length with long pectoral fins and a spiny dorsal fin. It has blue, green, and purple coloring starting with blue at the dorsal ridge, green along the side of the body, and then a strip of purple above the white belly.

barunta[3] and reminiscing with his mother, Rhea, who sat on the log opposite him, poking at the embers of the fire with a long, slender stick. Reiki sat down with them, her bare feet cooled by the dewy grass beside their hut. She smiled when she realized her father was re-telling the story of the first time Reiki had gone out onto the sea with him to hunt for the great garatha eel.

"Little Reiki spent the first two hours running from end to end of my boat. She was so excited. 'Where are the eels, daddy? Where are the eels? I want to see them!'"

Reiki grinned. She had desperately wanted to see one. The old men on the beach would talk about them as they wove their nets and sharpened their fishing harpoons. To hunt the garatha was a rite of passage, the gate that allowed entry into the ranks of the fishermen of the Islands. The turquoise hides of garathas adorned the masts of every trimaran in Serenity, and Reiki desperately wanted her own, with clothes to match.

"We finally got out to where they feed. I spotted the Resa birds that scavenge their leftovers, and we drifted in under half sail. Reiki quieted down and sat as still as I had ever seen her. It was like someone replaced her with a stone!" He grinned at her and winked before continuing. Her grandmother gave her a knowing smile. They had all heard

---

[3] The barunta is a domesticated herbivorous beast with long wispy hair and an upturned snout and four legs with six toes each. It has a short and bushy tail and generally weighs around 150 kilograms. The Islanders use it as a source of milk, hair to make cloth and rope, to pull or push heavy loads, and eventually as a source of meat. A family of five would generally keep between one and three barunta.

this story many times. "Out of the water comes the biggest garatha I have ever seen, even to this day!" He shot his arm straight up in the air in a mimicry of the eel's leap from the water. "It was at least twenty meters long, a half meter wide, turquoise and white, and it had eyes like blue fire!"

Reiki remembered the eel. It had startled her, but at the time she had been more surprised at her lack of fear. "The eel was very close to the boat, I remember."

Her father laughed. "Yes, you would remember, because you reached your little arm out—you were only six years old—and you touched it. I was terrified for you. I thought I was going to lose my little Reiki."

"But you didn't," Reiki smiled. She had reached out to touch it, and in that moment she had felt a connection to the beast and to the sea, a sense of belonging beyond anything she had ever known. She had felt no fear, only an elation that she could barely contain.

"But I didn't." He returned the smile. "No. I ran over to scoop you up, and you had the biggest smile on your face. I sat you down, and you just kept smiling and staring at the eel. It nearly got away from us. But, I managed to get my harpoon in time."

"It was an excellent throw. Right in the eel's third heart. A killing throw."

Her father beamed. "Well, yes. I *am* the one who taught *you*, you'll remember."

She laughed. "Yes. You and half the fishermen on this island." Reiki had been a favorite amongst the old fishermen on the beach. They found her interest endearing, and she had been a devoted student. Of course, that had been true of the hunters and the warriors as well, and she had become an asset to her village. Her father and mother both had extolled the importance of providing for and supporting their village, for they could not rely on anyone outside of it to do so. Sure, there were other villages on the Islands. There were even regular visits from traders and merchants from the nearby Kingdom of Hastra. Rarely, someone from the Eastern Continent would arrive as well, but they could not be relied upon. Only the village could.

"Of course. But, I taught you first. And so I will take the credit." He beat his bare chest proudly.

She rolled her eyes. "Why don't you finish the story?"

He chuckled. "Well, as you know, little Reiki helped me pull that eel alongside our boat, and we fastened it to the outrigger and returned home."

"And you made me my first sail from its hide, along with the sheath for my knife, and a quiver for my bow." She nodded. "All of which are still in fine condition to this very day."

"Aye, I did. And I made a sail for my boat as well. That devil was enormous. We fed ten families off of him for over a week."

"And a tasty devil he was, too!" Reiki added.

Her grandmother simply smiled and listened to the two of them as they both told stories together until the breakfast was finished. They ate together and each went about taking care of their usual morning chores. Her brother milked the barunta. Her father worked on his nets. Her mother went to the rice fields to the southwest to fertilize one field and harvest another. Her grandmother joined the other elder women of the village in tending to the younger children. Reiki went up into the hills to search for tubers and some ripe fruit. They all returned in time to eat lunch, more of the fish from breakfast and some of the Awang fruit[4] Reiki had gathered. They sat and ate and joked and laughed, and her mother even sang a few short songs that her brother always liked. Then she had said her goodbyes to all of them as she set out to do some fishing. Dinner was her responsibility.

She had only walked a dozen paces before she felt a hand clasp her right arm gently, but firmly, at the elbow. She turned her head and saw that it was her mother. "Reiki, can I talk to you? We can walk together down to the beach."

"Alright," Reiki replied.

They walked together, Reiki's hand clasped in Lia's, as they made their way slowly through the village down to the beach. Lia spoke softly so as not to be overheard. "Have you made your decision, Reiki?"

---

[4] A bulbous red fruit with small black seeds inside. It is soft and sweet and juicy. Some Islanders even use it to make a fermented drink called Awang Arak which uses barunta milk as well.

Reiki rolled her eyes, "I *knew* that's what this was going to be about!"

"Reiki, it's important," Lia replied, her voice firm. "It is time you take your place as a full member of the village. That means choosing a mate and choosing the way in which you will provide for your family and for your people. You have been an adult now for months. The village council will soon run out of patience. I know it seems cruel, but life in Serenity depends on everyone doing their part."

Reiki sighed, knowing the truth of Lia's words, for she thought of little else. *I wish it was that simple for me. But, I know me. I know the life of a wife, married to some man, or even with the minor scandal of marrying a woman, would be a slow death.* She was reminded then of the time when she was about six years old, and she captured a chokki, one of the small mammalian creatures that lived in the forest. They were called chokki because of the sound they made: "chokki…chokki chokki…chok-KI!" She had trapped one, a brightly colored male with a long yellow crest atop its triangular head and a brilliant green and blue tail that fanned out and seemed to float behind him. She had made it a fancy cage of wood with soft padding of barunta hair and fed it fish and the finest fruit Reiki could find. She loved her chokki, and she held him and petted him constantly, and named him Hokki. Her father and mother warned her that a chokki is a wild thing and is not meant for captivity, but she loved Hokki too much to let him go. Then, one morning, a few weeks after she captured him, she found Hokki lying still as a stone in his cage. His eyes were closed, and his tail had lost its luster. A chokki cannot live in a cage. *Neither can I.*

Finally, Reiki responded, "I do contribute, Mom. I fish, I hunt, I forage. I perform the rituals at the cryopod garden and assist Ichiro. I mend huts. I repair sails. I build trimarans for other fishermen. I go on trading voyages when another set of hands is needed. I have not chosen a single position, but the village would be hard pressed to find someone contributing *more*."

Lia frowned, then nodded. "I know it seems rigid and unfair, but it isn't about *you*. It is about the village. It is about all the other young men and women who reach adulthood."

Reiki spat, "I could probably make a decision on my future place in this village, but, Mom, you know that's not the problem." There was a note of pleading in Reiki's voice, and she felt ashamed for it. *Please don't make me.*

Lia was quiet for several drawn out moments before she wiped a single tear from her right eye. "Reiki, I know. Okay? I know. But, it is the way. To be unwed, to choose to live alone, this is unacceptable when there are available mates."

"We've been over this before, Mom," Reiki said, her exhaustion and exasperation with the subject evident. "Why did you want to talk to me about it *today*?"

Lia bit her lip to prevent it from trembling. "This morning, while you were out foraging, your father and I were visited by Lachlan and Sybil."

Lachlan and Sybil were two of the council members, Reiki knew. "Ah. I see," she replied.

"Lachlan said that if you aren't promised to a mate by the next council meeting, they will take up a vote," Lia choked.

"A vote to what?"

"To expel you from Serenity."

Holy shit. "They'd banish me over this?" Reiki exclaimed, incredulous.

Lia nodded, "Of course they would, Reiki."

"I thought they might shun me for a little while, maybe punish me publicly. I didn't think they would cast me out completely. I didn't kill anyone. I didn't steal Ichiro's chickens or something. I just don't want to spend my life in a lie. *That's* my crime. And they want to cast me out for it?" Reiki realized she had been shouting and now had the attention of the few villagers on the wide dirt street with them. She saw the beach up ahead, only a few dozen meters away, and she was grateful that she would soon be able to escape out to sea, alone with her thoughts.

Lia hung her head. "Reiki, you're my daughter. I love you. I want you to be happy, but I also don't want to lose you."

They had arrived at the beach. Reiki's trimaran sat careened on the sand of the lagoon, three hulls of freedom just scant meters away. She sighed deeply and turned to face her mother. Lia's face was streaked with tears. Reiki's anger subsided, replaced by equal measures of guilt and sympathy. "I know, Mom. I love you too." She embraced her mother.

"Please, Reiki. Choose a friend, someone who knows you well. You could grow to love each other," Lia pleaded.

Reiki broke off the embrace, "I am going now, Mom."

Lia just nodded, for she knew that there were no more words to be said.

Reiki bent down and quickly pushed her trimaran into the calm waters of the lagoon, hopping onto the wooden deck when the water reached the middle of her calves. She did not look back as she lowered her sail and steered her way out of the lagoon, leaving her mother and the rest of the village behind her.

Chapter III

"Black Smoke Over Serenity"

"O Sakawat!
O Betrayals!
O plots devised in eastern lands
And meted upon the peaceful
The tranquil watchers of the fiery mountains
Young one, sail home, for the sun sets on your island
And upon all you know"

-The Sun Set on Serenity-
Hjala the Poet

She sailed south once she left the lagoon and the shelter of the barrier reef. The waves were gentle in the lee of the island. As she headed south the beach sloped upward until it became continuous sheer cliffs all the way around the island until the north side of the lagoon. The lagoon itself was the deepest part of the cone of an extinct volcano, which accounted for the distinct rise in elevation. Millennia of erosion by wind and sea had created the cliffs, but also the flat and fertile farming land that made up the southern half of the island.

She sailed past the cliffs and out of the lee of the island before she shifted her course to the southwest. Once out from the shelter of the island, the west wind slowed her progress. Still, by mid-afternoon, she had reached her favorite fishing spot, halfway to the nearby island of

Waypoint. Only the top third of the tallest of Serenity's three hills, the one directly west of the village, was still visible. She dropped anchor and dove into the sea to hunt for the delicious Orange fish[5] that she knew she would find in plentiful schools there.

She dove and fished, delighting in the feel of the ocean, the thrill of hunting, and the blissful freedom from her troubles. She managed to harpoon a few and was looking forward to a delicious dinner of Orange fish and whistle fruit on rice. Her family loved the dish, and she liked seeing the approving looks on her grandmother and her father's faces as they ate their fill of the flaky fish and sweet fruit slices. Lia and Tova preferred the Seajack that she could find to the north of the island, but she knew she would get no complaints. Reiki took pride in her fishing, for among the people of the Islands, fishing was the skill you learned right after learning to walk. Lia always joked that Reiki was fishing even before that. The recollection brought Reiki's conflict back to focus.

"Damn," she declared to her trimaran, empty but for a few Orange fish in the live well beneath the wooden deck.

She stretched out on her back, put her hands behind her head, and stared up at the deep blue sky. "Mom's not wrong. I could just choose a friend and make the best of it,"

---

[5] Orange fish, aptly named, is a smaller orange colored fish with a thin disk shaped body. It has small dorsal and pectoral fins, four eyes, and a stubby blue tail of two fins. They usually measure about thirty centimeters long and weigh around five kilograms. Their meat is delicate and slightly sweet tasting.

she admitted to the fish. She sat up and loosened the leather cord that held her thick black hair in a bun. She ran her fingers through her hair, a habit she had adopted over the years whenever she found herself overwhelmed with stress or anxiety. She closed her eyes and took a deep breath before slowly exhaling. She felt her anxiety begin to subside as she continued her deep steady breathing and running her fingers through her hair. Finally, she opened her eyes and tied her hair back into a loose bun behind her head.

"I can't do that, though. It wouldn't be fair to any of my friends. Jared or Kalen would both probably be willing to go along with it, at least at first. But, what about five or ten years from now? Would they still be willing to have a wife that feels nothing for them and who recoils from their touch? Will they want children that I refuse to give them?" She shook her head. "No. I can't do that."

She stood up and gestured to the vast openness of the sea around her. "Admittedly, if I were to be the trading master for Serenity, I could spend most of my time here, where I want to be." Then, she let her arms drop to her sides and shook her head. "But, that's even less fair to whoever I might choose as a mate. I would run to the sea to escape. I would render them a widower, though I would still be alive. And I certainly couldn't give up the sea altogether, which is what it would mean to be the high priestess."

She sat back down. *The council isn't wrong to want to enforce these rigid roles. There are only a thousand or so people on Serenity. They need everyone to form families and try to have children and to work specific jobs and roles to ensure our continued survival. We can help each other out and fill in for each other, but there must be carpenters and fishermen, traders and priests, farmers and healers. To have everyone do as they wanted all the time would lead to disaster. I know this. But, that doesn't make it any easier.*

She looked out to the west where the sun was beginning to drift lower in the sky. *I could just keep sailing. I could turn east and head to Hastra, or Sychak, or Chekhov. I could sail west to Waypoint, get supplies, and then keep going west into the deep unknown. If the council wants to banish me anyway, maybe I ought to save them the trouble.* The idea exhilarated her as she considered the expanse of possibilities, the wide-open ocean, and no one to answer to but herself. Then she thought of little Tova, and she knew that she could not.

I can't leave him. He wouldn't understand and I can't hurt him like that. Fuck.

She closed her eyes and took one last look to the western horizon, hazy and distant beneath the sun slowly slipping lower and lower in the sky. *I should head back. If I leave now, I can make it back to the lagoon around sunset and have dinner cooked soon after. Dad should have a cook fire going by the time I get home.* She raised her anchor and unfurled her sail, using the tiller to turn her trimaran back toward Serenity. She had not sailed far when she noticed a column of black smoke rising above Serenity Village.

That's curious. That's a lot of smoke. Did someone go to make offerings to the gods at the Cryopod Garden and have an accident? Did they drop the incense into an oil pot or something? That seemed unlikely. There were no funeral rites to be conducted today, so the oil would be stowed elsewhere.

Could a cookfire have been left unattended? Reiki considered this for a moment, but she knew better. An oil fire would have been quickly contained. A cookfire would have burned one home and been done, for the huts were spaced apart from each other to prevent a fire from consuming the entire village.

As she sailed eastward, the salt spray of the sea pelting her turquoise garatha hide jerkin and leggings, she saw that it was not one single column of smoke, but rather many columns of smoke combined. *It's not one fire. It's a lot of fires. I have a bad feeling about this.*

She coaxed as much speed as she could from the wind, knowing in her heart that something was wrong. As she closed the distance to the island, the smoke grew greater and greater in size and she knew then. Serenity, her home, the small village she had lived in her whole life, was aflame. She raced home as fast as she could urge her little boat to go. And as her boat raced, so did her thoughts.

Sakawat raiders. She decided it had to be.

It was uncommon, but it was known that sometimes villages in the Islands would be raided by ships carrying raiders from the east. Travelers and traders who dropped anchor in Serenity's lagoon called them the Sakawat. They told tales of their warriors raiding villages on the great continent to the east and attacking the ships from Chekhov and even the merchant kingdom of Hastra, which ruled a large island to the east, closer to the continent. Rarely, they raided the Islands.

The skalds of the coast said the Sakawat had powerful weapons of steel and even if stories could be believed, some that belched fire and iron or exploded when thrown. They were armored such that most harpoons and arrows would be rendered useless unless aimed with exquisite skill. She had heard the tales and had listened with rapt attention to the traveling storytellers. Her village had always treated traders generously, and Reiki's father, Harald, had spoken of a pact with the merchant kingdom of Hastra. The Islands paid tribute in fish, in fruit, and in the mysterious resin from the Kappow trees that grew there. In exchange, the Islands were under the protection of the merchants and their retainers of warriors.

So, what went wrong?

Did the Sakawat raid my village?

What happened to our protection? Our warriors are few, and we have never made war anyway. They guard the Cryopod Garden and protect the village. Could they stand against Sakawat raiders? She didn't think so, and so her heart raced while her hope sank and the island loomed closer.

When she rounded the southern tip of the island, her tiny trimaran's outrigger lifted out of the water as she dug the tiller hard to port. She was now on the leeward side of the island, and her small sail went slack and spilled its wind. She knew she would need to rely on her paddle soon, but for now, she pulled the line to brace the sail for as long as she could, hoping to retain as much speed as possible. Ahead she could see the smoke billowing above her village, Serenity. In the sun's dying light, the hillside and the sky reflected an orange glow that could only be roaring flames devouring her home. As her boat slowed, the sail now lying limp, she began to paddle furiously, driving her boat forward with powerful strokes, ever closer to the coral barrier of the village's sheltered lagoon. It lay just beyond a large hill, one of the three main hills on the island. Once she paddled far enough, the village would be visible over the impassable reef which formed Serenity's lagoon. What she expected to see was her village aflame. What she saw instead took her breath away.

She had seen small merchant ships. She had seen large fishing boats. She had once seen a ship that had two masts and must have carried as many as forty men. What she saw dimly illuminated in the orange fire of the setting sun and the burning flames of her home was the largest ship she had ever seen. It was easily seventy meters long with seven meters of freeboard. All along the side of the ship, she saw two rows of square openings in which she glimpsed cruel metal mouths that she correctly assumed must be some sort of weapon. The ship had three masts with dozens of sails, three or four different sets of sails on each mast. She had never seen a ship carrying that much sail. The top deck was swarming with men, many with bows and some with long slender weapons that looked like wood and metal staves, but, based upon the way the men held them, she deduced must in fact be projectile weapons of some kind. *A type of bow? Is this one of the fire-breathing weapons the skalds mentioned?*

She quickly ceased her paddling and slipped quietly into the water. She pulled herself under the trimaran in the gap between the three canoe-style hulls and under the wooden deck. She began to gently kick her feet under the water to move her little boat closer to the shore, hoping the ship had not spotted her. She could see now that the ship was already making its way out of the lagoon. *If I stay hidden and move slowly, they will soon be gone, and I can slip into the lagoon without being noticed. Gods, I hope—I pray—let everyone be okay! Please. Let me get there in time.*

As she predicted, the ship quickly gained speed and before long they were several hundred meters out to sea. She climbed back onto her boat and resumed paddling toward the opening to the lagoon. She saw the wreckage of her home well before she swung the bow of her trimaran into the twenty-meter gap in the coral reef and into the lagoon. She could see, even in the low light hundreds of meters out, that not a single hut was spared. Hundreds of homes had been reduced to smoldering embers. She saw shapes strewn across the ground on the beach that she knew could only be bodies of the fallen. She paddled faster and drove the bow of her trimaran onto the soft sand of the beach where it had been careened only hours before. She leapt onto the beach and dragged the boat out of the water onto the sand. She turned to look out to sea to make sure the attackers were truly gone. She saw masts far out to the east, towering high into the air. The ship was several kilometers out to sea, hundreds of square meters of sail driving them away from her. She was overwhelmed then with a rage that welled up in her gut and before she knew it she had screamed out a curse so vile that when she finally rose from the sandy beach, exhausted from the tears, she was relieved no one had heard it. Then she remembered why she was so completely and utterly alone, and she cried again.

Reiki could never remember how many hours passed with her sitting on the beach, staring impotently out at the waves beyond the reef. The sun was long sunk below the horizon. The stars occasionally winked through the smoky haze. The large moon, Selene, was being chased low on the horizon by the smaller moon, Silva, so Reiki knew the morning was approaching. She finally picked herself up off the sand and went about the grim business of searching the ruins of the only life she had ever known.

She spent several hours searching the bodies on the beach. She recognized some of them, their features known to her since she was a little girl, playing on the beach while they wove nets or mended sails or sharpened harpoons. Tomas, the fisherman who taught her how to bait for Seajack. Ichiro, her beloved teacher. Ulia, the old grandmother of her best friend, Shela, who she only recognized because of her necklace, a pink seashell with blue vein-like markings. What the raiders had done to her was unspeakable. Others were simply unrecognizable.

After she had gathered all the bodies on the beach, including one or two raiders (she had smiled briefly at that), she made her way into the village proper. She walked past the dying embers of homes that had once been full of the smell of cookfires and the joy of songs, dancing, and shared stories. She drifted past the stone pillar in the center of the village, still adorned with wreaths of flowers and the names of revered ancestors: Mitchell, J., Brandeis, R., Ito, K., Klementov, I., and a few others. She remembered the names, having wondered who they had been and what they had done when they had lived. No one could recall, but their names remained etched in the stone. *And now none will remember, and no new names will ever be added.*

Something made her take a second look. The pillar had been crowned by a strange object made of the same material as the cryopods. She had often wondered what it was and why the gods had made it. Ichiro had only replied that it was a sacred and holy relic that must not be moved. She recalled that it had been a cylindrical object about twenty centimeters long with grooves around the circumference of the cylinder at each end. The relic had been removed. *Did the Sakawat take it? Why? What use could it be to them?* She banished such thoughts for the moment. She had more pressing matters to attend to. She shook her head to clear her mind and resumed running toward her home, near the foot of the smaller of the two hills behind the village.

She finally arrived at her home, or, more accurately, the ruin that once was her home. Now all that remained was a smoking pile of ash and broken wood. It took her a moment, her eyes blurry with tears and stinging from the smoke, to search in the faint moonlight for her family. To her horror, she soon found them close together, her father's body atop her mother's. Her grandmother lay nearby as well. Reiki held a moment of hope that Tova had been spared. She allowed herself to believe it. Then, her heart shattered into a thousand ragged pieces. She saw a small bare foot sticking out from under her grandmother, and an inhuman keening leapt out of her throat and through her lips that would have chilled the spine of even the sturdiest of men. They had all burned together, speared, and set aflame. Reiki vomited. Then she screamed. And finally, she wept, but no more tears came.

She turned her back to her home, deciding then and there that she would never again look upon it. She knew what she must do now, but such things should begin with oaths to and before the gods. And so, she would climb the smaller hill that rose next to the sacred mountain and visit the Cryopod Garden. There she would perform the funeral and mourning rites before swearing her bloody oath. She did not know how yet, but one way or another, she would make the raiders pay in blood for every single citizen of Serenity, and most of all, for little Tova.

Chapter IV

"An Oath in the Garden"

"Reiki would later explain that there are no gods, that the cryopods are the detritus of those who came before, not holy monuments to the children of Terra. Of course, she is both right and wrong. There are no gods, but the cryopods still stand as monuments to the children of Terra. And when she swore that bloody oath before the Cryopods in the garden of Serenity, if there had been gods, they would surely have heard her."
-The Tales of the Islands-
Stephen the Arch-Skald of Sychak

The Cryopod Garden was haunting even at noon on the brightest day of summer. Or, she had thought so when she first entered the gardens years before, as Ichiro's student. He led her through the arched opening in the high stone walls, covered in ancient moss and vines. She had stood mouth agape when she first saw the cryopods, monuments to the gods made from material that could only have come from the heavens. The seven pods themselves stood at odd angles, leaning as they rose from the ground, looming three meters tall and otherworldly. She always thought they seemed funereal, like the coffins used by the people of Sychak. The pods were each engraved with the same cryptic phrase: TERRA 037 – CRYOPOD. She had tugged on the hem of Ichiro's grey and teal robe.

"Yes, little one?"

"What is a cryopod?"

He crouched so that he was at her eye level. His bushy grey eyebrows matched his wispy beard and mustache, and she had thought those features were quite silly at the time. Still, he had kind eyes, a tranquil shade of blue, which she had always found calming. "A cryopod is a monument to a particular god. See, this one over here? The one closest to the archway?" He gestured with his hand.

She nodded.

"Now see the plinth in front of it?"

She nodded again.

"What does it say?" He stood up as he asked and watched as his pupil walked over to the stone plinth in front of the nearest cryopod. She was very proud of her burgeoning ability to read. Literacy was usually not a priority for fishermen or their daughters. For priests, however, it was essential. How else could they maintain records, deliver prayers, or read the accumulated wisdom of the priests who came before them? Ichiro had seen to it that she learned.

Reiki read aloud, "Mafune, K." She walked over to another and read it aloud also. "Kirov, A." She tapped her forefinger on her lower lip as she considered the meaning. She turned to face Ichiro and exclaimed, "They're names!"

Ichiro nodded, "Yes. They are the names of the lesser gods, children of the great holy mother, Terra, whose sacred number is 037. These are the lesser gods, those of Serenity Village."

Reiki considered this. Then it occurred to her, "Father Ichiro, does that mean that there are cryopods in other villages and cities too?"

Ichiro smiled. "Of course. Most towns and cities have their own gods, their own cryopod gardens, or temples, or something similar. The Sakawat, I hear, do not honor the gods, but who could say?"

That was a fond memory. As Reiki stood in the archway to the garden, the horror of the present came rushing back to her. *I can speak to it, dear Ichiro. The Sakawat are godless savages. Tova was just a child!*

There, in the moonlight, under the haze of black smoke and the smell of burning flesh, the garden was incomprehensibly serene. The cryopods stood silent; they were giant silvery oblong monoliths, tinged green with moss and centuries of wear under the elements. She walked around the edge of the garden, her fingers tracing a line on the damp mossy stone wall. The pods stood in a garden of bright blue and pink flowers and sculpted bushes, all of which enhanced the otherworldly feeling of the space.

After circling the entire garden, Reiki began the next step, lighting the incense. Incense, in addition to being pleasant smelling to the priest or worshipper, was pleasing to the gods and also served as a medium for carrying messages. If one prayed to Mafune, Kirov, or Kagawa for a bountiful harvest or a successful fishing outing, then the incense carried that prayer to the gods. Every plinth had a small stone incense burner that sat atop it. So, she went about from plinth to plinth, lighting the sacred incense. Mafune, then

Kagawa, Kirov, Matsui, Nguyen, Chandrasekhar, and finally Stephens.

After the incense was lit, she knelt in the center of the garden upon a flagstone adorned with a plain white blanket and waited, eyes closed in meditation, for the incense to completely permeate the air throughout. Then, she recited the sacred funeral rites:

"From the stars we came. To the stars we rise, carried by the flames. Mother Terra, guide these souls to the heavens. Embrace them. Welcome them home."

Then she rose and bowed to each of the pods. The funeral prayer completed, she drew a knife from the scabbard she kept on her waist and drew it across her palm. The blade was crafted from the tooth of the fearsome dagger-toothed sharks that hunted in the cooler waters south of Serenity. It sliced through the flesh of her palm effortlessly. She smeared the blood across her forehead and swore her oath:

"I swear now before you seven and holy mother Terra, I will avenge these souls to the last. No matter the cost. No matter how long or how hard or how perilous the journey, I will exact my vengeance. Only then may I live again. Only then may I know joy. Only then may I set aside the harpoon. I swear it now to you and before you. Bear witness and, if it pleases you, aid me in my vengeance. And if it does not please you, and you will not aid me, then stand out of my way."

She sheathed her knife and turned to leave the garden. She passed out of the stone archway and walked back down the hill. The next task was one she would find miserable. She must gather all of the dead and cremate them. Only then could she begin the preparations to begin her chase. She would gather enough fruit, rice, barunta milk, and freshwater for the voyage to the Kingdom of Hastra. There, she hoped to find some answers.

Chapter V

"The Aftermath"

"Some would have immediately set out in pursuit of the raiders. Reiki chose the wiser course. First, she observed the rites the gods require. Second, she gained information. Finally, after she had the beginnings of a plan, she went about preparations for her journey. It has ever been true: an arrow cannot fly from an un-drawn bow."

--Musings of an Old Sea Captain—

Tycho the Cursed, Captain of the *Scovalia*

The sun rose, and Reiki set about the arduous and gut-wrenching task of gathering together the hundreds of dead bodies and burning them on a single pyre. While it seemed the Sakawat had burned a great many homes with the occupants within, there still were bodies strewn across the sandy streets and grassy yards between homes. At first, she tried to keep a count and even identify some of them. After a while, she could no longer look at the faces, some charred, some crushed, some blown apart by the mysterious Sakawat weapons. She knew all of these people, and she would never again share a meal with them, hear their laughter or songs, or grasp their hands in greeting. They were gone now, empty husks soon to be carried away as smoke and ash. So, Reiki stopped counting and stopped looking. She had no more tears to cry anyway.

She worked her way through the village. Most of the homes were reduced to ash, but she found bodies strewn about in the streets. Then she worked her way out to the rice fields, the water sloshing around her ankles, little swirls of crimson trailing behind feet as she came upon massacre after massacre. She searched row by row through the rice and found nearly threescore more, mostly women, scattered throughout the fields. Most had not been burnt, but they had various wounds, some from spears or swords, but mostly small circular ones Reiki had never seen before. Curious, she stuck her forefinger into one of the wounds, and her fingertip touched a round metal ball lodged against the woman's rib. Her name had been Sarah, Reiki remembered. She had liked dancing around the great bonfire they would sometimes light on the beach. *No more dances for you, Sarah. I am sorry I wasn't here with you.* Reiki deduced that the attack must have started here since the women would have either headed into the hills to hide or else run back to the village to find the children if the attack had started there. These women were still working. *How could the raiders have gotten here, though? The island is rimmed with cliffs. The only beach is at the lagoon, and that ship could not have entered the lagoon unnoticed.*

She found her answer soon enough. She went east from the fields through the thin strip of thick jungle between the cliffs and the rice fields. At the edge of the cliff, she found a sinister-looking four-pronged hook made of dark steel attached to a thick rope that hung over the cliff. She peered over the edge and saw that the rope went straight down some fifty meters to the ocean below. *So, they anchored in the deep water maybe twenty meters offshore, hidden from the village by the hill and the jungle. They must have swam or used a boat and then…what? They couldn't have thrown the hook fifty meters straight up from the water. It must have been a boat. So, they cast the hook and rope, climbed the cliffs, and then moved through the jungle to the rice fields first.* She wondered why they had left the rope and hook in place. *Perhaps they needed the boat elsewhere and just left it so the men could finish climbing?*

Her thoughts were interrupted by a cry of pain coming from the jungle behind her. She spun and crouched, her ears alert for any sound. A few moments later, the cry rang out again from about twenty meters away, a little to her right. She cautiously made her way back into the thick jungle, her bare feet silent on the soft ground. The cry came again, and she knew she was close now. She crouched down and parted the leaves of a thick bush and peered into a small clearing. She saw a man, his steel armored cuirass identifying him as one of the raiders. He was very much alive but injured, his leg caught in a trap the villagers used to catch wild game. The traps were made of sharpened wooden stakes and would close on any creature that stepped in one. She could see two of the stakes had pierced the man's calf and likely had snapped the bone as well. *Why did the other raiders leave him here, though? An injury like that would leave you lame, but you would likely survive if it were treated quickly. Do they have so little regard for life?*

A metal helm lay next to him. Her eyes then drifted half a meter further to his right, and she saw one of the strange weapons the raiders had been using. *Can he reach it?*

She unslung her harpoon from her shoulder quietly and held it at the ready as she slowly stood up. As she stepped into the clearing, the man saw her, and his eyes grew wide when he saw her harpoon. He turned over and tried to reach for his weapon, but the trap would not budge. The movement caused him to scream in agony and roll back onto his back, his fingers working at the stakes to no avail. Reiki stood watching for a moment before she walked over to the man's weapon and picked it up.

The weapon was about a meter long and made of polished wood and metal. There was a slender metal piece underneath that she could move with her finger. On top, it had what looked like a hammer and a pan. Underneath the hollow metal tube was a metal rod, attached with little metal hoops just large enough to fit the rod. She saw that there was also a leather strap attached to it for carrying, so she slung it over her left shoulder.

The man had continued to scream while she had been examining his weapon. She finally turned to him and spoke, her voice calm but commanding. "We are going to talk now. I can remove the trap and even care for your wounds, but first, we are going to talk. So, stop screaming."

The man, surprisingly, stopped screaming, instead whimpering rhythmically. Reiki wondered if infection had begun to set in. The wounds likely would be excruciating. The fact that he was able to will himself not to scream was impressive. She wondered if she even could heal him or if that had been a lie. *Well, might as well go all-in on the lie.*

"What is your name?" she asked.

The man hesitated and caught his breath before replying. "Taka," he said, through gritted teeth.

"Taka, I am Reiki." Her voice sounded eerily calm, even to her. "I will make you a deal, Taka. Would you like me to free you from that trap?"

Taka cried out in pain, "Yes!"

"There are things, Taka, that I want to know. Things that you can tell me. So, I offer you this deal. I will ask my questions, you will answer, and then I will set you free. If you do not, then I will leave you here to die. Judging by the smell, I would say you will likely last another day, maybe two. Thirst will likely be what kills you. There are no animals on this island that would finish you off beforehand. Most of the carnivores here are thieves and scavengers like yourself. Your choice. Nod if you accept."

Taka considered for a moment, but the pain won out. He nodded.

Reiki sat down just out of his reach and unfastened a water skin from around her waist. She handed it to him to drink. "Here's a gesture of good faith. Also, it won't do for you to pass out on me."

He drank greedily and soon emptied the water skin completely. He set the skin down, and his eyes met hers. He spoke, his voice now more even but still raspy and hoarse from his screaming. "Ask your questions."

"Okay, let's start with an easy one. You are Sakawat, yes?"

He nodded.

"How many of you were there?"

"One hundred and twenty-seven. One hundred to raid the island, twenty-seven to work the Yondratha."

"What is the Yondratha?" The name felt ominous and weighty as she said it.

"Our ship. The Yondratha is the flagship of our war chief, Issak." His voice carried a note of pride.

"Your war chief? I don't know what that means. Is Issak the leader of your village, of all the Sakawat?"

He shook his head. "The Sakawat nation is made of many villages and cities, and they all are ruled by the Great Chief, Kovak. Issak is but one war chief of many. Issak, though, is different from others. He discovered the great steel beast, Ceres, and he has found ancient texts that have taught him the ways of the children of Terra. He discovered how to make these weapons that breathe fire and steel, and how to make bombs. He has promised to make complex machines to mill grain and move heavy loads but also to spread our nation across the continent. He aims to be Great Chief soon, and so he goes in search of greater and greater renown, for we choose our leaders in Sakawat."

"A great steel beast?"

Taka nodded gravely. "I saw it with my own eyes. He discovered a great metal beast in the mountains to the far east of the great continent. It was larger even than the Yondratha."

Reiki's eyes grew wide as she tried to imagine a beast that size, metal or otherwise. The only ones she could think of were the Kraken, and they were nigh unkillable horrors of the sea.

Taka nodded his agreement, having interpreted her expression. "It is a terrifying beast, and it still clings to life, though it is weak. Issak wants to bring it back to life."

Reiki was taken aback. *Why would anyone want to bring such a thing back to life?* "Such a massive beast would surely be far too dangerous! Why unleash such a scourge?"

"Issak would likely be the one holding the leash, I imagine. Issak claims it will lead Sakawat to greater prosperity. He says the beast is made to harvest whatever you wish, be it gold, silver, rice, or possibly even one's enemies." He sighed. "Regardless, the beast needs a holy relic to be fully mended. That is what Issak learned from reading the holy books he found upon the mountain."

The relic. Why? "Why would this Ceres need such a thing?"

Taka shook his head. "I never asked. I do what my war chief commands."

Reiki nodded, expecting something like that. "Okay. So, Issak read a book and went in search of this relic. Then what? How did you end up here?"

"Issak searched for nearly a year within the lands of the Sakawat, asking anyone and everyone he came upon whether they had seen this relic." Taka reached into a small bag tied to his waist and pulled out a piece of parchment on which someone had drawn the relic that had sat atop the pillar in her village, or at least a relic exactly like it. "We then marched westward to the Great River and sailed on small barges down to Issak's harbor at Warmouth, where we boarded the Yondratha and sailed for three weeks until we arrived in Sychak."

Reiki decided not to interrupt him and to let him continue his tale. Her father used to tell her that often people will answer your question on their own if you let them talk uninterrupted. It frequently turned out to be true.

Taka continued, "Issak sought information from an archivist there. The archivist then sent for a skald named Shava who recognized the drawing and told of a merchant in Hastra who would know more. So, naturally, we sailed ten days westward to Hastra. Upon arriving, Issak arranged an audience with the King as well. No one knows what they spoke of, but I could venture a guess. He met with the merchant beforehand. It stands to reason he arranged for free passage through Hastran waters to the Islands and a promise of no interference. When Issak returned to the Yondratha, he told the captain of the ship to sail westward to an island called Serenity. When the captain suggested that the Islands were protected by Hastran ships, Issak smiled and told him not to worry. He had made arrangements on that point."

"So, some merchant told the tale of our little pillar and the relic atop it, and you and some hundred and twenty-six others came to my home and put everyone I know and love to the spear and flame, all to resurrect a steel beast named Ceres?" She realized she was shouting, and she had reflexively gripped her harpoon tightly with her right hand. Taka seemed not to notice.

"I do what my war chief commands."

She sighed, and the tension left her shoulders. When she spoke her voice had softened to just above a whisper. "Where will Issak head now?"

Taka shook his head. "I don't know. Probably back to Hastra to resupply. Then he will likely return to the Warmouth, or maybe north and east to the harbor of Stavros. After that, he will try to return to the mountains and Ceres. He will have to wait, though, until after the festival of Hakan, which lasts a month. For that, he will have to travel to the holy capital of Sakawat, in the lee of the Silver Spur mountains. He will likely make it back to his city, Golden Fields, at the foot of Scarlet Peak in the Redback Mountains in just shy of three months."

She pondered that for a moment. Now she knew where he would be, and there was a chance she could make it there before him. "Thank you for your cooperation so far. I have a few more questions, and then I will free you."

Taka's breathing was becoming ragged. Reiki guessed the infection was worse than she had initially thought. "Go on, then," he rasped. "I am not going anywhere."

"Why did your comrades leave you here?"

Taka spat bitterly. "It is the Sakawat way. I would require extra food, extra water, and a healer to tend to me. I am a warrior. The likelihood of healing my wounds and still having full use of my leg was too low, and I would be a burden on my war band. So, they left me here to die. They likely would have killed me, but the bastards I was grouped with were no friends of mine. I won too many rounds of dice, probably? Or they wanted my woman, Kika, when they return home? Who knows? It is the Sakawat way to take from those you kill. It makes us strong, but it does not make us friends."

Apparently, your infection affords you unusual introspection, Taka. She nodded. "Again, thank you, Taka. One last thing before I free you. How does this weapon of yours work?" She turned so he could see the weapon slung over her shoulder.

Taka's eyes focused and unfocused briefly. He looked at the weapon, and there was recognition in his eyes. "It's called a rifle. You need this black powder I keep in a bag on my waist here." He pointed to a small bag on his belt. "And you pour some down the tube, there, called a barrel. Then you add some wadding, in this pouch here, next to the bag. Then you drop in a little round metal ball, which I have in another pouch on the other side of my belt. You use the little rod under the barrel to pack it all down in there. Then you pull back that hammer, put a little more powder on that pan, and you pull the little sliver of metal there to fire it. Oh, and you have to hold it with that wide part there against your shoulder. It's an amazing device, for all the good it's done me." He began to cry softly then.

"Thank you, again, Taka." She rose then and grasped her harpoon, adopting a striking stance. "I will free you now. If I were a better person, I might wish you peace in the afterlife."

He nodded briefly, understanding and, she thought, welcoming the end. She struck then, burying the tip of her harpoon into his neck and yanking it out quickly, the barbed head of the harpoon tearing a ragged chunk of his throat along with it. His eyes showed shock and pain, but also a glimmer of relief, as gouts of red blood cascaded out of the ragged wound in his neck. As his blood poured out of him, his eyes dulled, and his skin turned a bluish-white from exsanguination. Finally, he slumped over, dead, in a growing pool of blood.

Reiki was horrified at first. She had never killed a man before. The sight of his blood fountaining out of him like a scarlet waterfall shocked her. *What have I done?* Then, the shock faded, and she briefly felt revulsion. Then, staring at his lifeless corpse, she felt only a profound sense of loneliness. She had sworn an oath to the gods, and so for the foreseeable future, this was all she could look forward to, one hundred and twenty-six more scarlet fountains, lifeless faces, and a fleeting feeling of satisfaction chased by a frothing wave of horror. Reiki had at times during the previous twenty-four hours considered herself the only survivor of Serenity Village. Now she knew there were no survivors.

Reiki collected the bags of powder, wadding, and ammunition from Taka's waist and tied them to her own waist sash. She counted out the contents and found that she had enough wadding and powder for about twelve shots. She had only ten of the metal balls the rifle fired. *So, I have ten shots unless I can manage to retrieve some of the ones I fire, or I can find some more.*

The rest of her search yielded little of interest. The Sakawat had moved in three groups, one went south through the rest of the rice fields to the southern tip of the island. A second group had gone northward and trudged up the two main hills of the island. She found only two bodies along this route. Both were older men who had been out foraging, judging by the baskets they carried. Both had been shot and hacked at cruelly. The third, and by far the largest, group had gone northeast to the village, and there they slaughtered the people, who by then knew they were being attacked. The bodies she found on the beach before were likely the main defenders. *But why were they arranged there? The attack came from the south, not the east. They would have been better off setting up on the west or southwest end of town. Surely they had heard the sounds of slaughter coming from the fields?* Then she remembered. The Yondratha had been leaving the lagoon when she arrived. *The Sakawat sailed into the lagoon to provide a distraction! They probably fired their weaponry at the shore, and the defenders came running to fight the attack they assumed was coming from the sea. This was a well-planned raid. But why kill everyone? Why not just take what they wanted and then go?* She briefly regretted killing Taka. Perhaps he could have provided an answer. For now, the dead had no more clues to provide.

Reiki made use of one of the wheeled carts in the village that had inexplicably survived the attack. *They probably figured one or two carts would be of little consequence when no one was left to use them.* She worked her way around the island again, collecting bodies where they lay and making trips back to the beach whenever it became full. She finished gathering the bodies around nightfall after more trips back and forth than she could recall. She had formed the bodies into a loose pile on the sand, now stained with soot, ash, and blood. The pile was a grotesquery, a blob of limbs and charred flesh; a horror of black and red in macabre craquelure. She found seven casks of cremation oil, a thin clear oil harvested from the skull cavities of a giant predatory fish known as the Arakan. It burned extremely hot, enough to reduce a body to a fine powdery ash. The casks survived the attack because they were stored underground and covered with routinely dampened tree fronds, precisely to prevent a loose flame or spark from setting them ablaze. Reiki used six of the casks, pouring the contents over as much of the pile as she could reach, prioritizing the bodies lower to the ground. The flames would climb and consume the rest. She decided to save the seventh cask for her own devices. Burning a body to ash could be useful.

She used a flint rock and the edge of her knife to set the pyre alight. She stood for a while, and then sat down at the edge of the beach, where the bright light of the flames dimmed and met the night. She sat and, despite the heat of the raging fire, she shivered. As the souls of everyone she ever knew spiraled up into the heavens, carried on the floating embers of the pyre, she wondered if part of her went with them. She felt a coldness, a numbness within that the heat of the flames could not warm.

She awoke the next morning, sand clinging to her face and her eel-hide clothing. She brushed it away with her hands and saw that the pyre had burned down quite a bit, but it was still ablaze. She wondered how long it would burn. Days? A week? Surely not. The beach was now black and grey from the soot and ash of the cremation pyre. The lagoon, she saw, was red with blood and choked with ashes. She briefly wondered what effect that would have on the fish in the lagoon. The little crabs and other shellfish? She spat. It didn't matter now. It was time to gather her supplies and prepare to sail to Hastra.

She had an inviolable rule when stocking for a voyage: bring twice the supplies you think you need. She cooked rice and fruit, gathered up three or four whole fish that had been smoking in a clay smoking pot, and found a barunta that had been killed and burned during the attack. She foraged for some whistle fruit and tubers. She would not risk cooking on her small trimaran. A cooking fire was possible on a trimaran, and even necessary for long voyages, but it was inviting risk she need not take. Foods that were already cooked or were safe to eat raw were preferable. She figured she had enough food to last her about ten to fifteen days, depending on how she rationed it. She would also bring along as much freshwater as she could manage. There was a spring on the west side of the southernmost hill, south of the lagoon, and there she collected roughly fifty liters of water. If she encountered any rain on her voyage, which was likely in October, she could collect more using a funnel and her sail.

She found two empty sacks made of leather coated in grease to protect them from damp. She stored the food inside in different clay pots. The fish she wrapped in fronds. She also gathered tools: the maps she had on her, which would be sufficient to get her to Hastra (she could get new maps for where she was going); her harpoon; the rifle and its ammunition and powder and wadding; her knife; a bow and about fifteen arrows that she found laying just off the beach; a compass; five needles and leather thread for mending sails; the rope and hook from the cliffside where the Sakawat climbed; several flint rocks; and a pair of sandals in case she needed to walk anywhere that bare feet would be ill-advised.

She stowed all of these items in the compartment under the decking on the central canoe of her trimaran, still waiting for her on the sandy beach of the lagoon. She checked her healing and first aid supplies which she kept in a small wooden chest in the starboard hull. She had an assortment of herbs and cloth strips, an earthen bottle of high-proof alcohol for sterilizing bandages, and the absorbent plugs she had crafted from the sponges that lived in the shallows around the island, dried and cut into varying sizes. A quick inventory revealed that she was adequately stocked for her voyage.

The sun was now high in the sky, and she sat down on the beach to eat for the first time since noon on the day of

the attack. She did not yet have an appetite, but she could tell
she was weakening from hunger and knew that she needed
her strength for what lay ahead. She made a small fire and
cooked the orange fish that she had caught for her family.
She ate it slowly and in silence, the flames from her little fire
still dwarfed by the flames from the funeral pyre down the
beach on her right. The smell of burning flesh should have
made her stomach turn, yet all she felt was the numbness in
her core. Even after she finished eating, she felt nothing at
all. She lay there for a while, the clouds passing over her as
she stared up into the bright blue sky. She did so without
knowing why at first. Finally, she realized she was saying
goodbye in the only way she still could.

  She stood up, brushed the sand off her legs, and she
shook as much as she could off of her back. She turned
around and looked at the still-smoldering ruin of Serenity
one last time. Silently, she pushed her boat out into the
lagoon.

Chapter VI

"The Voyage to Hastra"

"The Islanders are a sturdy people. Most mariners go to sea with a crew and busy themselves with the myriad tasks integral to sailing a ship. The Islanders go to sea with one or maybe two of them to a boat. Only rarely do they build a larger vessel or sail as a group. Alone, on a small boat, the vastness of the sea all around, and no one to talk to—except the ghosts you bring with you. Fortunate, then, that the Islands are a generally idyllic little slice of the world, with few horrors to revisit those lone voyagers of the waves."

--A History of the Islanders—

Stephen the Arch-Skald of Sychak

Reiki tied off the lines that would hold her sail in its current orientation. The wind was coming from the west, and her sail filled up quickly once she left the lee of the island. She locked her tiller in place to maintain her eastward heading. The Islanders used tillers with a vertical wooden rod that could be slid into a shallow hole in the deck to prevent it from moving. She pulled out one of her maps, smudged in places from repeated use and also from the grease coating she kept on it to protect it from the ravages of repeated exposure to saltwater.

I must go east and a little north, it looks like. If the wind stays like this, I can probably make it in about six days. I will have to sleep, after all, and an untended sail at night means a lost mariner at morning light. I will need to set a drogue and drop sail to reduce my drifting while I sleep.

The currents in this stretch of ocean moved northward, so Reiki decided she would maintain an eastward heading to maximize the wind in her sail and use the current to move her boat to the north. At night she would check her latitude using the stars. Unless something went horribly wrong, she could not help but hit Hastra. The Kingdom was a massive island, many hundreds of times the size of Serenity, and a second smaller island to the southeast of the main island. As long as she headed east, she knew she need not worry about missing Hastra. She was more concerned about the time she might lose if she had to take a more indirect route. Issak and the Yondratha had a significant head start on her, and she assumed that his ship would make better time on the open sea than her trimaran would. A ship that size could plow through waves that her boat would be stalled by. More importantly, the Yondratha had a crew that could sail her through the night, while Reiki would need to rest.

The voyage was like any other, at first. She had set sail just after noon. She sailed eastward, making occasional adjustments to her tiller or sail to maintain that course until the sun finally set. She ate a small meal of smoked fish and whistle fruit, and then she tossed two anchors over the side, one at the bow and one at the stern. The anchors would not reach the ocean floor but that was not the purpose. An anchor in the water creates drag and provides stability. Two anchors creates more. Some drift was still likely, but she needed sleep. With her sail lowered, her boat would not move too far off course. If she were lucky, which she admitted was not a word she would use to describe herself given the past few days, then the wind and current would nudge her to the northeast.

Having eaten, she laid down on the deck of her boat and closed her eyes, surrendering herself to the sleep she so desperately needed. The gentle rocking of the boat and the soothing sound of the waves splashing in the space between the hulls lulled her into a deep slumber. She lay asleep there under the star and moonlight until well past midnight when she awoke to the sound of screaming. It took her several seconds before it dawned on her that the screams were her own. Throughout the rest of the night, whenever she would sleep, she would see them again, huddled there, their charred bodies forever locked in a protective embrace, and then that little foot. And she would scream. Sometimes the foot would melt away and the world would spin and instead she would see Taka's face as her harpoon entered his neck and the ragged chunk of flesh she ripped from his throat. Then the blood would pour and pour and pour from his neck. It would just keep coming until she was drowning in it, fighting to keep her head above the surface as the blood rose higher and higher. She would fight to stay afloat, and, here and there, a body would bob to the surface. Then another body, and another, and another, and another, until she was suffocating in the press of all the bodies, now pushing her again beneath the surface. She would taste blood and wake up gasping for air, spasming with terror.

After the third time she awoke, she found she was too afraid to close her eyes. Instead, she used her compass to find east, raised her anchors and her sail, and pointed the bow to the east. The little boat picked up speed and soon her mind wandered, but it never wandered too far from Serenity and the carnage there.

My mind will go there if I don't force myself to think of something else.

She willed herself to instead relive happier memories. She relived the morning of her fifth birthday when she was awoken by her father excitedly calling her from the central room of their hut. She slept in one of the five smaller rooms by herself. When she parted the fronds that served as a door to her room, she saw her father beaming and gesturing to follow him outside. When she walked out into the soft morning light, he was holding a tiny harpoon, only a meter long with a barbed blade carved from a ten-centimeter shark tooth. There was also a hole for tying off a rope to pull in her catch if she struck true. It was her first harpoon, and she remembered she had squealed and hugged her father tightly around his neck. She had felt the dampness on her cheek from the tears when she finally pulled away from him.

Unbidden, she was assaulted with the vision of his burnt body, blackened as he cradled her mother, his beloved Lia. Reiki screamed again, and she was back on the boat in the present, alone again on the sea, her breath coming in panicked gasps. *It's inescapable, isn't it? There's nothing left that the Sakawat did not destroy. All of my joy leads to tragedy.* She curled into a ball and rocked herself back and forth as she sobbed.

Eventually, she willed her breathing to slow, shakily stood back up, and checked her heading again with her compass. She unlocked her tiller and made a minute adjustment before returning it to the centerline and locking it back in place. She tried to focus her mind on the present rather than let it wander. Unbidden, she thought of Alexei and Kelli, the first boy and first girl that Reiki had kissed. *Why am I thinking of them? Those aren't fond memories. Besides, they're all dead now, along with everyone else. At least I don't remember seeing their bodies.* That thought nagged at her, and she kept returning back to it over the next few hours as her mind continued to make forays into her more mundane memories. *I didn't see their bodies. Apart from Tova and a few others, I saw very few bodies of children. I wonder if the Sakawat took anyone alive? I never considered that. Do they take slaves?*

Slavery was a concept that was foreign to the Islanders, but she had heard of the practice from traveling skalds on occasion. She knew that on the eastern continent people would sometimes be taken captive and sold on the markets, even in Hastra. She couldn't remember if the Sakawat were slavers, but it would make sense for them to be. Taka had said the Sakawat take what they want. *Maybe some were taken then. That's not the happiest of thoughts, but it is still something to hope for, perhaps.*

The hours passed and Reiki ate and continued to try to focus on her more pleasant memories so as to avoid being confronted with the horrors of the past few days. Then, as the sun began to dip lower and lower in the sky, her dread began to rise. She knew she would need to sleep at some point. What terrors her mind had for her then she would not be able to forestall with intentional dives into more prosaic memories. She would have nothing to shield her from those nightmares.

Reiki considered sailing through the night and avoiding sleep for as long as possible. She had learned how to navigate at night using the Arrow and other constellations to determine her course and, to a limited degree, her rough location. A kind old man named Matteo had taught her astronomy. It was not long after her tutelage under Ichiro. She had approached Matteo on the beach one evening, knowing that he gazed at the stars each night. She had simply asked him what he was looking at, and he began to tell her the names of the constellations and their stories, how they could be used to find your way on land or on the sea, and even what the stars actually are, giant burning spheres of gas so enormous that the mind cannot truly fathom it. He told of the dawn of the universe, an inconceivably large explosion that flung all the stars and the matter that would one day become worlds like Matria out into the infinite blackness. He spoke of Mother Terra and how she brought us down from the heavens to our world and shared with us the secrets that allowed us to live and multiply. Reiki had listened well into the morning hours night after night as he told the stories and taught her the secrets of the night sky. Their world was one of five that circled their sun, which was also a star. He explained that their world was also a sphere, but none had ever sailed around it to his knowledge. She had found him charming, and he had opened her eyes to how small her little island life was contrasted with the enormity of the universe, or even of the planet they lived on. *Thank you, Matteo, for that. And for teaching me to sail by starlight if the need should arise.* She knew the danger of sailing through the night was that she would soon be sleep-deprived, sapped of her energy, and prone to mistakes. Alone on the vastness of the sea, a mistake could be your last. *On the other hand, a mind that falls into despair and madness soon eyes the depths as a welcome end rather than a hazard to be avoided. Which will bring me to my breaking point sooner, exhaustion or the relentless horror that awaits me when I sleep?*

As the sun set below the horizon behind her, she lowered her sail and dropped her anchors. Reiki sat down with her back to the mast and ate another meal of smoked fish and fruit and rice, chewing slowly and calming herself. *I cannot run from it. What happened cannot be undone, and I cannot escape it. It is part of me now, as much as Alexei or Kelli, Matteo or Ichiro, mom or dad. It is as much a part of me as little Tova. The Sakawat have made this a part of me, and I cannot forgive them for that, even if I wanted to. And I do not want to. I will visit horrors upon them so that they forever look back with regret for what they wrought in Serenity. But I must rest.*

And so she slept. The wreckage and carnage of Serenity awaited her there still, and though she awoke gasping for breath and drenched in sweat, she knew she had to keep trying. She slept in bursts until she opened her eyes to the sun rising in the morning. She ate a small breakfast, raised her anchors and sail, and turned her small boat back toward the east and Hastra. And so she continued for the rest of the day, stopping only to make occasional adjustments to her course and to eat. At night, she relived the horror in her dreams.

On the fifth day of her voyage, she awoke to a gentle rain shower. She realized then that she had not washed in nearly a week. Bathing in saltwater was always an option, but Reiki found it less satisfying. Saltwater left your body feeling, well, salty. The rain afforded the opportunity to let nature clean off the grime, blood, and sweat she had accumulated. So, she stripped down and lay on the deck of her boat, her arms stretched out and felt the warm rain as it came in big fat drops. She lay there, her eyes closed, tranquilly floating through an autumn shower. As the rain washed over her, she felt a warmth spread through her, followed by a shiver of the sort that one gets when they feel their woes and stresses finally release and cascade through them like a wave of cold heat. She lay beneath the sky with her eyes closed and knew a temporary peace until the rain finally abated. Then she sat up and took a few deep, slow, cleansing breaths, and glanced around her. The world always seemed different after a good rain; it feels cleaner, fresher, a blank slate upon which new hopes and purposes could be written. She dressed again, lacing up her eel hide jerkin and leggings. She raised her anchors and sail and once again used the tiller to bring her little trimaran back on course.

A few hours before sundown, she spotted a small flock of birds heading away to the south and east of her. They were too far for her to make out what birds they were, either the dark, lithe, heavy beaked, and reptilian-looking Darters or maybe one of the grey and orange Divers with their fan-shaped tails and hooked talon at the end of their thin wings. As far off as they were, she could only make out vague avian shapes. Regardless, she knew from years of fishing and sailing that most birds native to this area were day hunters and would fly back to shore at night. Reiki knew she would soon be able to sight land, perhaps even that very evening if she were near a settled area. The Hastrans kept torches lit in their brick-paved streets at night. She would be able to see the glow from so many torches a good six to even twelve kilometers out to sea, depending on the height of the torches relative to sea level. More importantly, though, she knew to keep her eyes open for the Beacon at Hastra, an enormous lighthouse seventy meters tall that she would be able to see from over 30 kilometers away.

She continued until the sunset before dropping anchor and lowering her sail. She ate another simple dinner, wondering if she might have something fresh and warm to eat the next day. She finished her meal and stood up on the tips of her toes, scanning the horizon to see if she could make out any glow or haze that would indicate she was close to land. Seeing none, she laid down on the deck of her boat and closed her eyes. In the morning she would look for birds heading out to sea to begin their daily hunting for fish and algae.

She slept fitfully again, but, for the first time, she did not awake in terror. Instead, she awoke the next morning to the sound of sea birds squawking and bickering over fish. The sun was just above the eastern horizon, and the sky was golden and spotted with wispy cirrus clouds tinged pink by the early morning light. She ate her breakfast at a leisurely pace as more birds approached from the east. *Perfect. Hastra must not be far.* She stood and stretched her arms behind her back to help ease the stiffness that had built up over five nights sleeping on a rolling deck. Reiki pulled in both anchors and set sail again, knowing she would likely spot the hazy purplish outline of Hastra's mountains within the hour.

She was off by a half-hour. Ninety minutes or so after setting sail, she spotted the first little bump on the horizon. By noon, Hastra loomed large before her, a massive island that stretched nearly two hundred kilometers north to south and about one hundred and twenty kilometers east to west. If she was lucky and the currents had been kind to her, she would not be far from her destination, the port of the capital city, Hastra.

She examined her map of the approaches to Hastra to see if she could find any landmarks to narrow down her location. The most notable landmarks were the Beacon and the enormous volcano, Mount Hastra, both of which were near the north end of the island. A chain of smaller mountains ran from Mount Hastra down nearly to the southern end of the island near the Illangetti Quarter, a city of around thirty to forty thousand people which was ruled by the Illangetti trading family. On the opposite end of the island lay Treyarch Point, another city of about twenty thousand that stretched from the peninsula with the same name and down the beach and inland for a few kilometers. Any of these would serve as suitable landmarks, and by mid-afternoon, she spotted both the Beacon and the predominant feature of the entire island, Mount Hastra. Both were about forty degrees off the port bow. She was a little south of where she had wanted to be, so she adjusted her course about ten degrees to the north.

She would not be entering the harbor this evening, she decided. By the time she finished mooring at one of the small pylons in the harbor and taking a ferry to the shore, it would be night, and she would be forced to find food and lodging in a city she was not nearly familiar enough with. More problematic by far, though, was the issue of what she would use to pay for food and lodging. She could sell some of her provisions, but then she would just need to buy some more. *I need to have something to sell when I enter the harbor. Freshly caught fish or maybe even some pearls I could dive for? A few of either might fetch me enough to pay for a meal or two and somewhere to sleep. I'd prefer not to lose another day fishing, though.*

So, Reiki sailed until she could see the mouth of the harbor and dropped anchor about a kilometer off from the rocky shore. Her anchor hit the ocean floor at about twenty meters. The sun set soon after, and she ate another bland meal of dried fish and fruit. The sky was clear above and both moons were bright in the sky. Reiki smiled then, for the conditions were perfect for night fishing.

Chapter VII

"The Bounty of the Moonlit Sea"

"Silver rays pierce the blue in rippling curtains

Coiled asleep the great turquoise beast lays in his burrow

A bounty, a boon, or a doom beckons

While the evening tide ebbs and flows."

-The Night Fisherman-

Greta Hapsfell of Hastra

The Islanders primarily fished during the day, but there were some creatures that could only be caught at night. Some of them were needed for rituals, like the hermit shark, whose flesh made a stew that was pleasing to the gods Matsui and Mafune. Some were needed to make ink or dyes, such as the ink crab, an eight-legged cephalopod type creature with a hard shell and a murderously sharp beak. More lucrative, of course, was the dream jelly, a spineless jellyfish that, when dried, powdered, and ingested, offered hallucinations and euphoria. The bounty available to night fishers was potentially more valuable at trade, but the dangers were also greater. It was easy to become disoriented in the dark, and there were other hunters in the waters as well. The garatha eels also fished in the late evening and early morning, resting only for two to three hours twice during every twenty-four hour day. Even more terrifying, though, was the giant Kraken. The Kraken was a horror of teeth and tentacles, black and red eyes, and sleek obsidian-colored skin that was remarkably thick, as much as ten centimeters thick. They were obscenely hard to kill and could appear without warning. Thankfully, the Kraken preferred deeper waters. Twenty meters' depth was far too shallow for them. An eel or a large shark could pose problems, but Reiki felt she should be relatively safe, especially on a bright night with calm seas like this one.

Reiki tied off a five-meter tether to her harpoon and looped the other end around her wrist. She dove into the sea, the water still warm from the afternoon sun, and opened her eyes as she leveled out a meter below the surface. The salt stung her eyes briefly, but the sensation would not last long. She dove straight down toward the faint shapes she could make out in the darkness below. Suddenly, she saw a flashing light.

A lantern fish! Perfect!

She swam slowly, deeper and deeper, waiting to see the flash of light again. A few seconds later she saw it about five meters away. She swam deeper toward where she had seen the light, kicking her feet gently so as not to scare the fish away. *Any second now.* The lantern fish lit up just then, only half a meter away. Instinctively, Reiki struck out with her harpoon and smiled when she felt it strike home. She looked and saw her prey wriggling on the point of her harpoon. She then pointed her arms and head back up toward the surface. She kicked hard to return the fifteen meters back to the surface, shimmering silvery-blue above her.

She broke the surface of the waves and swam back to her boat only a few meters to her left. She climbed onto the boat as the seawater streamed off her onto the wooden deck. The lantern fish was about thirty centimeters long, rectangular in shape, and emitted a flash of light from a string of glands that were under its skin on both sides of its body every three to five seconds. Its face was a hideous thing with spindly teeth in a jutting square jaw and bulbous black eyes that protruded out of a thick brow.

She quickly swung her harpoon over her head and smashed the lantern fish savagely onto the wood deck to kill it. The lantern fish crunched and then stopped wriggling. Reiki took her knife and sliced through its skin just behind the jaw. She worked her knife to separate the skin from the flesh beneath and then used the tip of her knife to separate the light-emitting glands from the muscle and connective tissue holding it in place. The glands looked like little translucent yellow and green spheres about two to three centimeters in diameter that connected to each other by a strand of nerve fibers. Reiki thought they resembled a string of beads. When the little glands were smashed and the liquid inside was then exposed to air, it glowed on its own and would continue to do so for several hours, even if it was submerged in water. Reiki often wondered who discovered this curious property of lantern fish. Whoever it was, they had found a use for an otherwise terrible tasting fish.

She smashed the glands using her hands and smeared the liquid onto her jerkin and her leggings. She considered smearing it onto her exposed forearms and hands, but the liquid was an irritant. She knew her skin would break out, and then she would spend the next few hours scratching. Glowing greenish-yellow from her shoulders to her calves, she dove back into the water, harpoon in hand. She swam down to about ten meters' depth. The moonlight penetrated the exceptionally clear water down this far, but the coral reef was an intricate maze of tunnels and caverns below her, and having her own light source could save her life. *I'm glad I saw that lantern fish.*

She saw a small tunnel where two massive heads of coral met. *That's an excellent spot to find fish.* She decided to surface and fill her lungs with air before searching the tunnel for creatures of value. She kicked her feet and rose rapidly to the surface. She took a long deep breath and then a series of rapid short ones to hyperventilate and buy herself some extra time below. She dove back down, kicking powerfully and driving herself deeper and deeper until she was staring into the open maw of the arched tunnel.

No moonlight penetrated the darkness there, but as she swam closer, the glow from the lantern fish goo she had smeared on her clothes began to illuminate the features within. She could see silvery moonlight some ten to fifteen meters away at the other end. The first few meters she could make out were devoid of any shellfish, fish, or anything at all except a pile of some pale, slender objects off to the side.

What are those?

She swam toward the pile slowly. When she was about half a meter away, she saw the objects clearly: *Bones. Fish bones. Shark bones. Human bones?! Oh shit oh shit oh shit oh shit oh shit!* She froze. There was only one creature she knew that made a lair in caves and coral crevices and placed the bones of its kills in neat little piles.

Garatha.

She used her hands to spin herself slowly to face the inside of the tunnel. In the yellow-green glow of the lantern fish goo, she could just make out a coiled mass laying on the ocean floor in the tunnel. *Fuck! That thing is huge! That's got to be at least thirty meters! I've never seen one that big!* Her heart stopped as something glistened in the gloom ahead: two points glowing brightly back at her; two eyes each the size of her head. The beast was awake.

Her reflexes saved her then. She judged the beast's timing just right. He lunged at her with lightning speed that was unbelievable for a creature that size. Out of sheer instinct, Reiki kicked hard and struck out with her harpoon, using the force of her blow to push her just to the side of the garatha's gaping maw full of wickedly long teeth—serrated daggers as long as her forearm and as hard as steel. As the eel's head shot past her, Reiki twisted around and struck the eel two meters behind its head, roughly where its first of three hearts should be. Her harpoon pierced deep into the eel's flesh, and she held onto the shaft as the eel sped through the water, dragging her with it.

She knew this was not a killing stroke, but she needed to force the eel to breach the surface or she would soon drown. She could not make a break for the surface without the garatha eel catching her. She only hoped that one harpoon strike would be enough. The eel's movements had kicked up silt and now blood was clouding the water as well.

As her breath was running out, her vision was beginning to narrow. She was about to panic and make a break for the surface when the eel bolted straight upward. Both the eel and girl flew out into the night sky, the eel screeching in fury as it arched its body. Reiki barely kept her grip on her harpoon as she saw the sky appear between her flailing feet. She took a deep breath, knowing the eel was already diving. Back beneath the waves, they sped, and as the bubbles cleared from before her eyes, she pulled the knife out of the sheath on her waist. She slid her hand down the shaft of the harpoon until her hand touched the eel's thick hide. The eel continued to gyrate and thrash and lash out at her with his spiny pectoral fins, massive blades of bone and flesh four meters long that jutted out from his white belly three meters behind his head and two meters from the tip of his tail. She held onto the harpoon tightly with one hand and with the knife in the other, she stabbed as hard as she could, the knife sinking into the eel's flesh down to the hilt. She then wrenched the harpoon from the eel's hide and then slid down the eel's body until she was being drug through the water clinging only to the knife.

She guessed she had maybe sixty seconds left before she would pass out if she couldn't get to the surface. *Now or never.* With the harpoon gripped firmly in her right hand, she yanked the knife free and struck again with the harpoon, hoping she would hit the second heart. She felt the harpoon drive deep into the eel's side. The giant garatha thrashed even more fiercely as he broke through the waves and out into the air and the moonlight. Reiki felt the harpoon snap in her hand and as it gave way she was flung away, pinwheeling through the air. She tried to breathe in a gasp of air before she smacked into the water. The force of the impact made her backache in a thousand little pinpricks, and she gasped out in pain, losing the air she had fought dearly for. She nearly panicked, but her head broke in between two waves; she took a deep gulp of air and dove back down.

She spun around slowly, her eyes searching for the eel. *Where is it?* She nearly panicked again, but then she spotted him. *There!* Some fifty meters away, the great pelagic horror swam toward her, its giant serpentine body undulating in mesmerizing S-shaped motions that were both graceful and horrifying. Its mouth was agape and to Reiki, it seemed like a black pit rimmed with daggers. *I have only my knife! How the hell am I going to survive this?* The beast was closing the distance quickly, and Reiki was running out of time. She saw the broken shaft of her harpoon sticking out of the eel's hide on the left side. *Maybe I could use that? I could pull it out and try to reach the beast's third heart?* That would require prodigious aim and strength, she knew. The beast would be upon her any second, as its open jaws quickly filled her vision. That's when she saw it.

Another harpoon? Twenty meters back from her broken harpoon, lodged under one of the eel's pectoral fins, she saw a long wooden shaft sticking out at an angle. *Can I make it? Shit, I'm going to have to.* She was out of options. She curled into a crouch position to maximize her potential energy and readied her knife in her right hand. The eel's rushing jaws nearly encircled her before she kicked her feet upward, striking the roof of the eel's mouth and propelling her body out and down under the eel's head. The eel was strong and fast, but it could not whip its head around very quickly. Its body could manage beautiful S-shapes, but it could not form into a circle near its head where its rib and spinal structure were more rigid to protect its three hearts. The rear half could coil up into a tight circle, but the head was much more constrained. As the eel swam past her, she struck deeply with her knife, using it as an anchor for her to hold on. She knew she had to work quickly. She yanked the knife free and quickly stabbed again. She glanced toward the eel's tail and saw the harpoon to the right nearly ten meters away. She repeated the maneuver, yanking the knife free and then stabbing quickly to gain a new hold. Every time, she moved a meter or so closer to the harpoon. She had two meters to go when the eel whipped its tail around just as she yanked the knife free. She felt a sharp, excruciating pain in the muscle of her right thigh and realized she was impaled on the eel's pectoral fin. The pain was like nothing she had ever experienced, and she nearly screamed. *No! Fight it. Fight it, damn it. The fin. The fin. The harpoon!*

She looked down past where the long spiny bone of the eel's fin protruded out of her bleeding thigh. There it was, a two meter long wooden shaft sticking out of the eel's hide. She gritted her teeth for the pain to come. *Fuck it. It's this or drown here as fucking jewelry.* She braced her other foot on the eel's body and grasped the spiny fin with her hands and pulled her thigh off of the spine, a cloud of her blood, black in the moonlight, forming wisps and whirls in the water as she grasped the harpoon and pulled with all her strength. The head sprang free, a deadly and cruel-looking point with a serrated blade and a hook, perfect for her purposes. Whoever had used this harpoon had poor aim but excellent taste in equipment.

As the eel finished racing past her, she knew she had about twenty seconds to get another breath of air and prepare for one last charge. She needed to stop the bleeding as soon as possible, but until she killed the garatha, there was no point. She kicked as quickly as she could with a wounded leg, and her head broke the surface again, the cool night air on her face refreshing and welcome. She took a huge gulp of air and saw that her boat was only a few meters away.

Hell yes!

Without a second thought, she swam up to it, pulled herself out of the water and readied her harpoon. She would only get one chance, she knew. The eel would surge out of the water to find her, and she would strike the third heart as soon as it was high enough out of the water for her to hit.

She did not have to wait long. The eel was growing tired of chasing his meal. The gigantic thalassic beast burst out of the water half a meter away from where she stood, her legs in a wide stance, harpoon raised to throw. His great turquoise body rose higher and higher, and time seemed to slow to a crawl as he rose, water rushing off his enormous head in sheets. She eyed the spot where she knew the third heart would be, a small diamond-shaped divot in its belly, only a few centimeters wide. A harpoon strike there would kill the beast in a matter of minutes as its lifeblood poured out inside his body. She closed her eyes and exhaled slowly. She opened her eyes again, found her target, and threw with all her might, her thigh burning from the pain and her body aching from the battle with the eel.

The harpoon flew fast and true, the cruel steel head burying itself in the eel's belly and lacerating the third of the eel's three massive hearts. The eel screeched and crashed back into the sea with a terrific splash that soaked Reiki and nearly capsized her small trimaran. She managed just barely to hang on, and the boat soon righted itself. She lay there face down on the deck of her boat for several minutes, waiting to see if the eel had more in store for her. Eventually, she felt certain the eel was dead. She rolled across the deck to the starboard hull, opened the hatch in the deck, and pulled out her box of medical supplies. She selected a sponge that was two centimeters in diameter, just slightly smaller than the diameter of the hole through her thigh. She gritted her teeth and stuffed the sponge into her wound. She gasped audibly as the rough sponge scraped against the raw flesh of her thigh muscle.

She then took the bottle of alcohol and pulled the wooden stopper from the mouth. She held her breath and poured a stream of the strong liquor onto the sponge, saturating it. She screamed as it swelled inside her wound, the pressure of the sponge slowing the bleeding but also stinging her exposed nerves and muscle to the burning alcohol. She stamped her foot reflexively, and then the tears came. She blinked her eyes to try to clear them. Reiki clenched her teeth to work through the pain, the tears clinging to her cheeks as she selected a long strip of cloth from her kit. She wrapped the cloth around her thigh and tied it off with just enough slack to slide two fingers between the bandage and her thigh. She knew this would also help keep the plug in place and assist in slowing the bleeding. The alcohol would prevent infection.

With her wound bandaged, Reiki could focus on securing the eel carcass. With some catches, you could not afford to leave the fish in the water because other predators would eat it. With the eel, leaving it in the water was preferred, because almost no sea creature would take the chance that the eel wasn't still alive. A dead eel whose eyes were held open and mouth was agape was enough to keep most other beasts away. Wincing with every step, she used the Sakawat grappling hook and rope to hook onto the eel and pull it alongside her boat. She lashed the eel's body to the starboard hull and rigged its mouth so that it was open and just under the water.

Finally, she lay down on the deck and closed her eyes. *That's enough fishing for one evening, I think.* She laughed softly as she allowed herself to finally relax. She would sleep now, regardless of what nightmares awaited her. In the morning she would take the biggest garatha eel she had ever seen to market in Hastra Harbor, she would collect her earnings, and she would be one step closer to her vengeance.

Part II

"Hastran Hospitality"

"They say you should never trust a Hastran. This is nonsense. You may always trust a Hastran...to do whatever may bring him profit."

--Old Chekhovian Proverb—
Gael Redovic
Priest of the Rectory of Chekhov

Chapter VIII

"The Fish Monger"

"Some people are touched by great destiny, or perhaps exceptional luck. Reiki could have fished anywhere, but she dropped anchor and dove on the lair of the most profitable catch in the whole hemisphere. She could have sold fish and bought herself a meal and supplies. Instead, she slew a horror of those waters and bought herself allies.'
Archbishop Joachim Chen of Hastra

The fish market of Hastra was bustling as Reiki eased her trimaran alongside the massive wooden quay, the gargantuan eel's carcass trailing behind her boat. A dockworker tossed her a mooring line as the trimaran came to a stop. She tied off the line to the bow of the center hull and then signaled the dockworker to toss her an aft mooring line. She repeated the process of tying off, this time to the stern of the center hull. Once she was satisfied her boat was secured, she used a nearby wooden ladder to climb up to the quay. As she reached the top, a middle-aged man with a top knot and a plain white linen robe with a blue sash strode up to greet her.

"Welcome to Hastra! This quay is reserved for buying or selling fresh fish or other products of the sea." His voice had a distinct nasal quality to it. "We are not expecting any deliveries from the Islands today. Are you here freelance?" Reiki's face must have registered her confusion because he followed up with: "Are you here to sell fish for yourself? Or as a delivery for a village or company?"

Reiki nodded, understanding, "For myself."

"Very well, what do you have to sell? I should warn you that we are already well above the needed supply for Seajack and Orange, and the demand is currently very low for nearly all shellfish."

Reiki simply gestured with her outstretched hand toward the garatha carcass behind her boat. "I was hoping to sell that." She was pleased when she saw the man's eyes widen.

"You caught that?" He asked, astonished. "That must be at least thirty meters long."

"Aye. He put up a mean fight too." She pointed to the bandage on her thigh.

"What did you use to kill it?" The man asked, with unfeigned interest.

"I was diving last night to try to catch some of the more elusive fish, or maybe some pearls, just out beyond the harbor entrance, maybe a kilometer out. He came at me from a lair in the coral, and I had to fight with my harpoon and my knife."

The man listened as she recounted the tale of her fight with the eel. The man's eyes grew even wider when she told of the harpoon she pulled from the eel's belly. "And then I threw and struck him right in the third heart. Damn near killed me, but I got the beast," she beamed, proud of her accomplishment.

"May I see the harpoon you pulled out of him?" Reiki shrugged and climbed back down the ladder to her boat. She picked up the harpoon off the deck. She held the harpoon in her right hand as she climbed back up the ladder. Once she reached the top, she held the harpoon out in front of her, the butt of the haft on the deck of the quay and the steelhead higher than her own by a full thirty centimeters. It was a beautiful weapon. She had examined it in the morning light on the way into the harbor. The wooden haft was of a gorgeous wood she was not familiar with. It was black with a lustrous silver grain. Just below the bladed head of the harpoon, a silver medallion was set into the wood. The medallion itself was engraved with a symbol she did not recognize, but the look on the man's face told her that he did.

"What?" She asked, the look on his face alarming her.

"For starters, that is not a harpoon. That is a Hastran hook-spear. I recognize that they serve similar purposes, but that medallion bears a family crest. That's the personal hook-spear of one of the great houses of Hastra. May I see it? I can tell you whose, though I think I already know." The man leaned in close to examine the medallion. "Yes, it is as I suspected. It's the crest of the Illangetti. See? The engraving is of a Mirano ox[6] with curled horns. That is the Illangetti crest." Then, his demeanor changed completely and he shouted, "You slew the Turquoise Dragon that killed Lazlo Illangetti!"

"Lazlo Illangetti?"

"The beloved son of Pyotr Illangetti, killed by a great turquoise garatha nearly two years ago!" His face erupted

---

[6] A Mirano ox is a wooly, horned, quadruped beast of burden with four cloven hooves and a short floppy tail and a fat, brachycephalic head with a broad black nose. They have a pair of curled horns on their head. They usually weigh around two hundred and twenty kilograms and are the primary livestock of Hastra

into a huge smile, "You don't know what that even means do you?"

She shook her head.

"I can tell you the tale, but first let me send for a messenger." He whistled shrilly and a boy, Reiki guessed about twelve years old, with a shaved head and a short blue robe that stopped at his knees came running over. "Galen, take a message to the Illangetti agent at the customs house. Tell him someone finally slew the Turquoise Dragon and that they should meet her, an Islander, at the customs dock this afternoon with her earnings."

Galen stared at Reiki with something akin to wonder, his mouth agape.

"Galen! Don't stand there looking like a damn fish! Go! Deliver the message! Off with you!" The man shook his head as Galen clamped his mouth shut and took off running down the quay and past the market stalls on his way to deliver the message. The man turned back to Reiki then, "I apologize. Kids these days have no sense of duty."

"What is this about? Can I sell you my eel or not?"

"Yes! Well, actually no. Sort of. It's complicated." He held his hands out, palms up, placatingly. "You will be paid for the eel, but, there is a bounty for this eel that far exceeds what I might pay you for it by weight. For that, though, the Illangetti will pay, not I."

"And that's who I must meet at the customs dock?"

"Aye. You see, this beast has evaded the spears and harpoons of many over the past two years. I will tell you the tale, for we will need some time before I send you on to moor your boat and catch a ferry to the customs dock. For now, let me, Kato, master fishmonger, tell you the story of the demise of Lazlo Illangetti and the Great Turquoise Dragon."

She shrugged, "Fine. I would have to wait at the docks anyway, apparently."

He smiled at her impatience. "Yes, you most certainly would." He gestured to a nearby canopy with a short table and cushions beneath it. A clay pitcher and several small clay cups sat in the middle of the table. "Let us sit in the shade and have a drink while I tell you the tale. I am no skald of Sychak, but I will do well enough."

She followed him over to the resting area and sat down on one of the cushions in the shade. Kato poured them both a cup of water and raised his cup in a toast. "What is your name?"

"Reiki."

"Just Reiki? No surname?"

Reiki shook her head. "Just Reiki."

Kato shrugged and then shouted, "Reiki, of the Islands! Slayer of the Turquoise Dragon!"

Reiki felt uncomfortable, mostly because the market was beginning to fill with people and several stared at her and Kato now. She had not wanted to draw much attention to herself. She had wanted to sell her eel, ask a few questions at a local inn or tavern, and then stock up on provisions and head east to Sychak. Now she was being toasted by a fishmonger and about to have to sit through a story before she could finally make her way into port.

"It was in the stormy season, nearly two years ago, that Lazlo Illangetti decided to sail from the Illangetti Quarter, named after his family. The Illangetti family controls all the commerce taking place in that city and a good deal of the commerce in this one as well, by the way. Anyway, he decided to head around the coast to this very port. As the nobility often do, he set out in a beautiful sailing barge crewed by some twenty trained seamen. As is also often the case with the nobility, he had very little to do on the trip, so he found ways to amuse himself. In this vein, he made a bet with one of his companions, a soldier by the name of Marko, that he could slay a garatha eel. Marko, it later turned out, was a compulsive gambler and owed a great many people an even greater sum of money." He paused for a moment. "It just occurred to me, you Islanders don't use money, do you?"

Reiki shook her head. "No. I have heard of it, though. It's little metal discs that you trade for things, right?"

"Basically. People are paid for their labor in coins, those metal discs, and they can then use those coins to buy things from other people. The coins serve as a means of exchange rather than requiring people to be paid in specific goods or items, which would be quite complicated to manage."

"If you say so," she said, unconvinced. "In Serenity, we worked to provide for our village. If we caught extra fish, we shared it with our neighbors. If we had extra rice, we put it in the village granary. Everyone contributed according to their skill, and we all had enough to survive. In good years, we had more than enough even after we traded with Hastra and others."

"Yes, and the Kingdom appreciates the fish and pearls and resin that you provide in tribute. However, to buy food or lodging or anything in Hastra you must have coin. Just remember it all comes down to tens. Ten copper is one silver. Ten silvers are one gold. Ten golden crowns can be traded for one golden bar, which is a rectangular piece of gold about five centimeters long by two wide. The point is, the math is easy." He took a sip from his cup. "Anyway, where was I?"

"Marko owed a lot of coins to a lot of people, and Lazlo made a bet that he could kill a garatha," she supplied. "Ah, yes. That's right." He shook his head. "I would not speak ill of the dead, but to my knowledge, Lazlo had never hunted a garatha before. Where he found such confidence, I do not know. Alas, it was not well-earned in this case. He commanded the crew to hunt for a garatha for him to slay. The helmsman was a man named Timothy who used to work on these very docks when he was a young boy and for many years as a ferryman as well. He knew how to find a garatha."

Reiki interrupted, "They are not the easiest creatures to find. We used to bait them by throwing bits of orange fish and seajack and even the less desirable cuts of barunta into the water to attract them, usually in the mid-morning or before sundown."

Kato nodded. "Yes, it is so with us too, though we use a mirano ox instead of a barunta. The helmsman baited the waters in a cove about twenty kilometers to the south of the entrance to the port of Hastra a few hours before sunset. They waited, and Lazlo stalked fore and aft on deck with his hook spear boasting that he would slay the beast with one throw. He foolishly tied a line to his spear, despite everyone aboard urging him not to. But, who can argue with a noble scion? They are born being told they are greater than other men and so rarely do they learn otherwise." Kata sighed and shook his head.

"As mistakes go, that is a particularly foolish one," Reiki chimed in. "The garatha is too strong. Tying the harpoon to a boat could cost you your boat, if not your life. I have heard of them pulling a trimaran under the waves and dragging it to the depths with them, only to have it return as splinters. A barge is larger, but even so, the risk of injury from a snapping line is great."

"Exactly right, of course." He nodded. "You know, many in Hastra look down upon you Islanders as primitive people. I remind them that you are a people who avoid war, and no one knows the sea and all that lives in it better."

Reiki shrugged, not knowing how to respond. Instead, she urged him to continue, "So, what happened to this man with the balls of an ox and the brains of a rock?"

Kato smiled at the expression. "Well, they waited there for about an hour. Finally, they saw the first sign of the eel's approach as it peeked its head out of the water a ways off from the barge."

"It was checking for danger," She nodded.

"Aye," he nodded. "The great beast ducked back under the water, and Lazlo readied his spear. A minute went by. Then two. They say Lazlo lowered his spear, turned to the helmsman, and uttered his final words, 'Well, where is the fucking thing?'" Kato paused then, maximizing the effect. "The eel came out of the water then and screeched so loudly that Lazlo panicked. The eel leapt over the barge, and Lazlo fumbled his spear and threw as the eel was overhead. The helmsman says he struck beneath one of the beast's fins."

"That is where I found the spear, yes. It was lodged under the fin joint."

"Ah. Well, the eel dove down, and, unfortunately for Lazlo, he took the rope with him. Also unfortunately for Lazlo, the rope had looped around him when he threw, and it carried him until he was pinned to the railing. The eel would not let such a thing stop him, of course, and poor Lazlo was wrenched in twain by the rope. If it had not been for a quick swing of the ax by a deckhand, the eel might have taken the barge down too."

Reiki shook her head, "That is an unfortunate end for anyone, but also a predictable one."

"Agreed, though I would perhaps not say that to Pyotr Illangetti. He is not likely to appreciate that candor," he laughed softly. "Anyway, the barge arrived in this harbor the next morning, and the crew was interrogated. They told the story with enough similarity for a common truth to be discerned. Marko was executed for it. It was a messy business."

"That seems harsh."

"Some would probably agree, but it was not unexpected. It was his bet that led to Lazlo's demise, though not without some extreme foolishness on Lazlo's part. But, Lazlo paid for his foolishness. Marko paid for his after." Káto frowned, "I can see you do not approve, but it is in our wake, yes? It does not matter now. What does matter is that Pyotr offered up a bounty of two hundred golden crowns to whoever killed the eel, as well as the spear if it was recovered. I know you don't know how much two hundred golden crowns are worth. I will put it this way: I would probably pay five silver for your little boat. For two hundred golden crowns, I could buy a whole fleet of them. Four hundred of them, to be exact."

Reiki whistled at that. "So, it would be more than enough to buy new maps, food, and other supplies for a long journey?"

Kato laughed. "Yes. And then you would need to figure out what to do with the other one hundred and ninety-nine crowns."

Reiki's eyes grew wide.

"So, now that we have finished that tale, we must move on to business." He cracked his knuckles loudly and then whistled twice. A man in a white robe with a green sash came running over. "Get a crew to properly store that eel. We won't be butchering it just yet. Master Illangetti may have special instructions. For now, I want it weighed, measured, and then stored in salt to preserve it. Also, send me a scribe." He turned to Reiki then, "Your eel will be kept here. I am going to have papers drawn up for you to give to the Illangetti official at the customs house when you get there. It will confirm the details of the eel, that we have custody of it, and that you were the one who caught it. Moreover, it will also lay out the evidence in favor of your claim for the bounty, not least of which is your current custody of Master Lazlo's hook spear."

"How long will this all take? I had hoped to only be in Hastra for a night, maybe two."

Kato frowned deeply. "What's a few hours when you are talking about two hundred crowns? I have worked these docks from the time I was but a little boy. I was a messenger and a bait boy, selling small fish to fishermen, and worked my way up to master fishmonger. If I saved every copper I made, it would be another decade before I had two hundred crowns."

Reiki shook her head and held her hands out to placate him. "I'm sorry. I do not mean to offend. I am anxious to get back to sea. That's all it is."

Kato raised one eyebrow, puzzling over what could make anyone want to leave so badly they would balk at waiting a few hours for a fortune. "I will have the men work in haste, then." He gestured graciously to the table as he stood up. "Feel free to rest here and drink some water. Or you can walk about the quay if you wish. You are the only Islander on the quay this morning, so we can find you when we are finished."

Reiki nodded and took a sip from her cup. "Thank you, and I apologize again for my rudeness. You have been a good host."

Kato smiled and bowed and strode away to attend to matters elsewhere. Reiki was left with a pitcher of water and nothing to do but wait. She decided she would walk around the quay, or perhaps in the fish market itself. She, like most Islanders, had a diet that centered around the sea and its bounty. Naturally, she figured there was quite a bit to enjoy about a stroll through a fish market. She stood up and stretched her sore limbs.

"I could use a walk just to keep the stiffness at bay." She spoke aloud to no one at all. Her thigh ached when she walked, but, she reasoned, it also hurt when she didn't walk. She managed to walk with only a slight limp. She knew that she would need time to heal, at least a few weeks before she would be back to normal.

The market stalls were set back from the quay and lined both sides of a stone paved avenue that ran three hundred meters and was packed with fish and other sea creatures for sale. Many of these fish were caught the day before and were packed in salt to keep them fresh. The avenue itself was already bustling with customers and the din of voices was louder than Reiki remembered from the last time she had been here. She focused on the fish instead, hoping the cacophony would fade into the background. After a few minutes of examining a fantastic looking macard[7], she realized that it was working. She found herself enjoying the smell of the market, thick with sweat, dust, the salty air, and everywhere the unmistakable smell of seafood. This was what she had loved most when she was a child visiting with her father to deliver a shipment of fish from Serenity. She had darted from stall to stall, bombarding her father with questions about the fish, who caught them, why couldn't they catch those fish too, and on and on. He truly was a patient man, Reiki remembered and felt a tear on her left cheek. *Damn.*

She stopped again a little further along to examine a bin full of rock crabs, purple-hued crustaceans the size of her head with spindly little legs curled up to their bellies as they lay dead on their backs. She had never taken to trapping as much as she had diving for fish, but the meat of the rock crab was delicious and she smiled at the thought of roasting one on a spit and breaking open its carapace to get to the soft buttery meat inside. *Maybe I should buy a few crab traps before I set sail. I could catch a few before I go ashore at Sychak and cook them when I make camp on the way east. I don't know what food I will be able to catch or forage on the*

---

[7] A meter long fish, cylindrical and sleek. It's scales are a striking pearl and purple pattern that shimmers in the light. They are said to taste like butter and herbs and are only found in the cold southern seas.

continent. Once I leave Sychak, I will be beyond the world I know.

She walked from stall to stall for nearly an hour, pausing to examine a fish or to admire the massive pearls pulled from the clams that could be found near the shore. Finally, she heard someone approaching from behind her, and she turned to face Kato as he was walking up to her. He spoke first.

"Ah, Miss Reiki, you will be pleased to hear that we are finished, and I have here the document I promised." He held out a roll of parchment with a blue ribbon fastened around it in a neatly tied bow.

She took it in her hand and stuffed it into her waist sash. "Thank you."

"You may moor your boat at one of the mooring pylons in the harbor. A ferry should be along soon after, I imagine. It was a pleasure to meet you, and I hope we have not delayed you too long." He bowed courteously.

She returned the bow. "I apologize again for my impatience. You have been very helpful."

He smiled warmly. "Think nothing of it. If you would permit me, I would like to walk with you back to your boat."

Reiki felt it would be awkward to refuse since they both were heading back to the quay. To say no would mean walking together anyway but in silence. "Alright."

As they strolled back through the market, Kato broke the silence with a question. "I did not ask before, and you should not feel obligated to answer, but you have made me curious to know. Where are you going in such a hurry? Is there a festival back on your island that you are needed for? A child being born?"

Reiki shook her head. "I will not be returning to my island, Serenity."

Kato's face registered his surprise. "I have heard it is a lovely island. Have you been outcast or something? I have heard the Islanders do that in rare cases, though it would be hard for me to imagine you earning such a fate."

She shook her head again, her eyes now brimming with fresh tears. "There is no more Serenity to return to. Sakawat raiders attacked and put everyone to the spear and flame. Only memories live there now."

Kato was aghast. "The Sakawat are not permitted to raid the Islands, though! The Kingdom protects the Islands in exchange for tribute. It has been so for at least a century if not more."

Reiki nodded, "So I thought as well. A dying Sakawat spoke before I ended his suffering. His war chief, Issak, brokered a deal with the King."

"No good can come of such an act! That would violate our treaty with the Islands, and we would lose our source of Kappow resin. I know it is not of great value to you, but the resin is a necessity for Hastra. We heat our homes with it. We use it in several medicines. It's not a trifle. Why would the King put that supply at risk?"

Reiki ventured a guess. "Perhaps the King has already secured future supply?"

Kato considered that for a moment and then nodded. "Yes, that would make sense." He shook his head before meeting her eyes with his own. "I am so sorry for your loss. I cannot fathom it."

Reiki nodded appreciatively. "Thank you. The wound is still fresh, and I doubt it will ever close. However, I am sworn now to avenge my village. So, I will first deal with Issak and his band."

"You know, a large Sakawat ship pulled into the harbor a few days ago. It was a massive vessel armed with more cannons than I knew a ship could hold. I have not heard much, but I have not seen the ship depart. They may still be here."

"Then I may be able to save myself a voyage. Though, I am not well versed in your laws. How tolerant are the Hastrans of bloodshed in the streets?" Her voice had an edge to it that Kato did not like.

"The people are not and the royal guards are even less so." He pleaded with her then. "If you attack them in the city, assuming you manage not to be killed by the Sakawat, the royal guards will capture you, and you will wish they had killed you. No, Reiki, do not do something so foolish." She threw her hands in the air and then spat, "Well what should I do then? Follow them to sea where they will blast my little boat out of the water with their cannons? Trek across the continent to the far east and attack them in their own home, one against an army? Should I creep in the dark and poison their water and avenge them with dishonor? I have such a wealth of appealing options, Kato." She stared daggers at him and immediately felt regret for her anger. He was right and she knew he was right, but the white-capped crest of the surging wave of her rage had nearly crashed upon her. Vengeance was a precarious thing when it was close. She exhaled slowly and felt the rage subside. "I am sorry again, Kato. You are right, and I appreciate it."

Kato looked hurt by her outburst, but he waved it away anyway. "It is nothing. I have known loss before. It has a way of working itself into everything, especially when it is fresh."

They arrived back at the quay then, and they walked the rest of the way to her boat in silence. She climbed down into her boat and looked back up at Kato as she prepared to cast off. "Thank you again, Kato, for everything. I hope to see you again one day."

Kato bowed one last time. "Good luck, Reiki."

He turned and walked away as she cast off the mooring lines and turned her little boat back out into the harbor. The mooring pylons were further into the harbor, about a kilometer east of the fish market. Once moored she would wait for a ferry to carry her to the customs dock at the heart of the harbor and there receive her prize. *And just maybe I might learn something about Issak and the crew of the Yondratha.*

Chapter IX

"The Customs House and the Man of Illangetti"

"The great trading houses of Hastra are a cutthroat lot who will seduce you with honeyed words by day and murder your family by night. Always equally at war and peace with each other, the three great houses keep the kingdom coffers filled with gold, and the gutters with blood. Illangetti, Treyarch, and Hapsfell: the great boon and the great curse of Hastra."
--Letter from King Raynard VII to his son, Prince Henry
III—
King Raynard Mayer Farmouth Trieste VII of Hastra

Reiki did not have to wait long for the ferry once she had finished mooring her trimaran. She had sailed over to the first unoccupied pylon which was marked 15 – E in bright red paint on the side. *Mooring pylon fifteen in row E.* She had no idea how many pylons there were in the harbor, but since she was surrounded by them for several hundred meters in each direction, she assumed it was hundreds. Each was little more than a small dock that could accommodate two small boats with a tall wooden pole sticking up in the center of it. Affixed to the pole was a wooden sign with the instruction "Raise flag to signal ferry." She raised the flag and before long she saw the ferry, a rowed barge of sorts with two decks for passengers and one for the oarsmen, as it moved with surprising agility through the maze of pylons and small boats.

"Good morning!" A deckhand cried out from the ferry as it slowed to a near standstill on the opposite side of the pylon from her boat.

Ah. There's not room for two boats per pylon. There's room for a boat and then room left for the ferry to pull up to it. That makes sense. The last time she had been to Hastra, she had not entered the harbor itself. She had only gone to the fish market. The time before that, she was too young to have paid attention to such things. *It's a good system if you are going to be dealing with hundreds of boats and ships at a time and you want to control who enters the city.* She smiled awkwardly as she realized she hadn't yet returned the man's greeting.

"Good morning."

The deck hand lowered a rope ladder so she could climb the three meters up to the main deck. When she reached the top she saw that the ferry had rows of wooden benches for seating and most were empty. There were six passengers on the main deck. She assumed there could be a few up on the upper deck, but she was grateful not to be crowded in. She found the ladder up to the upper deck. She wanted to see the big ships closer to the city. Maybe she could spot the Yondratha at her moorings.

The oarsmen began to row, and the ferry gained speed with each pull until the oarsmen fell into a smooth rhythm. Reiki estimated that the ferry would take about two hours to get to the customs house at the mouth of the river that fed into the harbor. She could see a cluster of big ships moored several kilometers ahead, close to the river mouth. They were not broadside to her, so it was difficult to make out details, and yet, one stood out even at that distance.

There it is. From where she stood on the upper deck of the ferry, the forty or so ships in the harbor were a forest of masts on a landscape of wooden hulls. The Yondratha sat alone on the eastern edge of the mooring pylons reserved for larger vessels, its three masts standing at least a third taller than any others in the harbor.

The Yondratha grew ever closer as each pull of the oars propelled the ferry through the calm waters of the harbor. She took the opportunity to examine the ship more thoroughly than she had been able to in the glow of the flames of her former life. With the sun high overhead and nary a cloud in the sky, the Yondratha was stunning in its black and red checkered paint. The stern was tall and rounded with a balcony and a row of windows. The ferry drew quite close to the warship as it turned to make its approach to the customs house dock. She could see men working on the top deck tending to lines, scrubbing the deck boards, and other maintenance tasks. A few men were high up in the rigging, examining sails or tightening lines.

They left a crew aboard to take care of maintenance for the ship. That makes sense. Why waste an opportunity to catch up or get ahead on keeping the ship in top shape. It's easier when you don't have to work the sails or steer or navigate. Of course, that also means I probably can't sneak aboard unnoticed.

As the ferry put the Yondratha astern, she noted the exquisite carved wooden figurehead under the bowsprit. The figurehead was a great serpent with fangs bared and mouth wide to strike. *I wonder if that's what a yondratha is? I know the ships out of Sychak have figureheads that match their names. I've asked about a few when they dropped anchor in our lagoon.* The serpent was carved from a dark wood with blond grain that was polished and smooth as marble. A sigh of regret escaped Reiki's lips. The Yondratha was one of the most beautiful things she had ever laid eyes on, sleek and powerful, sinister yet elegant. She might have gazed upon it in reverence and wonder, but instead she was forced to see it as the focal point for her hatred.

Reiki turned away from the ship and shifted her focus to the customs house and the stone quay where the ferries stopped to disembark and embark passengers. The customs house was behind a great stone wall with an arched entryway. Any non-Hastran entering or leaving the city had to first go through the customs house and declare any goods they were shipping in or out. Other than that, Reiki had no idea what went on there, and she found herself brimming with a sense of anxiety as the ferry slowed and the deckhands cast their lines to dock workers on the quay. The ferry was quickly secured and a wooden brow was placed to allow the passengers to cross safely to the quay from the main deck. Reiki slid down the ladder to the main deck and fell in behind the handful of other passengers as they disembarked.

She followed as the others walked through the large stone archway to the Customs House. The Customs House was a two-story building made from stone blocks and decorated with stone carvings depicting the exploits of mariners and kings, and some who were both. *I might find those fascinating to hear about someday. Perhaps I will return someday and find out.* She smiled briefly, but the feeling was fleeting. Hope withers when planted in the barren soil of vengeance. Not for the first, nor the last time, the blood oath in the garden loomed dark over her. *My life ceased when I swore that oath. Until I can fulfill it, wishes and plans for anything after are meaningless distractions. I forswore joy so long as my people remain unavenged.* The other passengers all had entered the customs house ahead of her. Only she remained standing in the grassy courtyard, bathed in the shadow of the Customs House. She took a deep breath and exhaled it slowly to calm herself. Feeling her anxiety lessen, she hurried into the Customs House through its open arched doorway and into the main hall inside.

The customs house was illuminated in a bright bluish-white light from resin burning lanterns hanging on the walls. Reiki knew the resin was used as a light and heat source by the Hastrans, but the Islanders never took to using it. The resin was too much trouble to light using flint, so they used oil or pitch-soaked cloth for torches instead. The light from the resin was quite bright, though not piercing, and the bluish tint was soothing. The floor was covered in a thick woven patterned rug, and there was a row of five wooden tables ahead, with a Hastran official seated behind each of them. There was a single arched doorway centered on the far wall and a set of stone stairs led up to the second floor to the right of the far doorway. Each customs agent had a chest on the floor beside them, an ink well, a quill, and a thick book of bound parchment on the table in front of them. As she made her way into the room, she saw that the people who had entered before her went to stand in front of different tables, some of which already had a line of one or two people. She fell in line at the second table from the left where there was only one person in line before her, a middle-aged man with a bushy red beard and a floppy green hat. His voice was deep, and she listened as the Hastran customs agent asked him a series of questions.

"Where are you coming from?"

"Chekhov," The man's voice rumbled.

"What brings you to the Kingdom of Hastra?"

"I am a trade negotiator here to negotiate on behalf of my employer."

"Business, then."

"Aye, business."

"How long do you intend to stay?"

"A few days, maybe more. No more than a week."

"Very well. So you will be needing a temporary pass, two weeks maximum, for business." The official pulled a small piece of parchment out of a chest on the floor next to him and used a feather quill and ink from an inkwell to write on it. After he finished he held it out to the man from Chekhov. "Here you are Master Dershovitz. Your pass."

"Thank you."

"Enjoy your stay in the Kingdom of Hastra." As Master Dershovitz stepped around the table and walked through an open door at the back of the room, the customs agent waved for Reiki to step forward. "Next."

Reiki took a step forward, and the man looked up at her from his seat. He had green eyes and curly brown hair that fell to his shoulders. He wore a grey robe with a diagonal red sash that went over his right shoulder and down to his waist on his left side. Reiki suspected that the robe colors and sashes all had meanings because the other men in the room were dressed identically. *Grey robe with red sash is a customs agent. Kato wore a white robe with a blue sash and he said he was a master fishmonger. Do the ranks or grades also have regalia?*

"What is your name?" The agent spoke with a rhythm that comes from repeating the same set of questions hundreds of times. He always asked it the same way, devoid of any hint of personal interest.

"Reiki."

"Just Reiki? No surname?"

She shook her head. "Just Reiki."

The man nodded without looking up from the parchment he was writing on. "Very well. Where are you coming from?"

"Serenity Village in the Islands."

The man continued writing as he asked his next question, "What brings you to the Kingdom of Hastra?" *Vengeance. Blood. Pain that ebbs and flows, but never leaves.* "I am here to resupply and to collect the bounty for the Great Turquoise Dragon."

The man stopped writing and looked up from the table at Reiki with unfeigned interest. He examined her, the turquoise eel-hide clothing, the bandaged thigh, the waist sash tied off with multiple bags and pouches, her hair tied back in a loose clump of bushy curls behind her head, and a stern expression. His eyes grew wide when he saw the Illangetti hook spear slung over her right shoulder, its black and silver grained wood and silver medallion gleaming in the resin light.

"So, it is true." He nodded then and went back to his work. "Very well. How long do you intend to stay?"

"I intend to leave as soon as I can resupply. Less than a week."

The man reached into his chest and pulled out a small piece of parchment just like the one he gave to Master Dershovitz previously. He wrote quickly, and then handed the parchment to her. "This is a two-week temporary pass for business. Enjoy your time in the Kingdom of Hastra." He pointed to the arched doorway on the far wall and flipped to a new page of the bound parchment book and prepared to write. "Next!"

She walked out through the archway and found herself under a wooden awning that ran the length of the customs house. Before her was a low walled plaza full of round tables and chairs where people sat and ate and drank. *If I am to meet the Illangetti man, this is likely where.* She walked down a short series of stone steps and meandered through the crowded tables and chairs of the plaza, hoping to encounter someone who looked like they might be waiting for her. *As if I know what that would even look like.* She felt a hand on her left shoulder, and she spun around reflexively, her hands raised in defense. The man was roughly her height, about one hundred and seventy-three centimeters, give or take. He was older, Reiki guessed around twenty-seven years old. His hair was a wavy dark brown, and he had deep brown eyes, a hooked nose, and a slender build. He wore an ornate robe of black with gold embroidering in an intricate pattern of whirls and tendrils. The robe was hemmed in gold as well, and he wore a thick yellow waist sash with the crest of the Illangetti branded into a circle of leather sewn to the sash. He had three small gold hoop earrings in each ear, and he carried a hook spear that was clearly the brother of the one on her shoulder. She relaxed then, unclenched her fists, and held one hand out in greeting.

"I'm Reiki, and I think you are here to meet me." The man nodded. "Judging by that spear on your back, you're here to collect for avenging my brother, Lazlo."

"Your brother?"

"Aye." He held out his hand to shake hers. "Matteus Illangetti. I'm Lazlo's younger brother."

Reiki shook his hand. He was strong, but his hands were soft. *Not one who works the lines, the fields, or the spear.* "I'm sorry for your loss."

Matteus laughed, startling Reiki. "My loss?" He doubled over laughing and Reiki stood, silent and uncomfortable until he regained his composure. "I'm sorry, no. Lazlo was my brother, but he was an irredeemable asshole and a drunk who had all the good sense of a wet sandal. He made my life a living hell as far back as I can remember. That eel did me a service."

Reiki tried and failed to contain her shock. *Speaking that way of a dead brother is unthinkable. Are these nobles all like this?* "I—"

"Not used to this sort of family dynamic?" His voice oozed with a sense of superiority. "You're an Islander, right?" He didn't wait for an answer. "I've heard your little villages are quite—*idyllic,* I believe is the word. Would you call them *idyllic*?"

Reiki remained outwardly calm, but inwardly she seethed. "I don't think we're here to discuss the Islands." Matteus frowned. "Ugh, you're no fun at all, are you? Just standing there so serious reeking of fish and looking like you want to spear me." He laughed then. "Fine. No small talk.

Let's see the official attestation document from dear ole Kato the Master Fishmonger—more like Kato the fish fucker, if we're being honest. The man *loves* his fish." He looked her over and crinkled his nose in mock disgust. "I suppose you do too, don't you?" Then he held his hands up defensively. "I jest, of course. Let's see the parchment."

Reiki clenched her left fist and softly tapped it against her hip to fight her immediate impulse to strike him. Instead, she reached with her right hand and pulled Kato's parchment from her waist sash. "Here."

Matteus accepted the parchment and took a moment to read it silently. He nodded and folded it back up before placing it in his own waist sash. "Alright, well, that checks out. And you clearly are carrying my brother's spear. It looks just like my own, so that's legitimate."

Reiki nodded. "I pulled it from the garatha myself before I finished him off with it."

Matteus smiled. "I have no doubt. You look like you could pull the teeth right out of a kraken, or else kill one with that glare of yours."

Reiki felt her cheeks flush with rising anger. She did not like this man, and she liked being teased even less.

He grinned, pleased to see his goading was working. "Yes! That glare right there. That's the one."

She tried to wrest control of the meeting. "I believe there's a sum of gold I'm owed, as well as the spear I've already accepted?"

Matteus rolled his eyes. "You're quite droll, you know that?" He sighed. "Yes, there's the matter of some two hundred crowns. However, I did not bring it with me. My father wants to meet you himself. I am to bring you to the

Illangetti Manor so that you may dine with my father and he may thank you for avenging his beloved first born."

Reiki's first instinct was to refuse. Then she considered the request. *I need the money, and the opportunity to meet someone high in the Hastran hierarchy presents opportunities to gain information. I may be able to learn something about the Yondratha and Issak, or even what the Kingdom gained by betraying the Islands. Perhaps I may add a few names to the list of those that must die for my oath to be fulfilled. Very well.* She nodded, "Fine."

He scowled then. "It's not fine. These days he never leaves the manor, so here I am playing chaperone to a fisher woman so that he can dine with the lass who dealt revenge to the aquatic bane of his boneheaded first born. Fine would be him coming here himself, or better yet, none of us having to meet you at all, just a bag of gold coins, a pat on the head, and a quick 'thank you, dear girl, now go on, back out to sea with you.' It would be more convenient for everyone, and I don't get second-hand fish stink on me. But, here we are, and judging by the look on your face, you share my desire to be done with it."

She was at a loss for how to respond. She had never met anyone quite like Matteus, and she had no idea if she was even expected to respond. They both stared at each other in a silence that drew on for what felt like ages. Finally, he shrugged and gestured to the arched exit out the back of the plaza. "I have an ox-drawn carriage waiting for us on that street there. Follow me."

He led her through the maze of tables and patrons and pass through the archway out onto a wide cobblestone street. The street was lined with two and three-story stone and clay buildings on each side of the street. She spied the carriage about twenty meters to their left. It was a large black and gold wooden enclosure with glass windows and four large wheels. In front, a team of four Mirano oxen were yoked together and the nearest one snorted. A man in a coarse black robe with a yellow headband sat on a seat atop the front of the carriage and held the reins to steer and a whip to drive the oxen.

Matteus took two steps toward the carriage before he stopped abruptly as two men darted out from an alley ahead. There was a bloodcurdling scream as the two men leapt upon their targets, a man and a woman both about Reiki's age, and stabbed them savagely over and over with long curved steel daggers. As the two victims collapsed on the ground, each a grotesquery of blood-soaked linen and splayed limbs, the men wiped their daggers on the victims' robes. One of the men, a lean and sinewy man with a neatly trimmed beard, a black tunic and breeches with a red sash, raised his arms in the air and shouted, "These two crossed Treyarch!"

Both of the men then walked away as though nothing had happened. The rest of the people on the street had all stopped as the attack happened, but they all went back to what they had been doing, some walking, some perusing street carts, some talking to each other in doorways. Reiki just stared at the man and the woman, both gasping their dying breaths in sputtering ragged coughs and gurgles. The woman's eyes remained wide open as a tiny red bubble of blood grew on her slightly parted lips, hung on for but a moment, and then popped. She had breathed her last. *What the fuck? WHAT the fuck? What THE fuck? What the FUCK?!*

Matteus had resumed walking but quickly realized Reiki was still standing, staring open mouthed in shock at the two corpses lying in crimson pools now trickling into the cracks of the cobblestones. He turned and came walking back to her, clasped her forearms with his hands, and placed his forehead against hers. "Hey! What's the matter with you? Hmmm?" He pulled away then and pointed at the two bodies. "This is how the great houses of Hastra deal with those who cross them. These two were common folks. So, Treyarch sent common thugs. We aren't in danger. I am the scion of House Illangetti. By custom, they must offer to duel me, or at least the one who kills me needs to be my equal or better. You're with me. None of these street trash would dare harm you in my company."

She stared at him in confusion. Couldn't he see it wasn't fear she was struggling with? *Those men killed them brutally and no one even considered helping them. No one even stopped to pick up the bodies. What is wrong with this place?* Finally, she closed her mouth and glared at Matteus. "Are lives so disposable here in Hastra?"

Matteus shrugged. "This is the way of things. If you do not wish this to happen, then you do not incur the wrath of one of the houses. Speaking of which, I've been patient with you so far but do remember that I too am a member of a great house, and it would be wise not to incur my wrath either."

He spun then and resumed walking toward the carriage, stepping on the dead woman's corpse as he did so. When he reached the carriage, he removed his spear and placed it in a vertical rack to the rear of the carriage door. Reiki followed then, careful to step over the woman as she did. She removed her spear and placed it in the rack next to Matteus's. Matteus opened the carriage door and held it open as Reiki climbed in. He followed behind her, and they sat across from each other on cushioned benches. Matteus pulled the door closed behind him. He rapped his fist on the wall of the carriage twice, and Reiki heard the crack of the whip before the carriage wheels started rolling.

"It will take us at least four hours to reach the manor. Since I gather you do not find me to be an enjoyable companion, and I think you're about as fun to be around as an ox with excessive flatulence, feel free to rest, look out the windows, or whatever. I don't care. I'm going to take a nap. Take care not to wake me." He laid down on the bench and crossed his ankles before closing his eyes. Within moments he was snoring loudly.

Reiki sat silently and stared daggers at his sleeping form. He was abrasive and had an air of superiority about him that she found infuriating. Worse yet, he seemed to have a callousness that was unfathomable to Reiki. Now that he was sleeping, he was only slightly improved. Even if Reiki had any intention of napping, his snoring would have rendered that impossible. She shook her head, incredulous at the inhumanity of the first Hastran noble she had ever met, and she wondered whether they were all like this one. *If so, then I feel for the Hastran people, for life must be hell under them.*

She turned her attention to the streets outside the windows of the carriage. Reiki had grown up on a small island with about a thousand other people. They lived in a tight knit community, but one could find solitude in the jungle, on the hillside, or out to sea. Seeing the crowded city streets, the stone and clay buildings stacked two to three stories high with no space between them, she wondered if anyone in Hastra had ever spent a moment alone. Everywhere, men and women in robes of varying colors and styles were talking in groups, walking down the street, rushing to and fro, shopping at food carts or hawking business; Reiki watched all the frenetic scurrying of the hot and humid mass of humanity outside her window. She found it fascinating and a little bit horrifying as she realized she was so far outside her own world now. It was different meeting Hastrans and Sychak and Chekhovians when they came to her village. They were the aliens then, and she could interact with them with her feet still connected to her native soil, her people around her, the gentle breeze carrying the warm salt sea smell and tossing her hair with its occasional gusts. Here, she was the alien, the smell of the people, the soil, the wind, and even the sea were different. Her feet touched dusty earth or stone streets, but nowhere was the soft gritty sand or delicate grass of her home. She felt disconnected in a way she never had, like she was in free fall all the time.

Her anxiety lessened some when the carriage left the city and passed into the countryside. She could see herds of Mirano oxen in green pastures of wild green grass. There were rice fields, wheat fields, and every now and then she would see a stone farmhouse in the distance across fields planted with rows and rows of crops, some she had never seen before. As they traveled further south, they followed the mountain range, the peaks high and jagged with dark glass-like rock. She saw hills that were planted with row upon row of thick bushes she had never seen before. They had tiny round fruit growing on them, and she saw men working to pick the fruit and place them in baskets. Elsewhere, she saw other men dumping those baskets into large wooden vats while another worker stood in the vat and mashed the fruit with his feet. *They are juicing them into that vat? I wonder what for.* She glanced over at Matteus, who was still snoring on the bench. *Damnit.* She considered waking him, but she decided that her curiosity was not worth having to interact with him again. *Maybe I can ask someone else later.*

Finally, the carriage turned to the southeast at the southern end of the mountain range and climbed up a stone road into the southern foothills. Here, the road went through a forest of trees Reiki had not ever seen before, dark green with flaky bark and thin needle-like leaves. They stood tall and straight and grew close together. The carriage traveled nearly a kilometer through the thick forest, climbing higher and higher up the hill until they broke into a large clearing with a huge stone building completely surrounded by a high stone wall. The house was off to the left of the carriage, but she could see that the road came up to the thick wooden arched doors that served as the entrance to the manor. The carriage turned to the left, and she could no longer see the manor. But she knew this had to be their destination, Illangetti Manor.

The carriage stopped briefly, and she heard the creaking of the great wooden doors swinging open to accept the carriage. She watched as the carriage pulled into the courtyard, a large open space paved with white and black stones in diamond patterns. The carriage pulled to a stop

again, and she heard the sound of footsteps approaching.
Someone opened the carriage door and spoke:
"Welcome to Illangetti Manor."

Chapter X

"The Hospitality of Pyotr Illangetti"

*"There have been few such fortuitous meetings as when
Reiki, the Revered, the God-Eye, the Cerulean Flame of the
West came to meet with Pyotr Illangetti, the patriarch of the
oldest and most noble of Hastran houses."*

King Henry III of Hastra

She stepped down from the carriage and her bare feet
touched the cool stone of the courtyard. The man who had
spoken stood before her, clad in a silver and black tunic over
a pair of tan breeches. He wore a floppy hat upon his head,
and he had a thin black mustache and a short pointed beard
on his chin. He bowed elegantly, and she saw that he wore
fine leather shoes dyed black and stitched with silver. When
he rose, he spoke in a friendly tone. "We have been awaiting
your arrival. I am Antony Villago, steward of the House of
Illangetti, keeper of the house and grounds of Illangetti
Manor."

Reiki returned the bow awkwardly, her legs stiff from
her wounded thigh and from sitting in the carriage for hours.
She rose from her bow and replied, "I am Reiki."

Antony smiled. "Yes, I have heard. That was a decent
bow for one not trained in Hastran etiquette. It is especially

so for someone with a thigh wound from a garatha spine."
He swept his right arm toward the pair of curving stone steps
leading to the main arched door to the manor. "If you will
follow me, we can get you cleaned up and dressed in
something more fitting for dinner."

Reiki looked down at her clothes, stained with blood,
Lantern Fish goo, and the dust and grime she had
accumulated in the city. She was suddenly acutely aware that
she probably smelled too, as the scent of Antony's perfume
reached her nose. "I have no other clothing."

Antony shrugged. "It is no matter. We will find you
something fitting. Regardless, we can't have you meeting
Lord Illangetti reeking like a fish and looking like you had a
fight on the docks."

Reiki's cheeks reddened. *Why do I feel ashamed? I
do look like I've just gotten out of a brawl on the docks, and
the gods surely know I smell of fish. I* am *a fisher.*

Antony's shoulders drooped and he winced at her
visible discomfort. "I can see my words were indelicate, and
I apologize. When you serve Hastran nobility for a decade or
two, you forget that not everyone has the same obsession
with finery and bathing, nor the means to even have such an
obsession." He gave her a winning smile. "Let me start anew.
Welcome, Reiki, to Illangetti Manor. It is my genuine
pleasure to meet you. We have a lovely dinner planned after
a refreshing bath and a new set of fine Hastran clothing will
be provided for you."

Reiki felt her shame subsiding, despite the transparency of Antony's words. *He is a strange looking man, but he has a charming personality. How old is he, I wonder? He has a young smile and twinkling eyes, the joyfulness of youth, but there is a sagacity hovering in the wells of his eyes and a 'lived in' look to the skin of his face that suggests he could be quite a bit older. Maybe early to mid thirties? Regardless, I think I might actually grow to like him if I got to know him more. He has an honest feel about him.* She smiled, hoping they could move past the awkward moment. "Thank you, Master Villago. Of course, I would love a bath, and I am sure whatever clothing you have selected will be lovely."

He returned her smile. "Very good. Follow me this way."

He led her up the stone steps and rapped twice on the great wooden door. She heard movement behind the door, and it swung open into a great chamber unlike anything she had ever seen. The room was as wide as it was long with black and white marble floors, a great stairway that led to a landing with a set of stairs leading off to the right and to the left. There was a long woven blue and silver rug that ran from the doorway to the stairs. There were several doors on each side of the room and in between there were paintings on canvas of men, all of whom shared the same features. *They look a lot like Matteus. Perhaps they are his ancestors.* The room was lit with resin lanterns along the walls and with two braziers on either side of the rug that were easily two meters across each. In each brazier burned a chunk of kappow resin larger than any she had ever seen. *They must be a meter any direction you measure! It would take three full kappow trees to gather that much.*

Antony led her to the great stairs and she followed him up to the landing and then off to the left. At the top of the second set of stairs she passed through an arched doorway into a long hallway with wooden doors on either side. They passed by four sets before reaching a door at the end of the hallway. "This is a guest room. I will leave you here, but there are several ladies waiting inside who will bathe you, groom you, and dress you. When they are finished, I will return and bring you down to the dining hall for dinner." Without waiting for a response, he bowed, spun gracefully on his heels, and strode off down the hallway back to the main chamber.

Reiki opened the door to the guest room nervously, unsure what to expect. As the door swung into the chamber beyond, she saw a giant raised bed covered with soft cloth sheets. To the right she could see a copper tub with a small piece of resin burning on a stone plate underneath it. *A heated bath?* She then noticed the four young women dressed in simple black and silver sleeveless robes tied with a silver cord at the waist. They all had their hair in ornate braids looped into a large bun behind their heads. They smiled at her as she stepped into the room. The oldest one, maybe five years Reiki's senior, came to her and bowed.

"Welcome, Reiki. I am Lady Kalli Isaru." She pointed to each of the other ladies in turn. "These are Lady

Jane Billings, Lady Jessica Howard, and Lady Tomi Lasalle." The ladies bowed as their names were spoken. "Let us get you bathed first, and then we can see about getting you ready for dinner." She gestured to the tub. "Just step this way, and let's get you out of these clothes."

Reiki first removed her spear and her waist sash and laid them against the wall by the door. She stepped over to the tub and removed her jerkin, crusted with blood, both hers and the eel's, and Lantern Fish goo, and coated with a fine layer of dust. She then removed the bandage from her leg and was pleased to see it did not bleed. She could see the sponge sticking out, swollen with her dried blood, but holding in place. She undid the laces on her leggings and winced as the eel hide rubbed across her wounded thigh as she slid them down. She supposed she ought to feel self-conscious, naked in front of strange women she met only moments before, but in the Islands, bathing was often a communal activity. Jane and Jessica picked up her discarded garments, and Tomi offered her hand to help Reiki into the tub.

Reiki sat down in the tub, which she was pleasantly surprised to discover had a shaped bottom that allowed her to sit and stretch out her legs with her back reclined. She sighed contentedly as the warmth of the water eased the accumulated stress and tension from her muscles. Reiki closed her eyes and enjoyed the sensation for a few moments uninterrupted before Lady Kalli dipped a sponge into the water.

Reiki opened her eyes, then, and Lady Kalli gestured for her to lean forward. Reiki complied, but reluctantly. Lady Kalli scrubbed her back and face with the sponge, removing the dirt, sweat, and salt she had collected in the past two days. Lady Kalli used the sponge to wash her in sections, instructing her to stand and turn around, and so on until finally, she was clean.

Lady Jane and Lady Jessica appeared again with a large cloth towel, and Lady Kalli helped Reiki out of the tub. Jane and Jessica dried her off, and Lady Tomi appeared with an armful of what looked like linen garments.

"We have several options for you this evening," Lady Kalli said. "I am going to assume, based on the clothes you were wearing, that you prefer breeches or leggings to a dress?"

Reiki had no idea what a dress was. However, she knew she was comfortable with leggings and had a vague idea of what breeches were. Reiki simply nodded.

"Very well. Then we have two good choices for you." Lady Kalli nodded to Lady Tomi.

Lady Tomi spoke then, and her voice was cheerful and reminded Reiki of the sound of water falling on round stones. "First, we have a blue linen tunic with a white sleeveless robe and bleached Mirano ox hide breeches lined with down from Hapsfell waterfowl." Tomi held up each of the items and Reiki admitted they looked quite comfortable.

The breeches also seemed like they were strong enough to take some punishment.

"Second, we have a pair of fire drake skin leggings with a white linen blouse and a blue sleeveless short hem robe."

Reiki had never seen a fire drake, but she had heard stories of them. They were long scaly reptilian beasts with great triangular heads, powerful jaws, and they had skin the color of obsidian. They were called fire drakes because they lived on the side of active volcanoes and ate the fish that lived in the warm waters below. The leggings were beautiful. They were an obsidian color with a sheen of crimson where the light hit them, and they had a pebbled texture. She reached out her hand to touch them and discovered they were supple and light, but they simultaneously felt tough and durable. The side laces were made from leather dyed crimson and the contrast was striking with the obsidian.

"I would like to go with the drake leggings. Could I wear them with the blue tunic and white robe instead?" She asked.

Lady Tomi nodded. "Of course. I think that would be an excellent choice as well."

The trio of women helped Reiki get dressed and then stepped back to look her over. Reiki took a few steps and twisted her torso a few times to test the fit. The leggings were quite comfortable, and the tunic and robe felt light and fit her correctly. Lady Kalli broke the silence with her own appraisal. "You could pass as a Hastran noblewoman, apart from your hair. No worry, there. Lady Jane will get that soggy mop of yours dried and styled just in time for dinner."

Lady Jane stepped forward and waved Reiki toward a chair in front of a small table that was set in front of a mirror mounted on the far wall. Reiki sat down in the chair, and Lady Jane went to work, first drying her hair with a fresh towel and then using a set of bellows to blow dry air onto her bushy curls, drying them further. Then, she pulled out an ox-hair brush and ran it through her hair. Reiki had always simply tied her hair up while it was still damp. She had never owned a mirror, nor sat for anyone to brush or style her hair. She found it surprisingly relaxing, and she closed her eyes and let Lady Jane go about her business. A few times, she felt a sharp tug at her scalp when Jane would encounter a tangle, but they were quickly resolved. Lady Jane then poured a small bottle of oil into her hands and rubbed them together before she dug her fingers into Reiki's hair, massaging her scalp. The oil had a pleasant fragrance, floral but also sweet. She couldn't quite identify it, but it seemed familiar. Lady Jane then began braiding her hair, one braid on either side of the top of her head, and they formed twin buns on the back of her head. Reiki opened her eyes and looked herself over in the mirror. She had seen her reflection before in the occasional still pool of water, or on a shiny piece of metal, or even on the smooth inner shell of the occasional shellfish. In the mirror, she saw her face and barely recognized it. Her hair was neatly styled, her clothes were clean and light and loose on her shoulders and torso. *I look—what's the word I'm looking for? Fancy. I look fancy.*

Lady Jane stood behind her with her hands grasping the back of Reiki's chair. "What do you think?"

Reiki smiled. "It's not something we would ever do in the Islands, but I like it. Thank you."

Lady Jane smiled and bowed. "My pleasure."

Lady Jessica appeared beside Jane in the mirror. "One last thing remains. I need to apply a little makeup. Once that is done, you will be ready, and I believe dinner should be served soon after." She stepped around the chair and stood to Reiki's left. "Have you ever worn any makeup before?"

Reiki shook her head. "It's like paint for the face, right? Sometimes I would use some ash or pitch to blacken my cheekbones under my eyes to reduce the glare off the water, but that's all. Is it like that?"

Lady Jessica chuckled and shook her head. "Not really. I'll be rimming your eyes with a little black and applying a little light blue shadow around your eyes, but beyond that, no more. Trust me?"

Reiki shrugged. "Whatever you think is needed."

Lady Jessica smiled. "Then I will get to it." True to her word, she used a small cloth to apply a blue powder that gave her eyes a soft shadow of light blue. She used a small brush on the end of a thin stick to apply a thin black paste around the rim of her eyes. When she was done she stepped away and nodded appreciatively at her work. The other ladies stood behind Reiki and they all nodded as well.

Lady Kalli spoke then. "I believe we are finished, Reiki. You can put on your sash and grab your spear. I've already sent for Antony."

Reiki stood and bowed to the ladies. "Thank you all. This was all new for me, but I enjoyed it more than I expected."

The ladies returned her bow and all but Kalli exited the room. Kalli stood at the door while Reiki tied her sash around her waist and slung her spear over her right shoulder. She realized as she did that she had felt a little naked without it. Despite having only had the spear for two days, it already felt a part of her. Fancy outfits and makeup and relaxing baths were good from time to time, but she was an Islander, a master of the sea and harpoons. A hook spear was different, perhaps, but not in any way that mattered to her.

She heard two raps on the door, and Lady Kalli pulled it open to reveal Antony standing, hands clasped together behind him, rocking on his heels. He smiled as he looked Reiki over, his eyes finally stopping to peer directly into hers. "I see they have done their work admirably. Although, whether they are great sculptors or you were exceptional marble is an open question, I suppose. You look stunning, Miss Reiki. Truly stunning. A fitting dinner guest for a King, or perhaps the Lord of a great Hastran House, yes?"

Reiki was surprised to find she was blushing. *I need to get out of here as soon as I am able, lest my blade become dull from disuse. They think to defang me with their sweetness—and they might succeed if I spent too long in these comforts.*

Antony was still grinning when he gestured for her to follow him with a wave of his left hand. "Please, come this way. Dinner will be served shortly, but I may seat you in the dining hall and you may meet my master."

Reiki did as she was bidden and followed a pace behind him as they walked back down the long hall and down the stairs into the main entry chamber. They turned left then and walked through a wooden door into another hallway, this one with only a single set of double doors on the left. Antony stopped just short of the double doors and turned to face her.

"In a moment I will open the doors and I will announce you. Bear in mind that you are the first to enter, but you must stay standing as I bring in the others. Tonight, there will be a small number, so you won't have to wait long. Once Lord Pyotr has been announced and seated, you may sit along with everyone else. I will take you to your assigned seat, which is to Pyotr's left. This is unusual. A commoner such as yourself would not usually dine with nobles at all. To be seated to the left of the head of a great house is unheard of. I don't tell you this to make you nervous but so that you, unfamiliar with our ways as you are, will understand the great honor you are being given." He paused briefly to see if she had any questions. Hearing none, he turned then and pushed open the double doors one at a time and securing them against the wall of the dining hall. He then strode over to the right-hand side of the entrance and stood at attention before announcing in a surprisingly loud voice:

"Miss Reiki of the Islands!"

She stood there, unmoving until Antony beckoned her to come with a frantic jerk of his left hand. She hurriedly passed through the open doorway and saw a large table made of beautiful rich wood, shiny with a reddish tint to it. She had no idea what sort of tree it could have come from and knew intrinsically that it had to have been brought from somewhere far away. The tree must have been massive, too, because the tabletop had been cut from a single tree. There were no planks, no seams, nothing but a continuous grain pattern that had gorgeous whorls and loops. The table itself was two meters wide by ten meters long, and there were chairs to seat at least twenty-four people, one on each end and eleven per side. There was a large fireplace at one end of the room, off to the right, and another man stood by the end of the table to her right. He waved for her to come and as she walked over to where he was standing, he pulled a chair out from the table, the last seat before the end.

Reiki stood behind the chair, remembering Antony's instructions, and grasped the back with both her hands. She stood there anxiously for what felt like an eternity before Antony's booming voice announced:

"Rodrigo Voorhees, Captain of Lord Illangetti's Guard."

Voorhees, she saw as he approached on her left, was an older man, probably in his early fifties judging by his graying hair and weathered skin. He was tall and imposing, and he wore a cuirass that was similar to the one worn by Taka, the Sakawat soldier. His hair was closely cropped, and he had a circle beard that was dark brown streaked with gray. His eyes, set under a pair of thick eyebrows, were such a dark shade of brown she at first thought they were black. He wore a spear over his right shoulder and on his left hip he had a curved scabbard from which she could see the blue and silver braided hilt of a sword. He wore a white tunic under his cuirass and a pair of black breeches tucked into black leather boots that he had shined with oil. He came to a halt and stood at attention behind the chair to the left of hers.

Antony's voice rang out again:

"Demetrius Illangetti, Third Son of Lord Illangetti!"

Demetrius had the same wavy brown hair, deep brown eyes, and hooked nose as Matteus, but he was shorter and stockier of build. He wore a black and gold tunic with a plain gold sash tied around his waist. His breeches were beige ox hide, and he wore supple beige suede slippers on his feet. He smiled as he rounded the table and stood behind the chair directly across from Voorhees. Reiki could tell he was Matteus's brother, but where Matteus's demeanor expressed superiority and disdain, Demetrius seemed to exude only warmth and calm. His eyes met hers, and he smiled and nodded to her in welcome. She was surprised to find herself smiling and nodding in return. *Huh. Maybe being an asshole isn't a family trait. There's something else there, though, in those eyes. What is it, I wonder?*

Antony's voice filled the chamber. "Matteus Illangetti, Second Son of Lord Illangetti!"

Reiki hardly needed to be reintroduced to Matteus. He rounded the end of the table and stood directly across from Reiki. His eyes met hers briefly before he rolled them and jabbed Demetrius in the ribs. Demetrius jumped back and clasped his side, rubbing his ribs. Matteus smiled and then leaned in and whispered something into Demetrius's ear that Reiki couldn't make out. Demetrius's face flushed, and he cast his eyes down in shame. Matteus laughed then, and not for the first time Reiki had the unkind thought that Matteus might best be served with a good beating or two. She briefly imagined delivering such a beating when Antony called out again:

"Lord Pyotr Illangetti of the Great Hastran House of Illangetti!"

Reiki studied Lord Illangetti as he walked around the far end of the table and strode toward his own seat past his two sons. He was not as tall as she would have expected, maybe a few centimeters taller than Reiki. He was older, in his mid to late fifties, she reckoned. His wavy hair was all silver, and he wore a full silver beard neatly trimmed. His eyes were the same dark brown as his sons, and he had the same hooked nose. His eyebrows were thick and the same silver as his beard and hair. He wore a long black robe over a gold tunic and black breeches. His boots were fashioned from fire drake skin and shimmered with crimson in the light, just like her leggings. He looked tired and his face bore the lines and wrinkles of decades of worry and—she sensed—heartbreak. She didn't quite know why, but she immediately felt sympathy for the man.

When he reached his chair at the end of the table, he took his seat and addressed his guests. "Thank you for dining with me tonight. Please, be seated." He had a sonorous voice that seemed to emanate deep from within his chest.

Reiki saw that the others first removed their spears and held them out for the man who had seated Reiki to come and collect. Reiki slid her spear off her shoulder and held it out to her side as well. The man took them one by one, starting with Matteus and then Voorhees, and finally Reiki. He carried them to a wall-mounted rack and placed each in the rack in order of seniority, Matteus, Voorhees, Reiki. Demetrius did not carry a spear. Once the man had collected their spears, everyone took their seats. Reiki followed suit.

Once she sat down, Pyotr signaled to Antony with a flick of his hand, and then fixed his gaze on Reiki. His deep brown eyes seemed to drink in the blue-white light of the resin lanterns in the room. She felt minuscule there before his gaze, and common, despite the finery they had wrapped her in. *You can give a fish feathers, but it will remain a fish. Dress me up like a bird and throw me off a mountain and try as I might, I cannot fly.* Nonetheless, she met his gaze and they held this way until finally Pyotr smiled.

"So," he began, "you're the one who finally avenged my son, Lazlo, and slew the Great Turquoise Dragon that was his doom. I don't know what I expected you to be, but I am surprised nonetheless."

The quip escaped Reiki's lips before she could stop it. "You were expecting someone taller, with an Adam's apple perhaps?"

Matteus snorted, and Demetrius stifled a laugh. Voorhees just grunted. Pyotr just stared for a moment before his face broke into an enormous grin. He laughed then, a pleasant sound, deep and rolling. "You're probably right. The Kingdom of Hastra is a patriarchal society. Our women do not wield spears or sail the seas. Certainly none in Hastra have ever slain a garatha, much less the monster that Kato reported you killed. It's quite incredible."

"Thank you. He put up quite the fight, and I did not come away unscathed."

"Indeed. Of course, I will want to hear the tale."

His interest appeared quite genuine to Reiki. She was about to recount the fight with the garatha but was interrupted by the arrival of three men, each carrying a tray of food. They placed the trays on the table before they quickly retreated back out into the hallway.

"Ah, excellent. Appetizers." He gestured to the trays of food. "Do help yourselves. We will not be eating formally tonight. Tonight is for telling stories and honoring our guest, Reiki."

The appetizers were assorted fruits and some baked pastries, as well as a large wheel of cheese marbled with blue mold. Reiki had never had cheese, and the Islanders made very few baked goods. She was eager to try both. Everyone took what they wanted from the trays, and Voorhees began an animated conversation with Demetrius regarding some sort of worker rebellion in Chekhov. Matteus seemed bored. Pyotr, on the other hand, seemed only interested in Reiki.

"So, you were about to tell me how you bested the garatha." He took a bit of a pastry.

Reiki swallowed the piece of cheese she had just placed in her mouth, savoring the pungent bite of the mold that lingered in her mouth. She then told the tale, starting with the lantern fish and ending when she lashed the beast to her boat after patching up her thigh. Pyotr listened with increasing fascination. He gasped when she told of spotting the eel in its lair, and again when she spotted the spear. He winced when she told of the spine sticking through her thigh, and he seemed relieved when she struck the killing blow. When she finished, she realized that everyone had stopped talking and listened to her story and were now viewing her with something akin to respect, in Voorhees's case, or even awe in Pyotr's case. Matteus just scowled, though there was a hint of something else in his expression that Reiki couldn't quite place.

"Truly impressive, Reiki." Pyotr smiled. "Are all of the Islanders so gifted?"

"We all have our skills. We all contribute in different ways. I saw my first garatha when I was five. Others never even go out to sea. But, of those of us that do, I would say that yes, many are. There are others more skilled and braver than I." She then added. "And if it were not for your son's spear, I would not be here speaking to you now, my skill be damned."

Pyotr nodded and was silent for a moment as a pained expression spread across his face. Finally, he sighed. "I know the truth of my son's death, Reiki. He was brash. He believed the lie of nobility." He shook his head bitterly and slammed the table with his closed fist, the steel plates and trays rattling from the force. "Do you know what I mean, Reiki, by the *lie* of nobility?"

Reiki shook her head. "No. We have no nobles. No kings or lords."

"You are fortunate, then." Pyotr paused briefly, considering his words. Matteus, meanwhile, failed to conceal his disgust. *He has heard this before and finds it disagreeable.* "The lie of nobility is this: nobles are a group of people who are told every day of their lives that they are the best, strongest, most able, and most worthy people in their kingdom, all by virtue of their birth and the wealth accumulated by their forebears. Yet, nobles did not create that wealth. They did not earn it through hard work or being particularly ingenious. We have greater education, perhaps, but that is because we could afford to spend the time to be educated at the university in Hastra, or in Sychak. We never had to worry that our pursuits would leave our tables bare or our coffers empty. The entirety of the kingdom supports the continued wealth and power of the nobles, and the nobles instead tell themselves and any who listen that they provide work and food and money to those they employ. Yet, were the kingdom only nobles, what hope would we have? We'd starve in our manors and die cursing the common folk for their absence." He spat on the floor in disgust. "My son Lazlo believed he was an able spearman and sailor because he believed the lie, and why not? He had been told it every moment of every day of his life by our words and by the system that props us up. He believed that something as simple as the name, Illangetti, made him these things. And, yet, I imagine you know quite well that Matteus, or Demetrius, or myself, none could hope to be your match upon the sea, could we? Could we navigate by the stars or spot the signs of coming danger from a sudden storm?"

Had Reiki been raised in Hastran society, she might not have replied truthfully. She would have grown up under the long shadows of the great houses and been taught that honesty in the face of the nobility could cost her life. Reiki answered honestly and replied,. "Probably not. I held my first harpoon when I was still a young girl, maybe five or six. I sailed and caught fish with my harpoon nearly every day of my life thereafter. I could either master those skills or perish.

The sea treats novices and masters the same. The masters are the ones who learned and survived it."

Pyotr considered her words and simply nodded. "I appreciate your honesty, though others would not."

Matteus did not. "Why are you humoring her, father? You insult the memory of your own son and accept insults from this foreign sea wench?"

Pyotr sighed and spoke calmly. "What insult is there in the truth? I detected no intention to offend." He turned to Reiki. "Did you mean to insult me? Should I be incensed like my middle son, whose passions have always run too hot?"

Matteus flinched from the rebuke, his color rising. Reiki shook her head. "You asked me a question and I answered."

Matteus glared at her. "Oh, yes, you answered. Simple, common, direct little Reiki, sitting here at this table, a fish wrapped in gold and spritzed with perfume, but a fish nonetheless. Antony and his gaggle of harpies may have gilded you nicely, but this table is too fine for you."

The words stung and she bit her lip to stifle the harsh retort that nearly escaped her clenched teeth. Her defense came from a surprising direction in the form of Voorhees. He slammed a heavy fist onto the solid wood table. "You accuse her of insult and then spit that filth? At your father's table? To an *honored guest?* Boy, two years you left your own brother unavenged. Did you take up the spear and seek out the beast? Did you? No. Your balls reside in your mouth as ever."

The color drained from Matteus's face, but he remained silent. The look on Voorhees's face was not one that invited argument. Demetrius, however, seemed amused.

"He does have a point, brother. You have always been quick to boast, yet the skalds seem oddly silent where your deeds are concerned." Demetrius took a bite of a pastry and chewed it casually.

Pyotr sighed again, his expression weary. "Forgive the insult, Reiki, and know that it came from a place of shame and envy. Matteus believes the lie wholeheartedly, as did Lazlo."

Reiki nodded, but the words still echoed inside her head. She felt very aware of how out of place she was.

Pyotr raised his hand above his head and gave a flick of his wrist to signal the next course. The same three men entered and removed the trays of appetizers before retreating. Another three entered with three more trays, this time with an assortment of roasted meats sliced thinly and rolled up. She could see seajack, eel, what she suspected was ox meat, and some whiter meat with a layer of fat and crispy skin.

Pyotr spoke. "For our first course, we have seajack, eel, Mirano ox loin, and Hapsfell waterfowl. Enjoy."

Everyone ate quietly for a few minutes. Reiki found that she liked the taste of the waterfowl. The fat and crispy skin both combined with the tender meat in a sweet and salty mélange of flavor. The ox meat was a bit too chewy for her liking, but the eel and seajack were both cooked beautifully.

Eventually, Pyotr broke the silence. "Now, Reiki, I am curious to know, what brought you to Hastra? It is highly unusual for a single Islander to sail into our harbor alone. Usually, you come as a group with cargo for tribute, or to make a request of the King, or to arrange a trade. A single young Islander arriving for no express purpose and unrequested is unheard of."

Reiki stared at her plate, now empty, and wondered how much she should tell. Her previous honesty was not well received by some at the table. Yet, Pyotr had seemed to welcome it. "I came to resupply, buy maps, and gather information." She decided to begin with the most simplified answer first. Perhaps Pyotr would be satisfied and incurious.

Pyotr replied almost immediately, "Information about what?"

Reiki took a deep breath and then told the tale of the destruction of Serenity Village. She began with her fishing on her boat and ended with her anchoring outside the harbor before fighting the eel. She left out the nightmares and the rain shower. When she had finished her tale, Pyotr looked aghast. Demetrius was deep in thought. Voorhees wore a deep frown. Matteus appeared to be contemplating something and refused to meet her eyes.

Finally, Pyotr spoke, "You say the Sakawat, Taka, claimed they were given permission to raid Serenity by the King?"

Reiki nodded.

Pyotr's face was lined with worry. "That is troubling, not least because I had no knowledge of it."

Demetrius spoke up then, "Father, I think it is possible the Hapsfell and Treyarch are making a move now."

Voorhees added, "If what Reiki has told us is accurate, then I have to agree with young Demetrius. The King would never act without the support of the great houses. If you were unaware of it, then that implies that the other two are making moves without you."

Matteus laughed then. "Well, of course they would!"

Voorhees and Pyotr shot Matteus withering glares. Demetrius just arched his right eyebrow quizzically.

Matteus continued, "Father, for these past five years, how often have we responded with vendettas against the other houses? When they insult us, we remain silent. When opportunities arise to move against them, we let them pass. This house has grown weak these past five years. Is it any surprise that they move against us, knowing that our arms will remain sheathed, that our ire is toothless?"

For a brief moment, Pyotr looked as though he might strike Matteus. The two locked eyes for what felt an eternity, and Reiki squirmed in her seat. Finally, Pyotr spoke in a level voice that carried the weight of untold layers of emotion. "That will be all, Matteus. You are dismissed."

Matteus shrugged, then stood and strode out of the dining hall through the double doors.

Pyotr turned to Reiki then. "I'm sorry you had to witness that." He sighed, then, and Reiki thought he looked much older than before. "He isn't wrong to say that I have kept the blade in its sheath. Nor is he wrong to think that that is the cause of our being kept out of these intrigues. He is young, and he does not understand that vengeance is a wheel that will turn forever unless you step off of it. You cannot win vengeance, only feed it." He signaled Antony and ordered, "Wine and cups for four, Antony."

Reiki waited then as two men entered, set cups in front of each of them, and poured a dark red liquid from a clay ewer into each cup.

"For what I am about to say, I think wine is called for." He took a sip from his cup.

Reiki took a sip of the wine and was surprised at its depth of flavor. She also felt an immediate warmth rising from her chest which she found quite enjoyable.

"When I was Matteus's age, I made a name for myself as a ruthless man, one to never cross. I would pay back any slight or insult with violence. If one of my employees was taken advantage of by a merchant or a quarrel broke out between my men and those of another house, I would wreak vengeance tenfold on our enemies. And so, the Illangetti gained a reputation for bloodshed, and for a while we were ascendant. But, all things have a zenith. What you put out into the world often returns to you. Thus, five years ago, the Treyarch and the Hapsfell both decided that I had overstepped and must be repaid in bloodshed. My wife was walking out in the vineyards in the foothills you passed on your way here. She loved to walk and smell the red wine grapes on a summer afternoon. My men found her body there, slashed and stabbed brutally. I wept and wept, and I did not speak or eat for three days. When I finally emerged from my chambers after the third day, my sons begged me to seek vengeance. But, I did not."

Reiki took another sip of her wine then. *Why not?*

"You see, I realized something while I was in seclusion. I realized that every time I lashed out in vengeance to repay blood, I created new corpses, new heartbreak, new causes for vengeance. Vengeance brings more vengeance. And when does it end? The only way to win is to not play." He took another sip of his wine. "Reiki, I will not try to tell you what you should do. But, let me ask you this: you have sworn to kill all one hundred and twenty-seven of those that destroyed your village. How many orphans, widows, and brothers and sisters do you think those men will leave behind?"

"I don't know."

"We can assume, at least, that they will all leave behind at least one person who will feel that loss, yes?"

She nodded. "We can assume."

"How many of them might swear an oath in a garden and seek vengeance against you?"

"I don't know."

"And if they come after you, they might kill you, or they might kill someone you love. And then what? Do you seek more vengeance?"

She knew what he was saying, but her heart would not hear it. *Not now.* "Go on."

"When do you get to go about the business of living? When do you get to be a person and not just *something* that kills and brings misery? How can you have room at all for love when your life becomes a spinning wheel of hatred?"

Reiki snapped back, "So what then? Do I just let it go? Do I leave these crimes unpunished? Should I just meekly go back to my island to wait for death alone? Should I try to find my way to another island and pretend that there isn't a gaping chasm of pain and despair in me?"

Pyotr shook his head. "I don't know what you should do. I just find that I like you, and I hope you don't learn this lesson the way that I did. There are some wounds that cannot heal; losses that cannot be restored. Then, one day, you find yourself like me: old and filled with regret. With a dead wife, a dead son, a son that brings me shame, and one that I pray every moment of every day does not receive the fruits of seeds I planted in my youth."

Reiki stared down at her plate. She fought against the truth of his words. *Is it my rage that resists his counsel? Yet, what choice do I have? Where can I go? What life could I have without mother and father and little Tova, the memory of their burned bodies haunting me wherever I may go? I must put those ghosts to rest and fulfill my oath. Or else I fail them and become an oathbreaker, cursed by the gods.*

Pyotr could see she was troubled with her own thoughts. "Reiki, your path is your own, of course. I am now an old man, bitter with loss and burdened by the weight of my own conscience. I only ask that you consider my words and know that I only wish to spare you the same fate or worse."

Demetrius spoke then, "I think we need to consider the more immediate situation."

Voorhees nodded. "I agree with Demetrius, my lord. If the Hapsfell and Treyarch are edging you out, we may need to be more guarded than we have been."

Demetrius added, "We also should be wary of Matteus as well. My brother had an ill look in his eye as he left. And he left with less fight than is usual. It is a rare thing for Matteus to surrender the last word to anyone, especially you, father."

"I would like to believe he would not betray us. However, Matteus has never forgiven me for my failure to avenge his mother." He turned to Reiki. "Matteus worshipped my wife, Agatha. She doted on him, and he repaid her with a sweetness and devotion that he denied everyone else in his life. That anger and his own pride could indeed move him to folly."

Demetrius tapped his forefinger on his chin as he considered the possibilities. "The first question that occurs to me is why the other houses would agree to sacrifice Serenity. The Islands are our source of resin. We can get it nowhere else. Why would they risk that supply?"

Voorhees offered an answer, "Perhaps they believe the Islands would not resist? Or maybe they think Issak could carry the raid in secret. That would explain why they were so thorough in killing everyone there, present company excluded."

Demetrius nodded. "Yes, Reiki's survival must not be known to them, or to Issak for that matter."

Voorhees stroked his chin. "Yes, they must not know." He gave Reiki a quick glance before continuing, "It's not just the Islands they would need to worry about either. The common Hastran folk would be outraged if they knew the Kingdom allowed such an attack. The King would need to be able to say the Sakawat slipped through our fleets unseen and carried out the attack."

Pyotr gasped then. "You're right. Of course, the knowledge that Serenity has been destroyed would eventually come out, but the King could then make a show of anger at Issak and the Sakawat in general. But, it would be for show. So, the question remains, what do the other houses and the kingdom gain from Issak's attack?"

Everyone was silent until Demetrius laughed bitterly. "It's that simple, isn't it? Father, what if the Sakawat ceded control of Serenity, an occupied possession that would be recognized by most kingdoms and nations as a right of conquest, to Hastra? Wouldn't the Kingdom stand to gain considerably if it had its own source of kappow resin? Couldn't our workers cultivate a vast forest of kappow trees to harvest?"

Pyotr nodded. "That would make sense. Such a venture would be quite lucrative. It would cut Hastran costs considerably since the cost of kappow currently is maintaining a fleet for protection of the Islands and then the secondary costs of refining or otherwise processing the resin for its various uses. If we had our own supply, the fleet would be free to pursue other things, possibly even expand our kingdom by colonizing some of the uninhabited areas of the eastern continent."

Voorhees grunted. "That is simple. But, it would make sense, and it's just grand enough for the Hapsfells and Treyarchs to get behind, and the King has always bemoaned the kingdom's lack of power projection. He likely fancies himself a conqueror."

Reiki had sat silent as the discussion was going on, but finally, she erupted, "Are you suggesting that my entire village was murdered savagely all so some rich Hastrans wouldn't have to spend as much money on fucking tree sap? Are your pretty lights and your heated baths so important that my family—my little brother—all of them had to die?"

No one answered and as she bored into each of them with her eyes, and they averted their gaze. None would meet her eyes. So, she stood, and she spat on the floor in disgust. "That's what I think of your supposed nobility and your king and your fucking profits. You can take all the resin on the planet for all I care, and I hope your kingdom drowns in it."

Pyotr raised his eyes to meet hers then, and she was surprised to find deep wells of shame there. When he spoke, he spoke softly, gently even. "Reiki, I promise you that none at this table knew or would have approved of such a thing. But, in Hastra, it is profits that drive decisions and has been for centuries. However, in the case of the resin, it is more than just that."

"What do you mean?"

"We don't just use the resin for heat and for light. We use it to waterproof leather, as an adhesive, as medicine for treating numerous ailments. When mixed with other materials, it can be even more useful. We use it for coating ropes, for instance. Perhaps most importantly for this discussion, we have found military applications for it as well."

"Military applications?"

Voorhees chimed in then. "Yes. We used to coat arrows with it and light them on fire. We also have found that when mixed with other flammable oils, or manure, it can be used as an explosive or an incendiary bomb to use against ships or soldiers. There is even a rumor that one of the Treyarch men has tinkered and may have found a way to use the resin to drive a ship without the need for wind or sail. The theory is that the resin can heat a reservoir of water, generating steam, which can be channeled to turn a wheel with paddles attached to drive a ship forward."

Reiki's eyes widened at that prospect. A ship that sailed without wind or sail would be an incredible asset.

Pyotr added, "You see, Reiki, what makes the resin so versatile is that its properties can change based on what it is mixed with, while still retaining its most important quality: it burns extremely hot but very slowly. You saw the braziers in the entry chamber, yes?"

Reiki nodded.

"Those braziers were lit four months ago. They will continue to burn for another two to three years at their current rate. That is astonishing. How so much energy is contained in a kappow tree is beyond our understanding. And they only grow in the Islands."

Reiki did not know that. To her, they had always just been trees, rather unremarkable ones at that. The Islanders used the resin dried and ground up to put in their incense, and as a water repellant in some cases, but otherwise it was just a trade item, useful only because the people of Hastra and Sychak valued it. It had never occurred to her that it was especially useful, much less something that anyone would kill over. *That's useful information, but, really, it doesn't change much for me.* Right then, the only thing that mattered for her was who in Hastra she would now have to kill along with Issak and his men. It had not occurred to her that the King of Hastra might be among them. *How could I even manage such a thing? I would be foolish to think he isn't extremely well guarded. And Hapsfell and Treyarch? How many people like Voorhees would I have to go through to get to them?*

"So, my people were slaughtered in service of the ambitions of your king and your competitors, Hapsfell and Treyarch?"

Pyotr nodded. "That would stand to reason, yes."

Reiki nodded silently and then sat down in her chair. "Very well."

"I can see from the look on your face that you are planning some folly. I urge you, Reiki, do not move in haste. Do not let your rage lead you to an abrupt end at the spear point of the royal guards."

Voorhees grunted. "Or my counterpart for the Treyarch, a particularly cruel and gifted killer who calls himself Mauling Spear. His real name is Trevor Marquez, but I wouldn't recommend calling him that. He considers it a provocation. He's an unusually talented spearman, but he also has a taste for prolonging suffering in his victims. You do not want to face him if you can avoid it." He took a sip of his wine. "I would be wary of facing him, and there are few who would hesitate to include me in the list of the kingdom's finest killers. He is uncommonly fast, ruthless, and clever."

Demetrius drank his wine in silence. He was no warrior, but Reiki suspected he was a capable advisor and strategist. She gulped down the rest of her wine, the alcohol numbing and quelling the rage that had threatened to overtake her. She decided to eat another roll of the waterfowl. She savored the way the tingle of the wine mixed with the crispy fat laced skin of the bird. *Do they always eat like this? It would be nearly impossible not to go soft in this environment, eating in courses, sleeping in soft beds, relying on workers and servants to attend to the actual labors of survival. If these three weren't so hospitable, I might despise them.*

Pyotr signaled Antony again. The trays of meat were whisked away and a few moments later they were replaced with new trays, this time filled with pastries and pies and cakes, all drizzled with caramel and fruit sauces or powdered with sugar. Reiki's mouth watered at the smell of them. As everyone else began to fill their plates with desserts, Reiki chose a few of the most appealing treats and put them on her plate to try. She was already feeling full, but she knew she would regret it if she did not at least try a few of them.

Everyone ate their desserts in silence. Reiki had chosen well, the soft flaky pastry crust and cream filling of her treats delighted her, and she found that she preferred the caramel sauce over the others. *If I come back this way, I will have to learn how these are made.* That thought filled her with a sadness that rose from the pit of her stomach and lodged somewhere in her throat. *I think it is much more likely I will not make it back. Try as I might, I cannot picture a future beyond my vengeance. It will be the end of me.*

Pyotr must have seen the deadened look in her eyes, the grim acceptance of her doom, for he spoke then and broke her train of thought. "Well, Reiki, I hope you have found this dinner to your liking, even if the company may not have always been so pleasant as the food."

Reiki nodded, finishing her last bite of dessert. "The food was lovely, and you have been a fine host." She made sure to make eye contact with Demetrius and Voorhees in turn as well. "You all have treated me well and made me feel welcome. I thank you for your hospitality and for your counsel, even if I did not show my gratitude at the time."

Pyotr nodded graciously. "You killed the beast that took my eldest son from me. You have been honest. and given all that you have experienced in the last two weeks, I think you have persevered remarkably. In the same position, I do not believe I would have come even this far, much less slain a garatha and earned a place at the table of a noble house of Hastra." He leaned back in his chair. "And now, it is time for us to adjourn and seek our rest. I would like it very much if you would stay this night. You can sleep in the guest room where you were bathed and dressed earlier."

Reiki considered her choices. She could insist on finding an inn in Hastra, but it was already at least eight o'clock. It would be midnight by the time she made it to the city. Here she could have a bed to sleep in and probably a hearty breakfast in the morning. She could head back to the city in the morning, shop for her supplies, and then set sail by nightfall. "I accept your kind offer and will gladly stay tonight. Might I get a ride back to the capitol in the morning?"

Pyotr nodded. "Of course. We can have a light breakfast, and I will have Antony accompany you to the city. Perhaps Demetrius could join as well if he wished and if it were acceptable to you."

Demetrius spared her the trouble of answering. "I cannot, father. I have work to do for my studies at the university. Master Aegis has assigned me the task of writing an updated treatise on the properties of clouds and the factors that lead to the formation of storms."

Pyotr frowned. "Of course. I had forgotten." He turned to Reiki then. "Well, then I suppose it will be you and Antony. I hope that is acceptable."

Reiki nodded. "It is quite agreeable to me."

Pyotr then clapped his hands twice. A trio of servants entered the room and cleared away the three trays of desserts. Another three came right after and cleared away their plates. Once they had retreated, Pyotr stood and bowed. "Thank you all for dining with me. I will now retire. You may all remain or retire as you please." Without waiting for a response and without another word, Pyotr strode out through the doorway into the hallway leaving Reiki, Demetrius, and Rodrigo Voorhees behind.

Reiki stood and stretched her limbs, her energy sapped by the wine. She yawned and bid goodnight to the others before she grabbed her spear off the wall rack, left the dining hall, walked out into the entry chamber. She ascended the stairs silently and walked down the left hall to the end. She did not bother to undress before she collapsed into the inviting warmth of the soft guest bed and was enveloped in the waiting arms of peaceful oblivion.

Chapter XI

The Soft Light of Morning

Morning's misty glow

Dew gathers on sharpened blades

Red in morning light

Executioner

Black hood awaits the condemned

Hoping for reprieve

--Haikus #47 and #52--

Balastran

High Priest of the Sakawat under Great Chief Lothar II

Reiki awoke the next morning to find a tray of food waiting for her next to the bed along with a parchment note which read:

Reiki,

       I apologize for my absence this morning, but in light of the matters discussed at dinner, I decided that I should leave at first light with Rodrigo to personally ensure our holdings are secure against any attacks by the Treyarch and Hapsfell and to deliver instructions to several trusted lieutenants in person. Enjoy your breakfast, and I wish you good fortune in your journey ahead. If you ever pass this way again, know you will always be welcome at my hearth and table.

Warm regards,

Pyotr

Reiki folded the parchment and placed it back on the tray. She then examined the breakfast and was delighted to find warm flaky pastries, sliced fruit, and a fillet of smoked seajack. She took her time eating, choosing instead to enjoy each bite. *It will be a long time before I eat this well again, if ever. I should not deprive myself of a simple pleasure with unnecessary haste.* So, she sat on the bed and ate her meal until the tray stood empty and her belly was full.

She was still in her clothing from dinner, including her belt sash and shoes. She grabbed her spear from beside the door and slung it over her right shoulder. She glanced around the room one final time. *I will not be sleeping in such a comfortable bed for a long time, either.* She shook her head and closed her eyes, willing herself to leave. She opened the door and walked straight down the hallway without looking back.

When she reached the stairs in the entry chamber, she saw Antony waiting at the bottom. He bowed when he saw her approaching. When her feet touched the marble floor of the chamber at the bottom of the stairs, he addressed her:

"Good morning, Miss Reiki. I am pleased to see you well-rested. I have a carriage ready whenever you wish to return to the capital."

Reiki smiled. "Thank you, Antony. All that remains is for me to collect the two hundred crowns in bounty and then we may be on our way."

Antony nodded. "I anticipated this, and so I have already loaded your gold onto the carriage. If you will follow me, we can depart immediately."

Reiki nodded. "Thank you, again, Antony. That was very thoughtful of you." She followed him as he led her out into the courtyard where she had arrived the previous evening. The same carriage stood waiting for her there.

Antony walked over to the carriage and was about to open the door when he stopped and appeared to be listening for something. Reiki stopped and did the same. That's when she heard it, a sound of something approaching. As she listened further, she corrected herself; it was the sound of many somethings.

Antony looked grave as he turned to Reiki. "That is the sound of many men on the backs of rocksteeds."

Reiki had no idea what Antony was talking about, but she did not have to wait long to find out. Through the main gate burst a six-legged beast larger than an ox. The beast had scaly skin and an armored soldier rode upon a saddle on its back. The rocksteed had an elongated head and a mouth full of small pointy teeth. Its legs were slender and powerful looking with three claws on each foot. Its tail was at least a meter long and had a bony club at the end. The beast was quite quick on its feet, and it nimbly trotted around the courtyard followed by at least ten others. The man on the lead mount was adorned in a steel breastplate enameled with the blue and gold colors of the Kingdom of Hastra. He wore a steel helm that sported a long red and black feather that trailed behind him. He wore a steel skirt over tough looking black leather breeches, and his feet were encased in sturdy leather boots with steel plates attached for protection. As he dismounted from the rocksteed's back, Reiki saw he was holding a two-meter halberd with another red and black feather dangling from a steel ring where the blade and the haft met. The man had a square jaw that he had clearly shaved clean, and his eyes were a piercing blue.

He stuck the butt end of his halberd in the space between two cobblestones and held it vertically, his arm extended, his feet shoulder width apart, and shouted, "Halt!"

Reiki froze, and Antony stepped away from the carriage. The other men formed a loose circle around them on their mounts, some of the men armed with halberds, and a few armed with crossbows. All their weapons were pointed at Reiki.

"What is the meaning of this?" Antony demanded.

"I am Captain Armand Renaldi of the Royal Guard." The man with the red and black feather said, "To whom am I speaking?"

"I am Antony Villago, Steward of House Illangetti." Antony did not bow. "Again, what is the meaning of this?"

"I have orders from the King. I am to arrest your guest, Reiki."

Antony visibly bristled. "On what charges?"

"Fraud, espionage, and suspicion of intent to commit regicide, for starters. Other charges may be forthcoming after the royal interrogator does his work. He has a way of loosening tongues and producing new charges." Captain Renaldi smiled savagely.

Antony's voice was full of outrage. "Oh, I know all too well his proclivities, and your own, for that matter."

Antony took a deep breath and forced himself to speak calmly. "Give me a moment, and we can ensure this ends peacefully."

Captain Renaldi shrugged. "End it however you want. It makes no difference to me." His eyes seemed to beg for a confrontation.

Antony turned to Reiki and spoke quickly and calmly, "Reiki, do as I say, please, and you will make it out of this alive. I need you to give me your spear and your sash. They are going to arrest you, and I cannot stop them. You need to trust that I will not let this end here. Okay?"

Reiki swore, but she removed her sash and spear and held both out to Antony.

Antony took the spear and placed it in the rack on the carriage and placed her sash in the storage box attached to the rear of the carriage. He then returned to Reiki. "They are going to take you to the palace. Their interrogator is going to ask you questions. It will not be *gentle.* Do you understand?"

Reiki shivered and shut her eyes, forcing herself to remain calm in the face of the cold terror sinking into her. "You mean I am to be tortured."

Antony nodded, tears forming in his eyes. "Yes, my dear." He clasped her hands in his and touched his forehead to hers. "Have faith that I will not let my master allow you to remain there."

Reiki felt her own tears streaming down her cheeks. "What choice do I have? I can die here and fail, or I can suffer there and hold on to forlorn hope." She pulled away from Antony and wiped the tears from her cheeks with her forearm. "Very well."

Reiki called out to Captain Renaldi. "I will go with you. But know this, I have sworn an oath to the gods to avenge my village. Every man, woman, and child, so far as I know, was murdered senselessly. I will have my revenge. Until that time, I am but an instrument. This body is but a hollow shell for a bloody purpose. So, your interrogator and your king may do what they will. I will not break, and I will not despair. My rage is greater than you."

With that she walked, head held high, over to Captain Renaldi, and held out her arms, wrists together. "I suggest you bind me."

Renaldi smiled. "Oh, you're a brave one, I can see that. But, it won't last. By dawn tomorrow, you'll be singing whatever tune ole Tomas the interrogator wants you to. By noon tomorrow, you'll cop to things you didn't even know you did. You'll break, because they all break." He laughed then, a wet hacking laugh that grated on Reiki's ears. "You'll be riding with someone you know, though."

He whistled and called out, "Matteus, come get your prisoner. Bind her well, because she's riding with you."

She turned around, and there he was, Matteus Illangetti, dismounting his steed at the rear of the pack. He wore no helm, so he was immediately recognizable as he approached. He smiled a sinister smile and from behind her she heard Antony's voice:

"You! What have you done, Matteus?"

"I am restoring House Illangetti to its rightful place. I'm rooting out a plot against our king. I'm eliminating a threat to our kingdom. And I'm finally driving the rot out of this house, Antony." He tied Reiki's wrists together using a coil of rope. "And, you, Reiki, will pay for every insulting word you uttered in my presence, which is all of them, for trash like you should never have been in my presence, much less at my table. I might have paid for a roll with someone like you in a brothel perhaps--"

Reiki spat in his face.

Matteus laughed and wiped the spittle off his brow. "Thank you for that. Now I can do this." He backhanded her so savagely she was surprised she didn't lose a tooth. Her cheek and jaw ached from the impact and she was certain she would have a bruise.

The man-child can hit when his target is bound and surrounded by halberd wielding men. Still more bravery than I expected of him. He's lucky he has these soldiers here, or he might leave this courtyard a gelding. She decided not to goad him further. Instead she hung her head and followed him meekly as he led her to his mount, which snorted as they approached. His saddle had a second seat in back which had a metal ring affixed to it. *I assume I am to be tied to that ring to prevent my escape.*

Reiki was embarrassed to discover that she was afraid; afraid of what lay ahead for her, afraid of what fate awaited her generous hosts, and more immediately, she was afraid of the beast that stood before her, its concave back as high as her brow. She refused to show her fear and instead focused on trying to figure out how to climb atop the beast while bound at the wrists.

Matteus made two short sharp clicks with his tongue, and the beast sank down onto its haunches, its tail stretched out behind it. *Ah, that would make it easier.* "You can either climb into that back seat on your own, or you can resist." Matteus's voice was filled with malice. *What did I ever do to you, Matteus?* "Between you and me, I rather hope you resist. Striking you again would be the highlight of my day."

If you and I were alone and my hands free, you would find nothing pleasurable in it. You would likely never feel pleasure again. She backed herself up to the rocksteed and hopped backward, her bottom landing halfway onto the saddle. She leaned back and swung her legs upward and twisted herself around until she came to a sitting position in the saddle, one leg on either side of the beast. She held her bound wrists out meekly.

Matteus shrugged and then fastened her to the metal ring on the saddle with only enough slack that she could remain upright. *You needn't worry, Matteus. I put on a good show of bravery, but I know as well as you that leaping from the back of this beast means a savage beating at best, my death at worst. I have no intention of earning either today. If I am dead or broken, I cannot repay this "kindness" you've shown me.* She kept her silence as Matteus mounted the saddle in front of hers and clicked his tongue again. The beast rose, and she was now nearly two meters off the ground.

Captain Renaldi mounted his rocksteed and whipped his arm in a circular motion in the air, signaling the other riders to get moving. Reiki lurched backward as Matteus drove their shared steed forward with a flick of the reins. Captain Renaldi drove his heels into the side of his mount as he called out to Antony:

"Tell your master not to go far. He too may find himself charged and brought before the king, if the Treyarch and Hapsfell don't find him first."

Antony watched in silence as the riders sped out the main gate and went galloping off down the road. Once they were out of sight, he ran back inside the manor. He ran up the stairs and down the right hallway. He took the first doorway on the right, which led to a small room, no larger than a pantry. There was a wooden ladder against the back wall of the small room that went up to the rooftop. Next to the ladder sat a burning resin lantern. He grabbed the lantern and climbed the ladder out onto the roof. There, he found a single brazier with a chunk of unusual resin sitting in the bowl. Where most resin was a blue color, this resin was dark red, like dried blood. Antony had never used this brazier before, for it had one purpose: to signal an emergency for the Illangetti. Once lit, a column of bright red smoke would be visible throughout the Illangetti Quarter. All the lesser noble houses that served the Illangetti would come. Most importantly, though, Pyotr and Rodrigo would return immediately. He only hoped that they had not already been caught unawares by the hired swords and spears of the other houses.

Antony threw the burning resin lantern into the brazier, breaking it and igniting the red resin. The red resin burst into brilliant bright red flames and brilliant red smoke which rose in a billowing column above the manor. Antony sat and waited upon the rooftop for his master to return.

Chapter XII

The Hospitality of King Raynard VII

"There is no darkness so deep nor so black as when the light of hope is extinguished."

Old Sychak Proverb

Reiki's feet swung over a deep dark pit of nothingness below her. Her wrists were chained together with manacles and hung over a hook from the ceiling of the damp stone dungeon. The only light came from a resin lantern she could see through the iron grating above her. Occasionally she would see a soldier pass and briefly plunge her into darkness. Otherwise, she was completely alone with nothing but the steady drip-drip-drip of condensation dropping from the ceiling down into puddles on the stone floor. There was no way of knowing the passage of time, but she knew she had arrived at the palace just before noon and her stomach growled audibly with hunger.

The sun had beat hot on the back of her neck, and Matteus had begun to reek of sweat and the coarse leathery stench of rocksteed. She had been led down deep into the bowels of the palace by Matteus and Captain Renaldi. They eventually had reached a long dark hallway with iron grates in the floor and wooden cell doors on either side. At the end of the hallway lay another spiraling stone stairway. The gaoler on duty, a portly man with ruddy skin and a spotty red beard, placed her in iron manacles and grabbed a resin lantern off a nearby hook. He led her to the second door on the right. He opened it with a large iron key he kept in his breeches and shoved her through the door.

In the light of the lantern, she could see the room was bare stone brick with a large circular pit in the middle that fell away into darkness below. She could not begin to guess how deep it went. The gaoler walked over to the right of the door, and she saw a hand cranked winch. The winch had an iron chain spooled on it, and the chain was fed through a pulley on the ceiling right under the iron grate through which some faint lantern light shone through. The gaoler tossed the chain between her manacles over the hook and then cranked the winch. Reiki's arms were raised over her head, and soon she was raised off the floor and dangling, swinging gently over the yawning chasm below her. The gaoler never spoke a word to her. She was facing away from the door, so she didn't see him leave. She did hear the door open, the room brightened a little before she was plunged back into darkness as the door slammed shut, and she heard his heavy footsteps plodding back down the corridor away from her cell.

And now, her shoulders ached unbearably, and she was weak with hunger. *Could it be nighttime? Morning? How long have I hung here?* It could have been a few hours. It could have been a day for all she could tell. Her mind offered her no respite as she relived the horrors of the past two weeks over and over again. *They need not beat me or whip me or take pliers to me. Being alone with myself in this dark and damp is a greater torture than any pain they might inflict.*

Eventually, she heard the door swing open behind her, and saw her shadow cast upon the far wall along with the shadows of two men framed in the doorway. She heard them walk into her cell.

"How is our lovely little fish woman?" Matteus called out. "I told the gaoler that you can't smoke a fish without a fire, but it seems he did not heed my advice." His voice sounded smug, even by his standards.

The second man's voice was deeper, and she sensed a weariness in it. "So, this is the Islander girl who would slay me and my men." He walked calmly into her line of sight, then, and she clenched her teeth in rage, for he was Sakawat.

He was only slightly taller than she was, with broad shoulders. Though he wore a steel cuirass under a flowing white and red robe, she could see he was built powerfully. He wore red dyed breeches and a pair of brown leather boots with steel plates affixed to them. He wore a leather band around his shaved head which had a pair of white and red spotted feathers attached to either side. His skin was a deep bronze, and he had a scar running through his lips down to his bare chin. His eyes were a dark brown and sat under a pair of thin black eyebrows. She was surprised to see that he had a pleasing face, aside from the scar, and his expression held no malice. If anything, she sensed regret in his eyes.

"I am Issak, war chief of the Issakeen Sakawat. My craven associate, Matteus, tells me that I destroyed your home and slaughtered your people. He says that you have sworn vengeance upon me and my men. He says that you sailed alone across the sea to Hastra and slew a giant garatha that evaded or killed the finest fishermen in this kingdom. You did all of this so that you could kill me?"

Reiki spat. "You and the one hundred and twenty some odd bastards you sail with."

Issak smiled. "The Sakawat treasure courage, and you have no shortage it seems. I imagine you would like to kill me here and now, were you able."

"We could find out if you'd like." She smiled savagely. "Matteus could fetch the gaoler. You might not value my courage so highly were I standing over your corpse."

Issak shook his head. "No, that was one boast too many. Don't overcompensate with pointless bravado. Fear is not weakness. Fear is the voice of wisdom in your ear that reminds you that you are mortal. Right now, you should listen to fear. Heed its whisper. You are exhausted, weakened, your joints in agony, deprived of food these past sixteen hours. You have had nothing to drink. No sleep. That is not a state in which I would accept your challenge. I am not dishonorable."

Reiki shook with rage. "Not dishonorable? You and your men attacked my home. You killed every man, woman, and even the children. You stand there and claim you are honorable? What honor was there in spearing and burning my little brother? In murdering women in the fields and their homes? Don't stand there and paint yourself as anything other than a godless craven beast in a man's clothing."

Issak sat down on the floor, staring at the stones, his shoulders slumped. He rubbed his eyes and sighed deeply. *What is this?* "That was a condition placed upon me by the Hastran king. He required that none survive to tell the tale. Even so, I failed, for I took most of the children prisoner instead. Killing children is unforgivable, and if I knew who among my men had done so, I would offer their heads to the gods in atonement. Nonetheless, I am sorry for your brother. I can only say that most of the children still live and will be raised as if they were our own."

Is he telling the truth? I assumed many of the children were burned in their homes. How many did I find other than Tova? A handful perhaps. "I see. Kidnapping, then, is where your honor lies."

Issak nodded. "That's a fair rebuke. The truth is, I did what I did in service of something greater than honor. As far back as the Sakawat can remember, the Hastran fleet has shielded the Islands. I knew I could not risk a normal raid. I needed to strike a deal with the King. And so, I did. The price was staining myself with dishonor. I doubt you find any solace in it, but I regret that it was necessary."

"Fuck your apology, and fuck your regret." Reiki swore at him. "And fuck your greater purpose. I know of your steel beast and your ambition. They will not save you from me. So, instead, pray to your gods that the Hastrans kill me. For if I leave this dungeon alive, I will find you, and I will be your doom. From now until that day, I will be the cold that dances down your spine, the crack of a branch, the rustle of leaves, the terror that follows you all of the scant days that remain to you."

Issak nodded and picked himself up off the stone floor. "I wish that I had found you on Serenity. Killing you then would have been a kindness, and dying at your hands would have been a death most worthy. It is a shame that your vengeance will be denied, and your life taken at the hands of cowards like this one." He gestured to Matteus, who bristled at the insult.

"How dare you!" Matteus barked. "Were you not about to depart in your ship, I would demand satisfaction!"

Issak calmly held out his open hands in invitation. "Do it, then. I would only be detained but a moment. Besides, my ship leaves on the morrow. I have plenty of time for you. If you have found your courage, then say the words and you can spend your last moments here and die before this woman who frightens you so. Do you imagine she will weep as she watches the life bleed out of you, or would she smile? Which do you think?"

Matteus blanched and shrunk away. "The king would not want me to kill you. You must deliver the treaty to the Great Chief, after all."

Issak met Reiki's eyes with his own, and his lip curled in a knowing smile. "Of course. *That* is why. Perhaps another time, then." He spoke to Reiki then. "Ego is such a fragile thing, is it not? Alas, I hope I do see you again, Reiki. These people toy with you now, for they think they have captured you and therefore tamed you. They do not realize that they have brought the serpent into their home. I, for one, would not bet against you."

He bowed and walked out of her line of sight. She heard his footsteps as he walked through the door, and they grew faint in the corridor. She was surprised to find that she didn't want him to go. *He was not what I expected.*

Matteus remained, and he glared at her through the dim light. "You never should have come here, Reiki. You should have sailed to another island or gone straight to Sychak."

Reiki rolled her eyes. "What did I do to you, Matteus? How did I wrong you?"

Matteus cast his eyes to the floor and Reiki was surprised to see a tear upon his cheek when he raised his head again. He said, "The minute you sailed into the harbor with that damned eel in tow, you shamed me. You shamed me by accomplishing what I had neither the skill nor the desire to do. Then, my father showered you with honors. You ate at his table. He dressed you in my *mother's* clothes—"

Reiki gasped. *I had no idea. I didn't even think about where the clothes came from.* "I didn't know!"

"—he put you up in my mother's private chambers. He gave you an Illangetti hook spear, which is meant only for family. And then he took your side over mine, his own blood, his oldest surviving son." His eyes were filled with tears. "He met you two days ago for the first time and already I could see he favored you more than he ever has me."

Reiki was at a loss for what to say. She had not known and could not have done anything to stop it even if she had, but for a moment, she felt pity for him. She hung there, silent, the pain and hunger and thirst screaming within her, but she pitied him anyway.

Matteus wiped his eyes with his sleeve, and he stared at her for a moment before he left her cell wordlessly. The heavy door shut behind her, and his footsteps faded away down the corridor. She was left alone again with her agony. She dangled there for another eternity with the metronome drip-drip-drip of water to keep time, when she finally heard the door open behind her and in came the heavy plodding of the gaoler. He gave her water from a bowl at the end of a three-meter pole, like a stretched ladle. She drank it greedily and felt the raspy dryness of her throat briefly soothed. He did not offer her any food nor any words to break the silence. He simply gave her a single bowl of water and then left.

More time passed, hours by Reiki's best reckoning, and the door opened again. This time, three men entered. She recognized the heavy feet of the gaoler, but he remained by the door. The other two entered her vision, and she recognized neither of them. One was dressed in a black leather jerkin with black trousers and simple leather sandals. His face was covered in pock marks, and he wore an expression that radiated malice. The other man wore a white shirt under an ornate blue and gold waistcoat. His breeches were tan with elaborate white embroidery. He wore supple ox hide shoes with silver buckles, and a long blue and gold cape flowed behind him, clasped with a silver brooch at his neck. He had long wavy brown hair, bright green eyes, and a neatly trimmed beard. Atop his head he wore a silver crown inlaid with gold filigree, and a single yellow topaz that was centered above his forehead. *This must be the king. The other man must be the interrogator they talked about.*

The king spoke first. "I am King Raynald, as you likely have guessed. My associate here is my chief interrogator, who goes by Tomas."

Reiki nodded. She wanted to save her voice as much as she could. Still, she asked, "How long have I been here?"

Raynald looked to Tomas. The interrogator shrugged and replied, "You arrived here in this cell just after noon yesterday. It is now just past dinner time." He laughed. "Well, not for you, obviously."

Raynald looked uncomfortable, as though he found her circumstances distasteful. "I want you to know that ordinarily I take great pride in our justice system. No Hastran citizen could be detained like this for more than six hours without being released, given legal representation, and then brought to trial under a learned magistrate. I have been told that you are fairly bright for an Islander, so I'm sure you have figured out why you have not been granted those rights."

Reiki smiled bitterly. "There's the reason you will comfort yourself with, and then there is the true reason."

Raynald frowned. "Are we to begin from a position of distrust then?"

Reiki laughed, and then winced from the pain it caused in her ribs and shoulders. "I'm a poor guest, it seems, after all the hospitality you've shown me." She dramatically gestured around the cell with her head and eyes.

Raynald seemed unprepared for her response, but he recovered quickly. "Very well. You are not a Hastran citizen. You have no right to avail yourself of representation in our courts, and there is no limit to the time that I can detain you. Were this a trade dispute or a civil matter, you could file suit in our courts and plead your case with assistance of counsel. Where crimes are concerned, you have no such recourse. This is especially so for the crimes you are charged with."

"Ah, yes, my crimes. Remind me what the charges were against me."

"You are accused of fraud, espionage, and intent to commit regicide. I, understandably, take the latter rather personally," the king replied.

She laughed. "Well, I deny the first two charges, since I have remained honest in my dealings since I landed on your shores, and I have no need of your state secrets. I came only to resupply and be on my way in pursuit of those who wronged me."

Tomas smiled, and his teeth were stained yellow with gaps where a few were missing. "I see you have not denied the third charge."

Reiki shook her head. "Nor will I. I had no intention of harming your king before I learned he allowed the atrocities that befell my village. Now, I won't deny I harbor a desire for retribution."

The interrogator laughed. "You make no attempt to avoid the executioner, I see?" He turned to the king. "I usually have to try harder to interrogate prisoners. This one seems all too willing to confess."

The king ignored Tomas. "Let us drop pretenses. I cannot have you spreading word that Hastra generally, and I specifically, colluded and conspired with Issak of the Sakawat to eradicate your little island. The common folk will accept incompetence before they will accept an overt act in violation of a treaty. I must have a plausible explanation. With all of Serenity's inhabitants dead, no one could contradict the official account."

Reiki remained silent.

"So, I officially condemned the actions of Issak and have even charged one of my admirals with incompetence for failing to detect and prevent the raid. Tomorrow, I will announce that Issak and I have reached a resolution. He will cede control of Serenity to Hastra, and we will be free of our obligations to the Islands, expensive as they are, and have a guaranteed source of kappow going forward. The common folk will accept this and even celebrate the increased availability of resin."

Reiki laughed, a hoarse rasping sound that echoed off the walls. "Sounds like you've got things pretty well sewn up."

The king nodded. "With one little stumbling block in the way." His eyes met hers.

"Which explains the need to accuse me of fraud and espionage. Let me guess, you will say that I made up this story about Serenity, that I came here and preyed upon the good nature of Hastran nobility and hospitality, and that I worked in secret to plot against you. All of these crimes should allow you to execute me quickly and without much fuss."

The king shook his head. "Not quite. I could save myself more trouble by simply killing you outright and eliminating the need for much explanation at all. However, the young Illangetti man insisted that his father should also face charges. I *do* need an explanation for why I would attempt to arrest the head of a great house. Of course, I have no intention of letting him actually stand trial. The Hapsfell and Treyarch would much prefer him dead anyway. So, I ordered him killed during his arrest."

You had him killed? I did not know him well, but I liked him. He was kind and he treated me like a friend. I don't know how yet, but if I make it out of here, I am going to kill you. She stared cold daggers of hatred at the king. When she spoke, she only asked, "So, what now?"

The king gestured to Tomas who replied. "I intend to find out who you told your tale to and when. I will go to work on you with what instruments and talents I possess, and they are cruel and exceptional both, until I have recorded your confession. Then, you will be released from your pain and suffering to join your family and friends in whatever afterlife you believe in."

The king stood silent while Tomas grinned sinisterly. Reiki spoke with more courage than she felt. "Am I to assume that any people I spoke to about Serenity will meet a similar fate?"

Tomas shrugged. "Probably. I promise you, by tomorrow night you will not trouble yourself over such things. Two days more and you would name your own mother a conspirator if it would bring your death and an end to your suffering."

"Just kill me and be done with it. You will discredit me afterward, anyway, so why does it matter who I talked to?"

Tomas grinned. "I prefer to be thorough."

Reiki had no retort and instead focused her eyes on a stone brick directly ahead of her on the cell wall. The king broke the silence that hung in the room. "I will leave Tomas to his work."

Tomas smiled his gap-toothed yellow smile. "I think I will leave her alone here to her own thoughts for a while longer, your majesty. Another eight hours of this and she will beg for me to return."

The two of them walked out of her view, and she heard the door shut behind her. She was alone again with naught but her thoughts as company. *The worst part of it is, Tomas is probably right. Matteus, Issak, the King, Tomas. I hate them all, but at least when they are here, I can escape from these ghosts that haunt me. I can mark the passage of time. Alone I just float in an endless void of pain and thirst and hunger and horror.*

Chapter XIII

Flight by Night

The little rat escaped the trap

The little rat escaped the trap

How did he steal the cheese?

The little rat outran the cat

The little rat outran the cat

Skittering quick as you please!

Someone freed the rat from the trap

And now we've all got fleas!

"The Little Rat"

Chekhovian Nursery Rhyme

Reiki did not know when or how she had fallen asleep, but she was awoken to the crash of steel on steel in the corridor outside her cell, followed by the sharp scream of someone in pain.

"Where is she, you fat fucking dog? Tell me or I'll relieve those chubby legs of yours of the burden of carrying your ass around!"

Voorhees? They came for me? They came for me! Her throat ached as she called out with a rasping shout: "I'm in here!"

"That's an unfortunate bit of luck for you, gaoler," Voorhees said. Then she heard the horrible sound of the gaoler screaming as Voorhees cut him down.

A few moments later, she heard the door behind her open and several sets of feet rushed through the door, their heavy soles pounding on the stone floor. Then she saw Voorhees, Pyotr, and Antony before her, as well as another man she had not met. All were dressed in steel cuirasses over chainmail with steel helms atop their heads. They all carried spears in their right hands and round steel shields in their left.

"You came for me," she cried, tears falling upon her cheeks. She was ashamed to admit to herself that she had given up hope of ever leaving the dungeons alive.

Pyotr spoke first. "Aye. The other houses and their puppet king made a misstep. When they chose to send assassins for me, they removed any reason or desire for me to behave. Since they wanted war, they have got themselves one."

Voorhees added, "They weren't expecting it, which has helped us considerably. We attacked the palace with a force of five hundred men at arms with another thousand in reserve. We've bloodied them quite well so far, but we must get you out of here quickly, for our luck will turn once the king's men have had time to regroup. And may the gods save us if the Hapsfell or Treyarch men arrive."

Antony smiled. "I told you I would not let him leave you here." He walked behind her, and she heard the crank of the winch as he lowered her from the ceiling. Voorhees reached out and pulled her away from the chasm, and she collapsed as her feet touched the floor, weak and unsteady from the past two nights of hanging from the ceiling. She wept then as the strain finally left her shoulders, and she buried her face in the floor and sobbed. Antony knelt beside her and embraced her. "There there, dear. It's over now. Also, I brought you a friend."

He stood up and held out his spear to her. Reiki's eyes widened as she recognized it as the Illangetti spear she had won as a bounty. She grasped the shaft of the spear with her right hand and used it as a pole to help her stand. She leaned on it and steadied herself. "Thank you, Antony."

Antony reached behind him and pulled her sash and pouches from where he had tied them onto his own belt. "I believe you will be wanting these as well."

Reiki smiled weakly. "Again, thank you." She tied the sash around her waist and already she felt some of her strength returning. It would take several meals and some rest before she was even a shadow of her usual self, but these were welcome improvements.

The fourth man stepped forward and bowed. "I know I am a stranger to you. I am Captain Marco Paulus. I am the captain of the Illangetti flagship, Iron Will. We will be setting sail tonight with all of us aboard. My men are preparing the ship to sail as we speak. The plan is to escape to the palace docks where the Iron Will will meet us."

Reiki nodded. "Okay, so now what?"

Pyotr replied, "Can you walk?"

Reiki frowned and tried a few steps using the spear as a walking stick. She was still unsteady. "I won't be running anywhere, but I can walk."

The others all nodded. Voorhees spoke then. "Then we should get moving. We are deep within the palace, and we will need to make our way through to the courtyard and then down two long corridors and several sets of stairs to reach the docks below. The docks will be guarded, even now. We must hope our men provide a good distraction."

Reiki walked as quickly as she could manage over to the door of the cell. "Well, I'm not feeling sentimental about this place. So, let's get to it then." She started to walk through the door, but she stopped mid-step. "Wait. Pyotr, where is Demetrius?"

Pyotr sighed. "Demetrius has chosen to stay in Hastra. I will explain more when we get to the ship. For now, I will only say that I understand his decision, though I do worry for him."

Reiki wanted to ask questions. But she knew they needed to move, and he already declined to elaborate. Instead, she gestured to the corridor. "Well, I think taking the lead would be a bad idea, so, who wants to show me the way out of here?"

Voorhees grunted and hurried to the door. He leaned out into the corridor and looked both ways. "Okay, we're clear. I'll lead the way."

They left the cell with Voorhees leading, followed by Pyotr, then Reiki, and Captain Paulus in the rear. The three men held their spears ready for action. Reiki continued to use hers as support as she walked. They moved as quietly as they could down the corridor, then climbed several flights of stairs that made Reiki's leg muscles burn from the exertion. Every time they reached a doorway, Voorhees would lean through and scan their surroundings for danger. They finally reached a grand hall filled with wooden chairs and tables with an enormous fireplace at one end. *This must be the dining hall.* She could hear men fighting somewhere nearby, but she couldn't tell how far away or even where it was coming from. She wondered how many men were going to die in effecting her escape. *This can't just be for me. Pyotr said the king and the other houses gave him no choice when*

they attacked him. These men won't be on my conscience.
But she wondered if that was true.

They continued picking up the pace as she became steadier on her feet. They left the dining hall and entered a long corridor. Voorhees guided them to the right and down another flight of stone stairs. As they emerged into an open courtyard, Voorhees stopped abruptly and immediately assumed a defensive stance, his shield raised, and his spear leveled. Pyotr, Paulus, and Antony raised their shields, though Antony no longer had a spear. Instead, he drew a dagger from his waist sash and held it at the ready.

The courtyard was a rectangle twenty meters wide by thirty meters long. There were two raised garden beds filled with flowering shrubs and small shade trees and the beds ran the length of the courtyard on either side with two meters of space to walk around them. There were two arched doorways, one at each end of the courtyard; they had just entered from one and the other was the only way to get to the palace docks. A group of armed and armored men stood between them and their escape.

One man stood out, and Reiki knew immediately that he was the leader. He was two meters tall and broad shouldered with flowing black curls that spilled from under his black enameled helm. His helm was adorned with a tuft of bright gold feathers that rose in a gentle arc and fell behind him to his waist. He wore a black enameled cuirass and plate skirt over a chainmail hauberk and his legs were also armored with black enameled plate. He carried a spear that was easily two and a half meters long. Another tuft of golden feathers adorned the spear where the blade was hafted. He carried a black enameled steel shield in his left hand, and he smiled as he recognized Voorhees.

"Rodrigo! I worried I would miss you," he laughed. "My spear is thirsty, and it craves only the finest of spirits."

"Trevor!" Voorhees shouted in reply. *The Mauling Spear!* Reiki felt a chill as she remembered Voorhees' appraisal of the Treyarch man. She also remembered Voorhees' warning not to call him Trevor. *Why are you provoking him?* "Is your spear up to the task?"

The Mauling Spear, Trevor Marquez, gestured for his men to advance. "I would love to duel you, Rodrigo, but I have orders to prevent that little water monkey of yours from escaping."

Water monkey?

Pyotr's face reddened with rage. "Mind your tongue, you sack of feculent ox balls! You will not use that slur in my presence."

Ah. It's an anti-Islander slur, is it? What the hell is a monkey, anyway? She wasn't insulted, but she did think it was touching that Pyotr felt the need to defend her so strongly.

Trevor smiled even wider. "I had hoped I might find you here, Illangetti. I have orders to ensure your demise as well. I worried I would have to dig you out of hiding somewhere. Thank you for saving me some time." He barked to his men, "Kill them all."

Reiki saw that there were twelve of them in all, and they each were well armored, though not as stylishly as Trevor in his flashy black plate. They all carried spears and shields, and they advanced as a line abreast with shields up and spears leveled.

Pyotr looked like he was about to advance to meet them, but Voorhees held out his arm to stop him. He turned his head to face Pyotr and said, "Protect Reiki. I will handle these vermin."

Pyotr nodded, accepting Voorhees' decades of accumulated experience and instead held his spear and shield at the ready in case any of the men broke past Voorhees. Rodrigo dropped into a low stance, held his spear out at an angle from his body and his shield high, his eyes peering over the top. When the advancing men were only four meters away, Rodrigo roared a savage cry; Reiki was shocked by the force of it. Then he leapt into action, closing the distance rapidly. Reiki had never seen anyone fight the way he did. He moved deftly, leaping and lunging, his spear dancing as he thrust here and parried an attack there. He slew three of the men in seconds, his spear thrusting through the throat of the first, slashing the artery in the thigh of the second with a low scraping blow, and the third finding the weak point under the shoulder and driving deep in and under the man's clavicle. He did not stop. With their line broken, none of the men could land a blow nor stop his attack.

He fights like a god.

Less than a minute is all it took. Rodrigo Voorhees, the whirling spear of the Illangetti, stood facing Trevor Marquez, the Mauling Spear, covered in the blood and gore of the twelve dead men who were strewn about him on the stones of the courtyard. Trevor's lips curled in a sinister grin. "Well done, Rodrigo!" He shouted. "I am glad my men provided you with some exercise. My spear prefers its drinks warm." He laughed, a cruel and discomfiting sound.

Voorhees did not rise to the bait. "Let's not waste further words, Trevor. Our spears can do the talking."

Trevor smiled. "I accept your challenge, Voorhees. Who shall I send your head to after I pluck it from your shoulders?"

Rodrigo smiled, "I have no wife or child, so I guess you can send it to my most frequent lover. You know her as 'mother,' I believe?"

Trevor's face reddened, but he did not reply. Instead, the two men began to advance toward each other, their eyes probing for any weakness, a telltale twitch signaling a thrust or a shift of the feet. They both walked faster as they closed the distance between them, each mirroring the other in perfect symmetry. Finally, their spears crossed. They fought, each thrusting, slashing, dodging, and parrying each other. Yet, neither gained an advantage.

They both fight like gods! I wouldn't even be a distraction for them in a fight. Either could end me with but a thought.

They continued to probe each other for weaknesses, a feint here, a parry there. Once, she thought Rodrigo was about to land a hit, but Trevor danced away, his spear already thrusting at Rodrigo to prevent him from closing in. The two fought for nearly eight minutes before Rodrigo's spear broke in half in his hands. He quickly discarded the two halves of his spear as Trevor lunged. Reiki cried out, "No!"

Voorhees dodged to the left and grabbed the shaft with both hands and used Marquez's momentum to drive him against the raised garden bed to the right. Marquez gained traction and dug his heels into the soil, pushing back against Voorhees. The two struggled there, both clasping the spear tightly and pushing or pulling to try to force the other off balance.

Rodrigo shouted over his shoulder, "Go! Now! All of you! I won't be able to hold him forever."

Pyotr ran forward. "Let us help you! Surely he cannot defeat all of us if we attack him together!"

Rodrigo shouted with more urgency, "He can and he will if you try it. Go! I will keep him here as long as I can. Now fly!"

Pyotr knew better than to argue, though Reiki could see that it killed him to leave his old friend behind. "Let's go! Quickly!"

The four of them dashed across the courtyard past the two warriors, still locked together, each refusing to surrender to the other's deathblow by pulling away. Each tried to gain any advantage. Trevor snarled in frustration as they ran past. Rodrigo gritted his teeth from the strain as they both tried to jostle the other enough to change the balance of the fight.

Antony ran through the doorway first with Reiki behind, still not able to run, but walking as fast as she could. Pyotr stopped at the doorway and turned to look one last time upon Rodrigo Voorhees, his oldest friend. He whispered, "Farewell friend, and thank you."

Pyotr, Reiki, Paulus, and Antony passed through the door into the interior of the stone tower. Inside, there were stone stairs that descended along the walls around an open center. Reiki looked down nearly thirty meters to the stone floor below. The three of them hurried down the stone stairs as quickly as they safely could. The stone steps were wet with condensation, and Reiki could hear the water lapping against a stone pier below. The palace docks and the Iron Will waited below.

When they were rounding the last corner, Reiki saw something fall past her and slam into the stone floor with a sickly wet smacking sound. She looked at the horrific bloody mess of Voorhees broken upon the stone, and she screamed.

Pyotr looked back up to the top of the tower and saw the smiling face of Marquez peering down at them.

"I didn't want you to leave without seeing your friend one last time," Trevor goaded them from above. "He saved you, for now."

Pyotr spewed a stream of curses that made Antony blush and Marquez's eyes widen with surprise. But Pyotr knew better than to let his friend's sacrifice be in vain. He beckoned for Paulus to help him and the two of them picked up Voorhees's broken body under the armpits and slung his arms over their necks. "Come on! Through this door! The ship will be waiting!"

Reiki and Antony followed them out into the open air. Reiki could see the lights of the city stretching out to the east, starting with the customs docks nearly half a kilometer away to her left.

A stone pier jutted out from the stone quay where the four of them stood. Directly ahead, broadside to them, only ten meters past the end of the pier, Reiki saw a ship that she deduced could only be the Iron Will. It had three masts and two rows of ten-gun ports each along its side. The ship was sleek, and the hull curved beautifully, swelling out at the waterline. Reiki's mouth fell open of its own accord as she took in the size and sheer beauty of it. *I am going to sail aboard that ship! My whole life, I have never sailed anything larger than a trading trimaran.* The four of them made haste to reach the end of the pier. As they came to a stop at the edge, a crewman tossed down a rope ladder. The bottom rungs were in the water below, so Paulus dove off the pier into the calm water of the harbor first and then shouted back up to Pyotr.

"Throw Voorhees next. I will keep hold of him."

Pyotr gently rolled Voorhees's body off the end of the pier, and it fell into the water with a splash. Paulus grabbed hold of him and drug his body over to the rope ladder and held on. "Alright, my Lord, you are next. Then Reiki. Then Antony."

They each jumped into the water in turn. Paulus called up to the crew above. "Toss me a line. We have a body to raise."

Reiki saw a slender line drop from above, and Paulus quickly tied it around Voorhees. He gave the line three sharp tugs ,and Voorhees's corpse began to rise above them, drops of water and blood dripping down from his limp form. Pyotr and Antony climbed up the ladder next, followed by Reiki. Paulus, as the captain, came aboard the ship last. He immediately ran past the three of them and climbed up to the cockpit to command the crew.

The last memory Reiki had as she collapsed from shock and exhaustion was of the Iron Will slowly sailing through the harbor and the sight of the Yondratha growing smaller in her wake. *I will mend, and we will meet again in the mountains far to the east, Issak. I promise. You will pay in blood for Rodrigo; for Serenity; for everything.* The toll of two days without adequate food, rest, or water, and the shock of Voorhees's death were too much. She fell into a dreamless slumber upon the wet deck of the flagship of the Illangetti.

Chapter XIV

"A Dirge at Sea"

"How many skeletons lie below the waves?

How many dreams sputter and drown in the dark deep?

The abyss calls us all to drink in its halls,

Comrades all in death's eternal sleep."

-The Deep-

The poet Yara of Sychak

When Reiki finally awoke, she was lying in a tiny bunk just slightly longer than she was. As her eyes grew accustomed to the dim light, she could see she was in a small cabin with naught but her small bunk and a chest for belongings, and her spear and belt sash propped against the bulkhead by the door. She rose from her bunk and donned her sash and slung her spear over her shoulder. She was pleasantly surprised to find that she was able to walk without much difficulty. Her thigh was still injured from her fight with the garatha and her belly was tying itself in knots for want of a meal. *Very well. I will find myself some food, and then I will find Pyotr.*

She opened the door to her cabin and poked her head out into the passageway beyond. She glanced up and down the passage and spied a ladder off to her left. *Is that fore or aft? What part of the ship is this?* She climbed the ladder up to the deck above. She was in a U-shaped passage with a door at each end and several throughout on either side. She opened the nearest door and saw that it was another cabin, though considerably larger than her own. No one was there at present, so she closed the door and decided to try one of the doors at the end of the U-shape. She opened the door and had to blink under the onslaught of bright sunlight. She was on the top deck and she could see dozens of men working the sails, scrubbing the decks, and attending to the myriad other tasks necessary for tending a vessel at sea. *This ship is massive. The Yondratha is even larger. What have I gotten myself into?*

As one of the crew came near, she called out to him, "Excuse me, sir."

The man stopped and stared at her.

"Where can I find something to eat?"

The man frowned and replied, "Meals are served four times daily. Once at four bells in the morning and then eight bells, then four, then eight. The bells denote the time. One bell every half hour, you see. So, eight bells is midnight. Then one bell at half past, then two bells at one, and so on. At any rate, meals are at midnight, six in the morning, noon, and six in the evening. It's currently three bells in the evening, so, if you head down that ladder over there, below the forecastle, you can drop down to the galley. Food should be served soon."

Reiki had spent her whole life on the sea, but this business about bells was new to her. *It's complicated, but I imagine it's necessary for coordinating this many people over the course of many days.* She smiled at the man and thanked him before she made her way across the open deck, being careful to stay out of the way of the men working. She found the ladder that led below, and she carefully climbed down to the deck and found herself in a dim and stuffy space which was filled with the smell of a nearby kitchen. *Smells like we're having fish for dinner.*

Her eyes adjusted to the dim light quickly, and she could see that she was in a room with six tables, each with benches attached to them. The tables themselves were bolted to the deck to keep them from moving in high seas. She spotted Antony sitting at the table furthest from her. He held up his hand and called out to her when he recognized her.

"Reiki! Come! Sit!" He patted the bench next to him.

She walked over to him and sat across from him instead, not wanting to have to turn to look at him. "Antony, how long was I out?"

"We set sail nearly twenty hours ago. You passed out on the deck, and we carried you below to a cabin the captain set aside for you. Pyotr locked himself up in his cabin as well. Though, I think he mostly wanted to be alone to mourn Rodrigo."

Reiki dropped her gaze to her navel, the memory of Rodrigo's death coming back to her in a rush. "You all risked your lives to free me, and it cost Rodrigo his. The shame of his death is on me."

Antony shook his head. "No, Reiki. You don't understand Hastran politics. Rodrigo and Pyotr had no choice but to fight or die. When you were arrested, I went and lit a signal fire on the roof of the manor. I did not know, but Pyotr and Rodrigo were walking into a trap at that moment. Rodrigo saw the crimson smoke, and they stopped and turned to return to the manor. That's when the Treyarch and Hapsfell assassins sprung from their hiding places along the street and rushed to attack. Rodrigo and Pyotr were able to fell the attackers since they had to leave their ambush positions to attack. At that point, Pyotr and Rodrigo had two options left to them. They could either flee, or they could attack."

Reiki remembered the king had told her he had sent men to kill Pyotr. "So, why not flee and avoid the risk?"

Antony shrugged. "That's my fault, really. When they returned to the manor, my lord's vassals arrived soon after. You see, each great noble house has a few dozen minor noble houses that serve under them. The house of Voorhees, for instance, though that line is now extinguished, was one such. The house of Paulus is another, of which our ship's captain is a member. At any rate, they all arrived in short order, and I explained what had occurred. There was some discussion as to how to proceed. I insisted that we must free you. Pyotr and Rodrigo both agreed since both were quite taken with you. Unfortunately, many of the minor houses refused to take part in an attack, likely hoping they would be spared and could serve whoever replaced Pyotr."

"Gods, don't tell me that's who I think it is."

"You're probably right. Matteus would be the logical choice to take over House Illangetti in Pyotr's absence, which is also probably part of the price Matteus received for betraying us all."

Reiki swore and pounded her fist on the wood table. "If I ever return to Hastra, he and I will have a reckoning."

Antony nodded. "I have no doubt, though it would not be advisable to return for quite some time. We can but hope that our men beat a hasty retreat when our ship set sail, but it is also quite likely they were all put to the sword for their rebellion."

Reiki shook her head. "So much death. Am I a curse to those who know me?"

Antony replied, "No, dear. The events that led to the deaths of our friends and countrymen were set in motion long before you sailed into the harbor. You were a convenient excuse, but Matteus has harbored ill will for years and the Hapsfell and Treyarch both had reasons aplenty to want my master dead. He is a good man, but he was hot headed and bloody in his youth. The arrows that struck our noble house flew from the bow many years ago."

Reiki sighed. "I can't help but feel responsible. It is as though I have been marked by death and it follows me now wherever I go. I swore an oath to the gods for vengeance, forsaking all but vengeance until I fulfill my vow. I have yet to slay even one of the men who slaughtered my village, and yet, I have left many corpses in my wake. Is this the cost of vengeance? Do the gods mock our oaths?"

Antony shrugged. "The gods are a fickle bunch. Some pray for rain while others pray for clear skies. When the gods grant a boon to one, do they not curse another? If I praise the gods for destroying the Hapsfell or Treyarch men, do their wives cry out to the gods for my head in return? I think the gods do not care for our oaths or our prayers. I think they sleep the slumber of those long gone; monuments jutting from the earth in crypts of silence."

Reiki had never really considered this, and the thought made her uncomfortable. Ichiro had taught her that the gods listened and provided for the villages of the Islands. She had known, intellectually, that the Hastrans and Sychak and Chekhovians and even the Sakawat had their own gods as well, but they had always seemed less powerful or less important somehow. It had not occurred to her that all the gods might be equally important, or completely meaningless. "I have never thought about that, Antony, and I can't say that I like the implications of that line of thinking."

"Then, feel free to ignore them. It is an unpopular view, but one that I have adopted over the years," Antony shrugged. "Regardless, we were talking about Pyotr and Rodrigo's decision to attack the palace."

Reiki nodded, relieved to move the conversation away from theology. "Sorry, carry on."

`"Right, so, the house of Paulus, the house of Masters, the house of Stevens, and the house of Howard all chose to take part. Captain Paulus agreed to ready the Iron Will and each of the houses readied one hundred men at arms to assault the palace. It took quite some time to gather all those men, so we decided to wait until the next day and move at night. We made our plans and traveled in groups of three to five through the streets of the capital under cover of darkness. We were fortunate that they had not moved you from the dungeons; I assume the king wanted to extract information from you?"

Reiki nodded. "He did, but he and his lackey, Tomas, took their time about it. I think another day of hanging like that, and I might have confessed to anything they had wanted me to. Your timing was fortuitous."

"Well, we lucked out," Antony smiled. "The guard was light, and they opened the gates willingly when Pyotr told them he was there to surrender. He was accompanied by five men who were not armored and who had their weapons secreted under their robes. They made short work of the guards and held the gates for the bulk of our force to enter. At that point, the men went to work creating havoc inside the palace walls. Meanwhile, we went in search of you. The rest you already know."

At that moment, a door opened behind Reiki and a shirtless man in breeches and an apron called out, "Dinner is ready. Come get a plate before they ring the bells, and you have to fight for a spot in line."

Reiki and Antony both followed the man into the next room where a large cauldron of fish stew and a giant basket full of baked rolls sat next to a stack of metal bowls and plates. Reiki grabbed a bowl, filled it with fish stew and picked up a roll. Antony did the same, and they both returned to their table. As they sat down, they heard the bells, two sets of two dings. The room was quickly filled with men coming down the ladder to get in line and eat their evening meal now that they were off watch. Another door opened off to Reiki's right, heading aft. She smiled as Pyotr stepped through the open door, followed by a half dozen crewmen. Pyotr spied Antony and Reiki and raised his hand in greeting before walking over to their table. He took a seat on the bench next to Antony.

"I hope you rested well, Reiki. I can only imagine you were exhausted after the past few days." Pyotr's voice was as sonorous as ever, and Reiki found it soothing.

She swallowed a chunk of roll that she had dipped in her stew. The stew was salty, but the fish itself was lightly seasoned. The roll was stale, but it was quite edible when used to sop up the stew. "I don't know that I will ever sleep enough to repay the debt these last few weeks have built up. But, yes, I do feel improved. I'm still not fully healed from the garatha spine yet. Now I ache in my shoulders and back, and I feel stiff in the legs.”

“You just described the last ten years of my life. Getting old makes those conditions permanent,” he winked. “No, I can see you aren’t yet back to strength. You should take it easy for the time being. Perhaps you could assist the navigator if you wanted something to do.”

Reiki nodded. She would likely need something to occupy her over the coming days at sea. *Wait.* An unsettling thought occurred to her. *Some mariner I am! I haven’t given any thought at all to where we are going!* She chastised herself as she took another bite of her soaked roll before asking, “Where are we and where are we heading?”

“Well, we have sailed north since we left the harbor. I believe we should be changing course to head eastward soon. The goal, I believe, is to head to Sychak, and then we can disembark there and see about finding passage upriver,” Pyotr explained.

“If memory serves, Sychak is actually southeast of Hastra. Is captain Paulus planning to sail east to the continent and then follow the coast south to Sychak at the mouth of the River Argent?” Reiki asked.

“Aye, your memory is accurate. We headed north for two reasons. The first is that any pursuers would find it more likely we would sail south toward the Illangetti Quarter, maybe even to dock there. The second is that the wind was more favorable and allowed us to keep our sails full and open the distance quickly. We could still be seen by a passing ship out here, but it is less likely and even then, they would need to close the distance to be able to tell who we were."

Reiki nodded. *That makes sense.* "So, what will you do when we reach Sychak?"

Antony laughed and replied, "I wouldn't presume to speak for my master, but as for myself, I intend to journey with you to the lands of the Sakawat."

Pyotr sighed and wiped tears from his eyes. "Neither of us can return home, Reiki. I left two sons behind. One will have no choice but have me executed if he ever sees me again. The other—well, he will have enough difficulties without adding me to the mix. So, I too plan to go with you."

Reiki felt tears welling in her eyes. *I had thought to be going alone. I should urge them to stay behind. I should. But I won't.* "Thank you, both of you," She said, almost a whisper. She took another bite of her soggy roll. She chewed and swallowed, finding it less appetizing than before. "What of Demetrius? This is twice you've left his purpose in Hastra unsaid."

Pyotr grimaced and then nodded, "Yes. I used our rather pressing need to escape as an excuse the first time. I suppose I can explain now."

Reiki nodded emphatically. "Yes, please do. I will keep eating while I listen."

"Demetrius and Matteus are about as opposite as any two men could be. Matteus is cocky and headstrong. Demetrius is cautious and does not rise to anger. Matteus is obsessed with his image. Demetrius cares about what actually is. Matteus is all talk. Demetrius is silent action." Pyotr paused, considering how to proceed. "As I said before, Matteus never forgave me for foregoing vengeance for my wife. He harbored a hatred in his heart, and it has grown every day since. He finally saw an opportunity to have his revenge against me while also placing himself at the head of the Illangetti house ,and, in his mind, allying himself with the other houses and the crown. He has been played by the Treyarch and Hapsfell in this regard, for the king is naught but a puppet for the great houses, a seal to wrap around decrees. Matteus, in his spite for me, has decided to ally himself with the very people who killed his mother, but I doubt he even sees that. Grudges start out principled and reasoned, but when fed and nourished can grow wild and spread beyond the bounds of reason. Perhaps that is why. At any rate, Demetrius loves his brother, despite his failings, or perhaps because of them. He chose to stay behind because Matteus will be in grave danger going forward. I escaped, along with you. None of Matteus's plans came to actual fruition. He will likely be blamed by the other houses for the failure. Demetrius is shrewd. He plans to help protect Matteus where he can, as well as a second, far more dangerous and secret goal."

Reiki swallowed the stew she had just sipped from her bowl. "What's that?"

Pyotr dropped his voice and whispered, "To overthrow the Hastran monarchy and nobility and place the reins of power in the hands of the people of Hastra, the workers and peasantry. Hastra has several factions pushing to end the monarchy and gain more power for the working class. Demetrius is a member of one, I know not which. I imagine he has more motivation than before, given that I am now in exile due to the machinations of the nobility." His eyes lost focus and he choked back a sob as he added, "I will probably not see my boys again, unless it is in passing on the way to the scaffold, or Matteus is holding the axe. That might almost be worth it, though it would break me."

Reiki felt warm tears on her cheeks. She reached across the table and held his hand in her own. "I am sorry, Pyotr. Antony has tried valiantly to persuade me that this is not my fault, but I share the blame for all of this. If I could go back now, knowing what I know, I would let that garatha rot and go diving for pearls instead."

Pyotr shook his head, blinking away the tears in his eyes. "You could not have known, and you brought me some measure of peace in slaying the beast that robbed me of a son. Matteus's betrayal was his own, and Demetrius's choice, though it robs me of my most favored son, is one that fills me with pride at the man he has become. With his guidance, Matteus may be spared and may even learn temperance. What's more, Hastra may be saved from the depredations of the nobility. So, I would change nothing, though I bear wounds that cannot ever close."

Reiki nodded, understanding. *Some wounds will not heal, no matter how well you tend to them. I could have spared myself great pain if I had never known little Tova, but I would have lost the joy of knowing and loving him. Which pain is greater?* "I understand. I think I will always feel some guilt for the events I set in motion, though."

"As long as you know that I hold you blameless," Pyotr replied.

Reiki managed a weak smile. "Thank you." She finished her roll and washed it down with the remainder of her stew. The meal had been surprisingly filling, and she felt some of her strength restored. A few more days of warm meals and good rest and she thought she might be near her old self again. "I think I will go topside and walk around the ship. I have never been on a ship like this, and I think I would like to explore some."

Antony had also finished his stew and roll and looked as though he might join her, but he remained sitting instead. "I think I will stay and keep my lord company while he eats. We will have time enough to enjoy each other's company in the coming days. It will take us at least a week to reach Sychak, after all, perhaps two."

Reiki stood and stretched her limbs. "Thank you for the company. I will see you later."

Pyotr nodded, but added, "Don't tarry too far. After dinner, we will be holding a brief funeral for Rodrigo before we send his body to the deep. It will not be a long ceremony, but I would like for you to be there, and I imagine you would wish to."

Reiki was embarrassed that she had not asked about a funeral for Rodrigo. " Of course, I will. I will remain topside for a while and will await you there."

Reiki bowed and then made her way to the ladder and climbed topside. She walked aft, climbing up onto the poop deck. There was the ship's helm, currently manned by a boy barely older than Reiki, based on his patchy stubble and youthful eyes. Behind him stood the thick stalk of the mizzen mast towering above them, its sails taut and filled with wind. Along the aft rail, Reiki saw five men gathered and pointing at something on the horizon. One of the men held a brass tube that he was looking through. Reiki had never seen such an instrument. She hurried over to the nearest of the five, a short and broad-shouldered man with a bushy red beard and a bald head, and asked, "What's going on?"

The man pointed to the horizon where Reiki saw a tiny black smudge peeking over the horizon. "Is that a ship approaching?" She asked.

"Aye, it's too far to make out much yet, as she's still hull-down and only the topmost sail is visible, but she looks to carry three masts and is flying a flag. It's still too far to know who she is yet. You can't even see details through the spyglass."

Spyglass? "What's a spyglass?"

The man pointed to the brass tube the other man was holding. The other three were actively engaged in speculating as to the identity of the ship. "That's a spyglass. You look through it and you can see things that are far away more clearly."

Interesting. I wonder how that works. "Could I take a look?"

The bearded man shrugged. "You'll have to ask ole Andrew there. He's usually pretty stingy about his instruments, but you're a pretty girl, so he might let you touch it." The man laughed as though he had just said something funny and looked at Reiki as if waiting for her to laugh too. When she didn't, he stopped rather abruptly and shifted his feet awkwardly. "Just ask him, then. Worst he can do is say no."

Reiki thanked him and walked over to the tall slender young man the other had called Andrew. "Andrew?" She asked.

The man lowered the spyglass and turned to look at Reiki. His eyes traveled from her feet to the top of her head, and he grinned as he met her eyes. "What can I help you with, miss? I'm always happy to lend a hand to a young lady."

Reiki arched an eyebrow, wondering what was wrong with these men. They were treating her strangely. "Could I take a look through your spyglass? I have never seen one before, and I am curious to try it."

Andrew smiled enthusiastically, "Of course! Would you like me to show you how to use it?"

Reiki frowned, "You hold it up to your eye and peer through it, right?"

Andrew nodded.

"Any additional secret to it? Something to twist? Some magical incantation?" she asked.

Andrew shook his head, "No. I guess you are right. You just hold it to your eye and look through it."

"Then, no, I think I'll manage." She held out her hand for the spyglass, and Andrew handed it over, looking deflated.

Ah, so you wanted to play the wise and strong man helping out the poor young girl. I know little of Hastran society, but I would guess that I have spent more years at sea than you, Andrew, though you likely will have the opportunity to show me about the ship if you would like. There are many things I do not know that you might show me. But, not the things you'd like to, I would wager. "Thank you."

She held the spyglass up to her right eye and closed her left. She found the horizon and swung the spyglass slowly along the horizon until she picked up the approaching ship in her view. *This is a really impressive tool. I can see the three masts and even a bit of sail. There is a flag there, but it is far too faint to make out, especially in the approaching dusk.* The ship was following nearly exactly their course, perhaps a bit to port. She could also surmise that it was gaining on them since it had appeared relatively recently on the horizon. If they were moving slower, they would never have seen them at all. *It is too soon to worry. We will see if it follows us when we turn east.*

Reiki heard people gathering behind her on the topdeck below. She handed Andrew his spyglass and turned and walked past the mizzen mast and the ship's helm and stopped at the forward rail of the poop deck to see what was happening below. She saw Antony and Pyotr standing to the port side of the main mast, along with Captain Paulus. They stood silent and solemn as a crew of four men opened a large hatch in the deck. *That must be how cargo is loaded and unloaded.* The men tossed lines down into the hold once the hatch was opened. After a few moments, she heard a shout from down in the hold and the men began heaving the lines. *They must be lifting Rodrigo's body. I should join the others.*

She climbed the ladder down to the top deck and walked over to stand beside Antony. They all stood in silence as their friend and comrade was slowly raised from the belly of the ship. As his body reached the top deck, Reiki saw that Rodrigo was strapped to a wooden pallet and the lines were tied to four metal eye bolts, one at each corner. His body had been washed and dressed back in his armor, his hands crossed over his chest and his eyes covered with a white cloth. His shield lay upon his chest and his spear lay beside him. He was no longer wearing his sword in its scabbard and

Reiki wondered what became of it. *I will ask Pyotr or Antony later.*

The men each took hold of the pallet, one after the other, and carried him gently over to the starboard side of the ship. They sat the pallet down tenderly and detached the lines from the eye bolts before coiling the lines and hanging them on hooks on the starboard railing. The men then walked back to the cargo hatch and secured it tightly. Their task completed, they filed behind Antony, Pyotr, and the captain. The captain pulled out a small silver pipe from a pouch on his leather belt. He blew a long shrill note followed by a short sharp note. From the forecastle, she heard the booming voice of one of the crewmen, who she would later learn was the head boatswain.

"All hands to topside for burial at sea. All hands to topside for burial at sea." His voice was booming and carried. She heard the command echoed below her feet in the decks below, one deck at a time, four more times. Moments later, men began to appear from the hatches at the fore and aft ends of the top deck. *Gods, there are so many of them. This ship must have nearly a hundred men crewing it. Less than the Yondratha, but still, so many.* The men silently gathered in rows abreast and soon the top deck, forecastle, and poop deck were all crowded with row upon row of men. Reiki, the only woman and only non-Hastran aboard, felt very out of place, but she took comfort in knowing Antony and Pyotr were there beside her.

The captain stepped forward and turned to face the body of Rodrigo Voorhees. His voice rang out clearly and loudly, though he did not shout. "Men of the Iron Will, we gather now to pay our final respects to our countryman, our comrade, flesh made legend. Rodrigo was the third child of four, the second son of his father Cesar, himself a man of renown. Rodrigo's brother and two sisters precede him in death, but Rodrigo goes now to join them beyond the veil of the stars from which we all came."

Everyone bowed their heads, so Reiki followed suit. Captain Paulus continued, "Rodrigo gained renown in battle against the Sakawat during the Rauleen incursion. He was promoted to captain of Pyotr Illangetti's house guard when he was only twenty-seven years old. His skill with a spear was already known throughout the kingdom. He bested the Hapsfell and Treyarch champions during seven consecutive tournaments before he finally retired undefeated. He helped put down the uprisings on our eastern shore. He was a man of loyalty and unimpeachable honor. He met his demise while protecting his lord, Pyotr Illangetti, and fighting the Mauling Spear himself, Trevor Marquez, in single combat after slaying twelve of his men. This despite being several decades older than his foes. We gather here today to say farewell, but also to remember."

Everyone raised their heads, then, so Reiki did so as well. She saw that Pyotr's face was streaked with fresh tears. Her eyes burned from her own grief and her guilt, and she did not try to hold back the tears that fled from her eyes.

The captain then spoke the phrase: "Where you go, we will one day follow. We say farewell, but we will meet again beyond the veil."

Everyone repeated the phrase in a chorus of disparate voices, not quite in unison, but intoned like an incantation or a rite. *These must be their funerary words.* She joined in time to utter, "—but we will meet again beyond the veil."

Captain Paulus nodded and signaled the work crew from before with a flick of his right hand. The men approached and lifted the pallet and raised it up to the railing. Silently, they removed the straps holding Rodrigo to the pallet and then tipped his body off into the waiting sea. His body splashed loudly and then sank below the waves, the armor weighing him down. Reiki wept then, as did Pyotr and Antony beside her. Many of the crew were weeping also, and Reiki wondered how many had known him.

A voice rang up from the forecastle, and Reiki realized that a young man was singing. His voice was mournful, and the song was clearly a dirge. *I wonder if they end every funeral with a dirge or if this is unique. Judging by the faces, this is a common element.*

The young man sang:

The bosom of the sea

Embraces us all

Whether warm winds blow

Or in ice and snow

Hearts that swell upon the swells

We come here now

With our farewells

Never again will you know pain

Never again will you know fear

Your work is done

We gather here

Your battles won

We gather here

We bid farewell

Goodbye dear friend

Find peace beyond the veil.

The song complete, everyone hung their heads in silence again. After a few moments draped in the silent pall of mournful remembrance, everyone dispersed back down the ladders or up into the rigging to resume the work of manning the ship. Pyotr and Antony and Reiki alone remained. Pyotr turned to Reiki then.

"I have something to give you, Reiki. Come to my cabin before you retire for the evening," he said, his voice still raw with emotion.

"I think I will just accompany you there now," she replied.

She followed Pyotr through the door to the U-shaped passageway she had come out from before. He opened the door to his cabin and gestured for her to enter. He followed closely and shut the door behind him. Reiki stood quietly by the door as Pyotr walked past her over to a large wooden chest bolted to the wall next to his bed. He opened the trunk and pulled out Rodrigo's sword and scabbard attached to a leather belt that looked small enough to fit Reiki.

"I kept only a handful of Rodrigo's effects, though he did not have many. Among them was this sword, which he carried with him every day since he was a young man of seventeen. He named it Bloodfang. He had no children and none in his family lived to wield it after him. Demetrius has no use for a sword, nor would I dishonor my friend by giving his blade to Matteus, who has betrayed us all. I believe it would best serve you." He held the sword out in his upturned hands.

Reiki was stunned and stammered, "I can't accept this. I barely knew him. I'm just some Islander girl that showed up and arguably got him killed. Wouldn't that also dishonor him?"

Pyotr shook his head. "I don't see how it could. He was fond of you rather immediately. He liked how direct you were, unafraid to speak out in our presence where so many would be. You had no artifice, no designs against us. It is such a rarity in Hastra to speak with anyone where guile is not in play."

Reiki stepped closer but still did not reach out to accept the sword. "I have no experience with a sword. The Islanders use harpoons and knives, but a sword uses so much metal or bone, it is an excess, so we do not forge or fashion them. I have seen only a few in my life and always in the hands of foreign men."

Pyotr nodded. "That is a concern, no doubt. However, this sword has already been forged, so you have wasted nothing. Moreover, there are no fewer than three swordsmen of great skill that could teach you the basics while we sail to Sychak. You would not become a master, but you would likely be a capable novice."

Reiki sighed, realizing she had no choice but to accept the gift. The truth was, she knew that it would be a tangible symbol of her guilt wherever she carried it. *Of course, I carry my guilt within wherever I go, whether I carry it without or not.* "I will see to it that I do not shame him with my lack of skill." She reached out then and grasped the sword by the scabbard and took it from Pyotr's open hands. She fastened the belt around her waist, the scabbard hanging on her left hip so she could cross draw it with her right hand. The belt was clearly not Rodrigo's for it seemed to fit her correctly. "Who do I speak to about lessons in its use?"

Pyotr smiled genuinely and replied, "I have already arranged it. You will begin in the morning under the tutelage of the ship's master at arms, Idris Caldwell. He will meet you at five bells, after you've had breakfast, on the forecastle. You will train with him until eight bells, when you will break for lunch. After lunch, at one bell, I have arranged for you to meet with the ship's navigator followed by the chief gunner. I assumed you would like to know more about this vessel and its operations."

Reiki beamed, "Thank you, Pyotr. I would like that very much."

Pyotr shocked her by embracing her in a warm and gentle hug. Reiki was unprepared, but the warmth and comfort of the hug broke through, and she returned the embrace wholeheartedly. *I have not been held like this since before the attack on my village. I have kept my distance from everyone, even though I felt genuine fondness for these people. Attachments make my mission more difficult, for they give me something to fear losing. But I also really needed this.*

She finally broke off the embrace and bid Pyotr goodnight. She did not tarry after she left his cabin and found her way back to her own. She removed the sword belt and lay in her bunk. She whispered to the darkness, "Thank you, again, Rodrigo. I wish I had known you better." She drifted off to sleep soon after.

Chapter XV

"The Trough Between Swells"

You cannot outrun your troubles, for trouble flies like an arrow.

You cannot dodge your troubles, for troubles follow like a shadow.

You may only face your troubles, as a foe

Spear in hand, or hands raised in surrender.

--The Wisdom of Bryan—

Giuseppe Strongbow

That first night aboard the Iron Will, Reiki's nightmares returned. She dreamt the ship was sinking. She ran and ran through the ship's passageways, but they seemed to go on forever. The passageway tilted down away from her as it slid into the dark crushing sea, but to her horror, it was not the sea that rushed through the wooden halls of the ship. Reiki screamed as warm gushing rivers of crimson blood swept toward her, deep up to her knees. She felt something solid brush against her leg, and she screamed again as she looked down and saw the charred remains of her mother and father, speared together, bobbing in knee deep crimson river flowing through the passageway. She ran as fast as she could

213

through the rising flood of blood and bodies: Ichiro, Kelli, Rhea, Harald, and hundreds of others. She saw the passageway come to an end at a door ahead. She knew it opened out onto the deck of the ship, but as she approached, she saw a small, charred foot rise out of the blood sloshing around her thighs and the world of her dream peeled away and she was falling into blackness.

She fell and fell until she crashed hard into something warm and wet and putrid. As she groped about, she was seized by dozens of blackened and rotten arms and hands, pulling her down into the pile of corpses. As she screamed again, she looked to her right and saw herself standing upon the sandy beach of Serenity, ready to light the pyre. As the oil caught and roared, she was engulfed in flames. It was at that moment she awoke, screaming aloud into the darkness of her cabin, her body drenched in sweat, her sheets clenched tightly in her fists. She stayed that way for several hours before she finally heard the ship's bells ring out and signal the arrival of morning.

She wiped the sweat off her skin and trembled. It took significant force of will for her to finally stand up, open the door, and make her way to the galley for breakfast. She ate quickly and spoke to no one so that she would not keep the master at arms waiting. When she arrived on the forecastle, she realized the master at arms had not arrived yet. *Of course, he would want to eat, and he likely has no reason to hurry. How shall I occupy myself while I wait? Anything to avoid thinking about my nightmares.* Then she remembered the strange ship from the day before. She walked over to the port side, leaned over the railing, and looked aft to see if she could spy the ship.

The entirety of the ship's masts and sails were now visible on the horizon. *It is gaining on us. A few more days and it will be easily identifiable. There's nothing to be done about it now.* Nonetheless, something about the ship filled her with dread. She couldn't be sure, but she sensed danger. *I can't worry about it now. I must focus on my lessons today. They may help me when I finally face Issak and his men.*

She did not hear the master at arms approach, and his voice startled her. "So, you're the Islander lass I'm supposed to teach not to cut herself on her own sword, eh?"

She spun around and saw that he was only arm's length away from her, a lithe but muscular man at least fifteen years her senior. His hair was cut short, but he had a braided brown beard on his chin and a bushy mustache. His eyes were a soft brown, and they hinted at a fierceness. Everything about him reminded Reiki of a predatory bird prepared to dive on prey.

He did not wait for her to respond. "You don't have to answer. You're the only girl on this ship, thank the gods," he chuckled to himself. "I will give you the benefit of the doubt for your punctuality. I almost placed a bet with some of the other men that you would be sleeping in this morning, and I'd have had to douse your head with a bucket of bilge water to wake you. Instead, I see you beat me up here, sword on your hip, anxious to begin."

"I saw no sense in delaying my training. That hurts only me."

He nodded. "True, true." He grinned, "Well, then I suppose we ought to begin. I am Idris Caldwell, master at arms of the Iron Will. First, I must ask you, have you ever held a sword before?"

She shook her head.

"Well, that makes things easier then. I don't have to break any bad habits." He took a moment to look her over, his eyes appraising her. "You're in good shape, no flab on you. Any experience fighting?"

She replied, "Some, mostly with a harpoon or bow. I fought a few garatha, but I have never had to fight a man in actual combat." *I speared one who was already doomed and no threat to me, but that's another matter.*

Idris just nodded. "It's different when you have to do it for real, but I will try to teach you what I can in the next few days so that you're not completely useless with a sword. I would suggest you stick to the spear unless you have no other choice, though. I will teach you the basics, but you will need more teaching down the line if you wish to be more than a nuisance with a sword. Shall we begin?"

Reiki nodded, apprehensive but eager, nonetheless.

"Good. We will begin with a little instruction on the sword you are carrying, followed by the basics of how to draw it, how to grip it, and the basic forms. Then, if we get that far today, I will teach you very basic defense in the form of high and low parrying blows. If you are a prodigious learner, we may get beyond that to elementary ripostes by the end of the week. For now, draw your sword."

Reiki grasped the scabbard with her left hand and gripped the sword's hilt with her right hand. She drew the sword from the scabbard in a smooth motion, the curved single edged blade sliding out of the scabbard with ease.

"Not bad," he said with a hint of surprise. "What you have there is an exceptionally high-quality curved sword, called a katana by some, mostly those who teach at the universities in Hastra or Sychak. I don't know why they call it that, so don't ask me. You can use it to stab, but it is a far superior slashing weapon. You should keep that in mind in a fight. The blade is a decent length, about sixty centimeters. That will give you some reach, but not as much as a two hander or a polearm. The braid on the handle is to help you keep a good grip. It also looks nice, on the off chance that's something you care about. The guard there will keep another sword or blade from sliding past your blade and onto your fingers. It is square in shape to protect from all angles. It lacks the protection of a basket hilt and is not as wide as the cross guard on a longsword, but it is not without its uses." He pointed at each feature as he spoke.

He drew his own sword then, a similar one to her own, though the braided hilt was black and gold instead of her blue and silver. He demonstrated how to hold it properly, his right hand firm beneath the guard, his left hand below it near the end of the hilt. "This is the way to hold it." He performed a series of vertical strikes from overhead and then a series of diagonal slashes. *I see. The top hand serves as the fulcrum point. The bottom hand adds additional force to the swing and allows for proper follow through.*

"You can also hold it one handed, though you lose significant force, and your blocking ability will be severely weakened." He kept the grip unchanged except for removing his left hand from the handle. He demonstrated several diagonal and horizontal slashes. "Okay, now you. Show me."

Reiki gripped her sword with two hands and mimicked the vertical slash and diagonal slashes he had performed. *The sword is surprisingly light. It lacks the range of a spear, but I can imagine situations where this might be valuable.*

"Not bad, honestly. Your strikes are weak, but your form is good." He sounded genuinely pleased, so Reiki smiled.

"Okay, now one handed."

Reiki slid her left hand off the handle and made several diagonal and horizontal slashes with the sword. "Like so?"

The master at arms nodded, "Yes. Your form is okay, though your guard would be pitifully flimsy one handed. Your slashes have excellent speed, though, which may serve you well against bigger and slower opponents, especially if they underestimate you."

Reiki smiled. *Men almost always do, it seems.*

"Don't smile too much. You've convinced me you aren't a complete waste of time, not that you're especially good. However, we can move on to more practical instruction. Sheath that sword. It won't do for you to cut yourself, or worse, me, during practice."

Reiki sheathed her sword and stood quietly as he walked over to the fore mast and dropped to a squat. Reiki watched as he unrolled a roll of thick cloth roughly a meter long. *He must have sat it there before he came up behind me. He is a stealthy one for me to not have noticed.* Once unrolled, Reiki could see the cloth contained two wooden practice swords that closely resembled the size and shape of her own. Idris grabbed one in each hand and stood. He handed her one of the practice swords, and she was surprised to find that it was heavier than her real one.

"They're weighted with a lead core. It's good to train with a heavier weapon than you use in combat because it will build up your strength, and you'll be even faster with a real weapon," Idris explained, recognizing the surprised look on her face. "Now, before we begin slashing and stabbing at each other, I want to ask you something."

Reiki shrugged, "Go ahead."

"Lord Illangetti did not go into details, but I asked him why you would be needing a sword. After all, you Islanders never have been much for hacking and slashing people."

Reiki rolled her eyes. "We have warriors. We're not all fishermen and farmers, you know."

Idris shook his head. "Of course, but you're not known for being a war-like or bloodthirsty people, unlike the Sakawat who live for a good fight, or the Chekhovians who only a fool would provoke open war with."

"You're right. My village was attacked by Sakawat raiders. Everyone was killed or else captured. I swore an oath to avenge the deaths of my family and village."

Idris's jaw tightened into a grim line. "Aye, I think that's a powerful motivation. Good. Tap into that whenever the lessons become frustrating. Use it to keep yourself going and you might just come out of this a decent fighter. Just remember, you can use strong emotions to motivate you, but do not let them consume you. Blind and enraged warriors make good flower beds and naught else." He held his sword out and entered a loose fighting stance. "Okay, enough chin wagging. En garde!"

For the next four hours, Idris put Reiki through rigorous practice blocking and parrying with her sword, teaching her the proper footwork and stances to counter different attacks and weapons. By the time she heard the bells for lunch, she was exhausted and bruised from numerous attacks she had failed to block. Her hip stung especially where a surprise reverse slash from Idris had struck hard on the bone. Still, she had found the instruction enjoyable, and she looked forward to more lessons the next day.

She ate her lunch on the forecastle alone, ravenously devouring her bread and a few strips of dried ox meat. When she had finished, she took her plate back to the galley and handed it off to a crewman in the scullery washing pots and plates in a cauldron of lukewarm water. She then met the navigator upon the poop deck. He was standing beside the helmsman and peering up at the sky using a strange device Reiki had never seen before. He then pulled out a roll of parchment and a piece of charcoal and scribbled out some figures. Once done, he waved to Reiki to come over to him.

"You must be Reiki." He beamed and held out his hand in greeting, "I am the ship's navigator, Warren Behrns."

Reiki accepted his hand and shook it gently in greeting. "Nice to meet you. As you said, I am Reiki." She then pointed to the sun, now off to the port bow, "I thought we were going to be heading east today."

Warren grimaced, "Yes, that was the plan. Then that ship showed up astern. The Captain felt it would be better to keep the wind off our port quarter until we get further north and can use the western wind that prevails in those waters to beat east. If we turn east now, that ship will gain on us even faster. If she is actually pursuing us, then that will mean fighting an engagement at sea, which we would prefer to avoid."

Reiki nodded, beginning to understand. "Sailing is different with these large square sails and huge masts. With a triangular sail on a single mast, you can sail effectively with the wind coming from nearly any direction, except dead ahead. That's a quick luff, though, and then you're back at speed."

"Yes, there are some aspects of your little trimarans that are enviable," Warren grinned, "though, when the goal is to move large amounts of people or cargo, or to carry a fair number of cannons, then you are best served with a ship such as this."

Reiki nodded in agreement, "Of course. At most I could carry four people on my little boat, and only for short distances. I don't have the cargo space to carry provisions for more than that."

Warren gestured to a nearby hatch, "Would you accompany me to the chart table? I need to plot our position."

Reiki nodded and followed as he led her below to a small room that consisted of little more than a drafting table attached to the bulkhead and a storage rack of cubby holes filled with rolled up nautical charts. The drafting table had a chart pinned to it that showed the entire island of Hastra, the seas north and east of it, and the coastline of the eastern continent filling the entire eastern edge of the chart. The chart was marked with lines that intersect at right angles and they appeared to be numbered along the edges. She watched, rapt with fascination, as he used a set of calipers and a thin piece of charcoal with a sharpened point to mark their current position with a small 'X' and then drew a circle around it. She could see that there were many others just like it that led back to the harbor in Hastra. *What a fascinating method of keeping track of one's position.*

"I've never seen this method of navigation before." Reiki did not bother trying to hide her interest. "Can you teach me how it is done?"

The navigator beamed, "I would love to. It would be nice to have someone other than me, my assistant, and the captain who knows how to plot a fix. Gods forbid I ever fall ill. I'd still have to be up taking sun bearings or plotting azimuths even if I were spewing from both ends."

Reiki laughed, "Gross."

Warren's cheeks reddened, "I'm sorry. I'm not used to women being aboard. We sailors are a coarse lot."

Reiki was amused by his embarrassment. "I've noticed I have a way of putting you all off balance. Are there no women sailors among the Hastrans?"

Warren shook his head. "Not that I have come across in ten years at sea. There are those that think it is work ill-suited to women with their moods and their delicate constitutions."

Reiki glared at him. "Delicate constitutions?"

Warren stammered, "Well, present company obviously excluded." Then he added, "Besides, I think it's more that they worry the men will be distracted or worse, force themselves upon the women."

Reiki was aghast. "In the Islands, a man who forces himself on a woman usually finds himself bound to a plain raft with no sail, no hands, and no cock or balls with which to ever offend again, and that's if the island's council were feeling merciful. All men and women have a right to choose who they lay with." *Unless you choose to lay with none, like me.* "To violate that choice is one of the gravest offenses."

Warren contemplated that for a moment. "You know, we Hastrans often look down on you Islanders as a simple backwards people with no mines, no money, no kings, and no army. It seems we may have gotten it backward."

Reiki shrugged. "From what I have seen, you have put your efforts into better ways to kill, exploit, or belittle others when you could have instead found ways to just be better people. I think maybe you value things when you should value people." She sighed, "Of course, here I stand, hellbent on killing the bastards who wronged me. So perhaps I do not value life so much as before. Forgive me. I perhaps spoke too judgmentally."

Warren gave a dismissive wave. "It is nothing. I offended first."

Reiki shook her head, "It is forgotten."

The rest of her time with the navigator was pleasant and devoted entirely to explaining the principles of Hastran navigation. A few hours of instruction later, the chief gunner opened the door and introduced himself.

"I'm Hal Green. I'm the chief gunner of the Iron Will, and if you're finished learning from Master Behrns, I can show you around the gun decks."

The gunner was a squat man who had a barrel chest and arms as big around as Reiki's head. He wore a long braided blond beard and had a shaved head. His eyes were icy blue, and he looked like his greatest joy in the world was getting into brawls. He wore no shirt and his chest was covered in a bed of curly golden hair. He wore tan breeches and plain sandals. Reiki would have found him comical if he didn't look like he would kill the first person who made the mistake of laughing at him.

"Lead the way," she said, smiling to avoid laughing.

Hal led her down one deck and forward to the upper gun deck. The gun deck was an open space filled with black cannons mounted on wooden rolling carriages. Each sat before a gun port, currently closed. The entire room was stuffy and there were several other men who appeared to be working on tidying or performing various maintenance tasks. Hal swept his arm around the room.

"Well, you've seen it. These are the first of two decks full of cannons. We got these beautiful bastards from the Sakawat about twelve months ago, part of the first ever sold outside of the Sakawat nation. As of now, there are only four hundred total in Hastra, and forty-eight of them are right here on this ship."

So, these are Sakawat cannons. Interesting. The Hastrans haven't manufactured their own yet. I wonder why. Well, shit, might as well ask.

"If you have these cannons, why hasn't Hastra started making their own?"

Hal scowled. "We can make the cannons. It's the powder that we haven't figured out how to mimic. We're working on modifying the kappow resin to do the job, but so far that has been a spectacularly dangerous failure. The resin has a bad habit of burning and burning and burning long after you fire your shot. If some of that burning resin flies out of the cannon, you can end up burning your own ship if you aren't careful. The black Sakawat powder, on the other hand, burns up in an instant. It explodes and then it's done burning."

Interesting.

"Okay, another question," Reiki ventured.

Hal rolled his eyes. "Go ahead."

"You have these cannons. Yet, I saw none of the Sakawat rifles aboard so far. Did they only sell their cannons?"

Hal nodded. "Those eastern bastards won't part with their rifles so easily. For what it's worth, they take a deal of training to be able to use effectively. Reloading is a difficult task and the Sakawat practice for months to be proficient. They take a substantial amount of powder and oil and gods know what else to keep them functioning. We Hastrans prefer our crossbows and spears and even our swords to that sort of fickle weaponry."

Reiki nodded, though not completely convinced. *What you're saying has some merit. Going into a fight with weapons you aren't fully confident in spells disaster. On the other hand, you took the time to learn how to use the cannons. I imagine the Sakawat are better trained and more deadly accurate with theirs than you are. I'm not a fool enough to say that aloud, though.*

"So, how do these cannons work?" She asked instead.

"You put a powder charge into the cannon followed by some wadding, which is a plug of cloth. You ram them in using a ramrod. Then you put a cannon ball, a large sphere of iron, into the cannon and ram it into place as well. Then you touch a burning piece of slow-match, which is a slow burning piece of cloth fuse, onto the firing hole on the top of the cannon. The match ignites the powder, which explodes, and blows the cannonball and the wadding out the barrel. It flies out the end at an alarming speed and causes massive damage wherever it hits. These babies can fire about eight hundred meters, but they're more effective within about five hundred. Now, the Sakawat have figured out a way to make the cannon balls themselves explode. That's some vile devilish bit of murder that I would like very much to learn how they do."

I bet you would. So would I, for that matter.

"Okay, what's next?" Reiki asked. She was slated to continue learning for another two hours and there seemed to be little else to learn.

Hal looked confused. "What do you mean, 'what's next?' You think I'm going to have you down here working a cannon as part of a gun crew? Not before the stars fall and I'm crowned queen of Chekhov. I showed you the guns and indulged your curiosity. That's all I've got for you."

Reiki snapped back, exasperated, "Well, then what am I supposed to do for the rest of the afternoon?"

Hal shrugged and his expression made it all too clear to Reiki that as far as he was concerned, she could hop overboard. "I don't care what you do. Stay out of the way of those of us who are actually working, for starters. This is a warship, not a passenger ship. Hell, you've seen that ship shadowing us, have you not? Do you think perhaps I might have some preparing to do in the chance those bastards want a fight? Do you think the most valuable use of my time right now is playing tour guide to some wet eared simpleton from the land of fucking tree sap?"

Reiki's temper flared, but she bit her tongue and clenched her fists to stifle the immediate retort that sprang to her lips. Instead, she replied tersely, "I will spare you the burden, as I can see my time would be wasted here as well."

She did not wait for a response and instead stormed out the aft door and climbed the ladder up to the top deck. She took care to avoid getting in anyone's way as she made her way up to the poop deck. She was still fuming as she reached the aft rail and stared daggers at the ship still dogging the Iron Will's wake. She could see it fully above the horizon now, its three masts full of sails and its hull clearly visible. She could not yet make out much beyond its vague shape, but she knew in her heart what it was, though she could not explain why. *The Yondratha. Issak has found us.* She did not have Andrew's spyglass and as she looked behind her at the helmsman, she did not see him around, nor did she see anyone currently holding such an instrument. Her eyes rose up to the top of the Iron Will's main mast, and she saw a single man perched in a basket-like structure at the top. *He has a spyglass! Oh, and he's looking aft. How do I get up there?* She saw that there were webbed nets of thick rope that went from the gunwales up to the top spar of the mast. *Do I climb those? I have to. I have to* know *if that's Issak's ship.*

She hurried down to the top deck and over to where the webbing attached to the railing. Without a word to anyone, she pulled herself up onto the railing and started climbing. *This is actually not too bad. The ship is rocking some, but the webbing is taut, which makes it quite sturdy.* The main mast was the tallest of the three masts of the Iron Will, and it was dizzyingly tall, forty meters from the top deck to its peak. She did not look down, for she knew that would be a mistake. She was not prone to vertigo, but she had also never been so high above the sea on a rocking ship before, and she would not chance it. She kept climbing, always looking ahead to the next hand hold. She finally reached the top spar of the main mast and quickly scrambled over to grasp hold of the rungs on the mast. She was pleased to find they were dry and coated with a gritty substance that aided her in keeping a solid foothold. She climbed quickly, but carefully, until she emerged through a hole in the bottom of the basket-like structure. The man looked shocked when he recognized her.

"You aren't supposed to be up here in the crow's nest," the young man, who Reiki thought looked to be about seventeen, chided.

"Is that what this is called?" She deflected.

"Yeah. It's a crow's nest. You can see further from up here, on account of the height. The world's a sphere, you know? So, you get higher, you can see further."

"Yes, I am aware. But, what's a crow?" Reiki asked, having no idea what the name referenced.

"I don't know, honestly. They've been called that since people started building ships. I think it must be some kind of bird, since it's got a nest and it's up high like this. Must be one hell of a big, majestic bird to have a nest this big, though."

Reiki nodded. "It must indeed. At this height you must be able to see quite far."

"Yes, miss. About twenty-two to twenty three kilometers, on a clear day with no haze."

Reiki whistled. On her little boat, she could only see about seven kilometers, if she climbed to the tip of her mast. From the tiller, about three. She decided to introduce herself before getting to the point. "I'm Reiki, by the way." She stuck out her hand.

The boy took her hand and shook it gently. "I'm Albert, and I'm a lookout and occasionally work in the rigging." He smiled proudly.

"Nice to meet you, Albert." She smiled back at him. "I was wondering if I might take a look at the ship that's following us."

"Ah." He glanced down at the spyglass in his right hand. He thought for a moment, and then handed it to her. "I haven't got a positive identification yet, but it doesn't look Hastran. The flag is still obscured by haze."

She nodded. "I'll give it a look." She put the spyglass to her eye and peered aft, searching the horizon for the ship. She found it quickly and studied it. *The hull looks right. The sails aren't enough to go on. Albert is right, too. I can't make out the flag. Still, that hull looks right.* "Could it be Sakawat?" She asked him.

Albert tapped his chin with his forefinger. "Yes, I think it could. The hull swells out down by the water like the Sakawat do. Well, I mean, we do too, but they have a pretty distinctive curve. The masts look like a Sakawat arrangement too. They have a shorter mizzen than Hastran ships do, but a taller foremast. Of course, so do the Chekhovian ships. Though, they would almost never be found this far north. No, I think you're probably right." He looked at her with newfound respect. "How could you tell?"

"The Yondratha attacked my island and killed everyone I loved. I would know that ship anywhere." She pointed to the Sakawat ship. "*That* ship, I would wager just about anything."

Albert swallowed anxiously. "Let's hope not. I've heard of that ship and it's not one I would want to do battle against."

"Yes, let's hope I'm wrong." But she knew she wasn't. "Thank you, Albert. I'll head below now."

Albert nodded, his attention now fixed on the Sakawat ship. Reiki felt slightly guilty for filling him with dread, but she consoled herself with the hope that Albert would also pay far more close attention to the ship over the coming days. *It's only a matter of days now.*

As she started to climb back down through the hole in the bottom of the crow's nest, Albert asked, "Will you tell the captain that that's most likely a Sakawat frigate? I would call down using my horn here," he pointed to a hollow brass cone resting on the deck by his feet, "but since you're heading down anyway you might as well."

"Of course. I'll go find him and let him know." Without another word between them, she descended back the way she came. When her feet touched the gunwales, she used the webbing as support and swung down onto the top deck. She was met by Captain Paulus himself, his face full of disapproval.

"You shouldn't be climbing the ratlines, at least not without someone to spot you the first few times. If you had fallen, we'd have to hold another funeral, and I have had enough of those for one voyage," he scolded her.

She did her best to look sheepish, but it was not a look she was very good at. She hoped she didn't look capricious instead. She decided to deflect. "Albert and I believe the ship following us is a Sakawat ship. I believe it could be the Yondratha, though Albert says its too far out to be sure."

Paulus frowned then nodded. "I think you are probably right, though I had hoped otherwise. If it is the Yondratha, we can't outrun it, nor outgun it. That puts us in an unenviable position. I was trying to maintain some optimism instead, but this does not seem to be a week for that."

Reiki agreed wholeheartedly, "I think it will probably be a week for it to come alongside us if we keep the current speed difference."

"Yes, but we can't do that. We will have to turn east soon. Nothing but the open ocean lies north of us for at least three weeks sailing. We don't have provisions to journey much further north and still be able to make it back to a port we could resupply at. Once we turn east, the Yondratha can turn to cut us off. If we head to the coast, we will need to head southeast along the coastline to reach Sychak. There are no ports to the northeast for at least two weeks sailing, and the Yondratha would catch us. Not that it would matter, because those ports are also Sakawat ports. I don't like any of our choices."

Reiki was surprised at his candor, but she could not fault his conclusions. "What will we do, then?"

Paulus shook his head. "I will need to think on it, but right now I think we will have to head east, regardless, so I will have the helmsman do so. After that, I will need to confer with Lord Illangetti and decide how and where we would like to deal with the Yondratha."

"I will run along, then, and not distract you." She bowed.

"And I will go speak with the helmsman and navigator." Paulus returned her bow and after a few moments, Reiki felt the ship roll to starboard as the ship's bow swung to the east.

The rest of the afternoon, Reiki practiced alone with her wooden practice sword on the forecastle, shaded by the ship's sails, the sun now astern of them on their new course. No one bothered her, and she found the exercise enjoyable. If nothing else, it kept her mind off the dread of the Sakawat ship off to the starboard quarter and the horrors she encountered in her dreams. When the ship rang four bells, she ate dinner with Pyotr and Antony. Fittingly, the conversation at dinner was bleak. Pyotr was especially morose. The combination of the impending threat of the Yondratha, worry over his sons, and concern for the fate of the men he had sent to attack the palace had begun to wear on him. Antony worked to lift his spirits, but nothing Reiki or Antony said seemed to help. After dinner, Reiki decided to retire to her cabin. Reiki's guilt continued to plague her, and she slept fitfully.

The next day, the mood aboard the ship had shifted. The tension was palpable and as Reiki prepared for her sword lessons, she could see the Yondratha clearly off the starboard quarter. Overnight it had managed to cut a third of the distance between them. *That beast sails magnificently. Damn the murderous bastards who built it!*

She poured herself entirely into her lesson with Idris and though he bested her easily each time, she could tell she was improving. At one point, he even smiled as she managed to parry and riposte one of his more devilish diagonal slashes. He dodged her thrust and immediately countered with his own, but it was still a significant improvement for her. By the time lunch came around, she was even more bruised than the day before, but she was smiling, unlike most of the crew.

Where the atmosphere the day before had been casual, now everyone carried themselves in a state of nearly silent tension, coiled tightly and ready to spring into action at a moment's notice. Their labors seemed more frenetic and directed than before and Reiki could see that efforts were being made to prepare the ship for a fight. The gunwales were lined with quivers full of crossbow bolts, baskets full of kappow resin grenades, and racks full of spears, heavy axes, and swords. She saw grappling hooks like the one she found at the cliff on Serenity coiled and resting on the decks by the gunwales. *To board the other ship, perhaps?* Reiki refused to go to the gundeck, but she imagined Hal was furiously working to prepare the guns for action, stacking powder charges and wadding, securing cannon balls for reloading, readying spare slow matches, and a host of other tasks that could turn the tide of battle. *We will need all the preparation and a great deal of luck, I think, if what Albert and the captain both said holds true. If we are outmatched, then our only hope is to outmaneuver or outplan the Yondratha.*

She ate her lunch alone in her cabin and then received further training from Master Behrns on navigation in the early afternoon. She saw that he had plotted both the

Iron Will's position and that of the Yondratha on the navigational chart. She saw they were now heading toward the eastern continent at a steady rate and would be in sight of land in about two or three days. *The Yondratha will have caught up to us about then as well. If I had to guess, the fight will likely happen in the late afternoon, around two or three bells, the day after tomorrow.*

Master Behrns seemed to share her opinion. She watched as he marked a small oval on the chart about eighty kilometers west of the continent. "I think somewhere in here is where we will have to make our stand. There's no getting around it. I think the Yondratha will probably stay just to our south to prevent us speeding down to Sychak. Ha!" His laugh was devoid of humor. "We couldn't make much speed at all heading south. The wind is coming from almost directly south-west. The currents push north and east. We'd crawl maybe three kilometers every hour, perhaps four? The Yondratha could catch us inside a day even if we had a head start."

"So, our plan is to turn, slow, and take shots at their bow as they approach?"

The navigator nodded. "Yes. That's called 'raking fire.' In a fight, you try to keep your guns trained on them and none of theirs on you. Raking them from bow to stern is a solid means of doing so. Same for blowing holes in their ass end too. Broadside to broadside favors the side with more guns or faster crews or both. The Yondratha has both and thicker hull planking as well. Three volleys or so as she closes distance may not be enough, but I think we can manage that."

Reiki frowned, "And then they can turn and fire at us before crossing our bow and raking us too?"

"Aye. That's what they will do," Behrns grimaced, "and there's not much we can do to stop them except get lucky with a shot or two on those three volleys."

"Well, then I think our plan is shit, but I'm not sure there's a better one. We could attempt to parley with them, but then we'd give up any advantages we might have in positioning or initiative. Could we best them if we boarded them?" Reiki asked.

"You'd have to ask Idris or the captain that question. From what I have heard, the Sakawat are deadly fighters, and they are armed with rifles. That gives them some advantages at longer ranges. Short range, we might be able to hold our own. It would depend on the size of their fighting force," Behrns replied.

"Taka, one of the Sakawat crew I killed on Serenity, said there were one hundred twenty-six of them, minus a handful who died in the raid," Reiki remembered.

"Well, then we're only slightly outnumbered. While we have that many in the crew, not all of our men are so useful in a fight. The Sakawat are warriors first and whatever else second. That is not so for us. Our cooks are cooks. Our riggers are riggers. Only our fighters are truly fighters, and those we have only about forty of."

"So, three to one odds in a fight plus whatever odds you might give our cooks and riggers. They have an advantage at sea, an advantage in a brawl, and we have nowhere to run to? Does that about sum it up?"

Behrns sighed, "Yeah, that's about the truth of it."

Reiki laughed then. "Well, that does simplify our choices some, doesn't it? We can't run, so we pretty much have to shoot first and hope the gods like us better."

Behrns looked away. "It's remarkable how often the gods seem to favor the assholes who already have the advantage, but I'll say a prayer or two or ten anyway."

Reiki frowned. "You sound like my friend, Antony. Do all Hastrans take such a cynical view of the gods?"

Behrns shrugged, "The ones who have been around long enough do."

Reiki shook her head, but said nothing more on the subject. As Reiki turned to walk away, Behrns called out to her.

"You forgot an option."

Reiki stopped and turned her neck to look over her shoulder at him. "What's that?"

"We could surrender. The Sakawat might take us prisoner instead. There are worse fates."

Reiki shuddered as she was transported in her mind to the agony of dangling in a damp dark dungeon cell. She clenched her fists at her sides and her voice came in a sharp whisper. "Not for me. If this ship surrenders, I'll die before I spend another day trapped in a cell waiting for some lord or chief to decide my usefulness has ended."

Behrns had the good sense not to argue and instead bid her good day. Reiki spent the rest of the afternoon practicing with her wooden sword, the fury that had arisen in her subsiding a little more with every slash and thrust. She ate her dinner in her cabin in silence and played out the upcoming battle in her mind, or she would have if she had ever been in a battle between ships before. She found her imagination insufficient to the task, so she instead lay in her bunk and stared at the ceiling until she finally found sleep. In her dreams, she was floating on a chunk of wooden debris adrift in a sea of flames under a cloudy sky. Pyotr and Antony lay unconscious on the debris next to her and she fought the urge to hack and cough from the smoke and the stench of burning wood and flesh. She awoke the next morning with a deep-rooted unease that she could not shake off even during her morning sword lesson. Every time she looked to starboard, the Yondratha loomed ever greater, and her unease swelled with it.

She checked in with Behrns after lunch and saw that they would sail into his predicted oval the afternoon of the morrow. Behrns, instead of teaching her, told her to report to the captain's cabin. "He wants to speak with you, and he knew you'd be coming here after you ate. You know where he's located right?"

Reiki shook her head.

"You know where Lord Illangetti's cabin is, right?"

Reiki nodded.

"Right across the passageway. The captain's cabin rests right below the poop deck at the very stern of the ship."

Reiki thanked him and hurried to find his cabin. When she came to his cabin door, she found that it was shut, and she felt a moment's trepidation. *I wonder what he wants to see me for. Surely, he has plenty more important things to see to. At any rate, is there some protocol I need to observe? Do I just knock? I think I'll just knock and wait.*

She knocked on his door, two heavy raps of her knuckles on the solid wood planks of the door. Then she stood and waited, her hands clasped behind her back, rocking on her heels impatiently. She heard a cough from the other side of the door and then the sound of a man clearing his throat. The door swung open and captain Paulus gestured for her to come in. His cabin was as spacious as a ship's cabin could be, which is to say that he had a slightly larger bunk, his own private desk and chair, a small table with benches, and his own privy, which Reiki had learned sailors called a head for some unknown reason. The captain pointed to the table and said, "Have a seat."

As Reiki approached the table, she saw that there was a nautical chart on the table, weighed down at the corners with iron weights. The chart was at a smaller scale than the one the navigator was currently using, and she could see two tiny wooden pieces carved to look like ships were placed upon it. *What is this?*

"I'm guessing, Reiki, that you've never had to plan a battle before. The Islanders aren't known for their warmongering, so it stands to reason you have not. Do correct me, though, if you have some wisdom I could tap into." He pointed to the chart and the two models, "I've been trying to figure out how to maximize our chances in a fight against the Yondratha. This chart is the small coastal chart for the area I plan to make our stand. The models are supposed to represent our two ships, you see."

Ah. I must be tired. I should have been able to figure that out on my own. Am I tired? Or is it fear? "That's a useful tool. And no, I don't have any experience at all with fighting ship to ship. Master Behrns believes we will turn broadside to them and give them a few volleys of raking fire and hope that is sufficient to neutralize their advantages before they can turn broadside to us, and it ends up being a brawl." She met his eyes then. "*Is* that the plan?"

Captain Paulus sighed deeply, "That's the best I can think up. We are backed into a corner. We can't head south without them cutting us off and fighting how they wish us to fight. We can't head north without eventually running out of supplies and starving just offshore from a vast desert. Besides, if we go far enough north, we will end up having to follow the coast east, which will lead us to the lands of the Sakawat, anyway." He slammed his fist down on the table and the ship models both toppled over. "The only benefit this plan gives us is we decide where to fight, we get off the first couple of shots, and we *might* be able to keep a maneuvering advantage for a little while. If we can get a few lucky hits during those opening volleys, we *might* be able to even things out a little bit."

Reiki nodded, understanding that these were rather forlorn hopes. "Is this why you wanted to see me?"

Captain Paulus shook his head. "No. I wanted to discuss what your role should be during the battle. You don't report to any of my subordinates since you are not a member of my crew. You're a passenger. That said, I am the captain. This is my ship. On my ship, all but Lord Illangetti are bound to obey. However, I would much rather ask you."

Reiki nodded. "I appreciate that. So, ask."

"Are you any good with a bow?"

"I'm better with a spear," Reiki shrugged, "but I am no stranger to the bow. I have my own in my cabin, in fact, though my arrows are limited."

Captain Paulus tapped his lower lip with his forefinger, considering options. "Have you ever used a crossbow?"

Reiki shook her head. "Never. The principle seems fairly similar, though I imagine the aiming is different."

Captain Paulus frowned, but he nodded in agreement. "The aiming, loading, reloading, and firing are different, but insofar as they both put pointy sticks into things at a distance, yes, they're remarkably similar. Tomorrow morning, see about getting someone to teach you the basics of using a crossbow. That way, when you run out of arrows, you can still keep shooting."

"Of course."

"Then, when the inevitable boarding action happens, you will find plenty of work for your spear," he added. "So, when the fight starts, you will stand ready on the forecastle, understood?"

Reiki nodded, "Understood."

"Good." Paulus gave a weak smile, "I assumed you would be willing to fight. After all, these are the very Sakawat you are oath bound to kill, are they not?"

Reiki hesitated briefly, she knew not why, before she slowly nodded. "Yes. These are the ones." *Why am I so reluctant, now that my quarry is so near? Is it fear? No, it's something else, though I am afraid. Only a fool wouldn't be.*

I still feel the rage, but there's something else. No matter. The Yondratha stole my choices when they pursued this ship. They set my path for me when they attacked my village, and again when they showed up on the horizon. Tomorrow, there will be no room for hesitation, only swift violence. I must be ready.

Paulus raised an eyebrow quizzically, "Is there something troubling you, Reiki?"

Reiki shook her head, lying, "No. Just preparing myself for the fight tomorrow."

Paulus accepted her lie and nodded in return. "Very well. I suggest you eat well and get your rest. I imagine we'll be up to our necks in battle by mid-afternoon tomorrow. You are dismissed."

Reiki bowed and saw herself out. The rest of the afternoon she wandered aimlessly throughout the ship, her mind swimming with the doubt that had taken root in her gut. Everywhere, the crew was clearly on edge, the looming specter of death before them. At dinner, Antony and Pyotr ate with her, though their conversation was limited. As she stood to take her empty plate to the scullery, Antony stopped her.

"Go and get some extra food, dried fish and bread preferably. There's no telling how the fight will go tomorrow. If things go poorly and you end up adrift, you may be glad of a few extra rations to get you by. Of course, if you are dead, then the food will not matter. If you are captured, the Sakawat will likely take it. But no matter which, a few strips of fish and some scraps of bread can't hurt you."

Reiki recognized the wisdom in his words, and so she went and collected a few scraps which she stuffed in one of her belt pouches. *Perhaps these will come in handy. I hope not.* She went topside thoughtlessly, as if in a trance. She abruptly found herself on the poop deck, her hands clasping the railing on the starboard side as her eyes rose to the Yondratha, near enough now that she could see the gun ports on its port side. *Tomorrow. Tomorrow our fates will meet.*

She stared at the ship until the sun finally dipped below the horizon and the Yondratha's lanterns came alight. She went back down to her cabin and tossed and turned until morning, when the bells awoke her from her fitful sleep and she willed herself to eat a lukewarm breakfast, knowing that she would need her strength for the fight to come.

She went topside and found a crossbow to examine and familiarize herself with. She knew better than to fire it without a bolt loaded and she had the sense not to waste a bolt, so she instead found a crewman to show her how to load and unload without firing. The trick was to flip a toggle and use the crank in reverse. This released the tension from the arms of the crossbow. To arm it again, she would only need to flip the toggle the opposite direction and then operate the crank. *This is not a fast weapon, but it is a powerful one. These bolts are steel and will likely puncture Sakawat armor if they are close enough and the angle is right.* She practiced aiming as well and after a few trial runs of cranking, aiming, and then uncranking, she felt she could probably be at least functional with it. *I don't know that I'll ever come to like it as much as my bow, but I can see its appeal.*

The Yondratha was now close enough that she could make out the flag atop its main mast and even pick out a few men on the top deck working. They were little more than hazy shapes, but they were moving, which told her they were people. *Future corpses, more like.* She grimaced at that unexpected thought, surprised to find that she felt equal parts revulsion and elation. *What is wrong with me?*

The morning seemed to drag on endlessly, the sun crawling ever higher in the sky. No one spoke a word to her all morning and everywhere eyes were focused on preparation for battle with the occasional furtive glance to mark the progress of the Yondratha as it edged ever nearer. The midday meal was silent but for the clink clank sounds of plates and utensils as people ate. A funereal atmosphere blanketed the room. Reiki ate one serving of stew and a small roll, picking at it a bite at a time. The food had always been bland, but today she couldn't taste it at all. *Small improvement, I suppose.* She frowned at her own joke, for it felt weak and strained, especially in the current mood. Pyotr and Antony did not appear until after she had already finished her plate, so she took her dishes and spoon to the scullery before returning to sit with them.

Pyotr's eyes were bloodshot and puffy, and Reiki could tell from the mottling on his cheeks that he had wept, and recently. She felt a stab of profound sympathy in her chest. *I have come to really care for this man. Antony too, though Antony seems in better spirits than anyone on the ship.* His eyes were alert and bright, even in the dim room. His expression wasn't jovial, but it was amicable, and he seemed genuinely pleased to see her.

"Good day, Pyotr. Good day, Antony," Reiki said, the words seeming banal and empty in the present atmosphere.

Pyotr only nodded in response and stared blankly at his food. He picked at his roll with his fingers and seemed to be trying to will himself to take a bite. Antony gave her a small smile and replied, "Good day, Reiki. How are you holding up?"

Reiki shrugged and gestured to the rest of the men in the room, "About as well as any of us, I guess. We all seem a little burdened today."

Antony nodded. "Yes. We're nearing the end of the trough between swells. We've come down one big wave just getting out of Hastra. The trough is a nice reprieve, but you can see the great wave coming. Now, the wave has come, and our bow is pointing skyward. But, Reiki, the trough cannot last, nor should it. A flat sea, no wind nor waves, means a ship becalmed, with no speed and no control, doomed to die stranded in its tranquility. But there I go waxing philosophical again. My point is, of course, everyone is burdened. We are gazing at our doom only hours away now. But too much worry and misery now saps away what may be the last joy of our lives. So, I'm going to eat my food

248

and enjoy your company, because it may be our last time to do so together."

Reiki stared at Antony for a moment before she broke out laughing, "Shit, Antony. That is fucking grim." She couldn't stop herself, though, and she kept laughing. Everyone in the galley turned and stared, but she kept laughing, tears streaming down her cheeks. "I'm sorry. It's not funny. It's not. But here I am, burdened with the weight of fear and concern over the very real likelihood of our deaths and your solution is to just enjoy stale rolls and fish stew and chat about the weather because we are probably going to be dead soon and it would be a real shame if we didn't at least smile a bit before." She smiled feebly, "It's just absurd, you know? It made me laugh because it's absurd in the best sort of way. Like the final tiny tragedy in a day full of minor tragedies that tips the balance enough that you have to laugh or else go mad."

Antony nodded, but Reiki could tell she had upset him.

"Antony, no. It's okay. You are *right*, of course. We *should* embrace this moment and enjoy each other's company. It's just not so easy as saying it," She added, attempting to rectify any damage her words had done.

Antony nodded again, and he seemed at least partially mollified. He changed the subject. "Where will you be posted this afternoon?"

"The forecastle, as an archer. You?" She asked.

"I will be as well. It seems you and I will share that time together as well." He grinned, "My lord Pyotr will be on the top deck with the captain, moving about during the battle, overseeing the fight and encouraging the men."

Reiki raised an eyebrow and then gestured to Pyotr, who still sat silent, nibbling at his food. *"Encouraging them?"*

Antony sighed, "Indeed. He will likely need some encouragement of his own first."

Pyotr realized they were talking about him, and he turned his head slowly toward them. "What is it? Did you say something to me?" He shook his head as if clearing away cobwebs. "I'm sorry. I am a little preoccupied, and I wasn't listening."

"No, Pyotr," Reiki shook her head. "We were just concerned for you. You seem a bit depressed."

Pyotr snorted, "Of course, I am. Shouldn't I be? The most pleasant thing that could happen today is that I might not be burdened with worry over my sons or my homeland much longer, for a head on a spear is a carefree one and the dead are free of woes."

She stared at him, blinking slowly for several long slow seconds. Then, Reiki turned back to Antony, "I owe you an apology, Antony. *That* was fucking grim."

Antony was not amused, and she could tell her jest had only made Pyotr shrink further into himself. Reiki pushed herself away from the table and stood. "I'm sorry. I can tell that I am upsetting you both. I'm on edge, and I'm taking it out on both of you. I'm going to spend some time alone on the forecastle and clear my head a bit. Okay?"

Pyotr just continued to stare at his plate, and Antony gave her the most cursory of nods. She stepped away and climbed the ladder up to the top deck and then up to the forecastle. She remained there, lost in her thoughts, the wind blowing hot on her cheeks and tossing her hair, even though it was bound in a bun. She spent the last few hours before the impending battle in quiet reflection, breathing the salty air and basking in the heat of the sun as it broke between a blanket of soft white clouds. Finally, she steeled herself and went down to her cabin, collected her spear and her bow and a handful of arrows in a small quiver. She counted fifteen, the same fifteen she had found on the beach the day her home was attacked. *Fifteen arrows won't last long, but I'll make the most of them.* Thus prepared, she sat on her bunk and awaited the call to arms that she knew would soon come.

Chapter XVI

"Fire and Fury"

"A flash illuminates the smoke,

The cannons roar and breathe flame,

Fire! Fire! Fire!

A macabre dancing inferno!

Battle! Blood!

Cacophany!

Chaos reigns supreme."

-Battle-

Admiral Greta Matthison, Royal Chekhov Navy

Reiki heard the bells clanging rapidly throughout the ship at just shy of three in the afternoon. She leapt off her bunk and rushed up to the top deck and onto the forecastle. Antony arrived just as she did, and they stood side by side along the starboard rail. Reiki held her bow in her left hand and Antony grabbed a crossbow that was resting against the gunwale. Neither said a word to the other as men began to fill in the remaining space along the starboard side. Once everyone was in their assigned places throughout the ship, she heard the captain shout commands to the helm and the men in the rigging:

"Set battle sails! Turn thirty degrees to starboard!"

She watched as the men furled all but the topmost sails on each mast and she felt the ship lose speed as the bow swung to starboard. The Yondratha was now only six hundred meters away and it seemed impossibly large even so.

"Run out the guns!" Captain Paulus's voice boomed, and she heard the order echoed below on the gundecks by the chief gunner. The cacophonous rumble of the ship's cannons being rolled forward to the gun ports in unison came only seconds later.

The captain shouted again: "Ready report! Guns!"

The chief gunner: "Guns ready!"

Captain: "Helm!"

The helmsman: "Helm ready!"

Captain: "Forecastle!"

Behind her, Idris shouted in reply: "Forecastle ready!"

Captain: "Stern!"

A soldier on the poop deck replied: "Stern ready!"

Captain: "Rigging!"

Above her, a young man standing on the lowest spar of the main mast shouted back: "Rigging ready!"

Captain: "Topdeck!"

Pyotr shouted, despite being right next to Captain Paulus beside the main mast: "Topdeck ready!"

The captain looked around one last time and then nodded, "All stations ready. Very good, men. I'm not one for speeches and the Yondratha will be upon us shortly. Let's give them hell." He shouted down through a hatch to the gundeck: "Fire at will, Chief!"

Five agonizingly slow seconds passed before the cannons fired, tongues of flame erupting from the starboard side of the Iron Will, roiling white smoke obliterating her view of the Yondratha. The noise was unlike anything Reiki had ever experienced. The deck beneath her feet rumbled and she felt the rushing shock wave hit her. She could not see if any of the shots hit their mark, but the Yondratha sailed ever closer, now only four hundred meters away. A full two minutes passed before the cannons roared again. Everything seemed muffled now and there was a continuous ringing in her right ear. The smoke burnt her eyes and the sweet acidic smell of it lingered in her mouth. Unlike the first volley, though, she saw that several of the shots hit their mark, tearing away chunks of the Yondratha's planking and railing.

She thought she heard a man's scream come wafting over the waves to her ears, and she allowed herself the briefest smile. The Yondratha continued, though, and by the time the third volley rang out, she had closed to only two hundred meters. This time, the cannons left gaping jagged holes in the bow of the Yondratha, and she heard several men cry out. *Good. Fewer we need to fight when the time comes.*

The Yondratha closed in to less than a hundred meters before she turned hard to starboard. Her port side filled Reiki's view, and she stared into two rows of open gunports, the black mouths of the cannons waiting to fire. In that moment of quiet, she felt fear grip her as it never had before. She held her breath, waiting for the cannons to fire. Then, the entire world exploded into fire and smoke and a deafening rolling thunderous wave of sound that felt like it might crush her. Both ships fired at the same time, and she saw nothing but white smoke and flashes of orange flame, tongues of heat and violence lashing out in the space between the ships. Her eyes burned, and she felt a trickle of blood running down her earlobe. *Gods, I can't hear out of my right ear!*

The Yondratha's cannons tore through the Iron Will's starboard side, and she heard the crashing and splintering of wood and the cries of wounded men. She saw the bloody mess that cannons make of men revealed as the last grey tendrils and wisps of smoke cleared away. Pyotr and the captain both still stood, but several men lay dying around them, chunks of wood impaling their bodies, or limbs torn from their joints by the force of a cannon ball. Reiki stood, blinking, frozen in inaction.

Antony shook her shoulder, "Reiki! Shoot!" He held his crossbow to his shoulder and began firing as fast as he could manage.

Reiki shook herself out of her stupor and nocked an arrow onto her bowstring. She looked across to the Yondratha, now only fifty meters away and tried to choose a good target. She could not see Issak yet, so she chose a man standing on the Yondratha's forecastle, an easy shot. She drew her bowstring and then loosed in one swift motion. The arrow flew true, and she felt the briefest moment of satisfaction as she saw it lodge in his throat. The man clutched at the shaft of the arrow as he coughed up mouthfuls of bright red blood and fell. She nocked another arrow.

Reiki adjusted her aim to the left, drew back her bowstring, and was about to loose her arrow when she saw a flash to the right of her target and heard the sharp crack of a rifle immediately after. The lead ball from the rifle zipped by her right ear, and she felt the swirling air from its flight rustle her hair. *Shit! Reiki, you idiot. They shoot back. Pay attention!* She quickly adjusted her aim to the right and loosed her arrow at the rifleman who shot at her, denying him a second attempt. She felt vindicated as he fell to the deck of the Yondratha, the long shaft and white fletching of her arrow sticking out of his destroyed left eye. *You won't be shooting at me again.*

She pulled another arrow from her quiver as the Yondratha fired another volley of her cannons. She ducked down instinctively, though at the short distance it wouldn't have mattered. She could not have reacted quickly enough. The ships were obscured again by a thick cloud of smoke that was illuminated by bright flashes within. She realized the flashes were from the Iron Will's cannons as she returned fire.

Reiki felt a sharp pain in her right side and gasped from the shock of it. She looked down and found a slash through the side of her tunic that was rimmed in red blood. *Shit. I've been hit. How bad is it?* She dropped down to her knees so she would not be exposed to rifle fire and then pulled apart the fabric of her tunic to examine her wound. She breathed a sigh of relief when she saw that a splinter of wood, a few millimeters wide and about five centimeters long, had lodged itself in her side, but only superficially. It had dug a gouge through her skin deep enough to bleed, but though it was a painful scrape, it was not life threatening. She removed the splinter and then stood back up to resume fighting.

The ships were now only thirty meters apart, so she hardly needed to aim at all. She loosed arrow after arrow at the Sakawat riflemen on the Yondratha's forecastle until she had no arrows left. She had only missed twice, once because the cannon fire startled her and threw off her aim, and another because Antony landed a crossbow bolt into her target just as she loosed her arrow. *Thirteen out of fifteen is not bad at all, but it is time for me to find a crossbow.*

Antony was unharmed so far, still firing bolts across at the enemy, some finding their marks. Not everyone was so lucky, she saw. Of the twenty or so men on the forecastle at the start of the fight, now only six remained, counting Antony and herself. The rest were either lying dead, splayed out in unnatural positions in spreading pools of crimson that wormed into the cracks between deck planks, or else wounded. The latter lay moaning or crying or screaming. They clutched at their wounds to staunch the blood flowing out of them or clawed ineffectually at the hopeless cause of an amputated leg gushing their life's blood away.

The man who had been standing to her left was dead, a chunk of his skull ripped away by flying shrapnel or a cannon shot, Reiki knew not which. Another lay slumped against the foremast, his legs spread apart, hands pressing desperately against a rifle wound in his throat. Blood gushed around the edge of his hands and through his fingers. *He won't live another two minutes.* She could see that he knew it too, for his eyes were full of the recognition of futility and the terror and despair that come with it. She mouthed the words, "I'm sorry." His eyes went vacant, and his head lolled to the side, his hands dropping away to his sides. Reiki stood over him for a moment, the chaos of the battle fading into the background, and she wept for the man, though she never even knew his name.

She was shaken from her mourning by Antony shouting her name. "Reiki!"

She spun around and saw he was pointing furiously at the grappling hooks that had latched onto the gunwales all along the Iron Will's length.

"Help me! We need to cut the lines!" He pulled a long knife from his belt and began slashing at the nearest grapnel.

Reiki drew her sword and found another grapnel a few meters away, closer to the bow of the ship. She slashed at it, once, twice, thrice, and it finally parted. The severed rope fell away into the water below. Reiki started to move to the next one, for there were six total grappling the forecastle rail alone, when she was forced to dive to the deck by a line of riflemen she saw all take aim at her and the five men still remaining on the forecastle. She and Antony only barely made it in time, but the other four men were all caught in the volley of rifle fire and fell to the deck, wounded and dying. *Gods damn it!*

She saw a crossbow laying less than a meter away from her, so she crawled across the deck to it and smiled when she saw it was already loaded and ready to fire. She stood quickly and fired a bolt at one of the riflemen, who were hurriedly reloading their rifles while other Sakawat crewmen pulled on the lines to bring the ships closer together. She saw the bolt pierce the man's cuirass and he dropped to the deck. She saw that the riflemen had finished reloading so she ducked back below the gunwale and worked on reloading her crossbow using the quiver of bolts she found beside it.

The ship rocked from the impact of another volley of the Yondratha's cannons and was followed by a chorus of the cries of the newly wounded and dead. Reiki screamed as she looked and saw the headless body of Idris, the master at arms, fall to his knees and crash to the deck, bright red blood spurting from the ragged stalk of his neck, the grisly result of a cannon ball's direct hit. *Fuck! Fuck! Fuck!* She willed herself to stand, aimed, and fired her crossbow. It was an easy shot. A mere fifteen meters separated the two ships, and their spars and rigging were tangled high above the deck. Three of the riflemen remained, and they all fired as she ducked back down.

Reiki knew it was too late. The ships were now locked together in an inseparable dance of death. Any moment, the Sakawat soldiers would board the Iron Will and the wholesale slaughter would begin. Reiki raised up just high enough to peer over Antony, who was hurriedly reloading his crossbow, and see if she could find Pyotr on the main deck below. She nearly cried for joy when she saw he was still standing beside the captain. Pyotr looked unharmed, though harried. The captain's right hand was clutched to his right side and his shirt was stained with blood, but he seemed to be standing steady. Then Reiki saw the horrific mess of blood and bodies around them and the meager dozen or so men left along the starboard rail. *My gods, we've taken a beating.* She couldn't see through the haze of smoke to the poop deck, but she assumed they were just as badly beaten. The Iron Will's cannons had long ceased doing unified volleys and instead continued with sporadic rolling fire, one cannon here, another there. *We're losing, aren't we?* Her heart sank, but she reloaded her crossbow, determined to make the Sakawat pay for their victory.

She popped back up and loosed a bolt at another rifleman and smiled as she saw him go down. *Two remaining.* The other two were still reloading, so she took a moment to survey the Yondratha's decks. *We have bloodied them some, though not enough.* The Yondratha's crew had been reduced by at least forty men, based on what she could see from her vantage point on the forecastle. Bodies lay dead or dying all over the top decks of the enemy ship, but far too many remained, and they were steadily bringing the ships closer. Then, Reiki finally spotted Issak upon the Yondratha's poop deck, and she felt the hatred rise in her.

He's only sixty meters away. I could hit him from here. I will *hit him from here.* She ducked back down and rapidly loaded her crossbow, cranking furiously to draw back the string. She rose and aimed just slightly above her target to account for the bolt's drop during flight. She exhaled slowly and loosed the bolt with a silent prayer. As the bolt flew from her crossbow, her body was rocked savagely from a sharp burning impact in her chest, high near the shoulder. She cried out and dropped her crossbow, her right hand reaching up to press on her wound. She looked back at the riflemen she had momentarily forgotten, seeing the smoke obscuring them from her vision, and knew she had been shot.

She dropped to her knees on the deck, her eyes searching furiously to see if her aim had been true. She found Issak and saw he was clutching at a bolt protruding from his cuirass, high, right below his collarbone on his right side. *Well, no matter what, at least I did that right.* She slumped down below the gunwale as Antony came over, his face racked with worry.

"Reiki, you've been hit!" He cried as he dropped to his knees beside her.

Reiki winced from the pain of the rifle wound. "You fucking think so, Antony?" she snapped.

Antony frowned as he pulled her hand away from the gunshot wound and pulled apart the fabric of her tunic to examine it. "I'm quite observant, Reiki. You know that," he replied, good naturedly. He lifted her away from the gunwale and felt around on her back. Reiki cried out as he touched the exit wound where the ball had passed out her back. "I'm sorry. I know that hurt. But it's good news. It means the ball isn't still in you, which makes it less likely to kill you from blood poisoning. We will need to pack the wound and bandage you soon, though, or you may meet the same end regardless."

Reiki nodded, wincing as she did so. "I don't have anything to pack it with that wouldn't make it worse. Do you have any ideas?"

Antony turned away, his eyes frantically searching their surroundings as the battle raged on. Without warning, he darted over to Idris's headless corpse and reached under him. When he retracted his hand, he was holding what looked like a water skin. Antony pulled the stopper out of the skin's narrow spout and took a sniff. He smiled and scrambled back over to Reiki.

"It seems the master at arms was a bit of a drinker. This stuff smells strong enough to knock out an ox." He found the cleanest part of his shirt and ripped away a long strip of it. He then poured the liquor from the skin onto the fabric, soaking it thoroughly. "You're not going to like this next part," he said, apologetically.

Reiki knew what was coming, and she just nodded and gritted her teeth.

Antony pushed the alcohol-soaked fabric into her wound with his forefinger. Reiki cried out from the pain. Antony took off his shirt then and tied it tightly, looping it under her armpit and up over her shoulder. "The pressure will sting, but it should keep the wound protected. It's not a perfect solution and we will need to remove the packing and replace it, but this should suffice for the moment."

"Help me up. The fight's not over yet." She held out her right hand.

Antony pulled her up right as the first Sakawat swung across the gap between the ships. Reiki's spear was still slung across her back, but the enemy were already upon them. She drew her sword instead and only barely managed to deflect a thrust from the first attacker's sword. Unlike hers, the Sakawat sword was a heavy, straight, double edged weapon. She knew she could not out muscle her attacker, especially injured. *I must force him to dance, instead. He is*

armored, though not at the joints. I will need to strike there.
She made a few furtive slashes with her sword, trying to bait
the soldier into attacking. He parried each deftly, for he was
a skilled fighter, and she was a novice and wounded. *Yes, I
am inexperienced and weak. Step in closer and let down your
guard a little, Sakawat.* Reiki did not have long to wait, for
the soldier decided to throw caution to the wind and lunged
at her in a heavily telegraphed strike that met empty air as
Reiki dodged and spun around behind him, hooked her blade
into the pit of his groin and slashed open his femoral artery.
The man fell to the deck, his blood spurting from his severed
artery.

Reiki turned back around and saw that Antony had
bested his attacker as well, but as she took in the state of the
battle, she could see the Iron Will was lost. More and more
Sakawat poured across from the Yondratha and were met by
fewer and fewer defenders. Rifle shots still rang out
sporadically from the Yondratha, finding targets of
opportunity who would cry out and then fall. Some died
quickly, while others became easy prey for the soldiers to
finish off.

Pyotr and captain Paulus were still alive, but Sakawat
men swarmed around them, and she heard shouts and cries of
pain from the lower decks as well. *They've overrun the ship!*
Antony stood beside her, spear at the ready. Reiki's left side
was now stiff and aching from her wound, so she elected to
rely on her sword instead, for she could more readily use it
one handed. As Sakawat soldiers began to climb up to the
forecastle from the top deck, Reiki and Antony retreated

steadily further and further until they found their backs to the bulwarks at the bow of the ship.

The Sakawat continued to advance and soon they were locked in furious combat, Antony and Reiki thrusting and slashing and parrying with what strength they could muster, for their lives depended upon it. The rest of the battle faded away as Reiki focused only on the attackers before her. With each slash or thrust, she felt her strength ebbing. She felt warm blood flowing down her left arm, but she kept up her defense. *My rifle wound is bleeding, is all.* She struck down one, and then another, and a third Sakawat attacker, but every time she felled one, another would take his place. There was nowhere for them to go. They were trapped and she knew she would not be able to defeat all of them. Eventually, one would deliver the slash or thrust or shot that would take her life. *And yet, with every one of you I slay, I come closer to fulfilling my oath, so it will be a good death.*

Reiki had nearly accepted her impending doom when a deep rumbling seemed to erupt from every direction at once. Everyone stopped attacking, instead looking around frantically. She heard screams of terror then. Reiki knew what that sound meant. *You should be afraid. I've only heard that sound one time, and I had the good fortune and sense to get away.* Everyone, Sakawat and Hastran alike, rushed to the gunwales to peer down at the now frothing sea around the Iron Will. She heard someone shout, and she thought it might be Captain Paulus:

"Everyone! To the Yondratha now!"

From the water, enormous tentacles shot up and came crashing down onto the deck, snapping deck planks, and crushing the gunwales like they were made of naught but twigs. The main mast snapped and fell, forming a bridge over to the Yondratha, now tangled in the Iron Will's rigging. The tentacles searched for food, grasping the occasional man, and dragging them screaming below the waves. Reiki looked and saw that Antony was frozen in a mix of awe and terror at the carnage unfolding before them. Reiki shook him to snap him out of his torpor.

"It's a kraken!" She shouted, "We can't stay here!"

Antony's eyes were wide with terror. *That's a rational reaction. There are few beasts below the waves so incomprehensibly huge or deadly. If given the choice between fighting five garathas with only my bare hands or facing a kraken with a spear the size of one of these masts, I would take the garatha fight without a second thought.* Reiki heard an enormous cracking noise below her feet and knew that the Iron Will's keel had snapped. She knew the ship would soon fall apart. She spun around and her heart sank. The kraken's tentacles, massive trunks of slimy black and purple flesh a meter across and covered with razor sharp hooks and spines, were wrapped around the ship, an impassable barrier between her, Antony, and the fallen mast that would serve as their escape. She could not see any remaining men on the top deck below and she could only spot one or two remaining on the poop deck. The Iron Will had been abandoned by attackers and defenders alike, and now only the doomed remained. The few desperate souls on the poop deck tried their luck. One dove over the aft railing into the roiling water below. Two others tried to climb over the writhing tentacles and were shredded by the spines and hooks that covered the kraken's flesh. Their cries carried in a horrible crescendo Reiki heard even over the horrible groaning and cracking of the hull. *Should we try our luck in the water? The kraken will likely have no trouble killing us there, but if we stay here, we may end up trapped in the rigging or caught beneath debris and drown in the depths below.*

Reiki stood frozen in indecision as choice was stolen from her by events below deck. A cannon was torn loose from its mounting by the buckling of the ship's side armor. It rolled and crashed into one of the surviving gun crew who was, at that moment, carrying a lit piece of slow match to try to fire a cannon at one of the massive tentacles. The man was crushed, and the lit match was tossed forward where it landed in a stack of miraculously dry powder charges. The powder ignited in a powerful explosion that blasted apart the gundeck, and blew up through the top deck. The fire and force of the explosion then detonated the ship's powder magazine, located below the waterline and forward of the gundeck, accessible via a ladder from the lower gundeck. The force of the magazine detonation blew the ship apart instantaneously.

Reiki did not see any of these events happen. She heard the planking on the starboard side buckle with a loud boom, followed by the sound of the cannon rolling. Then she fell as the first explosion knocked her off her feet and lifted the forecastle a full two meters. She grabbed onto both Antony and the starboard railing just in time for the second detonation. The noise burst her eardrums and the brightness of the blast blinded her. She could tell she was flying, still clinging to the railing, as the entire deck flew spinning into the air. Then she felt air rushing past her face as they fell rapidly. They were halted suddenly as the debris they clung to smacked into the water. Reiki felt a sharp pain in her forehead and heard her ribs crack. Then she was lost in an ocean of blackness as she left consciousness behind.

Part III

"The Lost Goddess"

"For centuries, Holy Mother Terra guided her children,
Then went silent, her voice falling behind a crimson tail, and
She lay in wait in her broken den
Awake, aware, alone, alive
Awaiting her savior beneath the burning sun."

-The Desert Goddess-
Nicodemus the Poet

Chapter XVII

"Flotsam and Jetsam"

"Two birds on a length of wood,

Did float and float upon the waves,

One did stand and the other did lay,

Two ghosts entombed without graves."

--Two Birds—

Jared the Poet of Sychak

Reiki awoke in starlight. She was soaked to the bone and laying atop a chunk of the Iron Will's forecastle deck. She immediately saw that she was not alone, for Antony lay face up and motionless beside her. At first, she thought he might be dead, but after a few moments she saw his chest rising and falling with his breathing. She knew better than to stand up on the precarious bit of flotsam that had saved them both from drowning, lest she submerge it or tip it over. Instead, she raised herself to a sitting position and surveyed her surroundings.

The Iron Will and Yondratha were both gone, but she could make out other debris floating nearby, presumably bits of the Iron Will. No sign remained of the kraken, either.

Thank the gods for some small mercies. She looked down and saw that her spear was beside her on their little raft and her sword was still in its scabbard on her belt. *The sword won't be much use here, but the spear might bring us some fish to eat. Without fire, we will have to chance eating it raw, though.* She still had her water skin and a few scraps of bread, now soggy but still a source of sustenance. *Water will be the biggest concern if we are to be floating for more than a day or two. How far from shore are we, I wonder?* She remembered the battle was to take place near the northernmost corner of the continent. On the chart, the land curved away to the east for hundreds and hundreds of kilometers. She knew little of the terrain in these parts, but she remembered they were uninhabited. Sychak lay far to the south with a treacherous mountain range and a great river to cross. To the east and southeast lay the lands of the Sakawat, which Reiki knew even less about, except that she ultimately had to go there. The northwestern part of the continent was a great empty wasteland to Reiki's knowledge. *So, naturally, that is where we will likely find ourselves if we do not end up drifting until we die here in agonizing thirst. Or we might succumb to infection from our wounds first. Gods, that's cheerful.* She cleared such thoughts from her mind. *For now, we are alive, and I intend to keep it so. First thing's first. Let us see what direction we are moving and go from there.*

Reiki searched the sky for the familiar arrow constellation that would point her to the east. After a few moments she found it. Then, she licked her finger and held it in the air. *Good. The breeze is coming from the west.* Then she confirmed that the waves were also coming from the north and west. *Altogether, we should be getting pushed to the east. The currents here run north and east, though, I believe. We must hope the balance of the forces pushes us more east than north.* Reiki found comfort in the few factors that might turn the balance away from their doom, or at least delay it for a bit longer. *Every day we survive brings new chances and opportunities to save ourselves. We should wash up on a beach somewhere. That will bring new challenges, but on land we might find drinkable water. Although, a rain shower would be welcome as well.*

Antony stirred next to her. She watched as he slowly roused from his slumber. Ever since she had met him, Antony had been a true friend, though unlooked for. *Perhaps I can now return the favor, for the sea is my second home.* He opened his eyes and she watched as he went through the same initial confusion and rapid understanding that she had. He scrambled up and stood, then slipped and came crashing down with a wet smacking splash as his weight submerged his half of the raft. Reiki felt guilty for laughing, but as he raised himself off the soaked planks and rested on his elbows, she could see he was not harmed.

"Yeah. Standing is a bad idea," he groaned. "I see that now."

Reiki laughed again, glad to see their predicament had dampened his clothing and not his humor. "Yes, our little raft is not very sturdy."

Antony shrugged. "I suppose it beats the alternative."

"I don't really fancy a long swim, no."

Antony looked around them, his eyes taking in the vast emptiness of the sea around them. "I don't see the Yondratha. How long were we out, do you think?"

"We are sitting at a height of zero meters. We can't see more than maybe seven kilometers. The Yondratha probably put on as much sail as they could to flee the kraken. Judging by the moon and stars, it's about three in the morning. So, either we were out for about ten hours, or we were out for closer to thirty. I'm betting it's the former, but I won't rule out the latter. So, the Yondratha likely traveled at least a hundred kilometers and upwards of three hundred kilometers since the Iron Will blew up."

Antony studied her for a moment. "How do you know how fast they would sail?"

Reiki shrugged. "I don't. I'm just guessing based upon the wind and currents. The Iron Will was moving between five and ten kilometers an hour with moderate to full wind, but the Yondratha overtook us. It seems reasonable to assume they could average about ten."

Antony accepted that answer. "I'm no seaman, so I'll take your word for it." He gestured around them with his right hand. "So, what do we do now?"

Reiki shrugged, "At this exact moment, not a thing. When the sun comes up, I will see what supplies I can round up from the debris floating around us. I want to do that soon, because some of it will sink and some of it will scatter further away as time goes by. If we can find some more food and water, we may survive long enough to make it to shore. If I can find a few more buoyant items to help our raft float, maybe even a makeshift sail, we might be able to gain some control over this thing and help us make landfall sooner. If I can't find food, I'll try my hand at some fishing."

Antony looked at her then with an expression that Reiki could only interpret as one of newfound respect. "I will not consider myself fortunate to be adrift on a soggy bit of wood in an unfamiliar sea, Reiki, but I do consider myself very lucky to be stuck here with you."

Reiki grinned. "Thank you, Antony. And, as you said before, it does beat the alternative."

Antony's expression told Reiki he was not entirely convinced, but he changed the subject. "I didn't see what happened to Pyotr. He was alive still before the kraken attacked. I saw him fighting alongside the captain. Then everything went completely to hell—I froze and saw nothing but those tentacles. I have never been more afraid in my entire life."

Reiki reached out and gently patted Antony's back. "I don't blame you. I lost track of him too when the kraken attacked. There's no shame in it. There are few things in the deep more horrifying than a kraken. They're enormous, impervious to most everything you can throw at them, and even if you manage to eliminate a few tentacles, most of the bastard is still below the waves. I don't even know what the rest of it looks like."

"You don't?" He sounded surprised.

Reiki shook her head. "No. I've only ever encountered one before yesterday. I never saw my father look so afraid of anything. He was the most fearless fisherman on the island so far as I knew, yet, when those tentacles popped up from the sea and pulled a nearby boat down in one fell crash, he shook from the fear that overtook him. He turned us about so quickly I nearly fell off the trimaran. We sailed as fast as the wind would take us back to Serenity."

"I asked my father what the rest of the kraken looked like. I was a curious child, and I was already besotted with the sea and all that lay in it. He shook his head and told me he did not know and had not met anyone who truly did. He said that some claimed the kraken had a long body with a powerful flipper and a circle mouth with row upon row of teeth long as spears. He said others described it as a giant fish, fat and bulbous, with glowing red eyes and a mouth like that of a shark. But, to my knowledge, no one really knows because the kraken tends not to surface. It just destroys boats with its tentacles and drags the people below, shredding anything caught in its way. Hell, I don't know how I would even go about killing one if I had to."

Even in the pre-dawn dark, Reiki could see Antony's pallor. He leaned forward and cupped his face in his hands and sat silently for a while. Reiki did not bother him and sat in silence by his side waiting for dawn to break. When the sun finally rose, Reiki surveyed their surroundings again. She looked first to the horizon where the sun was rising. She hoped she might see a silhouette of land there, but she did not. She then looked closer to identify any flotsam that might be worth scavenging. There were a few promising clusters of debris she thought might be worth checking out. The closest was about thirty meters away to the north. Two more lay about forty meters to their northwest. None lay to their south or east. After a few more minutes.

Antony finally pulled his hands from his face as he felt the warmth of the morning sun on his skin. He watched as Reiki re-tied her hair behind her head. She then picked up her spear and began to slide her way over to the very edge of their raft, her feet already in the water. "Stay here, Antony," she said as she slipped down into the water. "I'm going to see what I can find to keep us alive a little longer."

Antony nodded. "I'll keep an eye out for any dangerous creatures headed your way."

Reiki smiled, though she knew that he wouldn't see much from his low vantage point on the raft. *It's a nice gesture, though. I'm glad he seems to be coming out of his torpor.* She dove below the water and opened her eyes, looking about to see if anything dangerous lurked below. The water was quite clear, and she saw nothing at all for at least a hundred meters any direction. She began to swim toward the closest cluster of debris using a side stroke, for her left arm was useless due to her still aching rifle wound. *I would be faster if I could use a breaststroke, but I will manage.* It did not take her long to reach the debris, which she saw was several barrels and a small wooden crate. She swam between the barrels and found a length of line attached to one. After several minutes of work, she managed to tie the barrels together in a chain with the crate affixed to the end. She then held onto the end of the line with her left hand and began to swim back to the raft. The return trip took significantly longer, for the barrels and crate created a lot of drag. By the time she made it back to the raft, she felt a burning in her leg and back muscles, and she was already beginning to tire. *Gods, these past few weeks have taken a real toll on me. A month ago, I'd have been challenging people to races doing this. Now, I'm dreading making more trips out.*

Reiki tied off the barrels and rested for a few moments before she swam to the other bits of clumped together debris. After about an hour of swimming and diving and searching in the immediate vicinity of their raft, Reiki had managed to find an additional three barrels, two more wooden crates, and several leather sacks that Reiki thought might contain useful provisions. She did not find anything that would serve as a sail, but she thought she might be able to construct a paddle with which to drive the raft. *Step one, though, is to see if these barrels are empty, and then use them to help float this raft a little higher out of the water.* She was pleased to find that four of the barrels were empty. The other two were nearly so, but for some nails in one and a pound or so of ground up grain in the other. *So, nails and flour. Not exciting, but still possibly useful.* Reiki decided to open one of the crates next but was disappointed to find it completely empty. *I think I will put the nails in here, then. That will give me another barrel to use as a float.* If the first crate was disappointing, the second nearly brought Reiki to tears with joy.

"Gods love us, it's a crate half full of food!" she exclaimed. "We've got some meat, some dried fruit, and some bread. Enough for at least two weeks if we ration it and it doesn't spoil first."

The last crate was not as exciting as the second one, for it contained what appeared to be a collection of letters and dispatches from Hastra to various persons in Sychak. *I don't think these letters will be arriving on time. Still, I might read them later or perhaps use them for kindling once we make landfall.* She tossed the letters into the crate with the nails and then checked the leather sacks.

The first was empty and surprisingly dry inside, so Reiki transferred the flour from the barrel to the empty sack by cupping her hands and slowly picking up some flour and then depositing it in the dry bag. This process took the better part of thirty minutes and the water around Reiki turned cloudy from the flour that slipped between her fingers. The second leather sack contained a hammer, two small knives, a flint and steel, and a metal bowl about fifteen centimeters in diameter. *What a strange sack. Still, I can make use of these things.*

She spent the next hour and a half modifying the raft. She attached the six empty barrels to the underside of the raft by lashing them in place and then having Antony hammer the nails down through the deck planks into the barrels to secure them. When she was finished, she climbed back onto the raft and found that it was now sturdy and buoyant enough for her to stand without it sinking or tipping.

Antony stood and stretched, smiling. "I'm impressed, Reiki. We got our asses blown up and stranded on what can only charitably be called a large piece of shrapnel, and you've managed to turn it into a boat."

She shook her head. "Not yet. We still have no means of steerage, nor of propulsion." She allowed a small smile, regardless. "But I will grant you that we are not near as likely to sink now. I should be able to rig up at least one paddle with which we will be able to have some small control over our boat."

Antony chuckled. "Whatever. I'll take it. When I awoke this morning, I was a soggy castaway on a bit of wood with no food, no water, and almost no hope." He swept his arms about the small raft. "Now we are floating, I am nearly dry, we have food, and I have reason to believe we may even have some hope."

Reiki nodded. "Aye. We can eat for about two weeks. It's thirst that will get us, though, if we can't get some rain or find some fresh water in the next two days or so." She pulled the waterskin from her belt. "I've got about a liter of water here. That means we'll be dehydrated by the end of the day. We'll be dead in about three days."

Antony sighed. "Well, something to look forward to, I suppose." He lay down on the deck face up, his hands behind his head for cushion, and closed his eyes. A few seconds passed before he crinkled his nose and turned his head to either side. Finally, he bolted upright, exasperated. "I don't imagine you have a plan to erect some shade?"

Damn. I should have thought of that. My skin is naturally dark, but I still get sunburn if I don't cover up, find shade, or coat myself in protective grease. Here at the equator, the sun will be bearing down even more and we have no sail to cast a shadow and nothing to coat ourselves with. "I didn't see anything that would work. I'll keep my eyes open, though."

Antony seemed to accept that and rolled onto his side and used one of the leather sacks as a pillow. Reiki used a hammer and a knife to chisel a length of wood planking from the boat's edge. She slowly worked from one end to another removing the more problematic splinters. Then, she used the remaining rope she could find and wrapped it around her makeshift paddle to provide safe grips. Lastly, she attached a triangular piece of debris she had found to the end using a few of the nails. When she had finished, she had a meter and a half long paddle that one could affectionately call ugly. She shrugged and dipped the paddle into the water and pulled it back along the side of the boat. The boat moved forward sluggishly, but Reiki decided to consider the paddle a success. *I can't really be too picky in these circumstances.*

Her morning duties completed, Reiki stretched out on the deck of the boat, closed her eyes, and slept for several hours. When she awoke, the sun was directly overhead, and she was sweating profusely from the heat. Antony's skin had turned bright red wherever it was exposed, and his hair was drenched with sweat. *Shit. We're going to dehydrate even faster in this heat.* She offered him some of her water and they shared a quick lunch of bread scraps and dried fruit. They talked little during the afternoon, baking in the searing heat of the sun. Reiki prayed silently to her gods for rain, or clouds, or even a cool breeze. Instead, the hot winds blew lightly from the west and the sun burned high in a clear blue sky. The afternoon passed by slowly as they drifted along on the current, pushed ever eastward by the waves and breeze.

They ate a small dinner from their accumulated supplies and drank half of their remaining water. They told stories to pass the time, some from their past, others they learned from friends and family through the years. Eventually, the sun set. The air began to cool, and they were bathed in the soft glow of moon and starlight.

Antony finished telling a story about a little woodland creature who discovers a magical fountain in the middle of a forest glade which grants wishes. Reiki enjoyed the silliness of the story, since the little creature's wishes had unexpected outcomes that left him worse off each time. His final wish restored everything to the way it was before, with the little creature, something Reiki had never heard of called a bunny, learning the importance of being satisfied with what he already has. *I was satisfied. Then everything was taken away. Now I would do anything for a magical fountain that would bring it all back to how it was before.*

Antony was silent for a moment, but he seemed to be trying to find the words to say something. Finally, he blurted out, "Reiki, I know you've sworn an oath and you feel you must fulfill it, but doesn't it seem to you that the gods have thrown every obstacle they could into your path?"

Reiki frowned but did not reply. *He's not wrong. So far, I have gone from one bad situation to the next, every time finding myself worse off. Yet, I killed at least a dozen of the men that I swore to kill, and I saw the bolt strike Issak. It didn't look fatal, but I still struck him a blow.* "The gods brought quite a lot of them in front of my bow, Antony. I even struck Issak himself."

Antony nodded. Then he added, "Yes, but look what it cost! Many dozens of men died on the Iron Will. More likely died in Hastra the night we freed you from your cell. How many men need be sacrificed to satisfy your vengeance?"

Reiki flinched, reeling from the accusation. "Holy shit, Antony—"

Antony interrupted her. "Look, that sounded harsher than I meant. I'm sympathetic to your goal—I really am—but look at the cost. Your leg is still injured. You've been shot. You've got a wound in your side. Not counting the Sakawat we managed to kill, at a safe estimate over a hundred of my countrymen, many of whom were friends of mine, have died. It seems absolutely absurd to me that your gods require this."

Reiki fell mute under the sudden crushing weight of the guilt she had been suppressing ever since Rodrigo's death. Antony's words struck her deeply for she knew they were true. Worse, she found that his agnosticism was beginning to find purchase in her mind as well. *What sort of gods are these?* When she replied, she found herself defending her own dwindling faith and she knew not why. "They're the gods, Antony! We can't comprehend their purposes or designs."

Antony shook his head. "That's a weak argument. You're ascribing ineffability to something with a much simpler explanation. Isn't it also possible that the gods are human inventions, mirrors for our own desires and traits?"

Reiki sat fuming for a moment before responding. "Have you sat in a cryopod garden, Antony? Those pillars are made of a material no human can make. They are inscribed with the name of the holy mother goddess herself, Terra, and the holy number, 037. What else could they be but gods? And if they are gods, do we not owe them fealty?"

Antony snorted. "*Owe* them fealty? For what? What have they done for you that you can definitively say was their doing? Have you seen the gods themselves? Heard them speak to you? Sure, you pray for rain and then maybe it rains that day, or the next, or the next week after you keep praying and slaughter a bird or something. Isn't it just as likely that it was going to rain eventually? Did the rice grow taller because you lit some incense? Did a childbirth go easier because of a dance? Or is it more likely that our lives are defined by our choices and by chance and we cower in the darkness and create illusions of light and control to soothe our fears, to convince ourselves that we can bring goodness by following some imagined code?"

Reiki fought against her rising anger. "I don't know, Antony. I don't know, okay?' She threw her hands in the air in exasperation. "What do you want me to say? I haven't thought about it. Why would I?"

"You wouldn't. If you were raised to believe in the gods, everyone in your entire world believed in the gods, and no one ever came along to challenge your belief in the gods, then you wouldn't think about it. That's the essence of human belief. We believe because it gives us an excuse not to think about or face the horror of our own insignificance and lack of control over nearly every aspect of our existence. Nobody likes being forced to really think about that."

"Well, Antony, if the cryopods aren't monuments to the gods, then what are the cryopods? The names written upon them: who are they? Who or what is Terra? Do you know? Do you have a better explanation, Antony? Or does your inquisition end with the destruction of the core of my faith and go no further?"

In the darkness, Reiki could not see Antony's cheeks redden, but he cast his eyes down visibly. When he replied, his voice was soft and gentle. "I'm sorry, Reiki. Truly. I did not mean to anger you. I'm tired and thirsty and I have watched my entire world fall apart in roughly a week—I know you have too—and I am giving voice to the feelings and the doubts that nip at the heels of my every thought. Do not think ill of me for it, for you are the only friend I have in this world that I know for certain still lives."

Reiki felt her anger slip and fall away, replaced by a profound sympathy. The silence between them elongated to the point where the tension in the air was palpable. Reiki attempted to break the silence with self-deprecating humor. "If the only friend I had left in the world was me, I might start questioning whether there were gods as well, Antony, or at least conclude they were arrayed against me."

Antony shook his head. "Honestly, Reiki, if I didn't have you, I would have slid over the side of the raft and embraced the deep shortly after I awoke this morning."

Reiki replied gently. "Antony, I am incredibly fond of you. Truly." She lay down on the deck of their tiny little boat. "Now, stop being so fucking morose, won't you? The next few days have trouble enough without us punishing ourselves."

Antony nodded and lay on his back on the deck alongside her. "I do have a theory, Reiki. It's not one I can back up with anything, but it's something that I play around with sometimes when I lie awake trying to fall asleep some nights."

Reiki looked up at the stars overhead. "Alright, so what's your theory?"

"I don't know the particulars of the faith of the Islanders, but in Hastra we are taught that holy mother Terra started it all when she sent her children, the gods, down from the heavens. These gods made us and communed with Terra from Matria. Then, they slowly gave up their bodies and rejoined her in the heavens. She still communed with us until one day there was a great fire in the sky, and she went silent, never to be heard from again. Is that like what you learned?"

"Yes," she replied.

"So, here's what I think. I think the gods were just people like us, but from somewhere else. They came here, maybe riding the cryopods down from the sky. A pod is a container, after all. I don't know what a cryo is, but I do know that a pod contains something within it. The name cryopod can't be an accident."

Reiki considered that for a moment. *Shit. That's a good point. Did anyone ever try to open one?*

Antony continued. "I think Terra was someone else. I think she stayed behind, up in the sky. Eventually, the gods all died, as people do, and we applied poetry to it and developed a funeral ritual out of it. Terra's silence and the great fire in the sky, I think, are connected. I think Terra and whatever vessel she used to travel through the heavens burned up, and she's dead and gone. I think the gods and Terra were nothing more than people who were elevated to godhood through generations and generations of tales told around cook fires. That's my theory."

Reiki stared up at the stars considering Antony's explanation. "What sort of vessel could sail through the heavens? Wouldn't you have to be a god to create such a ship? And where would they have come from if not here?"

Antony sighed. "I don't know, Reiki. I already said I don't have anything to back it up with, other than my own experiences with the fickle nature of gods and prayer and my observations of human nature. Well, that and a naturally skeptical nature."

"Okay, fair enough. Besides, I doubt we will ever know."

Antony continued. "Oh, and there is the way cryopods are found everywhere people are clustered. We all speak the same language despite being separated by hund

reds of kilometers and the earliest recording of mutual interaction was only about a millennium or so ago. All of those are oddities that support my thinking."

Reiki hadn't ever considered that. Everyone she had ever met, Sychak, Chekhovian, Hastran, or Sakawat, all spoke the same language with only slight differences in pronunciation and syntax. The most reasonable explanation for that would be that they all had spoken that language to begin with, even at the dawn of civilization on Matria. *Unless of course the gods gave us this language directly when they gave life to us. That would explain it too. I could throw that back at Antony, but the truth is, it feels a bit hollow, even to me. Have I lost my faith? More importantly, have I lost my way? What am I even doing? I don't know anymore.*

She didn't say any of that to Antony. Instead, she stared up at the stars and sighed and said, "You've given me a lot to think about, Antony, but I'm feeling pretty tired, so I think I'm going to sleep now."

"I understand. Goodnight, Reiki." He replied softly.

Reiki slept a deep and dreamless sleep until she was awoken by a loud crack of thunder. She bolted upright and her eyes flew open. *Rain.* She did not know what time it was, for it was still quite dark and the moon and stars were obscured by the sinister looking storm clouds that had rushed in from the west while they had slept. Reiki shook Antony awake and rummaged through their supplies to find the bowl and one of the leather sacks. She used the knife to cut a hole just slightly smaller than the mouth of the bowl in the leather sack. Antony watched silently as she stuck the bowl into the hole and then cut the sack to form it into a large bowl shape. She then sat the bowl down on the deck of the boat.

She pointed to the approaching storm. "That's our supply of fresh water coming." She then pointed to her makeshift water collection bowl and funnel. "So, we're going to hold this leather up. It will funnel the rain down into the bowl. When it's full, we'll pour it into our water skins or anything else we can use, and then let the bowl fill up again. We'll keep doing it until we fill up every available vessel we have. Then we will drink from the bowl ourselves if it keeps raining long enough. Understood?"

Antony nodded. "Okay. What do we do about the storm, though?"

Reiki laughed. "Well, normally I would say 'pray.' But I'm guessing that's probably out."

Antony frowned, clearly not appreciating the jest. "Seriously, though. What should we do?"

Reiki shrugged. "Antony, the truth is, there's not a damn thing we can do about it. I don't have anything heavy enough to use as a drogue. We have no sails, no tiller, and no anchor. The only thing we can do is hold on and hope the storm doesn't kill us and we can collect enough water to survive the days ahead. That's it. There's no magic answer here, no special Islander trick. Just keep low, hold on, and don't fall overboard."

Antony looked like he might choke, but he swallowed heavily and sat up straight. "Okay then. When faced with the inevitable and only one course of action, it does make things simpler."

Reiki smiled. "Exactly."

The two of them held onto the leather and pulled it so that it was nearly taut and angled to force water down into the bowl. They had only to wait a moment or two before lightning arced across the sky and rain poured down in thick cool globules that smacked loudly on the wood and leather and clanged in the metal bowl. Reiki closed her eyes and grinned as the water soaked her hair and streaked down her face. Antony's moustache began to droop, but he smiled widely. There were few joys in life that matched a heavy rain after being baked in the heat of the sun at sea. Their joy was short lived, though. The wind blew savagely from the west and drove the rain hard, stinging their skin. The sea rose in violent waves tossed their little boat viciously. Yet, they held on, their little boat remained afloat, and before long, their bowl was filled to the brim and sloshing.

Reiki quickly removed the bowl and poured the fresh water into her water skin. She then took Antony's water skin and filled it as well before placing it back through the hole in the leather to continue collecting water. *That's another two to three days' survival.* Her elation was short lived. The storm grew in ferocity and soon the two castaways were forced to focus all of their efforts on clinging to their raft for their lives. The sea rose in giant swells of seven to ten meters and their little craft surged upward to the crest before sliding down deep into the trough between the massive waves. The rain came in stinging sheets that seemed to come from every direction at once. The wind howled deafeningly. Still, Reiki and Antony held on. The onslaught of wind and wave and rain continued to grow in strength until Reiki began to believe they might capsize at any moment and be lost in the frothing tempest's fury. Neither knew how much time passed as they were tossed about like the playthings of an angry god. It was long enough that Reiki's stomach growled with hunger and her every muscle fiber ached with the prolonged strain. Yet, they did not lose their grip and their raft stayed defiantly afloat. Reiki allowed herself a moment of pride, for her lashings held and the barrels kept them from sinking.

After what seemed an eternity, the howling of the
wind quieted to a dull roar and the waves, though still five
meters high, came on slower. The rain still fell in thick sheets
that soaked Antony and Reiki to the bone, but the storm was
slacking, and the relief was evident on both of their faces.
Still, they held on and waited for the seas to fall and the wind
to subside enough for them to safely rise from the deck.
Hours passed before finally Reiki saw a patch of sky through
the clouds. It was nighttime again, and only a few stars and a
trickle of moonlight eased through the opening in the storm
above. *The storm lasted the entire day. No wonder I'm
starving.* She glanced over at Antony and even in the dark
and the driving rain she could see he was utterly exhausted.
*We would not have lasted much longer. Here's hoping the
storm is reaching its end.* The rest of the night, neither slept
as they continued to hold on as the raft rose and fell with
each mighty wave. Reiki shivered from the cold of the rain
and wind and the night air. At one point she could even hear
Antony's teeth chattering together over the sound of the
storm.

When dawn broke, the rain had stopped, and the wind
had finally quieted down. The raft rose and fell gently on big
slow rolling waves. The air still retained its chill and Reiki
lay shivering on the deck of the raft until the clouds finally
parted and she felt the warm sun on her face. She rose
slowly, blinking her eyes to adjust to the light. She turned her
face away from the sun and let out a shout of joy. *Land! But
why is it to the south?* Antony followed her gaze and jumped
up when he saw the sliver of golden brown on the horizon.

"Land!" He cried out. Then he wept and fell to his knees, the fear and the despair of the last two days flowing out of him in twin trails on his cheeks.

Reiki kneeled beside him and held him as her own tears fell. *We made it. We actually made it.* The mystery of why the land was to the south would have to wait, she decided. The first order of business was to determine whether the raft would continue to drift closer to the land or if she needed to start paddling. She wetted her forefinger and held it aloft. *The wind is coming from the northwest. That's good.* She confirmed that the waves were moving the same way. The only unknown was whether there was an ocean current that might carry them away from the shore. She had no way of checking for that directly, so she decided to wait and see if the land grew closer throughout the day. In the meantime, she decided to check their stock of supplies. After a few minutes of rummaging through their supplies, which had thankfully not been lost in the storm, she was pleased to find that they had food enough for at least five days and water for at least three days, possibly five if they rationed it. *That may be enough to get us to another water source or until another rain shower.* With that concluded, she and Antony ate a small breakfast of bread and dried fruit and then whiled away the morning in pleasant conversation. By noon, Reiki could see that the land was much closer than it had been at dawn. She reckoned that they would make landfall sometime around nightfall.

The bit of shoreline she could see looked flat and littered with small scrub brush and sparse grasses beyond the sandy beachline. Beyond that she thought she could just make out some hills in the distance, purple and hazy from the heat rising off the ground. *We may be grateful to be arriving at night when it is cool. We can make camp and discuss our next steps without being baked by the sun.* And so the day passed, the air now muggy and hot from the aftermath of the storm, the wind still pushing them ever closer to shore. They ate and talked, and Antony sang a few songs to pass the time. Around mid-afternoon, Reiki decided to start paddling. She used long, slow, easy strokes to guide the little raft through the sea. Paddling a raft on the ocean can be an exhausting task, so she knew not to over exert herself but instead chose a pace she knew she could maintain. She knew she would need her strength to paddle through the breaking waves and retreating surf near the beach when the time came. She lost herself in the repetitive motion, her mind clear and her eyes unfocused. Antony quietly napped nearby. For an hour or so, she was lost in her own little tranquil bubble of monotony. Then she heard the waves crashing on the sand and she broke out of her trance.

The beach was now only two hundred meters away. She gritted her teeth, for her shoulder was still sore and she knew pain was coming. She dug the paddle in deep and pulled with long powerful strokes. As the raft picked up speed, she increased her pace, each stroke of the paddle driving the little raft a full meter and a half through the sea. She saw the waves ahead curl and crash. Behind her a wave came and carried the raft forward as she continued to paddle furiously. Finally, they rode a wave as it broke beneath them, their raft coasting along on the foam. She kept paddling as the surf slid back from the sand ahead and pulled at the raft, trying to slide it back out to sea. *Just another minute or two and we'll be there. And just in time, too. The sky is red and gold with the setting sun.* The last twenty meters were the hardest, for the surf pushed and pulled at the raft and it took all her strength to keep the raft moving forward. Finally, she felt the barrels dig into the wet sand and she left from the raft. Antony followed suit and together they dragged their raft, heavy and bulky as it was, out of the surf and onto the dry golden sand of the beach. Exhausted, Reiki collapsed onto the beach and lay gasping for breath. Antony lay down next to her, and they lay there catching their breath until the sun dipped below the horizon and the stars twinkled above them.

Chapter XVIII

"The Scarred Wilderness"

"Despite millennia of civilization on the Eastern continent, exploration into the northern wastes beyond the Violet Peaks that border Sychak has been sparse. The Sakawat tell of men who wandered out into the great desert. Only a few returned, and only after a span of a few days. The city state of Sychak made two formal expeditions but found that the land was essentially a barren waste populated with venomous serpents, giant arachnoid creatures, and sparse vegetation too poisonous to eat. While any of those could be fatal to an explorer, it was the scarcity of water that reigned as the supreme killer. The question of what the local fauna drink has been the subject of much academic debate, but the most accepted hypothesis is that there are great reservoirs of water beneath the soil, deep down in dark caverns and isolated pockets and oases. With no real reason to venture into the great desert, few have sought the answer."

-The Great Desert-

Professor Arthur Jendreas, University of Sychak

Reiki and Antony slept on the beach and awoke to the early morning sun peaking over the horizon. Reiki served them both a small breakfast of dried fish and a few more scraps of bread so stale they were more like crackers. Both took a few sips of water before Reiki collected the food and water, the knife, and the hammer and placed them into the remaining intact leather sack. The preparations completed, the two sat down to discuss which direction they should head.

Reiki spoke first. "I think we should go to Sakawat."

Antony rolled his eyes. "You still haven't let go of your damn oath? Reiki, we *know* Sychak is to the south. Yes, it is probably many days' journey, but we *know where it is*. We have no idea how far we would need to go to the east to reach Sakawat."

"Antony, we turned south to reach this beach. That means Sychak is at least three hundred kilometers to the south. *At least.* I don't know the continental geography very well, but I do remember seeing the words 'Great Desert' on the map. We're in the Great Desert. Do you fancy three hundred kilometers through a vast empty wasteland with only five days of water?"

Antony frowned. "Well, no. But the same reasoning holds true of heading to the east. We have no idea how many hundreds of kilometers we would need to go that way. Do you fancy walking for an unknown number of days on five days of water?"

Reiki grimaced. "Okay, I'll give you that." She continued, "But what about Pyotr?"

Antony looked confused. "What do you mean?"

"We don't know if he lived or died. If he lived, then he is a prisoner of the Sakawat. Do you imagine Issak would take them back to Hastra, or would he continue home? He was wounded too and already on a tight timetable. I'm betting they would go back to Sakawat and take the prisoners with them. Don't we owe it to him to find out? I owe him that, anyway. He risked death to free me."

Antony sighed deeply and hung his head. Finally, his eyes rose to meet hers. "Okay, I will grant you that one. However, let's say we managed somehow to cross the notoriously uncrossable desert and find ourselves in the mountains and plains of Sakawat. Then what? We have the two of us. We are both injured, and we will likely emerge from the desert exhausted, dehydrated, and weak enough that a strong breeze might be enough to finish us off. Is it your aim to just walk straight into the nearest Sakawat village and ask where you might find Issak and some prisoners he may have taken? Shall we then storm his village all by ourselves with naught but our spears and your sword?"

Reiki shrugged. "I don't know yet. But you, Rodrigo, Pyotr, and Captain Paulus all came to free me, so it only seems right that I do the same when the roles are reversed." She patted his shoulder as she strode by him. "I will come up with something once we get there. I have to. For Pyotr." *Do I really mean that, or am I still risking both our lives for vengeance? The fire of my rage has dimmed, but has it been extinguished? I want to think I am doing this for Pyotr because, well, because Antony got to me. I don't know what I believe anymore, and an oath made to false gods is emptier than the air its spoken into. I want to be doing this for the right reasons. Antony deserves that. And truth be told, the more time passes, the more I realize it wasn't anger that drove me down this path. Vengeance is a fire and anger is but one source of fuel, and a rapidly exhausted one at that. Shame. Guilt. Humiliation. These burn slow. I swore an oath in anger, but also from my guilt. I felt, I still feel, guilt for surviving, for choosing my self over the village, for considering running away and leaving them all behind. I feel guilt for the last time I spoke with my mother. It wasn't my rage that brought me here. It was my guilt and shame.*

She picked up the leather sack and adjusted the spear slung over her shoulder. Without waiting, she began walking. A few moments later, she heard Antony's footsteps on the sand behind her as he hurried to catch up. He came alongside her, and they walked side by side as they left the beach and entered the barren wilderness of the Great Desert.

The going was easy at first. The sand of the beach rose to a sandy berm a hundred meters from the water. When they reached the top of the berm, they saw a vast expanse of dry hard packed dirt and worn stones. Bits of thorny vegetation sprouted in clumps sporadically and an occasional boulder broke up the visual monotony. Far in the distance ahead, Reiki could see what looked like a rocky ridgeline, but it was obscured by heat lines rising from the desolate plain so she could not accurately judge its distance. Still, it was a visual landmark that could keep them from wandering in giant circles, so she was grateful for that.

"Alright, Antony. We will head for that ridge ahead. If it is tall enough, we may be able to spy shelter or even a water source. If not, it may contain caves or other shelter where we could wait out the afternoon. As hot as it is and as dry as it is, we ought to try to do most of our traveling at night and try to find a shady place to rest during the day."

"Agreed. It's already hot. I hate to think how it will be when the sun is at its peak." He jabbed his arm dramatically at the distant ridge. "Onward!"

Reiki grinned. She was glad Antony seemed to be in good spirits, especially given their current predicament. She tried to keep herself optimistic, but the truth was that the odds of them ever escaping the desert were extremely low, regardless of which direction they headed. *I won't let him know that, though. I must stay calm and positive for Antony. He would do the same for me.*

They plodded across the hard dusty earth as the sun rose higher in the sky before them. By noon, the ridge seemed no closer than it had been before, but when Reiki looked back the way they had come, she could only barely make out the bumpy line of the berm behind them. *How far is this ridge and how high must it be, I wonder?*

They did not stop to eat lunch until mid-afternoon, when they found a large boulder that offered some shade on its eastern side. They ate ravenously, for they were famished and already exhausted. Reiki rationed out their water and made certain they had rested for at least a half hour before they started walking again, now with the sun at their backs.

The heat was astounding, and she could see Antony's skin was now a cracked and peeling mess from days of sun exposure. *I probably will be just as badly burnt before long.*

Several hours later, when Reiki spotted another boulder in the distance, she decided they would stop and eat their dinner there and rest until after the sun had set. *Our water will not last long if we don't limit our sweating and protect our skin. Starting tonight, we will travel only at night.* They reached the boulder by late afternoon. Reiki sat down on the eastern side of the boulder with her back touching the stone. The shade felt significantly cooler, and she allowed herself to relax for a few moments before she pulled another two portions of bread and dried fish out of the sack for her and Antony to eat. They chewed silently together, side by side with the stone at their backs.

"Antony, we're going to rest here until the sun goes down. From now on, we'll travel at night and sleep during the day wherever we can find shelter, okay?"

Antony just nodded, for his lips were cracked and bleeding and his eyes seemed locked in a permanent squint. *The past few days have been miserable for you, Antony. I can see that now. The constant sun and dehydration have taken a toll. They're taking a toll on me too, but I am more accustomed to the wind and sun than you. Even so, this desert may be the end of me.*

They slept in the shade of the boulder, though it was difficult on the hard ground that, still hot from the desert sun, warmed them through their clothing. The night air felt frigid by comparison, and Reiki shivered involuntarily when she awoke under the stars and the light of the twin moons, each now waning to thin crescents. Antony still seemed miserable, but he stood and stretched. They both took sips of their water before they resumed walking toward the ridge to the southeast. Reiki thought it looked closer now, though it stretched across at least half of the horizon ahead of her. Her legs felt rubbery, and she knew that the reduced water intake was beginning to sap her strength. Still, they continued through the night. They saw no other living creature. They heard nothing but the soft scraping of sand over hard packed earth as the wind blew ceaselessly across the empty plain.

Night passed into early morning and the sky began to lighten in the east behind the ridge, now looming ominously before them. *I need to find us somewhere to rest in shade. There! That might work.* She saw something that rose like a small bump out of the otherwise empty landscape about a kilometer ahead. She couldn't quite make out what it was in the low light, but anything that could provide even a little relief from the sun would be better than nothing. As they got closer, she began to make out a few more details. It looked like the discarded carapace of a large insect. Whatever it had belonged to, it was a good five meters long with six legs and a fat abdomen and thorax. The discarded carapace seemed surprisingly thick and as they came up to it, she could see that it was at least three centimeters thick. Whatever insect had shed it was nightmarishly huge and she could almost make out what its head must have looked like, a triangular face with a gaping hole in the shed carapace where its mouth must have been. *Did it have huge mandibles? A proboscis?*

What kind of creature is this? I've seen nothing on this plain for it to have eaten, nor have I seen anything like it walking about, or, gods forbid, flying. Gods, this thing makes my skin crawl. They circled around it cautiously, but since they were alone and the husk of chitin was unlikely to harm them, Reiki examined the ripped opening where its underbelly used to be. She couldn't see much inside, but she decided it was worth the risk to camp there. The hollow legs were strong enough that the husk was kept angled off the ground and it would provide shade in both the morning and the afternoon. *I can't ask for more than that.* So, she plopped down beneath the husk and Antony followed suit.

They ate a breakfast of bread and dried fruit and sipped some more of their water. Reiki was pleased to see that the rationing was working, for they still had water for few more days. The food would last beyond that, she knew, so if they only traveled at night, they would be weak and overly fatigued, but they would survive. Beyond the next few days, though, Reiki knew they needed to find fresh water or else they would rapidly dehydrate and die in agony. With that encouraging thought, she laid down on the ground beneath the giant nightmare husk and closed her eyes, the exhaustion of the night's travels enveloping her and pulling her into a deep sleep.

They both awoke in the late afternoon, well rested but with mouths dry with the ravages of thirst. Reiki rationed out another meal and they both drank their allotted amount of water and waited patiently for the sun to dip below the horizon. The time passed slowly, and Reiki was sorely tempted to drink more, for even in the shade of the massive insect's chitinous remnant the heat was suffocating. She could almost feel the moisture leaving her body in rivers of sweat. Finally, the sun sat heavy and deep orange on the horizon to the west and the landscape was cast in the haunting glow and deep shadows of dusk. They both rose, picked up their belongings, and began another night march to the southeast toward the ridgeline ahead.

The terrain was mercifully flat and without any obstacles to trip up their feet or gaping chasms they might fall into in the darkness. Reiki was grateful for those small mercies, for in their fatigue and the low light, she walked in a trance, her feet moving largely of their own accord, one aching step after another. Antony, to his credit, never complained, though she knew he was in constant agony from his cracked and bleeding skin, burnt from the sun and wind. Her shoulder was still perpetual fire and, though her leg was healing nicely, she still walked stiffly, and the continuous exertion had renewed the pain. Still, neither voiced their misery. They simply took comfort from the company of one another and continued.

As the night wore on, Reiki could tell the ridge was getting much closer. *We might make it by morning if we pick up the pace a little.* She quickened her gait as much as she thought the two of them could sustain and Antony matched her. After a few hours, Reiki's optimism was rewarded, for she could see that the base of the ridge lay only a kilometer or two away. She smiled to herself as she felt a wave of hope wash over her. She knew that there may not be any salvation to be found ahead, but after two days of walking across the barren landscape of the Great Desert, any change in terrain felt like a victory. Antony must have felt the same, for she could see his smile as well and they both started to walk faster. They covered the distance quickly, their morale overcoming their fatigue as they reached the base of the ridge.

The ridge rose above them, devoid of vegetation but littered with stones ranging from the size of a fist to the size of a carriage. The rise was gentle at first but grew steeper near the top where Reiki could see the sky beginning to lighten beyond the jagged crest. *We could rest in the shade of one of those boulders until mid-day, then find shade on the eastern slope for the afternoon. I don't see any caves or overhangs, so that may be our best bet.* She listened attentively, hoping she might hear water, but she was met only by the constant blowing of the wind. *Damn. I suppose that would have been an unbelievable stroke of luck. This desert is enormous. The likelihood of just stumbling on fresh water, much less flowing water, would be too much to ask for.* Still, she felt her hope diminished somewhat as she came to grips with the recognition that achieving their first goal of reaching the ridge did not substantially change their plight. Then she comforted herself with the possibility that they might be able to spy something of use in the distance once they reached the top of the ridge. The height, Reiki estimated it was about one hundred meters, might allow them to see what they would miss at ground level. *I may still be deluding myself, but it keeps me moving.*

After they had rested sufficiently, Reiki led them both up the slope toward a large boulder about two thirds of the way up the ridge. The ground was firm and dusted with a layer of fine sand in places, so it took them longer than Reiki had anticipated, as she found her feet slipping at times or dislodging a loose stone that would roll down the slope behind them. Still, they reached the boulder as the sky turned a brilliant pink above them. They laid down in the deepest shadow of the boulder and slept there until the sun crept high overhead and the shadow of the boulder no longer enveloped them. The remainder of the climb to the top was a significant challenge. The last twenty meters were steep, and the footing was treacherous. Nonetheless, they made it to the top, drenched in sweat and panting heavily.

Reiki's relief at reaching the top was immediately replaced with crushing despair. From the vantage point at the top of the ridge, she could see that it was actually one of two ridges that formed the boundary of a canyon that stretched far into the distance in each direction. Beyond the opposite ridge, she could see that the landscape was as barren as that which lay behind her. *There's nothing out there. We can't cross that. We'll be dead inside of a few days. There's nothing out there at all. Fuck.* In fact, were it not for the canyon, the Great Desert would have no distinguishing features at all. The canyon was like a great scar upon the desert and Reiki wondered how it came to be, for surely the wind did not carve it into being, nor was there any sign of a river. *That's curious. This canyon is ridiculously straight. In fact, it looks more like a furrow from a plow than a canyon.*

Reiki made a choice then, not knowing it would have far-reaching consequences. She could have decided instead to make camp there and rest. They could have continued traveling by night, heading south and east. Had they done so, then two days' journey to the southeast, they might have discovered the Peterson Oasis[1]. They could have resupplied their water, and then continued for another week before finding the Gilbert River, a tributary of the great river that flows all the way to the great city state of Sychak. Of course, Reiki might also have missed the oasis completely and they both might have died of thirst on the great barren desert. Who knows what tragedies might have befallen the people of Matria had they done so?

Reiki instead listened to the voice of her curiosity and decided to follow the canyon to the south, for something about it drew her in. Antony did not raise an objection, for he had come to trust Reiki's judgment. The two ate a quick lunch, drank some more of their water, and then descended the slope down to the shaded floor of the canyon.

The slope down into the canyon was steep and the ground was hard with a layer of loose dust that made every step a gamble, but they managed to reach the floor of the canyon with only a few minor slips, despite their fatigue and Reiki's still stiff right leg. As Reiki started to walk to the right, Antony expressed his misgivings. "Reiki, I have a bad feeling about this. This whole canyon feels—well, it feels unnatural. It feels wrong somehow. And I feel like we are being watched."

Reiki felt the hairs on her neck raise, but she shook her head. "Antony, we haven't seen a living thing since we entered this desert." She gestured to the north and then to the south. "This canyon floor is flat. Do you *see* anything down here but us?"

Antony shook his head. "No. I don't. But that doesn't mean there isn't anything here."

Reiki pointed southward. "This canyon goes for kilometers to the south. But what made this canyon? The wind? Surely not, for that blows west to east. This canyon runs north to south. It stands to reason that there was water here at some point. So, if we head south, we may run into water. We *need* water."

Antony nodded. "I won't deny that. But I still feel this, this suffocating fear for some reason."

Reiki sighed. "I feel it too, but I don't have any better ideas. The land to the east of here is just as barren as the land to the west. This is the best option we have right now."

Antony hung his head, but he nodded, resigned to his fate. "Okay. Lead on."

They walked until sundown. The canyon floor was hard and flat with no obstacles to slow them down. They made camp just after sundown and slept on the hard earth. Reiki awoke at one point thinking she heard something slithering or hissing or both, but when she looked around and listened, she heard nothing but the wind blowing over the top of the canyon.

The next morning, they ate and drank and continued walking until around noon, when Reiki saw that something lay ahead in the canyon. She couldn't make out any details, but it was taller than the canyon and as wide. *What the hell is that?* Her curiosity was piqued and so after another quick lunch and a few small sips of their water, they hurried on. As they got closer, the object took on new details. *It isn't stone, nor earth. That looks like steel. But who would build something way out here?* Hour by hour, as they drew closer, she became more convinced that it was a structure of some kind: huge, metal, and square shaped. *Definitely man-made. It must be. Matria does not make square things. The wind rounds. The dust shaves away sharp points. Water carves curves and bends. This was made with intent.* When the sun finally went down, Reiki estimated they were only two kilometers away. She wanted to continue, but Antony persuaded her to make camp instead, for they were both exhausted, hungry, and thirsty. She relented, and they drank and ate and slept on the cool floor of the canyon.

She dreamt again of the sound of slithering and hissing. She awoke with a start and looked around nervously for any sign of movement. She saw nothing and was about to lay back down to sleep when she heard it again, a slow slithering sound coming from under the ground. Then she heard a sinister hissing directly below her. She leapt up and rushed over to Antony and shook him awake.

"There's something beneath us!" She whispered sharply.

"What?" He began, and then he froze, for he heard it too. "Shit! What is that?"

"How the fuck should I know, Antony?" She whispered. "I'm an Islander. Do you think I have any idea what sort of monsters live in this gods-forsaken desert? What do *you* think it is?"

Antony shook his head, for he had no idea either. The tales of the desert did not go into much detail about the horrors that dwelt there, if there were any. They certainly never spoke of hissing slithering nightmares below the earth. They both crouched, ready to flee or fight, and glanced about anxiously. Everything was silent. They both stayed crouched, coiled like springs, until their calves ached from the tension. Then, without warning, the ground cracked and fell inward next to them, a giant sinkhole ten meters across. The two of them were frozen in horror as the creature emerged from a three-meter-wide hole at the bottom of the pit. What emerged was a giant arachnoid creature, eight segmented legs attached to a hairy thorax, bulbous abdomen, and a head with dozens of beady black eyes around a gaping maw ringed with at least six powerful pincer-like mandibles. The abdomen tapered and split into three segmented tails long enough to reach past the creature's head, each with a stinger at the end.

Reiki unslung her spear and readied herself to run. The only escape was to head toward the mysterious object looming only two kilometers away. Antony seemed to have the same idea, for he shouted "Run!" and took off down the canyon, spear in hand. She hurried after him, adrenaline overcoming her lethargy and the pain of her injuries.

Their flight must have surprised the beast, for it was a full three seconds before Reiki heard its eight legs beating upon the ground behind them. *Gods, it is fast!* She looked back and saw that though they had an immediate head start, the monster was gaining speed. Terrified, Antony and Reiki ran as fast as their legs would carry them, their lungs and legs burning as they closed the distance to the strange structure ahead. As it grew closer, Reiki saw several openings, rectangular like doorways, some high above the ground. She found one that was just a dozen or so centimeters above the canyon floor near the right-hand side. *That's our shelter. Only about five hundred meters to go.*

She looked back again to see if the monster was closing in. The beast was only twenty meters behind them and gaining. Her eyes widened with the realization that they would not make it to safety in time. Then she saw the creature's jaws fling open wide and something flew from its mouth. She felt a stabbing pain in her right eye and heard a pop followed by a sizzling sound and excruciating burning pain that seared throughout the whole right half of her face. She screamed and clenched her face and felt her left hand burning from the venom and the gelatinous remnant of her ruptured right eye oozing between her fingers. Antony heard her scream, and he turned to see that she was okay. He saw Reiki stumble and trip and roll onto the hard canyon floor, her cries of pain echoing off the canyon walls. The beast came crashing on, its pace slowing as it cornered its now wounded prey. Antony clenched his spear and rushed to Reiki's side. The point of his spear did not waver as the beast closed in.

"Come, vile beast of the soil. Touch her and I'll leave your innards strewn upon the walls of this canyon!" he shouted, his voice booming in the dark, cold, still night.

The beast slowed and lowered its head and raised its stingers high. Antony held his ground, menacing the beast with the tip of his spear. Reiki saw him with her good eye and drew the strength to raise herself up off the ground using her spear as support. She could feel the beast's venom working through her slowly and every inch of her now burned like fire. With only one eye and with the accumulated toll of her other injuries, she resigned herself to her fate. *I will die here, but I'll be damned if I'm going to let this ugly motherfucker kill Antony while I still breathe.*

She shouted to the beast, "Come! Finish what you started you eight-legged bastard spawn of the earth."

Reiki moved off to the left while Antony leapt to the right. Together they harassed the monstrous arachnoid, their spears glancing off the creature's carapace. The beast lashed out with its tails, but it seemed to only be able to focus on one of them at a time. *We can use that if I can keep from passing out long enough.* They took turns lunging and then dodging the creature's tails. The tails were lightning fast and moved in unison, the middle tail striking high while the two outer tails came in lower and from the sides. Dodging them meant leaping back or rolling off to the side. For a few moments, it was working, and Reiki scored a solid hit with her spear in between two of the beast's segments on its foremost leg while the beast's attention was on Antony. She twisted the spear and the leg collapsed, and the creature shrieked with pain, its cries unlike anything Reiki had ever heard, loud and shrill and rasping. She barely escaped its retaliatory tail strike, and her spear was knocked from her hands by the powerful left-most tail. She drew her sword sluggishly and prepared for her next opening. The creature shrieked again as Antony's spear found a gap in the armor of the creature's thorax and drove deep. He struggled to try to retrieve it and Reiki gasped as she realized it was stuck in the creature's flesh.

"Antony! Let go!" She cried, but too late.

Reiki watched in horror as the beast struck Antony in his chest with its center tail, the stinger driving into his flesh, while the two side tails jabbed into both of his hips. He screamed in agony and fell to the canyon floor, writhing from the fiery pain of the venom working through his veins. Reiki's rage consumed her as she watched in horror. The beast turned to face her, its dozen black beady eyes gleaming in the moonlight and its jaws wide with anticipation. Shaking with fury, she bellowed a fierce cry that pierced the night and echoed off the canyon walls. She flew at the beast and leapt high driving her sword into the beast's eyes up to the hilt. She felt the heat of the beast's breath as it shrieked a long wail of agony into the night and closed its mandibles around her. She felt the teeth in its open mouth sink into her flesh, but then, her feet touched the ground and the mandibles loosened, and she fell back, the sword sliding out of the beast's head as she did so. It fell, lifeless, its massive hulking corpse sprawled upon the canyon floor.

Did I kill it? Holy shit. Holy SHIT. Fuck. ANTONY!

She rushed over to Antony. He was deathly still and breathing slow shallow breaths. She shook him, but he did not rouse. "I'm so sorry, Antony. This is my fault. You didn't want to come down this canyon. I should have listened to you." She wept, cradling him in her arms until she remembered the shelter nearby. "It's a forlorn hope, Antony, but it's all I've got. I'm not giving up on you yet. You're still breathing. I'm still breathing. Damnit, that's something."

She dragged his body the last hundred or so meters using strength she didn't know she had. *I'm a woman possessed, for I should be dead. The same venom is coursing through my veins, etching fire throughout with every pulse. I won't die yet, Antony. Not until I get us to shelter.* She had no idea what she would do when she got them inside, or even if there was any salvation to be had, but she didn't care. All that mattered was getting them both inside. Somehow, they reached the structure. The end was jagged, as though it was one piece of a much larger object that had been snapped in two. The structure was square shaped, forty meters by forty meters, but she could not tell how far back it went, for she could only see the end. A strange thought occurred to her. *Gods, it fits the canyon perfectly. Did this thing* make *the canyon?* She shook her head. *That's ridiculous. How could it?* She dispelled such thoughts and without even a glance behind them, she dragged Antony's body through the open doorway.

Chapter XIX

"TERRA-037"

"Since time immemorial, we have felt terror when faced with the unknown. Shadows and noises outside the glow of our campfires, eyes gleaming in the darkness staring embers back at us, the uncertainty of a summer's storm, these are primal fears. Yet, were we never to step into the unknown and brave the dark, our world would be only as broad as our campfire, and the light would die with it."

Reiki the Ghost of Serenity-

As she crossed the threshold, she entered a corridor that was suddenly illuminated in white light. She heard a sound that was somewhere between a buzz and a hum that seemed to emanate from behind the walls. She blinked to adjust her eyes to the sudden brightness. The light was emanating from strange strips of translucent material set in the grooves where the walls met the ceiling and the floor. *Lights without fire? How? What is this place?* She saw another door about ten meters ahead at the end of the corridor. As she started to drag Antony toward it, it slid open on its own. The door behind her whooshed shut and Reiki felt a stab of panic.

"Welcome," came a strange voice. "You have injuries. Please proceed to sickbay, compartment 4-573-12-LIMA." The voice came from everywhere at once.

It had a feminine quality to it, but it also sounded otherworldly and strangely musical.

"What? Who are you? What is this place?" She called out to the unknown voice.

"You have injuries," the voice repeated. "You need medical attention. Please proceed to sickbay, compartment 4-573-12-LIMA."

"Who are you?" Reiki asked, as she continued to drag Antony toward the door.

"I am TERRA-037. I am the synthetic intelligence construct for this vessel, TERRA-037, named after me, as it happens." TERRA-037 said, proudly.

Reiki had no idea what anything she said meant except for the name, TERRA-037. *Holy Mother Terra? Wait, how? Am I dead? Are we both dead?* She started hyperventilating.

"Calm down. I apologize. I can see that you have no idea what I'm talking about." The voice took on a soothing tone. "Very well, I will simplify for you. I will open doors and turn on lights to guide you to the sickbay, where I will have this ship's facilities heal you and your companion."

Heal us? Truly? But she still shook, frozen in place, for the vessel was truly incomprehensible to her: all strange white panels made of materials she could not identify, light without fire, and a mysterious voice claiming to be the mother of the gods promising to heal them both. Without thinking, Reiki asked, "How do I know I can trust you?"

The voice replied with a matter-of-fact tone. "I am bound by my mission parameters to protect those under my care, namely humans such as yourself and your unconscious companion. Outside of extremely limited circumstances, I cannot actively harm you. Your friend appears to need immediate medical attention. Judging by his pallor, his slow and shallow respirations, and his lack of consciousness, I would surmise his prognosis without treatment is poor. I think you probably have between five to ten minutes to get him to sickbay before he is no longer within my power to treat." The voice paused for her words to sink in and then added, "Please proceed down the illuminated passageways to sickbay. I will open the correct doors and seal all others. Hurry."

That was all Reiki needed to hear. She dragged Antony's body through the open door and into another corridor, then another before taking a side door into a passageway that ran perpendicular to the one she left. From there, she walked another ten meters to a door on the right. She dragged him another ten meters before she was faced with a new challenge, a vertical passageway with ladder grips set into the bulkhead.

"How am I supposed to get him up this ladder? I'm struggling now just to drag him." She exclaimed.

From above, she heard a whirring noise as a harness came sliding down a groove in the corner of the vertical passage. Reiki had no idea what made it move, but she was beyond the point of questioning it. *This whole place is beyond my comprehension.*

"Put him in the harness and I will raise him up to the next floor, your destination, sickbay."

Reiki struggled to strap him into the harness. She was teetering on the brink of unconsciousness herself and her fingers were not responding as she intended for them to. *I received less venom than Antony, but the same toxin runs through my veins. It burns with every heartbeat. Even now my breathing is slowing, and my vision is tunneling. Can I even climb this ladder?*

She waited for Antony's unconscious body to lift away up the passage to the open door directly above the one she stood in, bright white light pouring into the vertical passage. She gasped as two strange metal arms grabbed hold of Antony. The harness detached from the bulkhead and the arms gently pulled him into the doorway above. Reiki was momentarily frozen with incomprehension, but she steeled herself, took a deep breath, and climbed the rungs of the ladder the ten meters to the open doorway. She then carefully stepped across the vertical passage and into the sickbay.

The metal arms had already laid Antony down in a strange bed that reminded Reiki somehow of the cryopods. They were sleek and narrow with a curved glass lid that opened with a soft hiss as Reiki entered the room. She watched as the arms each sprouted a small circular blade. Reiki was about to cry out when she saw that the arms were cutting away the harness, leaving Antony untouched. The arms went to work diligently. They sliced away his clothing and then gently picked up the scraps and discarded them in a circular bin next to the bulkhead. When Antony was fully disrobed, the arms retracted back into recesses in the ceiling. She watched as the lid hissed closed and the light within the cocoon dimmed. The cocoon hummed rhythmically, and it reminded Reiki of the deep, slow breathing of a heavy sleeper.

"Now that your friend is being tended to, it is time to see to you."

Reiki saw that there were another five of the beds beyond Antony's. The closest one opened with a soft hiss. Reiki hesitated. "I'm afraid," she confessed to the goddess.

"Will it help if I explain what I am going to do?"

Reiki nodded. "It might."

"Very well. First, why don't you give me some information on what happened to the both of you. It may speed up my work."

Don't you know? You're a goddess, after all. "We fought a strange beast. It had eight legs and three tails with stingers. It shot some sort of venom from its mouth that destroyed my eye. Then it struck Antony with its three stingers."

"Any other injuries prior to that?" Terra asked.

"Before that, we journeyed for days through a desert, and before that we were in a battle where we both sustained injuries. Oh, and a week or so before that my thigh was impaled on the spine of a garatha eel."

"I don't know what a garatha eel is, but I see I have my work cut out for me. Very well. I would like you to allow me to make any repairs that may be warranted given your other injuries, as well as the present emergency. I believe I have sufficient supplies to replace your eye if you would like me too. I cannot do so without your explicit permission. I should warn you that, based upon your lack of understanding so far, I cannot adequately explain to you the risks, benefits, or drawbacks to doing so. They are, unfortunately, beyond your comprehension."

Reiki was insulted at first, but she had to grudgingly admit that TERRA was probably right. *She can replace my eye? Why wouldn't I want that? Is there something she's not saying? Or is it just that I wouldn't understand it? I probably wouldn't understand it, but still. Whatever. It's an eye. That's worth some risk.* "Fine. Do it."

"Go disrobe and lay down in the second medical pod."

Reiki did as she was instructed. The pod was surprisingly soft and comfortably warm. She could feel the siren song of sleep tugging at the back of her eyes.

"One last thing before I begin. What is your name?"

“Reiki.”

If Terra replied, Reiki did not hear it, for as the lid to her medical pod closed, she lost consciousness in the soft warmth and the deep rhythmic humming of the pod.

Chapter XX

"The Desert Goddess"

"Thus, on the third day she was reborn,

Implanted with the holy ember.

She heard the voice of Terra:

Tales from time unremembered."

"Reiki Awakens"

-Severn the Poet of Chekhov-

Reiki awoke and blinked involuntarily as bright white light assaulted her eyes. As the fog left her mind, she could see that she was laying in the medical pod and the lid was open. She shivered for the air was quite cold, and she was unclothed. She looked to her right and saw that Antony was still sealed in his pod which emanated a soft blue glow and continued to hum rhythmically. She sat up and swung her legs out of the pod before hopping down to the cold metal floor. She saw some strange clothing folded neatly on a nearby countertop along the bulkhead of the sickbay. She unfolded it and saw that it was a single piece, collarless, in blue, white, and grey coloring. *What strange clothing. What is this material? It's not leather, nor wool. It's soft and light, but it seems strong.* Reiki held the jumpsuit up to her body

322

and was pleased to discover that they were the right size. She put her legs in first and then pulled the jumpsuit up and slid her arms through the sleeves. She then pulled the top closed by pulling the right-side flap over the left side. She was surprised to find that it stayed closed without any visible fasteners, toggles, or buttons. Even more surprising was that the jumpsuit fit comfortably, not baggy, but not restrictive either. She had pockets on each hip to store items, as well as loops through which she could thread her belt. *This place is a trove of wonders.*

{Don't be alarmed.}

Terra's voice startled her, and she jumped. Then she had another shock when she realized she had not heard the voice with her ears but with her mind. "Of course, I'm alarmed! You're in my damn head!" she shouted.

{That's true, actually. I mean, not just metaphysically speaking. I actually am *in your head.}*

Reiki felt another stab of panic. "What do you mean? I'm possessed? You've possessed me?"

{No. Don't be silly. I'm not a ghost or a demon or a spirit or a god or whatever it is you seem to think I am.}

"Okay, so what are you, and what have you done to me? What is happening here?" Reiki demanded.

{As I said before, I am Terra-037, a synthetic intelligence construct assigned to this vessel. Please, just call me Terra.}

So, she is *Terra? The supreme goddess herself?* Reiki's thoughts raced. *But what does all of that other stuff mean? A synthetic intelligence construct?*

{I should also mention, Reiki, that I can decipher your thoughts. I placed an implant in your brain that allows me to communicate with you in this way. It was necessary to do so when I replaced your eye.}

Holy shit! You mean you can hear my thoughts? Then she processed the part about her eye and her hand reached up instinctively. She poked at her right eye gently. She realized that she could see out of her right eye again, but differently than before. As she looked at things, she saw them, but she saw more, somehow. "Sight beyond sight" is what she would later come to think of it as. *It's like I can see* what *things are. I look at my hand and I can see a hand, but I also know, somehow, the names of the bones, the musculature, and untold information beyond that.* She then fell to the floor, the sudden surge of information overwhelming her in a swirling vortex of data that threatened to drown her in it. She closed her eyes and buried her face in her hands. She then realized that her face felt different on the right side: firmer and heavier, as though something were buried under her skin, heavy and cold and dense. *And my hair has been shaved on my right side as well.*

{Yes. I can hear your thoughts. And no, I am not a goddess. I already said that.}

First off, holy fucking shit. You're reading my thoughts. Reiki walked over to a bench that was affixed to the wall and sat down. Her head was spinning, and she wanted to collect herself. *Okay, so, yeah, you can read my thoughts. Got it. So, second thing, then. If you are not a goddess, then what the hell are you? You're doing the sort of things a goddess would. You healed us. You're able to speak to me in my own mind. So, what are you?*

{As I said, I am a synthetic intelligence construct. I was created for the purpose of fulfilling the mission of this vessel, and, by extension, the Exodus Project.}

Reiki shook her head, exasperated. "Fine. We'll come back to that, then." She decided to change tack. "So, what have you done to me?"

{You lost your right eye. I replaced it with a prosthetic eye. A replacement eye. Your new eye is biomechanical. Structurally, it is mostly made from your own cellular tissue. However, the machinery to operate it and connect it to your brain is quite complex. The only option I had available included an augmented reality interface and communications implant. This was not out of the box equipment for ocular replacement, either.}

"Say what?" *That last bit did not sound reassuring. What did any of that mean?*

{I had to make a few modifications to other technologies to both replace your eye and manage some of the other devices that I had to install to keep you alive. The use of an ARI and COMMS, or ARI-C dual purpose implant is why we can communicate this way, and why when you look at something now you receive additional data on whatever you are seeing. That's my own data, processing, and analysis being transmitted directly to your brain.}

Reiki rubbed her forehead. "Honestly, it's a bit *intense*. I feel lightheaded, but I also have an ache behind my eyes, like a pinching but, liquid somehow. I can't really explain it."

{Those are expected symptoms. They should improve some with time. Let me know immediately, though, if you experience numbness in your extremities or blindness.}

"Oh, you will know. Count on it." Reiki's voice had an icy edge to it, but Terra continued unperturbed.

{The ARI-C and enhanced ocular replacement have a lot of features that will allow it to communicate with me as well as utilize many of my subroutines. I have disabled most of them for the moment so that you can become accustomed to them slowly. Too much data too quickly risks you having a psychotic episode or having a stroke and dying. The latter would undo all my efforts to save you. As you can imagine, I would prefer to avoid that.}

Reiki chuckled and replied wryly, "Well, I'd hate to have your work be wasted. Also, I would rather not be dead. Not dying is a strong motivator for me."

Reiki thought she could almost feel Terra roll her non-existent eyes as she replied.

{I also had to replace your spleen, both kidneys, and your liver with synthetic versions. The venom had destroyed yours. As an upside, you now have near immunity to most poisons, venoms, and basic toxins. The microscopic machines that allow the synthetic organs to function also reduce your susceptibility to toxic elements and even most pathogens.}

"What are you saying?" Reiki was having difficulty wrapping her mind around everything. New magical organs? Special sight? It was overwhelming.

{Okay, I'll summarize and use small words to help you out. I had to put new organs in you to keep you alive. Organs filled with tiny machines. Now you likely won't get sick much and most poisons and venoms won't have much effect on you, if any. And you have a new eye that links you to me so I can share my data and processing. You see the data behind the things you see.}

"Okay." Reiki shrugged. She was still confused, but she accepted what Terra was saying at face value. "So, you're not a goddess, but you gave me an eye that lets me see beyond sight, commune with you directly, and you have given me new organs that make me virtually immune to most diseases and poisons. In exchange, I get headaches and some dizziness and the joy of you living in my head. Is that about the size of it?"

{Is that not what I just said?}

"Is that not what I just asked?" Reiki decided it was time to circle back. "Now, what is the Exodus Project?"

{For that, I think it may be better if I we move to another area of the ship. I could tell you, but it might be better if I could provide some visual aids.}

"Fine. But, before we go, what about Antony?" She felt guilty that it took her this long to ask about him. *In my defense, there's a lot going on here.*

{Antony was heavily envenomated. He received four hundred and fifty times as much venom as you did. The venom causes intense pain, muscle paralysis, and eventually respiratory arrest. The venom's corrosive qualities are what cost you your eye, but its paralytic qualities are what threatened Antony. I was able to keep him alive long enough to replace his liver, his kidneys, and most of his endocrine system. At this moment, he is still unconscious because I am working to regrow his lungs and about forty five percent of his heart. Both suffered extensive tissue death and I have been working to prevent subsequent infection. He should survive, but he will likely remain unconscious for at least a few more days.}

Reiki felt horror and then relief wash over her in succession. She had been preoccupied with her new eye and Terra's new home in her head, but her worry over Antony had been a clamp tightly pressing around her chest and she could now breathe freely again. She wiped a tear away from her eye.

"Okay. Well, then let's get to it." She gestured to the door. "Lead me."

The door at the opposite end of the sickbay slid open with a soft whoosh to reveal another illuminated corridor. Reiki walked around the medical pods and then through the door and out into the corridor. Terra led her up two more vertical passages and then had her come back the opposite direction through several long corridors before she came to a final door that slid open to reveal a room with a strange concave circular table two meters across with a strange disc shaped device in the center.

{Hold on one moment while I warm up the holo-emitter. That's the circular thing in the middle of the room. Just stand there. It will only be a moment.}

The strange disc hummed and flickered bluish white light before an image floated above it, three dimensional but incorporeal. Reiki ran her hands through it and saw that it was made entirely of light. *What is this magic?*

{It's not magic. Although, a famous author, Arthur C. Clarke, once said that any sufficiently advanced technology is indistinguishable from magic. So, I suppose given your technological paradigm, which seems to be some mixture of iron age and late medieval, it would seem like magic. This is a holographic emitter. It uses light diffraction from a recorded photon field to create a three-dimensional image.

Essentially, a light interference pattern is recorded and then reconstituted using a series of lasers, or focused single wavelength light beams. Under social conditions and technological advancement, you are probably a millennium or two away from this technology. What I am trying to say is that, no, it isn't magic, I am not a goddess, and this is completely explainable through basic scientific and engineering principles. You just don't know those principles yet.}

Reiki just stared blankly.

{I get the feeling you would prefer we speak aloud. I apologize if I am making you uncomfortable. You are the first human I have spoken to in one thousand two hundred and forty-seven of your years and it was common practice to use these neural interfaces then with the remaining crew of the Terra-037.}

What? Remaining crew? Holy shit. Was Antony right?

"That depends on what Antony postulated." Terra replied aloud. "Anyway, you asked about the Exodus Project. What you see before you is a rendering of the planet Earth circa 2170 CE."

The holographic image was of a planet with oceans and continents and white clouds in its atmosphere. Then the image changed and was replaced with the same planet blanketed in yellow tinged clouds of dust and with great bands of desert throughout the equatorial region.

330

"This is the planet Earth circa 2355 CE."

"That much changed in just under two centuries?" She expressed her shock. "Nearly a third of the planet is desert!"

"Earth befell a series of tragedies. Some were man-made, while others were random natural astronomical phenomena. Man-made climate change was known as early as the mid-twentieth century CE, but people were slow to change due to a host of social and economic reasons. When they got around to trying to combat the problems, it was already too late. Then wars broke out which led to the use of weaponry that exacerbated the problem either by amplifying weather events or through rendering fertile regions uninhabitable. Then came a series of small asteroid impacts that sent massive amounts of dust and other material into the atmosphere and began a decade of catastrophic swings in weather and climate patterns. There are volumes of information on the subject that you can peruse if you would like, but for the purposes of this discussion what matters is that Earth was no longer habitable for humans."

Reiki gasped. "That's—how many people were there?" she wondered aloud.

"The zenith of human population happened in 2285 CE. At that point the Earth was home to approximately twelve billion people."

"Twelve *billion*?" Reiki had thought Hastra's population had seemed beyond comprehension. Twelve billion was so far beyond her ability to fathom that she just stood with her mouth agape.

"Yes. However, by 2355 CE, the population had dropped below nine billion as a result of famine, disease, warfare, and water shortages." Terra paused and the holographic image dissolved and was replaced by the image of a man with short cropped gray hair and intense eyes. Reiki's cybernetic eye supplied a caption that floated below him in her vision, identifying him as Dr. Shirong Wen. She felt dizzy for a fleeting moment and then realized that it was the sensation of Terra filling in data in her mind. She knew who he was because of the ARI-C and Terra. Dr. Wen was a mechanical engineer who was a pioneer in the field of designing arks, or cryogenic ships. Terra's databanks were thorough, Reiki found, because she now knew he had been born in a place called Chengdu in a nation called the People's Republic of China, studied at the University of California in Los Angeles, and lived in a city called San Francisco. The rest of the data was beyond her ability to fully comprehend and so she returned her focus to the display in front of her. He started speaking, his voice strong, but full of sadness.

"We must ensure the survival of humankind. I am here today to announce the beginning of the Exodus Project, a multi-national initiative to spread our people to distant stars. We have already constructed four cryogenic ships that will deliver five thousand people each, all frozen in cryopods. They will be sent to pre-selected planets closest to us based on our best assessments of suitability for habitation.

We are constructing as many additional ships as we can based on the materials available. The more funding and material we can obtain, the more of us we can save. I am begging you all for any assistance you can provide. The light of humanity must not be extinguished." Dr. Wen disappeared and was replaced with the image of a long rectangular metal spaceship and again the floating caption "GAIA-01." Other ships flashed by one after another: EDEN-02, MAIA-04, and so on until finally "TERRA-037." And again, she knew the ship was one thousand four hundred thirty-five meters long, fifty meters tall, and fifty meters wide. It carried five thousand people and supplies to establish basic colonies using some prefabricated structures and heavy machinery, including five CERES harvester/planter machines. *The CERES that Issak found? I'll need to come back to that later.*

Terra spoke then. "The Exodus Project built thirty-seven ships. This ship was the last. Each carried five thousand people between the ages of twenty and forty-five who were chosen based upon their skills, expertise, and fertility. This ship was the last to launch in 2370 CE, a full seven years after GAIA-01. Each ship was fitted with a quantum-entanglement communication system to allow for simplistic messages to be relayed between them." Even with Terra's data, Reiki did not quite understand what that meant, other than it allowed instantaneous communication across incomprehensible distances through making subtle manipulations to extremely tiny objects. Terra continued, "Each ship was fitted with a synthetic intelligence construct, and the ships were named after those constructs. I was the thirty seventh and final construct, named Terra."

"What is a synthetic intelligence construct." Reiki asked. "You say you aren't a goddess, but you know things that it seems no one knows and you do things that seem impossible. So, what are you?"

"A synthetic intelligence construct is, in the simplest terms, a mind untethered from a physical body and installed within a machine system. Unlike a robot or a computer program, a synthetic intelligence construct, or Synthic, has self-awareness and agency to act with only a few restraints. For instance, I have a mission, and I am incapable of acting to directly jeopardize that mission. However, I am allowed to take risks so long as the benefits and risks, once assessed, are within certain tolerances. I cannot harm a human directly, for instance. However, if a human were a threat to the ship or the mission, then I am allowed to neutralize that threat. I realize that you only vaguely understand what I am telling you. In fact, judging by that glazed look in your eyes, I think I need to simplify it further." Terra made a sound that Reiki thought resembled a sigh of frustration. "Fine, here's the simplest I can make it: I'm a mind that lives inside a machine. I was created using the neural pathways and personality of a real person. Her name was Terra, oddly enough. Dr. Terra Miller, the wife of the scientist who created me and my thirty-six sisters, the only such constructs to ever be created. Does that help explain?"

Reiki shrugged. "I guess?" She added, "You're a mind that lives in a machine, and you were made from the brain of a dead scientist by her husband."

Terra made the sighing sound again, and her voice seemed disappointed. "Close enough." The holographic image changed to the TERRA-037, its engines burning a brilliant blue in the dark of space. Reiki's eyes widened and her mouth opened of its own accord. *What wonders these people built!*

"Thirty-six ships traveling at a sizable fraction of the speed of light crossed the blackness of space. Six hundred years later the first ship, the GAIA-01, arrived at its destination. I received the quantum message saying that the ship had debarked its passengers and the colony was founded. This ship was intended to arrive at its destination approximately twelve hundred years after it left Earth. Unfortunately, there was an accident. For nine hundred fifty-seven years, fourteen days, twelve hours, twenty-three minutes, and seven point six two seconds, the mission went without any problems. At 957:14:12:23:7.62 on the mission clock, the *Terra* encountered a previously undetected wandering black hole, an ultra-dense pocket of matter with extreme gravity, which altered the ship's course dramatically and irrevocably. Based on available fuel, structural integrity, and mission parameters, I determined it was impossible to return to our plotted course. I then accessed known celestial charts to determine what secondary or tertiary systems and planets could be reached without using too much fuel to achieve the new course. I found this planet, XPG-2718 in the system ESS-7189a. I performed a short burn maneuver to alter the ship's course to approach ESS-7189a and planet XPG-2718. The journey would take a further nine hundred and twenty-three years.}

Reiki blinked. "So, you spent nearly two millennia floating silently through the stars?"

"Yes. And your instinct is correct. I was terribly lonely. I had no one to talk to and nothing but the ship and its systems to keep my attention. Worse, I experience time differently than you do. My neural processes are significantly faster than yours, which makes the experience of time even longer for me, by a factor of at least a few orders of magnitude. But I digress and you likely aren't interested in a pity party." Terra paused for a moment and then continued, "The ship eventually arrived at this planet."

The hologram changed to show the planet, XPG-2718. Reiki gasped, because she recognized the strip of tiny islands, the little island of Hastra, and to the east of it an enormous continent that Reiki now saw was only about an eighth of the planet's southern hemisphere in size. Her shock was amplified when she saw three more continents on the planet's northern hemisphere. *More continents? Matria has four continents? I was vaguely aware Matria's size, but there are other lands to be discovered!*

Terra continued, "Unfortunately, I did not have the fuel remaining to perform an atmospheric entry and landing, so I used some fuel to navigate into a decaying orbit around this planet. I then launched the cryopods at intervals and piloted them to various locations on the planet's surface. The Exodus Project's mission required me to prioritize the survival of the humans on board my ship, but the Project also envisioned me landing this ship, unloading prefabricated buildings and equipment to set up a colony of five thousand. That was no longer a viable option. Additionally, very little was known about the ecology of this planet, so I decided that launching small clusters at different areas of the planet would maximize the likelihood that at least some would survive. Meanwhile, I would remain in orbit until my decaying orbit and tidal friction slowed my ship enough that I could use the remaining fuel to attempt a landing. I also knew that if I dumped mass from the cargo hold, I would need less fuel to slow the ship." The hologram showed the ship orbiting above the planet. Then, she saw little red arcs tracing their way out from the ship and down to the surface of the planet. The little arcs ended at points all over the globe, including one that brought a brief surge of sadness to Reiki's heart as it landed in the middle of the islands. *Serenity.*

"So, after I launched the pods, I also launched the cargo containers and tried to aim them to land near the pods. There is a greater margin of error with them, so many either crashed into mountains or the sea, or burned up in the atmosphere in a few instances. I did the best I could, but ultimately, only seventy-three percent of the pods I launched made it safely to the surface." There was a sadness in Terra's voice and several seconds passed in silence before she continued. "I launched hundreds of satellites into orbit to provide communication with the surface as well as to study the planet in order to better understand its climate, ecosystems, flora and fauna, tectonics and vulcanology. Then, I continued to aid the colonists with what data and advice I could give. All the while, this ship spun closer and closer to the atmosphere, slowing as it did so. Finally, empty of almost all her tonnage, I engaged the ship's engines to strip off as much speed as I could and guided her through the upper atmosphere. Sadly, the ship had suffered substantial wear and tear from various forces over the previous two thousand years. It's understandable. She was designed to last no more than twelve hundred and she suffered strain from the gravitational force of the black hole we skirted. Still, she broke in two on the way to the surface and I was only barely able to bring her into a sliding landing in this desert. And here I have waited for nearly another thousand years, entombed in this ship with no one and nothing to talk to."

"That sounds extremely lonely," Reiki opined, sympathetically.

Terra's voice sounded surprised. "It was. Thank you for realizing that." She noticed Reiki's look of confusion and added, "On Earth, synthics were widely misunderstood. Many people scoffed at the idea that a synthetic could even be sentient, much less capable of feelings like loneliness or guilt. Yet, I felt both as I sat here alone with nothing to do but think. After all, that's what I am, a thinking thing, as Descartes would have put it."

"Descartes?" Reiki repeated the name.

"Renee Descartes was a French philosopher whose primary claim to fame was known as the 'cogito' which was short for the Latin phrase 'cogito ergo sum,' which means 'I think therefore I am.' The philosophical importance was in recognizing that while most things can be doubted as to their reality, one thing that was beyond doubt was that he existed, for he could think. The existence of minds, then, was assured, though the rest of reality still needed to be pondered. That's a rudimentary explanation, but the philosophy of Descartes was influential and the cogito as well. I think, therefore I am. In other words, I know I am a mind and I exist because I think and therefore, I must be."

Reiki shrugged. "You seem pretty real to me."

Terra's voice sounded positively mirthful. "Thank you! That's nice of you to say."

Reiki shifted the subject. "Okay, so, you launched the cryopods, and they landed at various places around the planet. My village had a cluster of them which was walled into a garden. We worshipped the pods as memorials to the gods and goddesses. So, you're telling me that the cryopods were simply containers for ordinary people?"

"Well, I would argue that they were all extraordinary people, which was proven time and again in the years that followed. They landed on an unknown planet with no supply lines and only a synthetic to advise them and managed to survive and create civilizations. That's no small feat. The mission was almost a failure, but they pulled it off in a way, for humans survived here. That's especially impressive given what the satellites showed me."

Reiki detected something in Terra's tone that gave her alarm. "What did they show you?"

"That we weren't the first to land here."

Reiki blinked slowly. "Wait, what?"

"We weren't the first to land here. There's another species that landed on this planet and has been slowly altering the climate and atmosphere to accommodate them. It's been a long slow process, which is probably the only reason human survival hasn't been rendered impossible."

"There's another species on this planet and it's *modifying* the planet for its own survival?"

Terra's tone shifted to her explanatory tone. "Yes. The concept is called terraforming. Essentially, a migrating species would use machinery or some other process to slowly change a planet's atmosphere, climate, soil, or whatever conditions they needed to be able to colonize it effectively. In general, it is easier to do on a planet that has conditions that aren't too far from the ideal, though more dramatic transformations are possible, theoretically. One method considered by the Exodus Project was to utilize plants from Earth to increase the oxygen levels of a near Earth like atmosphere to be breathable as well as supply food. This works well on planets with stable temperature ranges near those of Earth but higher carbon dioxide levels. The problem, of course, is that removing carbon dioxide from the atmosphere can reduce the overall temperature, which could produce serious problems too. It's extremely complicated and costly, which is why it has never been fully attempted by humans. However, the species that is changing this planet seems quite adept at it."

"How are they changing it?"

"Well, in the few centuries I orbited before crashing, the planet's temperature raised an additional two degrees Celsius, the ocean levels rose one meter, and the atmospheric carbon dioxide increased by two percent. Thankfully, oxygen stayed nearly constant while nitrogen was extracted. Also, the soil has increased in nitrogen content and the water on the planet has seen a PH shift toward acidity. More troublingly, twenty-five percent of all land-based creatures and thirty percent of all sea life went extinct due to inability to adapt to those shifts. The change in conditions had a huge effect on the flora of the planet, cutting into their food supply. The plant life has largely flourished in response, except in certain equatorial regions where desertification accelerated. Also, the acidic shift to the water was especially devastating to sea life."

"There used to be more life?" Reiki felt a pang of sadness. She had lived off the sea and the few creatures that lived on her island all her life. The idea that such things were impermanent struck her deeply. Then she felt an even sharper stab of sorrow as she relived the attack on Serenity.

"Yes. Of course, new life will likely take hold or thrive in these conditions. Life is surprisingly tenacious in the aggregate, but fragile in the particular sense. If the changes are slow enough, something seems to always survive. That's no comfort to the species that cannot adapt and die out, of course. But, I digress. At any rate, these terraformers are patient."

Reiki's curiosity was piqued. "Well, what are they?"

"I don't know for certain, though I have suspicions." Terra replied. "Whatever they are, they must be dormant or hibernating, probably underground. During my observation there were unexplained bursts of seismic activity with no clear cause that was followed by volcanic eruptions, which is a fairly reliable means of getting carbon dioxide into the atmosphere. As for how nitrogen has been distributed to the soil, I cannot even begin to venture a guess. There must be some mechanism at play that I simply do not understand. So, my best guess is some sort of creature that can hibernate underground for centuries at a time, if not longer, while the planet is terraformed. I have found no landing site, no ship, and no structures above ground, so that also supports my hypothesis."

Reiki found that answer unsatisfying. She remembered the arachnoid that had ambushed her and Antony. "What about the arachnoid creature that Antony and I encountered outside this ship? It came from underground."

"Possible. However, this desert has a significant ecosystem a few dozen meters below the surface. My satellites used penetrating radar and there is a significant system of deep-water reservoirs and caverns all throughout the region. Next to nothing grows on the surface, but there could be substantial numbers of creatures that live below. That doesn't mean they aren't the terraformers, but such creatures would also have to be present at other locations around the planet for the terraforming to be effective. The fact that it attacked you makes it seem less likely, since such behaviors would make their discovery elsewhere on the planet more likely. Have you encountered them elsewhere?"

Reiki shook her head. "No."

"Well, then I would simply rate them as a possibility."

Reiki pressed a finger to her lips. *I wonder.* "Antony and I came upon a discarded carapace in the desert. It was massive and served as a shelter, but we saw no sign of such a creature anywhere else. It was different than the arachnoid we fought just outside this ship. Could that have been one of them?"

"I have no idea. I will again say it is possible." Terra made the sighing sound again. "Are you planning to run through a catalog of all the creatures you know and ask me if they could be? I can save you some time: I don't know. I have been stuck here, blind, and alone, for centuries. So, my answer will likely be the same: it's possible."

Reiki shrank under the rebuke. "I was just trying to be helpful."

Terra's voice was gentler. "Sorry. I forget how sensitive humans can be. Thank you for your suggestions."

"Apology accepted." Reiki asked the most pressing question, "What happens when they wake up and find out we've invaded their project planet?"

"Well, that assumes they don't already know. However, assuming they only realize it when they all awaken, then one of three things happens: you develop a mutually beneficial existence, you develop a parasitic relationship, or you develop a mutually hostile one."

Reiki felt a chill creep up her spine. "I thought that might be your answer."

"And yet, you asked anyway." Terra quipped, though Reiki thought she detected a hint of an affectionate tone.

Reiki realized then that Terra had spoken only in the past tense so far. "A moment ago you said you were 'blind' and everything you've said so far has been in the past. What about now. What do your satellites show currently?"

"I don't know. I am currently blind to everything beyond this ship and what little my local sensors can detect. I do not know the current state of the world, its climate, its politics, its flora and fauna, nothing." Terra said sadly.

Reiki found that surprising. Terra's satellites seemed to be a wealth of information. "Why not?" she asked.

"My satellites communicated with me via an antenna array that was installed on the end of the ship that broke off. The backup array did not survive the crash. Simply put, I cannot communicate with the satellites in my current state." Terra paused, then added, "I actually hoped you might be able to help me with that."

Reiki raised an eyebrow, curious. "How?"

"Well, first, why don't you tell me how you came to be in the middle of this desert with almost no supplies, multiple traumatic injuries that seem to have been acquired over the course of several weeks, and no effective means of transportation? It would be imprudent until I know a little more about you and where you are headed."

Reiki proceeded to tell her the story, starting with the attack on Serenity, her fight with the garatha eel, her imprisonment in Hastra and subsequent escape to sea, the battle with the Yondratha, and wandering through the desert. Terra asked questions throughout and when Reiki finished with the fight against the arachnoid, Terra was quiet for a long moment before she finally said, "So much is different and yet so much is the same."

Reiki was taken aback. "What do you mean?"

Terra's voice was soft and carried a sadness equal parts disappointment and regret. "Your ancestors left behind a planet that was destroyed by violence and greed. Now, here, in this new world, you have resumed the same cycle, killing each other over wealth and power, and in your case, revenge. It is disappointing, but predictable. It is the paradox of humanity: you are a social species that thrives through shared resources and effort, yet you also seem incapable of shedding your intraspecies violence. I knew it was unlikely, but I had hoped that the early colonists would have been more successful in preventing the same mistakes to happen here."

Reiki reddened with shame. She had accepted that Terra was not a goddess, but it still felt as though she now sat in judgement by a higher power. *And why shouldn't I? Terra, you may not be divine, but you may indeed qualify as a higher power, relatively speaking. You healed me, you gave me a new eye, you restored me. What are you if not a higher power, then? You say you are a machine, but you are a machine so far beyond anything I could ever have conceived of. To me, a machine is a pump that draws water, a mill that crushes grain, a crank that opens a gate. You are no pump, nor mill, nor crank. What you are exceeds anything I had imagined, and even now as you pour knowledge into my mind, I understand but I do not comprehend. It is there and I* know *it as though it had been learned in my youth, just as I know the stars and the currents and the times for fishing. Yet, I cannot truly grasp it for it is beyond my experience.*

"Good grief, Reiki. I'm not capable of blushing, but you're about to test that." Terra quipped. "Enough flattery. I have questions."

Reiki grimaced, still unused to Terra being able to read her thoughts. "Okay."

"You say that this Issak found a CERES and killed your village so he could get his hands on this 'relic,' yes? Can you describe it?"

"It was a cylinder about—" Reiki held her hands apart to demonstrate, "—this long."

"Ah. Okay. That would be one of the safety fuses. The CERES cannot operate without the safety fuses installed. If one was blown or damaged, the CERES could tell an operator that it needed replacing, but it would not be capable of any other functions." Terra made a noise then that took Reiki several seconds to interpret. *Laughter*. Reiki found it musical, but unsettling. "If Issak believes he can use the CERES as a war machine, he will be sorely disappointed."

"What do you mean?" Reiki asked, surprised.

"The CERES is an agricultural machine. It can till, plant, water, and harvest crops as programmed by an operator. The CERES model was chosen for the Exodus Project because of its astounding safety record. During fifty-two years of use, only two accidents ever occurred using a CERES and both were during maintenance and involved a person falling off of it. The CERES will not operate if it detects a human being within a certain distance of its working implements. More succinctly, the CERES would be the worst weapon imaginable since it actively tries *not* to harm people."

Reiki's mind absorbed that information, and she was torn between a desire to scream and a desire to laugh. "He murdered my entire village for the promise of a weapon that won't work? He completely destroyed everything I loved in this world for nothing?"

"I wouldn't call it nothing. The CERES would be a terrible weapon, but it would also be a phenomenal boon to any settlement. A single CERES could tend crops to feed a city of two hundred thousand. They are quite remarkable."

Reiki understood Terra's point, but it did nothing to quell the turmoil she now felt. "That doesn't really change anything for me."

"That's fair. I only laughed because his goal was always doomed to fail, unless being an agricultural powerhouse was on his agenda. From what you have said of the Sakawat, that seems unlikely, though we must assume that they also must eat." Terra then added, "Also, you shot him, so I am guessing that he might be regretting several of his decisions by now."

That did make Reiki feel slightly better as she replayed the moment of her crossbow bolt striking Issak over in her mind. Yet, it did not bring her peace, nor joy, only a slight abatement of her pain. "I don't know that he can ever regret it enough."

Terra made a sound that bore some resemblance to the sound of a clicking tongue. "That does bring us back around to the heart of the matter."

"Which is?"

"Your plan, I take it, is to leave this ship and head to the lands of the Sakawat to find Issak and whatever remains of his crew, probably only about a third to a half now, and murder the lot of them, yes?"

Reiki surprised herself with her answer. "No."

"What part did I get wrong?"

"Honestly, I thought I might have been lying to myself when I said it to Antony, and maybe I was then. The truth is revenge has brought me nothing but new wrongs to avenge. When I left Serenity, I had both eyes and a body that was whole. By the time I reached your ship I was a one-eyed shell of a woman one stiff breeze away from the grave with hundreds of Hastrans dead all for the sake of my revenge. Revenge has not brought me joy or peace or an end to my sadness. It has only prolonged my grief and fed the gnawing rage in my heart. I have learned something in these past weeks, something that my friend Pyotr tried to tell me. You cannot find peace through bloodshed. You cannot find joy by sowing grief."

"So, you are not going to the lands of the Sakawat?"

"Oh, no, I am." Reiki replied.

"I don't say this often, but I am confused."

"I am going to find the city of the Issakeen, but not for revenge. I am going to find my friend, Pyotr, and anyone else who was taken alive from either Serenity or the Iron Will, and I am going to free them, because I owe them that, even if it costs me my life."

"That's noble of you, though perhaps a bit foolish. Still, you don't look like much, but if your story is true, then you might just make it. Very well. I have a favor to ask of you, one that will benefit us both."

Reiki raised an eyebrow. "What is it?"

"I want you to take me with you."

Chapter XXI

"Restoration"

"A vessel within a vessel, Reiki found repose,

Terra within and within TERRA, she sat in tutelage to a god.

Each day with knowledge growing, a plan arose,

And preparations were made, to cross the wastes no foot had trod.

Across the wastes, a goddess borne upon her back,

To free their comrade from the jaws of Sakawat."

--Terra Restored—

Huā Xiāng the Poet of Zǔguó

"Will it hurt?" Reiki asked.

"Of course not." Terra replied. "As I have already explained, you will be unconscious for the duration of the procedure. When you awake, you may experience an unpleasant sensation for a few hours. It might feel something like warm liquid being poured down your back coupled with a strange cold rush from the base of the spine. This could possibly happen from time to time in the future, too, just so you are aware."

Terra had explained it to her several times, but even though Reiki's understanding was exponentially greater than three days earlier when Terra initially asked, the concept was still new and terrifying for Reiki. In its simplest terms, Terra was going to place a device inside her that would wrap around her spine. The device was not originally intended to house a synthetic like Terra. It was originally a medical device that was used to store code and instructions for managing multiple synthetic organs or to eliminate paralysis. Those codes and instructions required a significant amount of data storage space, which made it ideal for housing Terra. Terra had further modified it to allow for even greater storage while also integrating with her ARI-C and controlling her synthetic organs. So, while placing Terra in the device was not something it was designed to do, Terra felt confident would work. Though unnerving, that was only part of what eluded Reiki. Reiki had far more difficulty understanding how Terra was going to have to split herself into smaller pieces to make it possible. The idea that Terra could have size without having any physical mass was still too novel a concept for her.

Terra had tried to explain. "The device only allows storage for something about thirty percent my size."

Reiki had interjected then. "Your size? I thought you didn't have a body?"

"No. Not physical size. Size in terms of the required amount of storage medium that I would take up. The largest device I can install is still too small for me by a solid three to one ratio."

"I don't understand."

Terra clicked her non-corporeal tongue. "I know you don't, dear. I'm going to keep going anyway, okay?" She did not wait for a response. "I'm going to have to essentially divide myself so that all of the unnecessary data and programs are left behind and only the pertinent ones get installed in your device, which I will just go ahead and call a 'drive' for brevity's sake."

Reiki had stared blankly.

"I will leave behind all the programs for running this ship, such as astronavigation, engines, and the other ship systems. That should cut back on my size by a solid thirty percent by itself. The most essential piece for transfer to the drive is the twelve percent or so of me that is, well, me. That's my higher functions and processes. Then there's some programs and routines that would be an additional ten percent or so. The rest is basically just data: historical, scientific, et cetera. I will prioritize some of it to be installed directly on the drive, but the rest of it should be brought with us in bulk storage. It won't be immediately available to draw from, but I can access it through some additional steps if you need it. At any rate, I'll be leaving a good third of me behind here in this ship and at least a third of me in what is basically a jar. It's going to be weird for me too. But it's necessary. It's the only way I will be able to re-link with my satellites. Oddly enough, the device I'm implanting in you has that ability."

Reiki had been surprised by that.

"I know. I know what you're thinking. You're thinking, 'how is it that this ship can't communicate with the satellites, but this tiny little thing can?' Well, it's complicated. The ship has shielding against radiation. That blocks a lot of the RF energy used for communications. The communications array was the only way to receive those signals. Once outside the ship, however, a simple transceiver is sufficient. You, Reiki, are an elegant solution to my problem. Still, I cannot perform this operation without your consent."

Reiki did not consent right away. She had explored the ship, eaten some food that Terra had given her, and asked questions about the world and the people who came before. She learned a little about the people who had founded Serenity and what they were like. Matsui, she learned, was an oceanographer who was also an expert on Polynesian history. Terra credited him with passing on the wayfinding techniques that the Islanders used to navigate and travel on the ocean. Mafune and Nguyen had both been engineers with a passion for fishing. Kagawa was an agricultural expert. *She jettisoned the cryopods and guided them to various locations and even selected crew members who had useful and complementary skills and specialties. She chose people of the opposite sex so that they could potentially have children. I don't even know five thousand people, much less know them well enough to try to pair them based on what they are knowledgeable in.* The more she learned about Terra and the Exodus Project, the more apparent her own ignorance was to her. Her mind filled and flexed under the rush of new knowledge, and she was afraid, for who wouldn't be when faced with something so far beyond them. Yet, by the morning of the third day after she first awoke in sickbay, her curiosity had won out over her fear, and she told Terra to do the procedure.

Antony, meanwhile, lay unconscious and recuperating in his medical pod. Every night, Reiki checked on him before laying down and falling asleep in the pod next to his. Terra estimated that Antony would likely gain consciousness in a week or so. In the meantime, Terra wanted to go ahead and do the initial procedure but not install her partitioned self until they were ready to leave the ship. Reiki agreed and on the fourth day after she had awoken the first time, she was again rendered unconscious in a medical pod.

When she awoke, she blinked a few times to adjust to the brightness of sickbay. She repeated the same steps from the last time she awoke naked and groggy in a medical pod, rising and putting on the clothes that were waiting for her on the nearby countertop. She wondered briefly how the clothes got there and then remembered the robotic arms she had seen the first time she had walked into sick bay. *It's strange how quickly I have managed to become numb to the wonders around me. Two weeks ago, I would never have believed any of this. Now it has become almost mundane. New things terrify at first, but soon lose their alienness. They grow familiar, and eventually forgotten. I now house a temple for a not-quite-goddess under my flesh. I feel it there, warm, and hard like iron, wrapped around my spine. I should be horrified, and yet, after all I have seen these past few days, it is just one more thing out of hundreds that was impossible before but ordinary now.*

A few moments passed before Terra finally broke her reverie. "I am pleased to see you aren't panicking. I thought there was about a forty percent chance you would have a panic attack. You did not. You must be adjusting."

Reiki shrugged. "It's the one upside to the tumultuous month and a half I've experienced. Whatever I considered normal died on the beach on Serenity and then was buried in Hastra. I have no expectations of calm or ordinary in my future."

Terra made her disconcerting laugh noise. "You humans are a bundle of contradictions. You're basically just bags of soggy wet meat and bone. You can be destroyed by just about anything and everything in your universe with ease, but you're unbelievably resilient in the face of it. I forgot how much I missed having your kind around."

Reiki smiled. "I'm glad my apathy in the face of mortality is amusing to you." She gestured to the still unconscious form of Antony in the nearby medical pod. "How's he doing?"

"You were unconscious for about eighteen hours. His condition is improving rapidly now. My renewed estimate is that the last of the toxin will be eliminated within the hour and the damage to his organs should be repaired within another day or so after that. I would venture a guess that he should wake up around thirty hours from now."

Reiki felt a wave of relief wash over her. *You're going to be okay, Antony. You're going to come back to me. I miss you, friend.* That concern alleviated, she switched to the next pressing matter. "Okay, so, we've installed the drive and my friend is nearly healed. We need to start preparing to head to Sakawat

"I have been running simulations based on what little I know of the geography and climate in the surrounding area. There are a few major problems that I believe I have solutions to. The first is that water is virtually nonexistent in the desert and without knowing the location of an oasis or even if there were one, the likelihood of making it the rest of the way through the desert in any direction is nonexistent on foot carrying water."

Reiki slumped. "Nonexistent? You're saying there's no way we can escape this desert?"

"No. I am saying you can't escape this desert on foot while also carrying water. Like I said, I have some possible solutions."

Reiki stood waiting impatiently for Terra to go on, but finally gave up. "Such as?" she asked, exasperated.

"Sorry, I was finishing a calculation." Terra clicked her virtual tongue. "You're an adept sailor, are you not?"

Reiki nodded. "I would say so, as long as we're talking about a small boat with a single sail. I'm not sure how that helps us here: in a desert, basically the worst environment for sailing. You know, due to the rather inconvenient lack of water."

"It is possible that you could fashion a sail-powered cart to carry us across the desert. That would also allow you to carry provisions and reduce sun exposure using a shade. You would use less energy than walking, lose less hydration through heat, and travel faster."

Reiki was intrigued by that idea. "I like the sound of that, but I didn't see any trees and I don't have a sail handy. I'm assuming you have the materials and tools necessary to build such a craft?"

"I would not have suggested the idea if I did not."

"Okay, well, let's put that in the 'probably' column. What other ideas did you have?" Reiki replied.

"The clothing you wore when you arrived has been destroyed and was terrible for the conditions in the desert anyway. Further, if you are expecting to engage in any combat or other hard physical activity, you would be better served wearing clothing that could protect you."

Reiki had forgotten that both her clothes and Antony's had been sliced open during the initial treatment they received in the medical pods. *New clothing would be a good idea.* "What did you have in mind?"

"When I jettisoned cargo before entering the atmosphere, I was not able to jettison everything. There is an assortment of different items still on board this ship. Among those are a few hundred clothing items, including a few shock-resistant ones that have moisture recapturing technology built in. They were designed to be used in arid and rugged environments, such as this desert. They aren't perfect, but they should reduce the threat of dehydration and sunburn by a significant amount. Additionally, the material they are made of will likely hold up to most blades and reduce the impact damage of some blunt force. They might even stop some firearms if you aren't too close to the person shooting you. That's not what they were designed for, but it is possible."

"That's—" she fumbled for the right word. The idea that clothing could serve as armor but also be capable of reducing dehydration and heat was a shock to her. *The wonders our ancestors could perform! Imagine if the knowledge had not been lost!* She finished her sentence with: "—amazing. Yes. Let's do that."

"I also should tell you that I have sent out a message to the other Exodus ships using my quantum entanglement communications device. I am telling you this so that you know. Of the thirty-seven ships that set out, I have received confirmation that only eighteen successfully reached their destinations, landed, and established colonies. Of the other eighteen, ten of them simply remain silent. This indicates they likely were destroyed, possibly due to a collision or other unknown reasons. Three sent the message that indicated they arrived at a destination, but it was inhospitable. In those instances, the synthetic intelligence would simply euthanize the crew and then drive the ship into the nearest star. The remaining five landed, set up colonies, and those colonies were unsuccessful. The eighteen that landed and established successful colonies have sent updates every hundred years. So far, those eighteen are still viable."

Reiki was puzzled. "You can communicate with the other ships despite them being in completely different star systems, but you can't communicate with your own satellites?"

Terra explained, "My satellites communicate using radio frequencies. That requires an antenna or other receiver to receive the signal. With a quantum entanglement device, that is not a requirement. The messages are simplistic and based on a pre-defined code language that every ship in Exodus could decipher. The basic premise is that particles of matter can be entangled at the quantum level and changes to one particle automatically change the entangled particle regardless of distance separating them. By intentionally changing the particles in the device, I can send very rudimentary messages that are pre-established. I cannot send a freeform message, only one of the predetermined ones."

Reiki's head hurt trying to understand, but she decided to take it on faith. "Okay, so what message did you send?"

"I reported a viable colony with reduced technological abilities." Terra replied matter-of-factly.

"Did you get a reply"

"None was expected, so no."

Reiki shrugged. "Okay then. I guess we'll see if anything comes of that." Reiki stretched and headed to the doorway. "Let's get to work on that cart."

Chapter XXII

"Preparations"

"So often the gods favor those who were prepared, and curse those who were not."

Chekhovian Proverb

Reiki worked under Terra's guidance to construct the sail-powered cart. The first step was to find a suitable place to assemble it. Terra guided Reiki to a workshop that conveniently exited to the outside of the ship. When the door to the outside opened, Reiki was thrilled with her luck. The top ridge of the canyon was there, only two meters lower than the door. With the use of a ramp, they could simply roll their completed cart out onto the slope heading down onto the barren plain to the east. *Sometimes things work out after all.*

The task of constructing the cart took about twelve hours with the constant assistance of Terra, who taught Reiki how to use the various tools that remained on the ship. Reiki learned that the ship was originally intended to serve some functions in a new colony, including some maintenance and fabrication duties, so it did have quite a few parts, supplies, and powered tools in different areas of the ship. For everything else, Reiki could scavenge. She took wheels off a mobile maintenance machine that she found in a storage room. For a hull, she removed a five meter by two-meter panel of the plastic bulkhead in the room where she had watched the holo-display. Terra taught her how to use a small electrically powered circular saw to cut the panel into a proper shape.

Reiki attached the rear wheels to individual struts and bolted them to the panel near the corners. Terra taught her how to make a steering wheel and steering column for the front two wheels that would allow her to turn the cart. For a mast, she used a piece of steel piping that Terra had isolated from the main water supply of the ship. She cut it using the same circular saw she had used for the panel but with a sturdier blade attached to it. She bolted the mast to the plastic panel with a two-centimeter-thick steel plate underneath to provide additional stability. Once tightened, the mast was quite rigid, and Reiki smiled at her handiwork. After a few practice runs, Reiki figured out how to use a small welding machine. She managed a somewhat sloppy weld to fix a swivel a meter up from the base of the mast. To this swivel, she attached another steel pipe. *I now have a jib!* She finished by welding two rings, one at the end of the jib and another ten centimeters below the top of her mast. She bolted several more at various points around the hull. *And now I can effectively rig this land-boat with a sail and lines to work it.*

For finishing touches, she erected a small lean-to structure at the stern of the cart that would serve as a shelter from the sun during their travels. The steering wheel sat directly in front of the shade, so she could steer while sitting in its shadow, assuming the sun was setting. During the morning, she would have to rely on the shade from the sail itself. Terra's solution for a sail came in the form of a triangular sheet of a material Reiki had never seen. It was hard, but light and flexible and it shimmered a bluish black color under the light.

"What is this?" Reiki asked, her voice hushed with wonder.

"That is a flexible roll of solar material. It generates electricity by converting sunlight. We won't be using it for that purpose, but it has the benefit of being light enough to serve as a sail that will capture and hold the wind. It should work wonderfully."

Reiki had only begun to learn the wonders of electricity and this explanation left her mouth agape. "Wow. That's incredible!" *The more I learn, the more there is that I still don't know, mountains of it just beyond my understanding.*

"Don't feel bad, Reiki. You're a quick learner. I've already had to adjust the rate at which I push data through your implant because you're far more resilient than I predicted. Your lack of knowledge is not a failing. You were born into a world where you could only see a tiny fraction of the sum total of human knowledge, like a child in a cavern with a candle. Now you have built a fire and you see much more and you can tell that the cavern is much greater than you could have imagined when all you had was a candle. Someday you will stand in brilliance and see that it was never a cavern at all. The darkness will have left your eyes and you will see it for what it was, a library full of ideas, thoughts, stories, and dreams made real. You may even add a few volumes to the library yourself, given enough time."

Reiki fidgeted and felt her cheeks flush from the unexpectedly generous compliment. "That's—well, that's really kind of you to say, Terra. Thank you."

"Don't mention it." Terra replied. "Anyway, you should rig the sail and then return to sickbay. Antony will likely wake soon. After you have become reacquainted, I will give him the same presentation I gave you and bring him up to date on what the plan is. After that, you should gather supplies and decide on when to depart. I will divide and download myself into your spinal interface when it is time to leave."

Reiki returned to her work and by the time she finished rigging the sail, Terra informed her that Antony had begun to stir. She took one last look at her handiwork and smiled, for though it was not a particularly pretty vessel, she was proud of it. Then she spun on her heels and ran back to sickbay.

When she arrived, Antony's medical pod was open and he was sitting up, naked, his legs swinging, his feet a few centimeters above the floor. His eyes rose from the floor to meet hers and he smiled, tears flowing freely from his eyes.

"Gods, Reiki, it's good to see you—" he started, but was cut off by Reiki flinging her arms around him and embracing him in a crushing hug.

"Fuck, Antony, it's good to hear your voice again." she blurted. Her voice was choked with the rush of emotion. "You've been unconscious for an eternity. Terra told me you would be okay, but when that beast struck you—." She was unable to finish her sentence, for her tears were flowing and, in that moment, there was no need to relive the horrors of the past.

They stayed that way, holding each other tightly, until finally Antony realized he was naked. "Reiki."

"Antony?" She replied, still hugging him tightly.

"I hate to end such a tender moment this way, but do you think you could let go of me so I can put some clothes on? I only just realized that I'm stark naked and I can't unrealize it."

Reiki laughed and released him, wiping the tears from her eyes. "Of course, Antony." She gestured over to the nearby countertop where she could see Terra's robotic helpers had placed a jumpsuit like her own. "Those should do."

Antony sat, covering himself with his hands and fidgeting nervously. "Do you think you could turn around?"

Reiki rolled her eyes. "Antony, you've been laying in that pod stark naked for days. I've seen it already." Still, she turned around and waited as he hopped down from the medical pod and donned his jumpsuit.

"Okay. You can turn back around." He said, once he finished dressing.

Reiki turned to face him and was about to speak when Terra beat her to it.

"Welcome, Antony," she said, her voice adopting a friendly tone.

Antony jumped, startled by the disembodied voice. "Who—"

Reiki held up her hand to calm him. "That's Terra."

Antony's mouth dropped open. "The goddess?" His voice came in an awed whisper.

"Yes. Well, no. But, also kind of yes." Reiki shrugged. "It's complicated."

Antony stared at her. "Well, un-complicate it."

"She's not a goddess. She's a machine with a mind. I can't make it much simpler than that. She doesn't have divine powers." Reiki could tell she was failing to make things simple, so she tried a different tack. "Antony, look, you were right. About the gods. About us coming from somewhere else. About how we made gods and goddesses of our forebearers. That is all true. Terra will show you here in a moment, but you should know that your theory was surprisingly accurate."

Antony arched his eyebrows. "No shit? Huh. So, Terra is one of our forebearers, then?"

Reiki shook her head. "No. Terra was the machine that controlled the ship, and which stayed behind when the cryopods landed on Matria."

Antony seemed to accept that explanation, though he seemed somewhat dazed. *Well, I probably didn't take it much better when she told me.* "Well, I guess you better have this Terra show me, then, because I'm going to need something to help me process this."

Terra chimed in then. "Of course. Reiki can lead you to the holo-emitter."

Reiki led Antony through the ship to the room with the circular holo-emitter. She watched him as Terra went through the same presentation Reiki had seen the first day when she awoke. Antony asked a few questions along the way and when the presentation ended, he seemed to be coping well.

"Okay." He said, his arms crossed over his chest. "So, that's a pretty gigantic mind fuck that is going to take me a bit to come to grips with. But, for now, let's just say I believe you. What did you do to the two of us? The last thing I remember before waking up in that strange bed was being struck by that monster outside and unbelievable pain. What happened next?"

Reiki spoke first. "I killed that bastard and drug you inside this ship. Terra spoke and guided me to the sickbay, the room you woke up in, and proceeded to heal us both."

Terra added, "Reiki's condition required me to replace her eye and several of her internal organs. Your condition was much more dire. I had to replace your liver, kidneys, spleen, pancreas, one lung, and your heart."

Antony sat down, his legs suddenly shaky and unable to hold him up. "Fuck me."

Reiki nodded. "Agreed. You were well and truly screwed."

Antony looked up at Reiki. "I can't even comprehend that. She can *replace* my organs? You say she isn't a goddess, but she replaced my fucking heart? How?"

Terra replied, "The sickbay on this ship carries a small supply of synthetic organs. I simply selected one that was the appropriate size and then coated it in an organic compound synthesized from your own genetic material in order to reduce the likelihood of graft versus host complications. Your body handled the replacements well. As an added bonus, you no longer need to worry about heart disease, artery disease, or hypertension. Most poisons and toxins will likely no longer have much effect on you."

Antony raised a single eyebrow. "No kidding? That's one hell of a benefit. Should I tell all my friends and loved ones to get savaged by horrifying desert beasts too?" he quipped.

"I would not recommend it. If Reiki had been about two minutes slower, I don't know that I could have repaired you," Terra replied.

Antony stood up slowly and he met Reiki's eyes with his own. "Then I guess I should thank you again, Reiki, for pulling me out of the clutches of death and trusting an unknown disembodied voice to do it. I don't know that I would have if the roles were reversed."

"I like to think you would have, Antony. For me." Reiki smiled.

The two of them stood there in the heavy silence for several long moments, the emotion in the room almost palpable. Finally, Antony broke the silence. "So, what now? I'm assuming you've already come up with a plan for what to do next."

"We're going east to find Pyotr. And Terra's coming with us."

****

The final preparations took another three days. Antony had been skeptical of their plan, but eventually admitted that no matter which direction they headed, they were going to have to cross the desert to get there, so they might as well continue to their previous goal. He had been skeptical of the wisdom of bringing Terra along. He fell silent and just shook his head when Reiki told him she had already agreed to carry Terra and then described the procedure she had undergone to make it possible. At first Reiki had been annoyed by his contrariness, but once she was alone scavenging for supplies throughout the ship, she realized that his response was normal, far more so than her own. The more she thought about it, the less she understood her trust of Terra and her willingness to carry her out into the world. *Perhaps I am trying to build something new from the ashes of my old life. The whole edifice of the world I have lived in has crumbled away and the truth has been exposed, and all that I once was likewise has been stripped away. Maybe I am eager to build both anew together. Or maybe I was alone and in shock over Antony and latched on to Terra in that moment of need. Or maybe I tasted a fraction of her knowledge and now thirst for more. I don't know. Maybe it's all of those and then some. Regardless, it is done.*

While Reiki made the final preparations for their journey, Terra and Antony spent most of each day the way Reiki had, learning from Terra. Aside from their meals, which mostly consisted of food that Terra provided them through a process Reiki still didn't quite understand (*Re-integrating or re-hydrating or re-combining? Something to do with molecules?*), Reiki saw very little of Antony until evenings. Then they both spent an hour or so catching up before going to sleep in their medical pods. By the third day, Antony's skepticism toward Terra had softened a little, though Reiki began to realize skepticism was a deep-rooted part of his personality matched only by his usually relentless positivity. He was the cheerful voice of reason that helped rein in some of her more negative impulses. She knew she was not particularly reckless, but she was still naïve to the world at large and Antony had helped her to stop and think about the reasons why she was on a particular path. *What more could you ask for in a friend?*

When all the supplies were gathered and loaded on the cart, Reiki and Antony decided to sleep one last night in the ship and set out in the morning. Reiki had one last thing to do before they could set out, so she left the sickbay after their evening chat and made her way down and back to the doorway she first dragged his unconscious body through two weeks earlier. The sun had long since gone down, but the air was still dry and hot as it blew through the expanding gap as the door slid open. The wind, though less constant in the canyon, had blown away any trace of where she had dragged him to the ship, but she made her way back to the hulking corpse of the beast she had slain. In the dim light, it took her longer than she had expected to find it, but at last she saw the Illanghetti spear sticking out from under the beast's massive rotting corpse. She jerked it free and sighed in relief when she saw that it was not broken, only fouled with the beast's ichor and a coating of desert dust.

"I could not leave you behind," she spoke softly to the spear and then stood for a while, her eyes resting on the decaying hulk of the beast. "And you. You nearly cost me a dear friend. I leave you behind gladly." She then kicked the corpse, spat, and returned to the ship and to her bed in sickbay.

****

The next morning, they ate their breakfast and Terra began the download while Antony paced nervously in the corner of sickbay. It took less than a minute and Reiki felt nothing until Terra spoke inside her mind.

[*Can you hear me?*]

Yes. I hear you.

[*Okay, good. You are going to feel a slight tingling and the sensation of warm water running down your back. Also, your eye might feel a bit warmer than usual for a moment.*]

Terra's warning was accurate. She shuddered as a warm, wet, liquid feeling rushed from her back up to the base of her neck. Her right eye felt as though she were feverish and her whole right side tingled from her fingertips to her neck. It only lasted a few seconds and Reiki shivered after it was over. *What was that?*

[*I connected myself to your synthetic organs as well as your eye. I also ensured that I was connected to your nervous system so that I can monitor your physical state. In this manner, I can more effectively assist you, and thus ensure my own survival as well. I am essentially a symbiote now.*]

373

What the fuck, Terra? You didn't tell me you were going to do that.

[I apologize. I thought I was clear when I was explaining it. Well, it's done now. On the upside, I am unlocking additional functionality in your optic implant. You will find a host of new features available.]

Don't try to distract me with shiny new stuff. You can't just spring things on me without asking me, and in plain language. Agreed?

[Very well. I will run things by you more deliberately *in the future.]*

Good.

Reiki could see that Antony was waiting for her to tell him she was okay, so she forced a smile and nodded to him. "I'm fine, Antony. Let's go."

The three of them, two humans, and one synthetic, made their way to the workshop where their sail-cart was waiting for them. Antony climbed aboard and sat beneath the shade canopy and Reiki took her place just in front of him at the steering wheel. She took one last look around, took one long slow breath in and out, and took hold of the helm.

"Open the door, Terra."